WI

'Enthralling and multi-layere‗‗‗‗‗‗‗‗‗‗‗‗‗ ‗‗ the Month

'Gripping . . . Deeply moving . . . A love letter to London, seething with outrage' *The Times*

'A propulsive crime novel. Thomas ably captures local community anger, interracial tensions and especially the foreboding atmosphere . . . This ambitious work on a big canvas is an admirable attempt at portraying a fraught and fracturing nation' *Guardian*

'Captures the searing energy and polarised nature of the capital in the late 1970s and early 1980s . . . Thomas creates a potent drama from the counterculture of a period when Rock Against Racism and the Anti-Nazi League were battling prejudice. *White Riot* adroitly blends fact and fiction' *Independent*

'*White Riot* is a timely, powerful and gorgeously readable novel that represents everything that is good and important about the crime fiction genre' *Irish Times*

'So impressive in its unpredictable and uncliched choice of characters, this is highly effective historical fiction about class war – but crucially for its success as a novel it is also a story of people, recognisable in their conflicts, hopes and mistakes' *Morning Star*

'With real life and fictional characters rubbing shoulders in a turbo-charged and multi-layered narrative, this is truly a State of Britain thriller . . . A genuine, undiluted punk epic, with a ready-made soundtrack and I can't wait for the next instalment' *Crime Time*

'Police and thieves, punks and spycops, *White Riot* captures the raw energy of the times in spectacular fashion, evoking a visceral narrative of power and corruption' **Jake Arnott**

WHITE RIOT

JOE THOMAS

First published in the United Kingdom in 2023 by Arcadia Books

This paperback published in 2023 by
Arcadia Books
An imprint of Quercus Editions Limited
Carmelite House
50 Victoria Embankment
London EC4Y 0DZ

An Hachette UK company

A CIP catalogue record for this book is available
from the British Library.

ISBN (PB) 978 1 52942 339 6
ISBN (Ebook) 978 1 52942 338 9

1 3 5 7 9 10 8 6 4 2

Typeset in Minion by MacGuru Ltd
Printed and bound in Great Britain by Clays Ltd, Elcograf S.p.A.

MIX
Paper from
responsible sources
FSC® C104740

Papers used by Quercus Books are from well-managed forests and other responsible sources.

Author's Note

Though rooted in certain factual events of 1978–83, *White Riot* is a work of fiction. Where possible, and in the context of a work of fiction, I have used or adapted the recorded words of real-life figures, in some instances weaving these into my own dialogues, though the interactions and situations they share with my characters are imagined. Acknowledgements follow the main text and include a comprehensive Bibliography of all sources consulted and a Notes section of all quoted material.

The Acknowledgements itemise instances where fact and fiction meet, what happened and what I have imagined; I provide information as to which is which – as far as that is possible in the context of a work of fiction – as well as where further information can be found. A guiding principle: the scenes in which real-life figures appear are fictionalised versions of real-life events, or fictional situations created to deliver factual information based on their testimony and footage. The police officers in the novel and their actions are entirely fictional. Whilst the bands, the music and the magazines in the text are real, my characters Suzi and Keith are fictional and therefore the portrayal of their work and their interactions with those real people and groups is wholly imagined. Other principal and minor characters and their associates, including Shahid Akhtar, Jon Davies and his family, Godfrey Heaven, Gideon, Dai Wyn, are fictional.

Throughout the text, factual quotations are attributed and referenced in the Notes section. Quotations from the speeches and writings of well-known and less well-known figures, and from other texts pertaining to them, are a matter of the historical record and also cited in the Notes section; any conversations or interactions they have with my characters are entirely invented.

This novel is dedicated to the memory of Altab Ali and Colin Roach, their families and friends, and all those who have worked, and continue to work, to fight injustice in Hackney.

'The obligation of subjects to the sovereign is understood to last as long, and no longer, than the power lasteth by which he is able to protect them. For the right men have by nature to protect themselves, when none else can protect them, can by no covenant be relinquished.'

Thomas Hobbes, *Leviathan*

'The past is a foreign country.'

L.P. Hartley, *The Go-Between*

'I believe very strongly in fascism. The only way we can speed up the sort of liberalism that's hanging foul in the air ... is to speed up the progress of a right-wing totally dictatorial tyranny ... Adolf Hitler was one of the first rock stars ...'

David Bowie, interview, *Playboy* magazine, 1976

'I think Enoch's right, I think we should send them all back.'

Eric Clapton, onstage in Birmingham, 1976

PART ONE
Heroes

Shahid Akhtar is drunk.

He's wearing a tracksuit, and he's very drunk.

At eight o'clock in the evening he says goodbye to his wife and good night to his kids and leaves his council house on Mildenhall Road to go jogging.

But instead of going jogging, he delivers himself to the off-licence around the corner and buys the most expensive bottle of Scotch they offer: Bell's.

Biggest-selling brand in Europe, the shopkeeper tells Shahid Akhtar, cheerfully. A million people can't be wrong.

It is, Shahid Akhtar concedes, definitely working.

He doesn't know where to go after making his purchase, so he walks his usual jogging route while drinking Europe's favourite whisky and thinking things over.

Now, he finds himself on a bench on the towpath next to the canal, just beyond the busy Lea Bridge Road, just beyond the bridge itself.

Cars are passing above him, North Millfields Park is behind, and he is looking across at the deserted building merchants' yard, and it is dark.

It is very dark, Shahid Akhtar notes, his head spinning.

Really dark.

He can see, if he turns and cranes his neck, the lights on at the Prince of Wales and Ship Aground pubs, and there is a moment where he thinks he might just stroll over there and walk in and have a few in the public bar and see if anyone has any ideas regarding the pickle he is in.

But the Prince of Wales intimidates Shahid Akhtar with its saloon rules and its faux-gentility, and the Ship Aground has a strict 'No Asians' door policy, so that's out.

Shahid Akhtar laughs loudly at these thoughts.

That it's come to this: alone in the dark, drunk, and not knowing what on earth he should do.

He has certainly made things worse this evening.

Earlier, from the phone box on Fletching Road, he had called his mistress, a woman called Dawn.

A few days before, Dawn, a white woman, had told Shahid Akhtar that she is pregnant with his child.

In the urine-heavy air of the phone box, Shahid Akhtar offered Dawn a sum of money.

Blackmail, she called it.

It was a fairly large sum of money, he reflects now, bitterly.

He's got a fair bit of money, Shahid Akhtar, what with his business interests in Brick Lane, and his community-minded leadership of the place. Not a lot of produce passes into the Brick Lane area without Shahid Akhtar having something to do with it.

He was surprised at Dawn's reluctance to accept this sum of money.

He was surprised, too, when she told him that tomorrow, the very next day, she is planning to march round to Shahid's council house – that's what she said she'd do, *march* round there – and tell Shahid's wife and three children exactly what's been going on between them.

It's a pickle, he thinks again.

He really messed it up, that phone call.

He wonders if he should call one or other of his contacts at Whitechapel police station. It's likely a bad idea, he reasons, they'll only laugh at him getting into trouble like this or use it as leverage. Either way, he owes *them* after last weekend, the march and the concert, keeping his interests – *their* interests – safe and well protected.

He finishes his whisky and tosses the bottle into the canal. It makes a satisfying noise as it hits the water and sinks.

He thinks about all he's done for Dawn; all he's given her.

Insurance, he told her, if you ever need it.

I don't understand, she said to that.

He remembers smiling then, giving her a wink, saying, If you ever need it, love, you will.

It is very dark, and Shahid Akhtar is very drunk, and he should go home, not least because it's not long until chucking-out time, and one of the pubs round here, well, he thinks, he doesn't want to be walking past when it's chucking-out time.

He decides to lie down for a moment and clear his head.

It feels good to lie down.

He breathes deeply and examines the sky, the stars, opens and shuts his eyes, one eye then the other, seeing stars, so many stars, flashing and spinning stars, and he tries to stand, but he doesn't stand, and he slumps, and he trips, and he thinks, I must get home, but what on earth am I –

The pub lights glow, the traffic flows –

He hears that song by David Bowie, thinks, We can be heroes –

There are voices in the dark, whistles in the dark, laughter in the dark –

Shahid Akhtar sleeps.

1

Punky Reggae Party

The Weekend Before
30 April, 1978, Carnival Against Racism, Victoria Park

Gideon

They'll accept you 'cos you're one of them. You're not too worried about going to the meeting, you'll shape up. You might as well get stuck in, get straight in there. It's what you want, after all. What you want is to show them that you are one of them. And you are one of them. You were born in Hackney Mothers' Hospital on Lower Clapton Road. You lived on the Pembury Estate before it was overrun with Jamaican and Nigerian families. You went to Rushmore Infants' School, then Juniors, then Hackney Downs. Then you didn't know what to do. There was no chance of college, there was nothing doing business-wise. You were a bright enough lad. You had a bit of violence behind you, nicking car stereos, bit of receiving, but nothing that meant actual time. There was quite enough painters and decorators knocking about the borough, and you thought, what's there for me exactly? Now: twenty-four years old and no job and some minor previous to go along with it. No one's taking you on. There's an old bloke called Harry who lives close by and he needs a pair of hands on a couple of building jobs, but it's day by day, there ain't a future. He's just doing the old man a favour, truth be told. What you're feeling is frustration. What you're feeling is displacement. What you're feeling, they're telling you, is alienation, alienation 'cos of the government. What they're telling you is every outsider, every foreigner, every illegal immigrant is doing better than you are 'cos that's what the government wants – they want them to do better than you and at your expense. You hear this off your mate Phil who's gone and shaved his nut and bought some boots. You hear this down the pub from the old geezers at the bar, drinking their benefit cheques in the mornings and scrounging scraps in the afternoons. You hear this from the kids on the estate, sniffing glue and spraying graffiti. You hear this in the bookies, in the job centre. You hear this at the football, West

Ham. You hear this at the music, Sham 69. You hear this fucking everywhere, and you start to believe it and that's when they get you and that's when you decide, yeah, I'll join, I'll come to the meeting, yeah.

Locker room, West End Central police station.

Detective Constable Patrick Noble is kitting up for the day. He's off to Victoria Park to have a look at this festival so he's in his civvies. Seconded to Hackney –

Racist attacks and all hands on deck.

And this is what, Noble thinks, a fact-finding mission?

Giving up his Sunday.

The Clash are all right, he's thinking, what Joe Strummer said the other day makes sense –

'People ought to know we're anti-fascist, we're anti-violence, we're anti-racism and we're pro-creativity. We're against ignorance.'

'Oi, Noble.' A yell from across the room. 'You better pack your hand-kerchief, son.'

Noble turns. It's Big Ron Robinson, Detective Constable and all-round 'character'. A real charmer is Big Ron.

Noble says, 'Leave it out, eh, Ron.'

'And keep an eye on your wallet, too,' Ron says.

'What are you on about?'

Big Ron leers. 'Punks and blacks, mate,' he says. 'At your little concert this afternoon.'

Noble shakes his head. Noble mutters, You wanker.

Big Ron leans in. 'One'll spit in your face and the other'll lift your cash while he's doing it.'

'Fuck off, Ron.'

Noble closes his locker, heads for the door.

'Be lucky, Chance, old son,' Ron is laughing. 'Be lucky, Paddy boy.'

Chance Noble: one small bit of good fortune, *once*, one lucky break, and the nickname stuck.

Doesn't help his name's Patrick –

Luck of the Irish ain't a phrase you hear in a London nick.

Same day, a few hours earlier.

Suzi Scialfa's at a squat party on Charing Cross Road.

At four in the morning, someone puts on Junior Murvin's 'Police and Thieves'.

The party ripples quiet. Reggae vibe.

Someone shouts, Isn't this a Clash song? Everyone laughs.

Suzi's looking out the window. There's a procession, hundreds of people making their way down the road.

Suzi, quite drunk, leans out of the window. She calls out, 'Where you guys headed?'

'Where you *from*, love?' someone yells back.

Laughter. Shouts: oi, oi!

Suzi laughs back, hams up that all-American drawl of hers. 'New York, New York, darling.'

She takes her camera and snaps. 'You're not going to tell me where y'all are going?'

Another voice says, 'Trafalgar Square, sweetheart. March against racism.'

Suzi goes, 'Now? It's four in the fucking morning.'

'May as well get there early,' someone else shouts.

Junior Murvin's bass player rumbles through the night.

Someone puts on The Clash.

Suzi's boyfriend joins her at the window. She points at the crowds.

Fucking hell, he says.

Mildenhall Road, Clapton, a little later.

Jon Davies lies in bed with his six-month-old son, Joe, his wife Jackie downstairs making the tea.

She calls up. 'You going to want to go to the march, love? Or just the music?'

Jon's been thinking about this for a few days. The march is Trafalgar Square to Victoria Park, a decent few miles. They'd be going a long way west to come back east again. What would the boy make of it all? Jon never knows what he'll make of anything. He seems happy enough with whatever's put in front of him, until he's not.

It's a hassle, the march, is what it is. But it's Anti-Nazi League and the music's Rock Against Racism, and Jon works for the council, so it might be diplomatic to do both –

As if anyone cares.

'Just the music, love,' he shouts downstairs. 'I want to make sure we see Steel Pulse.'

'Steel who?' Jackie yells.

Noble knocks on DS Foreman's door and goes in.

Foreman's smiling. 'Got your glad rags on, Chance, I see. Very trendy.'

'Very funny, guv,' Noble says.

'At least you'll fit in.'

Noble's not sure how true that is.

Foreman says, 'Take this.' He hands Noble a piece of paper. 'These are a few names to look out for.'

'OK.'

'This is a recon exercise, Chance, that's all. You're just there to observe.'

'Yes, guv.'

'And this –' he hands Noble an envelope – 'is some ready money and a backstage pass.' Foreman smiles again. 'We thought you'd like to knock boots with the glamour crowd.'

Noble nods.

'We want you at Trafalgar Square, do the whole route. Get a sense of it, OK?'

Noble examines the piece of paper.

At the top, a title: PERSONS OF INTEREST ON THE LEFT

And a list of names:

Red Saunders, founding member Rock Against Racism [RAR]
Syd Shelton, central RAR committee member
David Widgery, central RAR committee member

Ruth Gregory, central RAR committee member

John Dennis, central RAR committee member

Wayne Minter, central RAR committee member

Kate Webb, central RAR committee member

Roger Huddle, Socialist Worker Party and central RAR committee
   member

Peter Hain, founding member, Anti-Nazi League

Paul Holborow, founding member, Anti-Nazi League

Halfway down, another heading: PERSONS OF INTEREST ON THE RIGHT

But there is no list of names.

'Guv,' Noble says. He gestures with the piece of paper. 'What's this?'

Foreman smiles. 'You're supposed to fill that in yourself, son, that's
what this is.'

Noble nods.

Foreman softens. He says, 'You've got your skinheads and your head-
bangers on one side, right? On the other –' and here he raises his left
hand – 'you've got your subversives. Easy enough to keep an eye on the
skinheads. They're hooligans, end of.'

'And the National Front?' Noble says. 'They're not of interest, guv?'

'They're an official political party, DC Noble,' Foreman says. 'Legit.'

'I thought, guv,' Noble says, slowly, 'that I was looking into racially
aggravated assault, GBH, that kind of thing.'

'You are, son.' Foreman breathes out.

He's all right, Foreman, Noble knows this, he's just –

Well, he's just more worried about his job than anything else.

Foreman says, 'A word of advice, Chance.'

'Go on.'

'The skinheads won't fancy this lefty mob marching straight through
their patch, know what I mean?'

Noble nods. 'Brick Lane.'

Foreman shakes his head. 'That's not a problem.'

'No?'

'You know Gardiner down at Whitechapel, don't you?'

Noble nods.

'He'll be at the top of Brick Lane with the uniforms. Go and say hello.'

'Right.'

'And when you get close to Bethnal Green,' Foreman says, 'I'd get near the front, if I were you.'

'In a manner of speaking,' Noble says.

Foreman laughs. 'Good one, Chance, clever boy. Arrivederci.'

Suzi's half-listening to a man talking loudly about how the stage at Victoria Park has been occupied all week by some old-school dockers and like-minded West Ham fans, and it's already been attacked three times by National Front thugs, but they were seen off no problem, sounds like it was a laugh –

Suzi turns to her fella. 'What time is it?'

'Six-thirty.'

'*Six-thirty*? How did that happen?'

Her fella taps his nose, gives a big sniff. 'How do you think, love. We better go soon, eh?'

Suzi nods that they should. They'll both be working all day, after all.

She's grinning and wired in a good way and checks her bag for camera equipment, notebook, pen.

Pats down her pockets for keys, money, fags. Check check check.

'Let's go,' she says. 'Let's go!'

People are already leaving the squat and the stairwell echoes excited chatter and shouted slogans:

'The National Front is a Nazi Front, Smash the National Front.'

People are singing in the street. They hear 'London's Burning' by The Clash.

Suzi leans into her fella's shoulder. She likes the word fella, makes her feel more English, somehow.

'You excited, babe?' she asks.

Keith, her fella, wraps his arm around her. 'I am, love. It's a big deal, today. You excited? You should be, girl.'

Suzi smiles, she noses her way further into Keith's corner, the crook of his neck.

She can't wait, truth be told.

There's a dampness in the air – it's rained three days solid – but the light's bright and cuts through it, and the streets *gleam*, and there's a bounce in everyone's step. A West End Sunday morning is a bleak business, normally, Suzi thinks. The patches of vomit. The *debris*. Not today though. Today, it feels, they're all on a mission.

Keith is the sound man for The Ruts, and The Ruts are set to perform on a truck the whole way from Trafalgar Square to Victoria Park, and Suzi is going to be on that truck, on assignment, taking photos for *Temporary Hoarding* magazine and making a few notes, getting a few quotes.

Someone's bounding down Charing Cross Road yelling 'here we go, here we go'.

They turn. It's Syd Shelton, one of the organisers and the graphic designer for *Temporary Hoarding*, so, in a way, Suzi's boss.

He slaps Keith on the back and gives Suzi a big kiss.

'All right, Sweetheart,' he says, grinning.

So many people called Suzi sweetheart when she first arrived on the scene as a seventeen-year-old, she took it as an official nickname, half-ironic. Suzi 'Sweetheart' Scialfa. Co-opting it, is what she said she was doing. It stuck.

They do that, nicknames, they stick.

Keith says, 'You're up early.'

'Couldn't sleep.' Syd winks at Suzi. 'You Suze, you lose, get it?'

'I'm American, Syd, I'm not stupid,' she says. 'I've lived here all my life – *man*.'

Syd laughs.

'You're looking very pleased with yourself, Syd, if I may,' says Keith.

'Hear that?' Syd stops them, cocks an ear, puts a hand to it.

They're halfway down to Leicester Square and it's too late – or early

– for any Soho carousers, and the tourists are still tucked up, but there is a lot of noise coming from somewhere.

Suzi says, 'That sounds like a crowd.'

'There's about ten thousand here already, we reckon,' Syd says. 'Coach loads from Scotland, Manchester, Liverpool, Sheffield, Middlesbrough, South Wales, all over. They wanted to beat the traffic,' he deadpans.

'Ten thousand?' Keith whistles. 'Well, we shouldn't have any problems today then.'

'Unlikely, mate,' Syd says. 'I just chatted to a load of punks from Aberystwyth. They're rugby players, most Sundays.'

They laugh.

Suzi feels a touch of relief. She wouldn't admit it, but she was a little bit concerned about the possibility of trouble. Sham 69 are playing later – well, Jimmy Pursey is rumoured to be doing *something* – and there's been a lot of it, trouble, she thinks, at their gigs. National Front skins at Middlesex Poly causing a ruckus was the worst of it.

Suzi's been thinking that the truck on the march might come in for a little attention. But ten thousand *already*? They'll be dandy.

'It's not just punks,' Syd adds. 'There's all sorts. Young, gifted and black, white, brown. Teds, mods, bikers, punks, greasers, disco kids. All ages. The reggae sound systems are setting up in the east. And it's not even seven.'

'Fucking hell,' Keith says.

'Look,' Syd says, 'I need to get a wriggle on. See you on the truck, my lovelies.'

They watch Syd fly down the road.

'Where the fuck is Aberystwyth?' Suzi says.

'Babe –' Keith ignores her – 'I don't know about you, but I fancy a cup of tea and a bacon sandwich before all the fun begins.'

Suzi squeezes Keith's arm. 'Lead on, squire,' she says.

Keith takes her hand and they swerve right into Chinatown.

Suzi makes a face, confused. 'Love?' she says.

Keith grins. 'I know a place.'

'Course you do, love.'

*

Jon Davis is sitting in his big brown chair by the window watching the football highlights, balancing a cup of tea and small plate on the arm, and the boy in his lap.

The boy's wriggling about a bit, his tiny hand crammed into his mouth. Jon Davis is slurping tea and taking quick bites out of his bacon sandwich. The brown sauce adds a lovely tang.

Jackie's downstairs making more sandwiches to take to the carnival. 'Ham and cheese do you, Jon?' she yells up the stairs.

Jon Davis yells back, 'Lovely, love, thank you!'

One thing about moving out of a flat and investing all your money in a small, terraced house, Jon thinks, is how much more shouting you do, up and down the stairs.

The football highlights are grim. Jon's team, West Ham, have lost away to Liverpool, conceding goals from McDermott in the thirty-eighth minute, and then Fairclough in the sixty-sixth. Liverpool appear to have made fairly easy work of West Ham. Relegation beckons, Jon thinks.

He says to the boy, 'You've a lot to look forward to, son.'

The boy gurgles and smiles.

Jon fancies taking the boy to Upton Park. Six months old and the lad's already in his claret-and-blue sleepsuit. Jon's been West Ham all his life, but still, where else is he going to go? Arsenal? Fucking Spurs? Don't even think about Chelsea.

They put on a bit of show at the Boleyn, he'll give them that.

Charming, the fans, some of them. It's a minority, he reckons, and he'll just about put up with some of it, but it's not all good fun. There's your naughty boys, they're all right, they're on the North Bank or the Chicken Run, and they'll only go after like-minded. Whatever floats your boat, is Jon's feeling.

No, it's the geezers in the main stand Jon doesn't like. The catcalls. The brazenness of it all. A few of them making their feelings known quite openly. Go on, Clyde, they'd yell, until Clyde left the club a season or two ago.

Go on, Clyde, go on. Kick their coon.

A stylish man, Clyde Best. Handsome devil. Good on the ball. A worker.

One of Jon's neighbours, a fairly sexy woman of about his age, claims to have bedded Clyde Best, West Ham's first ever black player.

'More tea, love?' Jackie yells.

'No thanks!' Jon yells back.

The boy chews his hand, thoughtfully, Jon thinks.

Trafalgar Square is heaving. Noble is impressed. He's listening to some ponce barking into a microphone. Some bloke called Tom Robinson, Noble's worked out. A lefty singer, on later, the Tom Robinson Band. Good name, Noble thinks, spitefully.

This Tom Robinson is talking a lot about positivity but the sound's a bit crackly and Noble only really gets this bit:

'The message of this carnival, not only to the loonies of the National Front but all bigots everywhere, is hands off our people: black, white, together, tonight forever.'

Some other geezer follows. Corduroy and hair.

Noble notes the name: Peter Hain. Noble notes the face: this Peter Hain is on his list.

Peter Hain says something like, 'We're building a people's movement to defeat the Nazis.'

Nazis? Noble scoffs. He surreptitiously checks his piece of paper. Peter Hain, Anti-Nazi League.

Well, that explains it then.

Noble's edging through the crowd, keeping his head down and his fake smile wide –

'Smash the National Front!'

And so on. It's a sentiment he is sympathetic towards.

At the corner of the square, at the top end of Whitehall, Noble clocks a distinguished-looking bloke with a notebook and a press card. *Telegraph*. Now that's a surprise, Noble thinks.

The crowd sways and sings. Music roars into life on one of the flatbed trucks parked and ready to go.

Noble recognises the song, but not this reggae-version bollocks. 'Police and Thieves.' He smiles. We're all at it today, he thinks.

'Didn't think your lot would turn up for this,' Noble says to the reporter.

The distinguished gentleman thrusts his notebook at Noble. 'This is what I've written,' he says. 'Have a good look.'

'Why don't you read it to me?' Noble says.

'I will.' He glares at Noble, nods down the road. 'I was only here to cover a veterans' event.'

'Well, go on then,' Noble says. 'Read it.'

The gentleman flips a page: 'This is the most despicable group of miscreants from every lowest dregs of society that you've ever seen,' he reads. He snaps the notebook shut. 'I'm talking about you, young man.'

Noble smiles. 'Look around you,' he says. His arm sweeps. 'I don't think you're talking about anyone.'

'That's not what it'll say in the paper tomorrow, lad.'

Tom Robinson hops aboard The Ruts' float. The band are setting up, Keith conducting.

Suzi's watching Tom Robinson bounce about.

The fucking numbers, he's saying to the band. There must be tens of thousands. What a feeling! Solidarity and strength, boys. The sheer fucking numbers!

With her camera, Suzi snaps away.

She hears another chant.

'We're black, we're white, we're dynamite.'

Suzi spots David Widgery, a *Temporary Hoarding* colleague. He's waving a placard with words from his first editorial, his manifesto:

WE WANT REBEL MUSIC, STREET MUSIC, MUSIC THAT BREAKS DOWN
PEOPLE'S FEAR OF ONE ANOTHER. CRISIS MUSIC. NOW MUSIC. MUSIC
THAT KNOWS WHO THE REAL ENEMY IS. ROCK AGAINST RACISM. LOVE
MUSIC HATE RACISM.

He approaches the side of the truck, smiles at her, yells, Read this! and
hands her his notebook.

Suzi reads:

'Trafalgar Square raked with colour. Yellow ANL roundels, punk-
pink Rock Against Racism stars, DayGlo flags oscillating in approval to
the speeches.'

Suzi thinks: spot on.

'What time do you think we should leave then, love?'

Jackie is yelling again.

Jon, carrying the boy down the stairs, says, 'I reckon it'll start quite
early. Say, ten-thirty? We can walk along the canal.'

'Good idea, love.'

Noble eases his way back into the crowd as it disperses, begins its long
walk to Victoria Park. He snakes towards the stage. There, he spots one
of top brass, the deputy chief constable, in uniform, speaking to one of
the organisers. Noble gets closer, thinks, Hang about –

Brass is saying, Thank God everyone wanted to march off in a hurry
because we couldn't have contained the situation.

The bloke brass is talking to says, This is not a crowd in the mood for
confrontation, officer.

Noble thinks it's time to get to the head of the thing and he turns –

The Ruts' float is about a third of the way back from the head of the
march. Misty in Roots are playing further forward and Suzi can feel
their bass-heavy reggae throb. Keith gives the signal: louder, *louder*.

The band are screaming along through their set and Keith's got a great big grin plastered across his beautiful face –

Punky reggae party! Keith's yelling.

They do 'Dope for Guns', 'Jah War', 'Savage Circle', 'Human Punk', 'Something that I Said' –

The Ruts' crowd are a mix of kids and adults. Glue sniffers and socialist activists.

Suzi's taking photos. Everyone dancing and walking, singing and chanting. Her idea to talk to a few people and get a few quotes is a non-starter, she realises. The *noise*. There are, she gathers, something like ten thousand whistles being blown all at once. Tom Robinson, before he hopped off, was bragging about getting them from the head of EMI, making everyone laugh.

They reach Bethnal Green Road and Suzi feels a little edge creep up.

The sink estates that flank the road further down, that overlook the main drag, set back a little, ominous, are notorious Front breeding grounds and if there is going to be anything like a response to the enormous cheek – the *face* – of marching thousands of people through a right-wing hinterland, then it's going to happen here.

She focuses her camera on a placard, clicks:

QUEER JEW-BOY SOCIALIST SEEKS A BETTER WORLD

The canal is quiet. It's lovely, actually, Jon thinks, as they walk towards Homerton and then Hackney Wick and then across and up into the park.

Millfields Park is bleak, the grass full of fag ends and dog shit. The pylons hum and buzz. They rear up over the trees. Jon thinks of *War of the Worlds*, of *Day of the Triffids*.

The water's not especially lovely.

They're playing a game they've played for years, ever since they were courting teenagers. Shopping trolley, traffic cone, fishing rod, TV, deckchair, tyre –

They're pointing at the water as they walk.

'What's that?' Jon says.

'Where?'

'There, look.' Jon points at the murk. '*There*, just below the surface.'

They peer into the murk.

'Looks like a car stereo,' Jackie says. 'You should jump in and fetch it, love. We need a new one, after all.'

Jackie takes the boy down the pool at Hackney Downs school every Monday afternoon for mummy–baby swimming. About once a month, the car window is put in and the stereo nicked.

Jon's had it with paying for these swimming lessons.

Jon nods. He examines towpath graffiti. Rain falls.

The boy sleeps in his buggy. It's lovely, Jon thinks.

Everyone's moving slowly, so it doesn't take Noble long to get to the head of the march. They're fast this lot, he thinks, for a bunch of hippies and layabouts.

It's a scruffy crowd, he sees. A lot of punks, sure, but a lot of others too. A lot of second-hand clothes and long hair, a lot of leather. A lot of sharp-suited types, belts and braces, girls *and* boys. Wide lapels and trousers that fall just short of the ankle. School-uniform chic. A lot of corduroy. A lot of denim. Flares and boots. Funny how many of them could pass for football hooligans, Noble thinks. Even the soft-looking ones have a lairy swagger in their apparel. The odd heavy-knit fisherman's jumper. A fair few hats about the place. And a lot of Asians, a lot of brown faces. This, Noble thinks, is the first time he's seen so many Asians among the blacks and whites. He thinks this might mean something.

At the top of Brick Lane there are uniforms and mounted police.

It's an impressive show in a very specific place: the shops and businesses of Brick Lane have long been targeted by National Front foot soldiers, and Noble's thinking there might be a few of these about, not taking kindly to the opposition's presence. It's a message, Noble thinks, if word gets back.

Noble spots Gardiner, nods at him, slips through the line of uniforms out of sight of the crowd. They shake hands.

'Foreman told me you were coming,' Gardiner says.

Noble gestures at the horses. 'You didn't fancy any riot shields then?'

'Yeah, well.' Gardiner shrugs. He nods down the road. 'We're helping out.'

'Helping out who?'

Gardiner smiles, shakes his head. 'None of my beeswax.'

'Leave it out, eh.'

Gardiner points at a group of Asian men standing not far away. 'Community leaders had a word with someone who had a word with me. The gist is nothing happens today in Brick Lane.'

'Just today?'

'Like I said, none of my beeswax.'

Noble nods. 'Conflict of interest, I expect.'

Gardiner snorts. 'More like my enemy's enemy is my friend.'

'Very profound.'

'Cowboys and Indians, mate, is what it is.'

Noble nods at the group of Asian men. 'Make a donation, did they, to the retirement fund?'

'Something like that.'

Noble narrows his eyes. 'You know any names?'

Gardiner nods again at the Asian men. 'The friendly one's called Shahid Akhtar, a businessman.'

'Legit?'

'Semi.'

'And this little show is for the Front, is it? Keep out?'

'Have a look at the faces on some of them uniforms, son,' Gardiner winks. 'Like bulldogs chewing on wasps they are, itching to have a pop.'

Noble smiles. 'I'll be seeing more of you then.'

'You will. Stay safe.'

Noble heads back through the line of uniforms and into the crowd.

Staying safe isn't a problem today, he thinks.

That brass in Trafalgar Square had it right: it's not a confrontational mood.

He thinks about what Gardiner has just told him – or *not* told him.

What Gardiner's saying, or not saying, he thinks, is that there's *some* relationship between Brick Lane and Whitechapel nick, but that he's not part of it.

More than that even: not everyone is about stopping the National Front terrorise Brick Lane and the surrounding area.

Back in the thick mess of the crowd, Noble examines the flags and banners. Yellow and black Anti-Nazi League placards, red everywhere. Socialist Worker Party signs and your Marxist slogans and the odd Anarchist black. Pinned to just about every lapel, every collar, some sort of right-on badge.

It's kids, mainly, larking about. A lot of kids, a lot of *young* people.

Older Rastas with their dreadlocks and spliffs, that stoic look to them, inscrutable, unconcerned, nodding to a band on the first float in the queue, Misty in Roots, Noble has learned. British reggae: looks like a tasty scene, he thinks.

He's more a punk man, Noble. He enjoyed The Ruts as he passed. It's the energy he likes, that and the seriousness, the *intent*. They're an earnest bunch, the punks. Noble admires that, the politics.

The march turns down Bethnal Green Road and Noble keeps his eyes peeled –

Ahead: the Blade Bone.

A National Front pub.

Skinheads and sixteen-hole boots on the troops. Nasty racist scumbags in cheap suits directing operations from the back, stirring them up with who's taking our jobs and who's stealing our women and we want England back –

There ain't no black in the Union Jack.

Noble lets the crowd drift a little further ahead of him. He gets himself across the road, same side as the Blade Bone.

From her vantage point on the truck, Suzi hears chanting –

'Sieg heil, sieg heil, red scum.'

She rubbernecks, gets on her toes and sees a few dozen evil-looking thugs standing outside the Blade Bone giving Nazi salutes and spraying the marchers with lager.

There's jeering and V-signs flying around, taunts of get a job and go back to where you came from.

There's a single line of police –

Suzi tenses.

As their float approaches, The Ruts break into their biggest song, 'Babylon's Burning'. Keith presses a button and winks at Suzi and the sound of a siren pours out of the speakers just like on the record but louder – *louder!* – and then the ascending descending guitar line and there's a roar and a measured sort of pogoing starts up –

Singalong. Arms waving, yelling about burning in the street, burning in your houses, Noble thinks, something about anxiety –

The Nazi salutes falter.

They haven't got the legs! someone shouts.

Suzi thinks: that's right. They can't keep it up for two hours, and it'll take that long for fifty thousand people to file past.

Someone else yells, Use your right arm for wanking, you cunts!

That gets a laugh.

An old boy pulling a shopping basket is swearing about something, gesturing at the crowd.

The crowd cheers him on.

Suzi focuses her camera on a blue plaque, the Corporation of The City of London, the St George's Cross smack in the middle of the logo.

Beneath, multitudes throng.

Jon, Jackie, and the boy reach Victoria Park. They come in at the south-east entrance and struggle through the mud with the buggy. The stage, when they see it, makes Jon smile.

Above, across the top, white lettering on a red banner that stretches from one end of it to the other proclaims:

CARNIVAL AGAINST THE NAZIS

There's something charming, something amateur about the capitalisation, Jon thinks.

Beneath that, another banner, in black letters on white:

ANTI-NAZI LEAGUE

It looks, Jon thinks, like a school project.

Lower down, behind where the bands will play:

ROCK AGAINST RACISM

They pause for a moment, the three of them. They're some distance from the stage but they can see someone on it, they can hear *something*.

There is a smattering of people, at best. A few hundred and spread out.

'Looks like we're early, love,' Jackie says.

Jon, distracted, nods.

'Who is this?' Jackie asks.

Jon's not impressed with the PA, but he knows who it is.

'X-Ray Spex,' he says. 'The singer's called Poly Styrene.'

'She looks nice,' Jackie says.

'Where is everyone?' Jon says.

Noble is one of the first into the park.

He left the flatbed truck behind just as it went the wrong way down a one-way street and got stuck on a central reservation trying to reverse. The band, Noble noted with some pleasure, played on.

They're all piling into the park and heading east where the stage is set up. Kids screaming and laughing, there must be a thousand already.

Some bird in a turban is onstage yelling into the microphone about bondage and up yours and little girls should be seen and not heard –

Noble's smiling. Not such a bad Sunday, after all. Not that he's made any progress, work-wise. He thinks about what he could put in a report, not sure he even has to write one. He pulls his backstage pass, or what these amateurs consider one to be, and arrows towards a side entrance, just to the right of where the band are spitting through their repertoire.

He'll have a nose-around; he's pretty sure he's not going to find any right-wing persons of interest, but it'll be helpful to put a few faces to names –

Oh, fucking nice one, that's just fucking great.

This is John Jennings – Segs – having a moan. The Ruts' bass player is pissed off. Suzi can see why: the truck is stuck.

Segs – this is Dave Ruffy, the drummer, yelling – the driver can't hear you, you muppet!

Suzi's half-listening. Keith, she sees, has a wry smile on his lovely face. He always does, she thinks.

The gears crunch and the truck lurches. The narrow roads around Bethnal Green are proving a bit of a bugger to get through. Council estates are grey, forbidding.

Suzi can see the crowd filing in through the main gate of the park.

From her vantage point, she sees thousands of people.

The truck chunters along behind. The crowd divides. Like the Red Sea! someone yells and waves them through.

Someone else is brandishing some kind of radio telephone. No signal! he's yelling. Can't get through. Useless fucking pongos.

On Victoria Park Road they're trying to manoeuvre the truck through the north gate, right by the Hemingway pub. Kids perch on the estate walls, taking the piss, throwing stones, flicking V-signs. All good-humoured, Suzi grins at them, waves. Someone shouts, Get out of it, you mouthy little tykes!

The gate is locked – at least the bottom bit of it is. There is some debate about this.

Then Syd Sheldon's bounding over again.

The bloke who's supposed to let us in is fucking stoned! he's laughing. We gave him a bottle of Johnnie Walker this morning and he's been off with the Steel Pulse cooks ever since.

The band, taking a break, laugh at this.

Here, Syd says. He couldn't find the keys, but he gave me this.

He hands the driver a sledgehammer. The driver smashes the lock.

There are cheers. The air is charged, Suzi feels, with some righteous energy.

They enter the park; Suzi climbs onto a speaker.

'Careful, love!' Keith calls out.

Suzi grins and waves.

Trees sway and drip. The sun is out now. The wind soft.

In the distance, she sees a band taking to the stage –

The Clash.

She waves again at Keith, mouths I'm off, mimes taking photos and legs it across the park, round the eighty-thousand crowd, the heaving crowd, to the side entrance at the right of the stage, and climbs the steps just as Jimmy Pursey –

'The state of the crowd,' Jon says. 'From nowhere!'

Jackie nudges Jon. 'The state of the *band*.'

'All right, easy on, Jacks,' Jon says, grinning. 'They're good, they're serious musicians, political.'

'Very,' Jackie says. 'They look very serious.'

Jon is grateful they're so far back.

Noble wriggles his way to the side of the stage as The Clash rip into 'London's Burning'.

They look good, The Clash, Noble gives them that. Strummer's in a red T-shirt and white rude-boy jeans. Simonon's in a blue jacket, studded belt around leather trousers, platform boots. Jones is all in black, menace and chains –

The crowd erupts. It looks messy down there, Noble thinks, the charge to the front a crush of bodies, flailing.

Noble clocks Jimmy Pursey from Sham 69 standing not too far away. Noble knows all about Sham 69 and their nasty skinhead following. He clocks a little group of skins near the front throwing bottles.

The crowd, alive, surge at this nasty little group. They're swallowed up, eaten, spat out.

There's tension stage left and Noble feels it. Arguments about how long The Clash are supposed to play. Some flash cunt in a red shirt squaring up to a long-haired Scot. They've pulled the plug, someone's yelling.

Noble's jaw is set and he lurks.

Tower blocks across the park shimmer through the trees.

Then Pursey's bouncing on in a striped red-and-white T-shirt, very French, and braces and boots. Shouting white riot into a microphone that someone promptly switches off.

The pogoing. The fists punching the air. The *crush*.

Strummer's singing into Simonon's mic.

I wanna riot, the crowd sing back. *I wanna riot*.

Then it's all over and the band file off stage, looking like rock stars, not punks.

Noble edges forward.

Red Shirt has pushed some wanker in a leather jacket swigging Special Brew onto the stage, and this wanker's yelling More, more Clash, more Clash into the microphone, and the Scot shouts Get this idiot off the stage, and Leather Jacket is smirking, and Noble does not like the cut of this lad's jib, so Noble steps out, sees the crowd beneath him, banners and whistles, Mohicans and safety pins, and he grabs Leather Jacket by the lapel and he pulls him back and he says, right in this wanker's face, he says, Get the fuck off the stage, you try-hard cunt, you understand? and the bloke looks at Noble and he sees, Noble sees, that Noble is serious, that Noble is not someone to mess about and Leather Jacket shrinks, nods, and Red Shirt's giving it the all right, calm down, and then Noble's off, down the steps, and he feels a hand on his jacket and he turns –

'That was pretty cool,' Suzi says to this fella who just helped clear the stage of The Clash's idiot road crew.

The fella shrugs. 'A real heartbreaker, that lad in the leather.'

Suzi smiles. 'Ray Gange.'

'Eh?'

'His name. Ray Gange. He's an actor, sort of. They're making a film about The Clash and he's playing a member of their road crew.'

'How very clever of them,' the fella says.

'*Rude Boy* is what the film's supposed to be called.'

'Well, the pair of them were certainly that.'

'Can I take your photo?' Suzi asks, twitching her finger. 'Click click.'

'No, sorry, love,' the fella says. 'I look like a criminal in photos.'

Suzi watches him walk away into the crowd. She snaps two pictures of his retreating figure.

She climbs back up the steps and waits for Steel Pulse.

'A lot of families here, aren't there, Jon?' Jackie says.

'Carnival atmosphere,' Jon says. 'It's a bloody circus.'

Jackie laughs. 'I expect that lot from playgroup are in the thick of things.'

It's Jon's turn to laugh. 'I expect they are. Hippies, eh?'

They're eating their sandwiches. They've found a quiet bench just back from the crowd, a little further east of the stage, and Jackie's feeding the boy while they eat their lunch.

Jon's looking out at the old swimming pool, the tennis courts in a bit of a state, an adventure playground that's seen better days. The lake, he remembers, has a sign on it that reads something like:

NO FISHING, NO SWIMMING, NO BOATS

A fun lake, he's always thought.

Better than some of the graffiti he's seen.

'Makes a change, love,' Jackie says, 'from our usual Sunday.'

Jon nods. He checks his watch. 'Steel Pulse up next,' he says.

He's excited, to be fair. The Clash were quite something, that 'White Riot' a real moment, true. But British reggae: pure class.

Their Sundays have been the same since the Queensdown Road days, their first flat –

Jackie sticks a chicken in the oven, dead low, and they cross Millfields Park and have a drink in the Prince of Wales on the canal, right next to Lea Bridge Road. They can't take the boy in, so Jackie waits outside while Jon orders in the saloon bar: a pint of ordinary, a glass of white wine and a couple of bags of plain crisps in his pockets. He nods and smiles at Harry, his next-door neighbour, an old lad, a builder not far off retirement, who drinks in the public bar on the other side, where there's sawdust on the floor and men standing, their pints sunk and mugs refilled at quite a lick.

It's all right, the Prince. There's one of those seafood stalls outside and Jackie likes a pot of cockles, a tray of prawns. She likes the vinegar. She drinks the stuff left over, *slurps* it down.

There are a few blokes fishing; a few kids climbing the pipe that runs across the water. There's a sort of lock gate on the other side that Jon doesn't understand but it looks pretty, and there's a little house that may or may not belong to a lock keeper or whatever they're called, and that always seems to Jon like an idyllic sort of life when you're down the canal on a weekend.

Yeah, it's all right, the Prince. Sometimes they'll wander further up the canal, cross at the footbridge, have a gander at some Sunday League, at the fishermen hunkered down with more kit, pulling carp, saying nothing, then keep going, watch the rowers at the bottom of Springfield Park – *rowers*? Jon always thinks, in *Hackney*? – cross back and have their pint of ordinary and their wine and their crisps in the Robin Hood with its sorry-looking playground, or outside the Anchor and Hope, a pub with no tables, no women, no kids.

Yes, they like the Prince.

They used to go to the pub next door, the Ship Aground, from time to time. Strange one, that is. A concrete block with a concrete patio. Not quite the pub at the bottom of an estate but not far off; the estates here are further back from the Lea Bridge Road. The Ship was useful when the tables outside the Prince were full.

But they don't go there anymore.

That sign at the Victoria Park lake –

It pops, again, into John's head.

A year or so ago, they were sitting outside the Ship Aground and suddenly it pelted it down. The landlord stuck his head out the door, called the families in.

Good lad, Jon thought.

But just after they got settled inside to wait it out, he watched as the landlord put his hand up, said 'no thanks' and blocked the Bengali family Jon knew lived nearby from coming in.

A couple of weeks later, the wall outside the Ship had some fresh graffiti.

NO DOGS, NO BLACKS, NO IRISH

'Do you mind if we get a little closer, love?' Jon asks. 'For Steel Pulse.'

Jackie's nodding. 'Is that them now?' she asks, pointing at the stage. 'It's gone awful quiet.'

'Yeah,' Jon says. 'That's them.'

'What's that they're wearing?'

Jon's not sure. They're kitted out all in white, with white robes – and great big white hoods. The crowd, Jon realises, have gone dead quiet. The band kick into their song 'Ku Klux Clan'.

'Fucking hell,' Jon says.

As Noble leaves the backstage area someone else claps him on the back –

'Thanks for that, big man. On stage, I mean,' the bloke is saying. 'We could use someone like you. Here.'

He gives Noble a card.

'Cheers,' Noble says.

On the card, a name: Red Saunders.

As he leaves the park, Noble makes for the uniforms gathered near the Bethnal Green exit to get a sense of what they're about. He spots Gardiner again, laughing.

'All right, Chance,' Gardiner waves. 'Enjoy the show?'

'Which one?'

'Don't be cheeky, son.'

Noble grins, walks away thinking: the music or Brick Lane.

Suzi's stage right when she gets the shot that makes her name and captures, for her, what the day has been all about. The crowd, in the background of the shot, a mixture of black, brown, white faces, a mixture of expressions, of awe, wonder, determination, joy and, above all, she thinks, just before she snaps it, shock, yes, that's it, shock.

There is a look of shock on a lot of faces.

In the foreground, Steel Pulse, dressed in white robes and white hoods, play some serious political reggae music.

2

Skinhead

May 1978

Gideon

Your mate Phil says, It's on, tonight, you should come. You decide you should. It's an important one, Phil says, top brass are going and there's some announcement. You pick Phil up on the way. Bag of chips, Phil? you ask, shall we? I've got a bag of something else, mate, Phil says, we'll have that. You stop at the edge of the estate, sit on a wall and Phil pulls out a little plastic sachet of yellowing amphetamine. Traveller speed, Phil says, mixed in some lairy gyppo's pocket. You both laugh at that. It'll get you nice and psyched, Phil adds. You don't doubt it. You both have a big snort and the drugs come on immediately, that sulphur burn in the nose and in the head. Phil says, Let's go and get a drink, it'll be starting soon. So the pair of you march up past the Cambridge Heath Hackney Road junction and down alongside the train line, chucking stones and spitting, and turn right past the tube and along Bethnal Green Road looking in at the pubs and everyone in the pubs gives you a look, it might be a nod, yeah, go on, or it might be a raised eyebrow, or it might be a turned back, but you notice it all right, a couple of big, scary-looking lads in bovver boy boots and jackets, cropped hair and wired, and you do get a bit of attention, like you're being cheered on or at least acknowledged, and that feels good. The pub is full. You're nodding and buzzing and grinding your teeth, which are right on edge, but there's a grin trying to get out through your buzzing teeth, and Phil is shouldering through the crowd to the bar where there are lagers and bitters already poured and lined up and a couple of empty pint glasses with notes in and Phil drops a few into one of them and hands you a lager which is flat and sour but tastes good anyway, cools your chattering teeth. Phil's nodding at one or two others, shaking the odd hand, introducing you, and you're sized up and there's nods in your direction, the odd twist of the mouth that seems to say, yeah, he looks tasty, and there's a right old racket in the room and it puts you in mind of the pubs around Green Street and Plaistow on match day when you'd go with your old man and all the noise and the optimism and the laughter, something like that, but with more edge, more meaning, or something, more significance. You look around and see grey faces and red faces and white faces, you see skins and boots, braces and leather, you see brown suits and sideburns, you see grey suits and ties, you see work coats and dust-covered overalls, you see men, a lot of men, and three tarts behind the bar serving these men, serving them with their big smiles and their big tits and their big teeth, chattering too, their big teeth, smudged with red lipstick and laughing, laughing, laughing, pouring pint after pint after pint. Phil nudges you and juts his chin. That's Tyndall, and that's Webster, he's saying, they're top boys, right, and there, over there, and he nods, that's Derrick Day, he's the firm's organiser, and you nod and you grind your teeth, and you think you know that name, and Phil's saying, I'll introduce you later to Little Derrick, no relation, we call him that on account of him being fucking massive, and Phil's laughing and you're laughing, and Phil says hang about, it's starting, and the room hushes and quiets, and you fumble for your notes and get you and Phil a top-up, and then Tyndall or Webster, you're not sure which one of them it is, but it is one of them, Tyndall or Webster bangs a gavel on a table, yells order, order, and then Tyndall or Webster is up on a chair, Tyndall or Webster is speaking.

METROPOLITAN POLICE
APPEAL FOR ASSISTANCE

MURDER

THURSDAY MAY 4, 7.40 PM

**ALTAB ALI, aged 24, was stabbed in Adler
Street, E1 (off Whitechapel Road).**

WERE YOU IN THE AREA?
DID YOU SEE ANYTHING?

Please contact the Murder Squad at
LEMAN STREET POLICE STATION
Tel: 01-488 5212

All information treated as strictly confidential

Whitechapel police station, 5 May 1978.

It doesn't take Whitechapel plod too long to find the three little toerags who knifed poor old Altab Ali by the park in Adler Street on the night of 4 May.

Noble reckons the village elders made sure of it. The old-school faces. He reckons they would not have been at all happy with the casual, vicious, *public* nature of the attack, drawing attention.

Three young lads in custody. Noble called over from his base in West End Central, part of the Met Initiative on Race Crime.

He nods at DC Gardiner. 'Told you we'd be seeing more of each other.'

Gardiner says, 'Two downstairs in holding and we've got one of the scumbags in an interview room.'

'They do it then?'

Gardiner winks. 'That's the word.'

'Right.'

'Only a matter of time. You've got the leader, if you can call him that.'

Gardiner hands Noble a piece of paper. On it, a statement:

If we saw a Paki we'd have a go at them. We would ask for money and then beat them up. I've beaten up Pakis on at least five occasions.

'He said that, did he?'

Gardiner shakes his head. 'The younger one, but it's a start.'

'It's not a confession though, is it?' Noble says.

Gardiner shakes his head. 'He was showing off.'

'Charming,' Noble says. 'The other one say anything?'

'The cunt was crying for his mum.'

'She visit?'

Gardiner laughs. 'Briefly.'

'What a country.'

Gardiner nods down the corridor. 'All yours, mate.'

In the interview room, a room without windows, a room with a bolted-down table and a fixed ashtray in its centre, Noble looks into the dead-ened eyes of the suspect, seventeen years old, a history of violence etched into his face and knuckles, a forehead squat and creased, lined by fury and hate –

Noble lights the suspect's cigarette, an Embassy, and Noble watches him smoking his Embassy while handcuffed.

It screams previous, form.

Noble says, 'This won't take long. One of your pals has confessed and fingered you and your other mate.'

'OK,' he says.

'I'm not interested in the what or the how, son,' Noble says. 'We know exactly what you were doing and where, how the victim – *your* victim – staggered a few yards into the park and then bled out.'

Noble notes the suspect's demeanour is unaffected by this description of the crime.

'No,' Noble says, 'I'm interested in *why*.'

'No reason at all,' the suspect says.

Noble nods. 'We believe the victim was on his way to vote.'

The suspect shrugs. He looks hard at Noble. 'I didn't know Pakis could vote,' he says.

Noble nods again. 'What you're saying is this is a motiveless crime?'

The suspect draws on his Embassy. The smoke climbs the walls and stains the linoleum ceiling, stains the dirty floors.

'Well?'

He grinds his Embassy into the table. 'I want my brief,' he says.

Noble nods. 'You'll need him.'

Back down the corridor, Gardiner is waiting.

'There's some clown at front desk who wants a word,' he says.

'With me?'

'Why not, mate?' Gardiner laughs. 'Might as well be you.'

'Who is it?'

'Just some clown. You might find it interesting.'

Gardiner straightens up. 'Cuppa, while you're here? Kettle's on.'

Noble nods. 'Three sugars.'

'Good man.'

At front desk, Noble ushers Shams Uddin into an office for a word.

Shams Uddin tells Noble that he has information about Altab Ali.

'So, what was your relationship with Altab Ali?' Noble asks Shams Uddin.

'He was a friend,' Shams Uddin says. 'We used to watch wrestling on a Saturday afternoon. I was the last person to speak to him, apart from – well, you know.'

Noble nods. 'Off to vote, was he?'

'He was. I'd just been,' Shams Uddin says. 'I was feeling excited, I was a big boy, casting my vote for the first time.'

'It's a big moment,' Noble says.

Shams Uddin goes on. 'Mr Ali was on his way back from work, same textile factory as me, carrying bags of shopping. He told me he needed to go home because he had some cooking to do and after that he was going to go out and vote too. It was a big day for us.'

'Why's that?'

'There've been racist incidents in the area that we just ignore. We know there's no place for us unless we fight back. So, everyone joined together – Bangladeshi people, Caribbean people, Indian people, Pakistani people. Everyone is involved.'

'By voting in local council elections,' Noble says.

'Absolutely,' Shams Uddin says. He looks at Noble. His eyes blaze. 'The activist Ansar Ahmed Ullah has said that "it's difficult for Bengalis to go out on their own because you're often abused. If you live on a council estate your neighbours can be very hostile towards you. They break your windows, they push rubbish through your letterbox

– basically make your life miserable." We're voting for change, you understand? And we won, didn't we, in a way?'

Noble nods. They did win, in a way. The National Front took a hammering, at least.

Shams Uddin says, 'Black and white, unite and fight.'

Noble thinks about the previous Sunday, about where he was.

'One of our community leaders told us,' Shams Uddin says, 'that if we kill racism from the political ground, it will automatically die on the streets.'

Noble nods.

'So,' Shams Uddin says, 'we're going to take Altab Ali's coffin all the way to Downing Street.'

Noble thinks about the previous Sunday. He thinks:

Fat lot of good that did anyone.

Hackney police station, 8 a.m., 6 May 1978.

The day after Noble interviews the murderers of Altab Ali, he's sitting in a meeting in another Hackney nick, this time on the Lower Clapton Road.

Gardiner's there, looking chipper, and a couple of lads Noble doesn't recognise, older, a tired look to them. Rough skin and hangover tans.

There's a bloke he does know, he thinks, Kieran Caldwell –

A Hackney boy with a chip on his shoulder.

Irish, funnily enough, with a name like that, and bullied at school, Noble's heard. They're the same age, more or less, and Caldwell doesn't like Paddy Noble much. Something about Noble not growing up on the Murder Mile in Belfast. Hardly my fault, *that*, Noble's always thought.

Five men gulp sweet tea. Five men smoke Embassy cigarettes.

The meeting was called late the night before, and there's brass in attendance, part of the racially aggravated assault unit, the Paki Squad, as it's known at West End Central.

The meeting's chaired by a division head, a Welsh bloke, DS Williams.

He's saying, 'The body was pulled out the canal last night, down by the Prince of Wales pub, under the Lea Bridge Road. The deceased lived in the small estate on Mildenhall Road, just down from Clapton Pond, and he'd been out jogging, according to his wife, and never came home. She had the family out looking for him—'

'So, half of Brick Lane then,' someone mutters.

Sharp looks.

'She had the family out looking for him,' Williams says, 'as she doesn't trust the police.'

Nodding at this, mainly from Caldwell, Noble notes.

'He's a community leader, whatever that means, so there were a lot of people involved in the search. Some kids saw the body caught up in some blue plastic sheeting, half-sunk. They thought it was a bit of furniture, a shopping trolley, and were throwing stones at it.'

'Nice surprise for them, should've been in school,' someone says.

'The deceased's name is Shahid Akhtar,' Williams goes on. 'Thirty-eight years old, father of three. He was missing for approximately forty-eight hours.'

Noble glances at Gardiner but he's miles away.

Caldwell says, 'He's a big wheel at the mosque at the Lea Bridge Roundabout. He's a businessman too, interests on and around, yeah, don't laugh, Brick Lane.'

'Thanks,' Williams says. Williams looks at Noble. 'Yesterday, DC Noble interviewed Carl Ludlow, Roy Arnold and a third suspect, who will remain anonymous as he is a minor, for the murder of Altab Ali in Whitechapel on the fourth of May.'

Noble nods. He feels the cynical stares of the older lads, knows Chance Noble is a Hollywood-case-only sort of a geezer, promoted beyond his years –

'These three have since been charged with the murder of Altab Ali.'

Someone goes, Nasty little cunts.

Someone else goes, Job done.

Someone else, Well then.

'Guv,' Noble says, 'with respect, it doesn't exactly sound like the same MO.'

'It doesn't have to, Chance,' Caldwell says.

'These lot and their sort,' Williams says, 'drink at the Ship Aground pub on the Lea Bridge Road, about two hundred metres from where the deceased was pulled out.'

Right, Noble mutters.

'Arsing around by the canal, the poor sod jogs past and Bob's your big brother, another random hate crime.'

'I—'

'Leave it, Chance. The timeline fits.'

'We're sure the death should be treated as suspicious?'

'For now. Autopsy's a cunt, the waterlogging takes forever.'

'We better get some faces out and about reassuring the elders,' Gardiner says. 'Both mobs.'

Williams nods. 'Word from above is clear: despicable acts of abhorrent racist violence. Three thugs or other swing, end of story.'

'If he's a community leader,' one of the older lads says, 'they're going to kick up a bit of a fuss.'

They fucking well should, Noble thinks.

'Crowd control,' Williams says. 'Community outreach. Got that? Ongoing investigation, *not* a criminal investigation. OK? We'll run a notice in the *Hackney Gazette*, keep a lid on things.'

Nodding.

'Read this.' Williams circulates papers.

On them, statements. Noble reads three:

There was a marked increase in racist graffiti, particularly NF symbols, all over Tower Hamlets and in the presence both of NF 'heavies' and clusters of alienated young people at key fascist locations, especially in Bethnal Green

Ken Leech, Anglican priest for Brick Lane

… the Bengali youth, who have joined enthusiastically with their white friends in combating a menace which in its ultimate form will spell the death knell of a democratic Britain

Tassaduq Ahmed, educational worker in the East End

45

How many more racial attacks? Why are the police covering up?

From the statement announcing the carrying of Altab Ali's coffin to
Downing Street

'Officially, of course,' Williams says, 'this means our detail is considerably enhanced.'

More nodding.

'Higher profile. There's an opportunity here for any ambitious types among you.'

Noble thinks: too right there is.

As they leave the room, Caldwell nods at Noble.

'Enjoy yourself, did you, at the concert?'

Noble smiles. 'All right, Kieran?'

'Bunch of fucking wasters, that lot,' Caldwell says. 'All mouth. Your sort of a scene, like.'

'The reggae was something else.'

Caldwell frowns. 'Don't piss about, eh, Chance.'

'Take it easy, Kieran,' Noble says.

Suzi's listening to Keith snore in their bed as she drinks her tea and has a roll-up.

She's looking out the window at a grey May morning. The squat is quiet this time of day. Suzi's an early riser and this suits her. Their little studio is six floors up and has a view over the canal. You can see down to Stratford on a good day, up to Springfield Park. A disused textile factory is what it was, institutional chic now. The units, if you want to give their rooms an estate-agent makeover, are big and white-walled, like a hospital. A mental hospital, Keith says. Once you're in, he laughs, you're only going out one way.

Point is, it is an old place of business, so there's facilities on every floor, shared toilets and kitchens, a room with a big bath and a couple of showers. Everything works and there's enough of them to police it; it's like a co-operative. They even had to go through an interview process to get a unit, she and Keith.

46

Oh, you know *The Ruts*, the co-op board laughed when they turned up. You should have said.

We did, Suzi told them.

Yeah, yeah, *Keith*, we know *you*.

Suzi loved these boards of men, these leaders. They didn't have a fucking clue, most of them. Slogans and corduroy, un-showered and shy – at least when it comes to doing the washing-up. And using contraception, the state of their broods. Never mind monogamy.

They said to Keith, You just make sure our sound system is amazing next party we have, man, and we'll get on just fine.

Groovy, Keith said.

That was three years ago, when Suzi was just eighteen and this was all she could afford. Not much has changed, she thinks, and anyway she likes it here, she's happy.

And squatting's an art like anything else: you need a vanguard to figure out how to get the electricity on, pay rates, get a certain legitimacy. Those floppy-haired graduate politics students at Enfield Poly were good for that, at least.

And Keith's nice to them. He was doing the music at a big reggae crowd's birthday party the year before, up in Dalston, and he invited the whole squat. Bring your own booze, he told them. Lots of it, preferably.

So, everyone is all excited and dressed up in their tweed and their desert boots to impress the blacks, bags and bags of Red Stripe and pouches of hash, expecting a dub party or something. All the Rastas, Suzi remembers, were drinking brandy and listening to Lonnie Donegan and Waylon Jennings, laughing at the white man, in a nice way, mind.

Keith loved it and he wasn't taking the piss. It was kind of him, what he's like –

Doing them a favour, *sincere*.

Suzi glances at him now and smiles. Y-fronts and drool, he's still a looker.

Out the window, there's a thin mist above the water and Suzi sips her tea and smokes her roll-up in one of Keith's shirts. She'll have to get dressed properly if she wants more than a cuppa, but it's one of those mornings when anything takes a little while longer than it should.

The Ruts were playing the night before and the post-carnival vibe was strong.

Suzi's piece in *Temporary Hoarding* is done, she's just checking the photographs. She knows which one'll get the attention, if one does. And it won't be the one she snapped of the grumpy-looking lad walking away, though that is going in, what with its accidental panorama of the whole scene.

Keith groans but doesn't wake up.

Suzi hears a van pull in at the front of the building. Two men get out. Suzi can't read what it says on the side of the van.

The men are carrying a load of envelopes, a roll of what looks like posters. Probably some event or other to advertise, though they don't look the type.

One of the men is carrying a toolbox, which he opens. They step up to the front door and that's when Suzi loses sight of them, the blind spot.

She listens out for knocking or the bell – there is one and it does work.

But that's not what she hears –

She hears nails, nails being driven into wood, nails being driven into the doors and the window boards they've put up to protect the ground floor.

'What the fuck is that racket?' Keith says.

'I don't know, love,' Suzi says. 'It sounds like we might be getting notice.'

'Not now, eh?' Keith says. 'How about a cup of tea instead?'

Suzi smiles at her fella. 'I'll make a fresh pot.'

'Don't forget to warm it first, love,' Keith reminds her.

Hackney town hall.

Clapton Pond is a desperate place –

Jon Davies shakes his head – rueful. He's in a meeting, Jon is, but he's not listening. It's more piss than water, the pond, he's thinking. The ducks look like they're on smack.

What a place to live.

He cycled past that morning, up from his three-bedroom terraced on Mildenhall Road, his son sitting in a baby seat on the back, saying nothing. Up to the playgroup in the United Reformed Church on Lower Clapton. *What a place to bring up a kid.* A kid and a cat; what a family. The chair of the Housing Committee, some no-mark councillor, is droning on. Something about squatters. Something about the right to housing. Something about ethnic integration. Something about building communities.

'What do you think, Jon?'

Jon looks blank. 'What do I think?' he says.

'About the proposal, Jon. Will it work, you know, for your department?'

Jon nods. He likes the euphemism *for your department.*

Is it legal, is the question?

And yes, broadly speaking it is.

Chucking out squatters with a minimum of necessary force, of *welly*, is very legal if you do it the right way.

'My department,' Jon says. 'On board.'

The councillor, the chair of the Housing Committee, Godfrey Heaven, smiles. 'Glad to hear it,' he says.

Jon raises his eyebrows.

These committee chairs: elected councillors living off their expenses, their allowance.

The more committees you chair, the more you pocket.

He's eyeing Heaven. He's all right, this Heaven, but still, a bit too much fucking about in meeting rooms, moderating, delegating, *chairing*, to really respect him.

Heaven sent, is the joke: Thank Godfrey.

The meeting drifts; Jon drifts.

Jon's wife, Jackie, found their cat, then a kitten, in Clapton Pond.

Some old perv was trying to drown a whole bag of them. Fat chance. Might as well have tried in a puddle, to be fair. Jackie marched over, yelled something unsavoury and the bloke legged it. Five kittens: lovely result. A couple to cousins up the road, one next door, one to the lady who runs the corner shop and one for them, Eric. They called the cat Eric. Eric from Clapton. Very funny, it is, when Jon cracks that joke. Talk about auspicious beginnings.

Then real-life Eric says all that awful stuff about Enoch Powell and the joke's not funny anymore and Jon doesn't play Eric's records much these days.

Why did we ever stay in this place?

Well, that's an easy one: money. Seventeen grand for a three-bedroom terraced and a pregnant newlywed in tow: no brainer. And the job, of course. Why he's in this meeting. Solicitor for Hackney Council. *What a place this is, eh?* Bunch of hippies, mostly. Hippies and thugs. Council run by flared collars and heavy black boots. The corridors echo like a mental hospital. The walls glare at you, dare you to have a go. They're hard, these walls. You could bounce a head off them, no doubt. Marxists and racists, the loony left and the organised right. Nasty business, Hackney Council turned out to be.

The meeting slides. The meeting drags itself along by its knuckles, its legs fucked.

Then: a name is mentioned.

Derrick Day.

Jon's from round here, not too far away, he's local, so he might as well nail some East End colours to the mast, especially with his son born in Hackney Mothers' –

And he knows the name Derrick Day, all right.

Fat Bastard, to his friends.

Derrick Day, *politician*, to his enemies.

Derrick Day: Hoxton activist and parliamentary candidate for the National Front. Old-school racist, old Fat Bastard.

The problem is 73 Great Eastern Street, London EC2 –

Recently purchased, undergoing renovation and now: a planning application to use the building as a publishing and storage facility for the National Front.

Right on the council's doorstep.

The corridor. The hard, echoing corridor. The walls curve. Heels click on a dirty, polished floor. They're like public baths, Jon thinks, these corridors. A sort of damp or dankness, in all seasons. A door opens.

'So?'

Jon smiles. It's his colleague, Kate, from the legal team at Hackney Council.

'It's all go,' Jon says.

'How exactly?'

Jon waves at the empty corridor. 'Applications,' he says. 'There'll be applications. You know how it works. Building communities.'

Kate does know. 'Communities, right,' she says. 'Hardly the same thing as forcible ejection of squatters.'

Jon nods.

Kate crosses her arms. Her lips pucker, purse. 'And Great Eastern Street?'

'Like they said in the meeting,' Jon says, walking away. 'It's a planning application. The building is owned, Kate, it's not the same thing as the squatters.'

His heels click; his clicking heels echo, really ring out.

'Owned by who, though?' Kate says, quite loudly.

Without turning, Jon tells her that it doesn't matter.

'You know that's no sort of an answer,' Kate calls after him.

He raises one arm, doesn't look round.

The Met Race Crime Initiative hub is Whitechapel nick and Noble's past the front desk, down a long corridor, up the stone stairs, down another long, echoing corridor, buzzed through a security-controlled door, down one more long, echoing, cold corridor, he arrives at a door and he knocks on the door, he opens the door and he pokes his head round the door and says –

Guv, a word?

He's speaking to Chief Inspector Maurice Young, top man on the Met Race Crime Initiative. Young himself hand-picked Noble.

Another nickname for old Chance 'Paddy' Noble: Golden Bollocks.

'Have a seat, DC Noble,' Young says.

Noble sits down.

'What can I do for you?'

'I need a man, guv, a new-recruit type, unknown.'

Young nods. 'Go on.'

'I want someone on the inside.'

'That's an ambitious goal, DC Noble.'

Noble nods. 'Opportunities, guv, right?'

Young tells him he's in the right place.

'I think I am, guv.'

Young considers this. 'Right or left?'

Noble holds Young's look. 'Left, guv.'

'Of course.'

Young plucks a fountain pen from a pot on his desk. He takes a smart, embossed notepad. He writes on this notepad with a flourish. He tears, carefully, a sheet of paper.

'Speak to this man here. Go and see him.'

On the sheet of paper, a name, a telephone number, an acronym, SDS –

Special Demonstration Squad.

Young opens a desk drawer and takes from it an envelope.

'He'll be expecting a call. Give him this envelope.'

Noble pockets the envelope and nods.

'One other thing,' Noble says. 'Shahid Akhtar?'

'Ongoing investigation,' Young says. 'You know that. I won't see you out.'

Suzi and Keith and some of the co-op board are standing outside the squat examining the handiwork of the men in the van.

It's thorough, they'll give them that.

You can hardly see the plywood for paper.

The board are saying things like, But we're on the same side, and, There are plenty of other places that do not support the council's policy of right to housing for all and the building of communities, that's what we are, a community, at least broadly, and, What the fuck are they playing at? and, How are they going to house immigrants in a fucking abandoned factory?

Things like that.

Suzi watches Tiny Tony, a very tall, thin man, and chief co-op 'head', go back inside. Keith is chuffing away and slurping tea in vest and jeans. Suzi looks at her watch. She's due at the RAR HQ in not too long – the pub, that is – and plans are afoot, she's heard.

One of the board says to Keith, 'What you working on these days, Mozart?'

That's their nickname for Keith: Mozart. It's called irony, apparently.

'Studio stuff,' Keith says. 'Down the Sonic Bunker, producing and engineering some new punks' new single today.'

'Right.'

'Yeah, they're all right. The Buzzcocks, they're called. Song's about falling in love with someone you shouldn't have fallen in love with, something like that. Keep an eye, they'll be massive.'

'Will do, Keith, will do.'

'Sounds catchy,' someone else says.

'Yeah, yeah,' Keith smiles.

Suzi smiles. She loves her fella. The Sonic Bunker is his little hideaway, a room with a drum kit and a 16-track just off Victoria Park. The owner lives upstairs and gives Keith the run of the place. Suzi tends to steer clear; these young punks are like the co-op hippies in terms of their less than enlightened views on women.

Tiny Tony's back.

'Right,' he announces. 'Not being racist, but. Here's the thing. The Bengalis, I see, have set up squats in the following parts of London's East End.' Tiny Tony brandishes a piece of paper and reads from it.

'Matlock Street, Varden Street, Walden Street and Old Montague Street, in Jubilee Street, Adelina Grove, Lindley Street, Redmans Road, White Horse Road, Aston Street, Flamborough, Westport and, for a bit, Arbour Square. So,' he says.

'Not being racist,' Suzi says.

'So?'

'Why would that be racist?'

'It's the council, isn't it? They're not targeting them, are they?'

Suzi shakes her head. 'I don't know.'

Someone says, 'Next week they're going to carry that lad Altab Ali's coffin from Brick Lane to Downing Street. We should go, you know, solidarity.'

Tiny Tony nods. 'Yeah, we should. But a few of us need to stay here.'

He taps one of the many posters plastered on the boards. 'Look, we've got a month to fight this and we will. We're a part of this ethnic integration malarkey and all we need to do is prove it.'

There are murmurs of That's right, Course we bloody are.

'What we'll do,' Tiny Tony says, 'is petition this councillor and make our case. That'll buy us plenty of time, either way of course.'

Suzi watches Keith nod. They'll be OK, she thinks, for him this is just another part of the life he's chosen, the life he leads –

More like the life that chose him, she thinks.

'Who's the councillor?' Suzi asks.

'Godfrey Heaven,' someone says. 'Chair of the Housing Committee.'

'Since when did an old factory mean housing, I ask you?' someone says.

'Yeah, yeah,' Tiny Tony mutters.

'Godfrey Heaven can go to hell,' someone shouts.

Jon and Jackie moved into their three-bedroom terraced twelve months before, after a couple of years in a flat on Queensdown Road overlooking the park. It hasn't changed. Today the press is all about some poor sod knifed to death in an unprovoked racist attack up the road in Whitechapel. The lad was called Altab Ali, Jon sees, job in a textile factory. On his way home from work, apparently, carrying a load of shopping, about to cook a meal for his missus and her family, and all excited as he was set to vote in the local elections for the first time. *What a waste.* The three nasty little cunts who did it are unrepentant to the point of indifference. At least that's how it's reported. The younger one, sixteen years old and therefore unnamed, is the one they quote: *No reason at all*, he'd said, when asked why they'd done it. *If we saw a Paki we'd have a go at them. We would ask for money and then beat them up. I've beaten up Pakis on at least five occasions.* Jon knows very well that on the same day poor Altab Ali had a six-inch blade stuck in his neck, forty-three of the council seats were contested by the National Front. *What a place this is,* Hackney. The casual nature of the kid's language, the easy use of it – sickening. *We'd ask for money.* Ask. Poor old Altab Ali rushing home to vote in an election in which the fucking National Front featured so prominently – *what a country.*

There's another notice in the local paper that Jon reads with interest. A neighbour of theirs, across the road in the low-rise housing estate, Shahid Akhtar, missing for a couple of days, now found dead. Local businessman, community leader. Police investigation is ongoing but at this stage it is not a criminal investigation.

Jon takes a moment to digest this.

He didn't know Shahid Akhtar well but they were on nodding terms.

He was quite flash, very friendly.

Big smile, most of the time. His wife teasing him, his kids.

Shame. A real shame.

Ayeleen: I push open the door of the café that my uncle owns, where my mother sometimes waits for me, where my father works and spends time with his friends. He's the manager, my father, but he's never here when I come after school.

'All right, Leenie?' asks Lea, the waitress.

I smile and nod. 'Yeah, all right,' I say, and it's true as school has finished. I find a table in the corner and open my school bag and take out my homework.

Lea brings me a glass of milk. 'Homework at your age?' she says. 'I don't know.'

'I'm seven and a half,' I tell her. 'I'm in the juniors. Spelling, that's all.'

'I went to Rushmore,' Lea says, her eyes all wide, 'once upon a time.'

She's talking to a man I've seen here before.

They're laughing about something but I don't know what.

The man stands up. 'I've got a spelling for you,' he says to me. 'How do you spell tip?'

'Very funny,' Lea tells him.

'T-I-P,' I say.

'I've got a tip for you,' the man says, opening the door. 'Don't eat yellow snow. Ta-ra.'

The door shuts but I can still hear him laughing.

'Ignore him, babes,' Lea says.

'I wouldn't eat snow of any colour,' I tell her.

'Clever girl,' Lea winks. 'Your mum will be along in a little while. You want anything while you wait?'

I shake my head, suck on my pencil.

'Suit yourself,' Lea says.

She goes back to the counter and in a sing-song voice tells me, 'Shout if you change your mind!'

She's nice, Lea.

I scribble in my schoolbook, suck my pencil, kick the chair –

My uncle Ahmet is outside on the street. He's talking to two younger-looking Turkish men and an Indian man, and it looks like he's shouting at them. The Turkish men keep nodding and looking down. My uncle Ahmet is shaking his head and waving his arms about, going a bit red in the face. After some time, he stops and sends the men away. They walk to a car and get inside and drive off.

Uncle Ahmet comes into the café, he nods at Lea, he stands over the table where I'm sitting and he pats my head.

'Working hard, I see, as always!' he laughs and claps his hands together.

'Yes, uncle,' I tell him.

He's nodding, Uncle Ahmet. He's looking around the café, out to the street.

'And where is that father of yours when I need him, eh?'

'Mr Ahmet,' Lea says, 'he was in first thing.'

Uncle Ahmet mutters, 'I bet he was,' then smiles at Lea and says, 'Thank you, darling.'

'My mum will be here soon,' I say to Uncle Ahmet.

His smile is very wide when he says, 'But I need to see your father, love.'

I don't know how to answer him, so I don't. Instead, I say, 'Why were you shouting at those men, uncle?'

He smiles. 'Some … sadness. A man I know, a business partner, a friend at the mosque. That's all.'

'Oh.'

'It's fine, really. These things, they … happen.'

I nod. 'Yes, uncle.'

Uncle Ahmet then sits down at a table with Lea and he asks her some questions and they look at notebooks and he writes some things down, and Lea does lots of nodding and sometimes shakes her head, and Uncle Ahmet closes the notebooks and smiles at her and stands up again.

I'm still doing my spelling homework when my mother arrives.

'Hello there, sister-in-law,' Uncle Ahmet says to her.

My mother smiles but I can see she is surprised to see him. 'Hello, brother,' she says.

He smiles at me. 'My niece makes me very proud,' he laughs.

'She makes us all very proud.'

'She does.'

'Ayeleen, time to go.' My mother gestures at me to hurry up.

'Tell your husband I want to see him,' Uncle Ahmet says.

'He's *your* brother,' I tell him, and stick my tongue out.

'Very proud,' he says, winking.

I wave goodbye to Lea and we walk home. My father isn't there.

Noble elbows his way into the Britannia pub on Mare Street, next door to the Hackney Empire. It's 11 a.m. and there's a queue at the public bar. The place smells of disinfectant and sawdust, stale smoke and fresh smoke.

Noble waits patiently. The light is piss yellow through the dirty frosted glass. In front of him, on the bar, a jar of pickled eggs has seen better days. At the other end, saucers of tripe and onions for the really committed.

An old man shuffles off with his mild, glaring at Noble.

He's used to it, Noble is, this antipathy towards the Old Bill, though he doesn't think he looks too much the part this morning.

He's wearing a work coat and a fresh shirt, clean-shaven chops and Chelsea boots.

Perhaps that's the problem –

The state of the clientele is desperate.

Noble points at a pump. 'Two of them, mate, and two whiskeys, Irish.'

The barman raises an eyebrow. 'Mick breakfast, is it?'

Noble smiles thin. 'Keep the change,' he says.

He takes the tray of drinks to the back of the bar where it's dark. Sitting at a table with his own pint and Irish whiskey is a man Noble knows is called Bill Stewart, the name on the piece of paper given to Noble by Maurice Young.

'Top of the morning to you,' Stewart says in a thick London accent. He raises his pint.

Noble nods. He passes Stewart a pint from the tray, a whiskey too.

Stewart examines the drinks, then examines Noble. 'Course,' he says, 'I forget myself, it's the fucking Scots who are mean cunts, not your mob.'

'This your local then?' Noble asks.

'Of a sort, mornings, anyway.'

'Oh yeah?'

'I work nights, son. This ain't a full Irish, don't be cheeky.'

Noble smiles. 'Wouldn't dream of it.'

'Good lad.'

Noble reaches into his inside pocket and takes out the envelope given to him by Young. He places the envelope on the table and pushes it over to Stewart.

Stewart takes a Rothmans from the packet on the table. He takes a disposable lighter and brings it to his Rothmans. He reaches into his own inside pocket and pulls out his reading glasses. He balances these little half-moons on the bridge of his nose.

He points at them. 'Know what they call me in here?'

Noble shakes his head.

'Old Bill.' Stewart roars then shakes and splutters with laughter. 'They've got no fucking idea.'

'That's funny,' Noble says.

'I know it's fucking funny, that's why I told you.'

'Right.'

Stewart opens the envelope and thumbs through the contents. He takes out from the envelope a sheet of embossed paper and he reads –

Noble waits. Noble sips his beer, sips his whiskey –

Stewart smiles. 'You need someone then.'

Noble nods.

'Someone young, someone who can look after himself, yeah?'

Noble nods. Noble sips his beer, sips his whiskey.

'Strikes me,' Stewart says, 'it might be favourable if this someone has done a stretch, right?'

'It might be, yeah.'

Stewart nods. 'Know what I do, do you?'

'Not exactly, no.'

'I'm with SDS, Special Demonstration Squad. Covert.'

Noble nods. Noble sips his beer, sips his whiskey.

'What I do is work with young officers. I find them and prep them. The sort that might fancy the Special Patrol Group that sort of thing, but are, in fact, better than that. See?'

'I think so, yeah.'

59

'And you, son, are flavour of the month, it seems.'

'Does it seem that?' Noble says.

'It does. Maurice Young doesn't call me very often but when he does, I listen.'

'That's good to know.'

'It fucking should be.'

Noble nods. Noble sips his beer, sips his whiskey.

'Right.' Stewart picks up his pint, the pint that Noble has bought him. He gulps down his pint. He bunches a fat fist around the whiskey glass that Noble has bought him and he throws his whiskey down his neck. 'Much obliged,' he says. He stands. 'Now you're coming with me.'

Noble finishes his beer, finishes his whiskey.

Noble nods.

Suzi's thinking that a lot of the men she knows wear dungarees.

It must be the half-Yank in her, she thinks, wanting to call them coveralls. Suzi's not been to the States in donkeys, and she's been in England long enough to use the term donkeys, but she learned as a teenager that a bit of mystique, a bit of foreign, doesn't half go a long way, so she's Suzi Sweetheart, American bird, when she wants to be.

She wanders down from the squat to the canal.

She's headed to the Prince of Wales, where the RAR Central Committee are having a get-together to bask in the glory of the carnival and make some decisions about the next issue of *Temporary Hoarding*.

The graffiti spells out NF roughly every twenty paces or so. It's on the walls, it's on the towpath, it's on any canal boat that's stupid enough to stay still for longer than five minutes. The odd Anarchist 'A' with its line through the middle sticks out a challenge of sorts. The NF flourish is just easier: one squiggle and a dash and there you have it –

A threat. Multiple threats, all over the place.

The canal heaves with rubbish and foam and oil.

A body was pulled out a little further on just the other day, Suzi gathers. In blue plastic, kids trying to sink it.

It doesn't bear thinking about.

The pub is a solid landmark. Just across is the Ship Aground but none of Suzi's lot will drink in there. The NF graffiti feels less like vandalism and more like a manifesto. Scrawled beneath, until last week:

NO DOGS, NO BLACKS, NO IRISH

What a country.

On the steps, up to the pub's saloon bar entrance, canal side, a rat pisses and then jumps into the water.

A group of kids cheer, sitting on the tables by the wall, their bikes scattered on the ground.

Above, sitting on benches outside the pub's 'conservatory', Suzi sees the RAR gang crowding the narrow terrace that looks down on the rats and the kids.

Suzi Sweetheart! someone calls out.

The kids look up at her. Calls of Oi, oi, and, Get your tits out –

Suzi gives them the finger, smiling.

Red Saunders is in ebullient mood. Syd Shelton is winking at Suzi as Red Saunders conducts the group in a cheer.

'This is just the beginning,' he's saying, 'we push on. This is only the beginning and it means nothing without actual progress.'

Suzi's drinking her half of bitter, half listening.

She's looking at the layout of *Temporary Hoarding*. They've used her captions under the photographs, like a commentary.

'It's a photo essay, is what it is,' Syd Shelton says to her. 'New journalism.'

'Just luck,' Suzi says. 'You kept this one in, then?'

She's pointing at the photograph she snapped of the moody hardman.

'Yeah, course,' Syd says. 'It's a glorious depiction of the day, perfectly sums up the diversity, you know? Look at the lad walking away from you – could be anyone.'

Suzi nods. She hopes this everyman doesn't read *Temporary Hoarding*. She suspects he doesn't.

'Drink?' Syd Shelton says. 'Same again?'

Suzi nods. 'Cheers, Syd,' she says to his back.

'September,' she hears Red Saunders saying, 'we'll do carnival two in September and we'll do it in the south. Give the man in Brixton something to shout about, am I right? Brockwell Park.'

There are mutters of Good idea, Let's do it bigger, Too fucking right you are.

Syd Shelton sits down with Suzi's half and his own pint. 'Elvis Costello's in already, apparently.' He nods at Red Saunders. 'Aswad, too. Misty again, no doubt.' They clink glasses. 'Keith heard anything about it yet, from The Ruts?'

Suzi shakes her head.

'Let us know, will you,' Syd Shelton says, 'if you hear anything, yeah?'

'Course, Syd,' Suzi says.

Suzi sees that David Widgery is about to say something. She focuses. He's clever, David Widgery is, Suzi thinks, a doctor, a sharp mind –

'First up though, Red, we're all going on the fourteenth, OK?' David Widgery is saying. 'The Bengali community is gathering thousands, almost ten thousand, maybe, to march Altab Ali's coffin from Whitechapel to Downing Street. It's happening and we are all going to be there.'

More mutters: Hear hear, and, Too fucking right we are, and, Yes yes –

David Widgery keeps talking. 'We all know that these racial attacks are a National Front plan to provoke the communities into blind retaliation, as they know that our political system will favour them when it comes to handing out punishment.'

Suzi thinks this sounds about right.

'It's been getting worse for a while,' David Widgery says. 'Worse since the National Front came on the scene, worse since Thatcher's turned up, and Callaghan and his government are doing nothing.'

More agreement. David Widgery, Suzi sees, is building to his point.

'With her alien culture speech,' David Widgery says, 'Thatcher has single-handedly recuperated overt racism into the parliamentary tradition.'

Well said, That's right, It's a fucking shame.

'Again and again, I'm seeing the consequences,' David Widgery says, his audience drinking their pints and their halves and listening intently. 'An elderly Asian hospital porter sacked for looking ill. A Bangladeshi woman sectioned in the seventh month of pregnancy. A white trade unionist driven to insomnia by window bashing after he's defended his Asian neighbour. And these are just a few examples. I could go on.'

David Widgery sits back and drinks thirstily at his pint. His audience claps.

Red Saunders says, 'Thanks, David. Your work on the frontline is more than any of us could ever do.'

David Widgery, Suzi notes, does not disagree.

The meeting winds down. The drinking is heavier now, mid-afternoon.

Red Saunders plonks himself down next to Suzi. She's watching as kids shuffle along the enormous pipe that runs across the canal along-side the bridge. They move cockily around the spikes.

'Suze,' Red Saunders says. 'Before I forget, well, before I get too drunk and forget, someone called for you at the office the other day.'

'Oh, yeah, who?'

'Didn't leave a name and didn't ask yours.'

'What does that mean, Red?'

'Well,' Red Saunders says, shuffling his backside along the bench, 'it's funny, actually. This bloke just asked the name of the bird who was back-stage taking photos. I assume he meant you.'

'Did you give him my name?'

'Course not, love,' Red Saunders says. 'You think I'm an idiot?'

'Course not.'

'Well then. I said I didn't know who the bird was. I just thought you should know.'

'He tell you what he wanted?'

'Some work opportunity, he said. I told him I'd ask around and to ring back.'

'Thanks, Red.'

'My pleasure, Sweetheart. Now –' and Red Saunders, beautiful bear of a man, wraps an arm around Suzi – 'same again?'

Hackney town hall, council office, reassuringly empty.

Jon Davis sits at his desk, sighs. He fishes a file from the cabinet under his desk. The file is named: 73 Great Eastern Street. He sifts through papers. He examines clauses. He studies contracts. The root cause of the case is a planning application from NF Properties Ltd with ownership and tenancy shared with two wholly owned, off the peg subsidiary companies. One of these is to handle printing and storage, and the other publicity, for commercial purposes of some form. In the paperwork, who the publicity is for, what they'll be printing and what they want to store is not made explicitly clear at any point. The whole thing is murky; planning applications being what they are, the council is prepared for this.

Jon Davis sighs again. NF Properties Ltd claim their initial does not stand for anything. 'It's a coincidence,' Jon reads. This is Tony Reed-Herbert, a lawyer from Leicester representing NF Properties Ltd. Jon has heard, unofficially, that Reed-Herbert is a National Front 'organiser'.

The problem is that the building, a disused warehouse, has been bought – for £47,000. Jon thinks that one way in here might be to work out where that money came from.

Jon reads testimonies. One, from Stuart Weir, Labour Party candidate:

Even in the Labour Party, I have experienced a reluctance to take on the far right. The most extreme example of this came some years ago when I was one of three people standing for election in Hackney. The agent (a man with real anti-fascist credibility) ordered us not to take part in a debate with the National Front candidate, Derek Day [sic], a violent thug and prominent racist, on the estate where he lived and not to canvas the estate. The agent even came to the meeting to order us out. We stayed, trounced Day in the debate and won over people on the estate as we canvassed. In the pub one evening, my colleague's handbag hit the table with a big thud. She was carrying a hammer, 'just in case'.

Another, from 'Anti Nazi League – a critical examination. A Resistance pamphlet'.

There was a relatively successful attempt to kick the NF off their pitch at the top of Brick Lane on the Sunday. Local NF leader Derrick Day and his Hoxton thugs were routed, with Day running and attempting to hide under a parked lorry. Unfortunately, the fat bastard couldn't fit and attempts by our comrades to kick him under were not appreciated by Derrick. Not even a thank you!

A small TV and VCR have been brought into Jon's office and he pops in a VHS cassette tape to watch a thirty-second clip he has been told he should study.

It features Derrick Day.

Day jumps out of a council-estate flat's ground-floor window. It's in Hoxton, Jon knows, not far up the road.

Day runs at the cameraman, a flash-looking thug in hat and suit right behind him.

Day looks deranged, Jon thinks, spittle flying, his white combover waving about the place.

Day vaults, quite athletically, the low wall of the estate's perimeter.

And then Day is yelling at the camera:

Want something on how many people have been mugged?

Day squares up, yells something Jon can't understand, then:

I'll break your fucking jaw –

He yells, his fist clenched.

Yes, he shouts, I am a racist and why?

Day is banging his chest, his fist clenched.

Who's made me a racist?

Day points, thrusts his finger, shouts more. He howls at the estate.

This government, he shouts, the Conservatives.

His sinews strain, his face creases with anger, with hate –

And every standing, stinking councillor, he yells, who sticks up for the nigger.

Jon Davis presses pause and breathes out. Jon Davis sighs, again. He presses play.

Day, calmer now, saying, And I'll stand by my words.

As he says this, two young black women are leaving the same estate. They pass around Day, oblivious it seems, to his bile, his hate.

Because I don't like these people, Day points at the young women, never will do.

Day glares, content, at the camera.

Jon shakes his head. Is this what he's up against? he thinks.

He switches off the TV set, ejects the VHS cassette, puts it back in its flimsy cardboard case and switches off the VCR.

Jon flicks on through the file – half-hearted. He is feeling faintly hopeless, Jon is, with all this. He flicks on and reads a little. He just wants to get to the end, to feel like he has done something useful, has made some sort of progress.

He shakes his head. He doesn't know how anything ever gets done. There are meetings about scheduling meetings. There are memos about sending memos. There are phone calls about the problems of phone calls. He sighs. He turns the last page –

A tight, brown envelope. The envelope has his name on it. The envelope is sealed. He opens the envelope. Inside: two photos, black-and-white. The first photo he recognises immediately: Great Eastern Street, number 73. The second photo takes some time to register. It is of a man, beaten. The man is prone. The man's face is bloodied. The man's eyes are swollen. The man's legs are splayed. Jon does not recognise the man. He thinks that may not be the point.

Jon sits. Jon considers this development. It does not feel especially welcome.

Later, the phone on his desk rings. Jon cradles the receiver.

'Yes?'

Call, Jon. Shall I put it through?

'Please.'

The call is patched through. There is a pause, a tone. Then a voice:

Jon Davies?

'Yes.'

Seen them photos, Jon? On record, in that file of yours?

'Yes.'

Mind them photos, Jon, if I were you.

Jon replaces the receiver.

This threat, this intimidation, is something new.

Someone, he realises, has been poking around in his office.

Old Bill Stewart parks his Escort, *jams* his Escort, into a tight spot round the back of the Chinese takeaway on Lea Bridge Roundabout, Dan's Island –

The gears sound shot, the handbrake groans.

Noble says, 'Nice wheels.'

Stewart glares and lights a Rothmans. 'Follow me.'

One of the chefs is standing at the back door, smoking.

He nods at Stewart.

He says, 'Ah, William, upstairs.'

He points and cackles, his mouth yellow and shy of teeth.

'Cheers, Panda,' he says. 'Come on,' he says to Noble. 'Upstairs.'

'Right,' Noble says.

As they tread grease-spattered carpet, Stewart says, 'He's all right, Panda, we've used him for years.'

'Why's he called Panda?'

Stewart stops mid-staircase. 'You ever heard of Brilliant Chang, Chan Nan?'

'Can't say I have.'

'Someone should teach you some history, son. Chang was the big man a long time ago, ran parts of London. Old Panda here is family, firm-wise anyway, third generation.'

'Really?'

'Yeah, he might not look it, but he was a naughty boy once upon a time.'

'He turn, did he? That how you know him?'

'Something like that.'

'So why is he called Panda?'

Stewart smiles. 'His modus operandi as a criminal, as an enforcer.'

'Oh yeah?'

'Oh yeah. Guns first, out the door, ask questions later.'

'OK.'

'And he's a skinny cook.'

'Right.'

'So, think about it, you plonker: Panda.'

Noble says, 'I don't get it.'

'Panda. He eats shoots and leaves.'

Stewart, for the second time this morning, convulses with laughter.

'Very funny.'

'I know it is, I fucking made it up. Come on.'

They climb the stairs.

Stewart stops again, turns, says to Noble, 'He's a fucking Chinaman, the joke writes itself.'

Stewart continues up the stairs.

Noble says, 'Benny Hill.'

'What about Benny Hill?'

'I'm pretty sure you've nicked one of his jokes.'

'Well fucking arrest me, then,' Stewart says, shaking his head.

At the top of the stairs, a door. Stewart opens the door. Inside, a room, a bare room with a foldout table and three foldout chairs. On the table, an ashtray, smouldering. A young man is sitting at the table. He is dressed in bomber jacket and jeans, boots, a very close crop on his bonce and some lairy jewellery.

'All right, Bill,' the young man says.

'Parker,' Stewart says. 'I've got a job for you.'

Noble raises an eyebrow, points. 'This guy?'

Stewart's smiling. 'Abso-fucking-lutely.'

'But how did you know?'

'Know what?'

'Know what I need.'

Stewart laughs. 'I'm not just a pretty face, old son. I know which way the wind blows and I know you ain't getting anyone inside the National Front in the current political climate. I guessed, boy. You were going to pull a fast one.'

Noble thinks: Stewart knows I've told Young a porky about which outfit I'm putting this boy into. Stewart knows I'm putting this lad into the Front.

He must think it's the right move.

Noble's smiling. 'Beautiful,' he says. 'And he's been inside?'

Stewart winks. 'Assaulting a fellow officer, GBH, affray – got four months, did twenty-eight days for good behaviour.'

Parker shrugs.

Noble looks at this Parker, looks back at Stewart. He says to Stewart, 'That you, was it, the fellow officer?'

Stewart grins. 'Not just a pretty face, are you, Chance, old son?'

Home again, quite drunk now, Suzi cuddles up to Keith.

'Good day, love?' she asks.

'It was, love. This new band are good, I'm telling you.'

'Ever fallen in love with someone you shouldn't have done, is that them?'

'It goes something like that.'

'Have you?' Suzi asks. 'Have you ever fallen in love with someone you shouldn't have?'

'Not lately, gorgeous,' says Keith.

'Me neither,' says Suzi.

PART TWO

You're the One that I Want

1

Summer of Hate

June–August 1978

Gideon

And the gist of what Tyndall or Webster is saying is, We need to make a stand here, we need to show these lot whose place this is, and that it's not right that they can march a coffin, unopposed, right through our heartland, right through our plot, our space, and right up to those jokers in Downing Street who did nothing about it and let them have it, let them have their day, well their day is coming, I can tell you, their day is certainly coming. And there are cheers and Phil goes, Altab Ali, innit? and you nod as you know all about that, thousands of Bengalis marching, they'd had enough, and a bit of you thinks, well, fair play, but most of you don't think that at all. And then Tyndall or Webster is talking again, talking over the hubbub, talking over the cheering, talking over the jeering, talking over the shouting and the braying, and he's saying, We've got right on our side and we've had a little result anyway, you know why? as we're in this together and we will not be defeated, and we have right on our side, and you know how I know? look at this, OK, that march, that demonstration that went through our heartland, through our plot, through our space, that march, that demonstration was thousands strong, thousands there were, but who knew, outside those thousands? Because there are millions of us! Cheering, yelling, shouting and braying. You look at Phil, whose mouth is twisted, with spittle forming at its corners, in its meaty knot, and he's drinking fast, Phil, and you look at the pub as it heaves and it sways, and Tyndall or Webster says, That march, that demonstration received no coverage in the Daily Mail. *That march, that demonstration received no coverage in the* Daily Telegraph. *That march, that demonstration received no coverage in the* Express. *There are cheers and yells, shouts and whistles. Lager is flying, splashing the crowd, but no one cares. Tyndall or Webster makes the gesture to simmer down. He* says, *That march, that demonstration received thirty-five words on page four of* The Times. *That march, that demonstration received thirty-one words in the* Financial Times. *That march, that demonstration, Tyndall or Webster is saying, is nothing, that march is nothing at all and we will prove that, we will prove that on the eleventh of June. On the eleventh of June, we will march, we will demonstrate, we will march and demonstrate right down Brick Lane and show these people that we will not be intimidated and we will not be taken for a bunch of fucking mugs in our own fucking land. Applause and cheering, shouting, Olivia Newton-John and John Travolta on the stereo, everyone laughing and then Phil nudges me and says, Come on, I'll introduce you around, and you elbow your way across the packed pub, aiming for the side entrance where just beyond you can see a few likely-looking lads, young, like you, smoking and laughing. You get outside, and there's a moment of fresh air, then that disappears as a truck chunters down Bethnal Green Road, belching exhaust. Phil says, All right, Derrick, to this lad who has the look about him of someone in charge, he's not too big but he has that look about him, authority, and he's sitting up on a wall with his fag in his mouth and a few others flank him like they're his minions, his underlings. All right, Phil, he says. He nods at you, Who's this then? Phil says, He's with me, you'll like him. All right then. Derrick hands Phil a piece of paper, which Phil pockets. That's the meet and time, right? You'll both be there, this Derrick says, and Phil says, Yeah, course, we'll be there. You better be, son, says Derrick, winking. Jog on then, he adds, and Phil nods, Yeah, nice one, and he leads you away from the pub. We not staying then? you ask. Nah, we have what we need. Phil brandishes his piece of paper. That geezer, Phil says, Derrick Junior. He's on the firm, looks after the youngsters. Like us? you ask. Yeah, Phil says, And younger. They start at them at school these days. Commie teachers need looking after, Phil sniffs. Right, you say. What's on the piece of paper? Phil grins: Saturday. Saturday comes and Phil picks you up and you head up to the Whitechapel end of Brick Lane. There's a fair bunch of you, skins and suited boys in boots. You'd put it at three hundred or so, which is hardly the millions that Tyndall or Webster was banging on about the other night. There's some placards, some flags, some chanting. Phil nods at some of the lads, and you recognise one or two and nod at them. You march, all of you, right down Brick Lane, cutting the traffic and chanting and yelling and brandishing your placards and waving your flags. You feel strong, significant, powerful. That's what this is: power, a show of power, of force. There's Old Bill about but they're well back and laughing and winking at some of you, so there ain't a problem likely there, and there's a bunch of the community behind them, giving you the wanker sign, shouting, but on you march, and then a signal, Phil nods, and you and a splinter group duck down Curtain Road.*

She sits, a woman, at her spartan desk, just off the corridors of power. She's close to these corridors – she can smell them, smell the stink of power, breathe it in. She is, to use a phrase she has heard on the lips of one or other of her constituents, within spitting distance of these corridors.

She remembers what she read a year before, a tract written by Nesta Wyn Ellis, a liberal. Nesta Wyn Ellis claims in this tract that Britain is ripe for fascism. She has this tract open on her spartan wooden desk. Again, she reads:

> ... *breakdown of traditional values, a militant working class/trade union caucus opposed to the capitalist status quo, monopoly capitalism (both state and private), economic crisis, high unemployment, state of war and therefore of emergency in relation to Ulster, the existence of the immigrant scapegoat, increasing powers of central government. Such a society is especially threatening to a seemingly bewildered bourgeoisie of small shopkeepers, business people and professionals whose status and security are thus at risk.*

Her eye returns to the phrase *existence of the immigrant scapegoat*. Earlier this year, January, she gave an interview to *World in Action* and she remembers what she said:

We are a British nation with British characteristics. Every country can take some small minorities and, in many ways, they add to the richness and variety of this country. The moment the minority threatens to become a big one, people get frightened. People are rather afraid that this country might be rather swamped by people with a different culture.

If she is honest, this is not exactly how she feels.

The year before, she told a meeting of Young Conservatives: I think we are trying to get rid of discrimination wherever it occurs.

Expediency, then.

Exploit the feeling, discredit the movement that feeds it, take the votes and make their politics mainstream.

She thinks power, power at all costs.

Power, then, comes at a price; there is an expense, it comes at an expense.

Power is a compromise of sorts, she thinks.

That demonstration, that marching with the poor young lad's coffin, those thousands – what did that achieve, really, what did they achieve? What did Callaghan *do*?

There is a cleverer way.

There are sides to play.

She picks up the phone.

Labour really *isn't* working, she thinks.

She, Thatcher, picks up the phone and calls her favourite chief inspector. She has an idea.

Power, her version of it, will start with an idea.

Jon Davies lies in bed with the boy on his chest. Jackie snoozes, post-feed, and Jon's keeping the little one busy with his dummy and his little blue bunny rabbit and, most successfully, Jon's bookmark.

The boy loves his bookmarks.

It's not long after six and Jon is thinking.

He's decided not to tell anyone about the rather unpleasant letter.

He will do, but not yet.

It is, he thinks, the sort of thing that might come in handy later, if conventional means haven't worked.

It's not like Jon to think this way. He'll admit that he quite likes it, though.

The boy gurgles and wriggles. Jon smiles, strokes his cheek. 'He's a big baby boy,' he says, 'he's a little baby boy.'

The boy smiles, squawks.

Jackie lets out a soft groan. 'Here,' she says, arms outstretched. 'Go and get yourself ready.'

'Thanks, love,' Jon says.

He pads down the stairs and washes his hair in the bathroom sink.

Chatsworth Road, early, and Noble sips tea and fingers a bacon sandwich in a caff. The seats, he notes, are bolted to the floor. There's no one else in there, too early.

He nods at the blonde behind the counter. 'You open nights, darling?'

'You want us to be?' She's smiling.

'Slow down, love,' Noble says. 'I mean your seating arrangements.' Noble gives the chair next to him a shake. It barely wobbles. 'Hardly tea at the fucking Ritz, is it?'

The blonde laughs. 'Kids like to come in before school and then again after they've had their dinner. Like a boys' club, it is. What are you going to do though, eh?'

'There used to be a boys' club down the road.'

'Where?'

'Part of Chats Palace, before it went all hippy.'

The blonde, now leaning on the table next to Noble's, again laughs. 'How do you know it's gone all hippy? Doesn't look like your scene.'

'It ain't.'

'Well then.'

Noble smiles. He sees Parker approach, bounce down the street. 'Tell you what,' he says. 'I'll come in again one day soon and tell you.'

'Oh yeah?'

'Why not?' Parker's at the door now.

'You do that,' the blonde says.

'I will. Now be a good girl and get the same again for my young friend, will you, love?'

'Coming right up, sir.'

'Beautiful,' Noble says.

'Oi, oi,' says Parker.

They both laugh.

Parker folds his long limbs into a seat. 'Fucking hell,' he says, 'I was thinking of nicking one of these.'

The blonde brings over Parker's tea. He thanks her and she smiles at Noble. Noble winks. Parker shovels sugar into his mug.

He slurps. 'That's better,' he says.

'You're looking a bit civvy today, son,' Noble says.

'Got to calm down the get-up first thing.'

'Fair enough.'

'It's still in character, don't get me wrong, just a touch softer.'

'All right.'

The blonde is back with a bacon sandwich. 'You want anything else?' she asks Parker.

'Maybe your number.'

The blonde laughs. 'You might be about fifteen minutes too late.'

'And about fifteen years,' Noble says.

'What?' The blonde feigns horror. 'You still in school then?'

'Leave it out,' Parker sniffs.

Noble claps his hands. 'All right, darling, can you give us a minute, bit of business?'

'Suit yourself,' the blonde says, but she's grinning. 'Business, eh? God knows what kind of business the two of you are in.'

Noble looks at Parker who makes a face: yeah, yeah.

'How's business?' Noble says.

'Slow.'

'What does that mean exactly?'

'Not a lot has happened but it will do soon.'

'I'm not sure you've answered my question there, young man.'

Parker makes another face: all right. He bites into his sandwich. 'Got any sauce?' he asks Noble.

'Brown or red?'

'Both.'

'Classy.'

'What I mean is,' Parker says, 'that over several weekends this month, starting on the eleventh of June, there will be a show of National Front strength in Brick Lane.'

'We know. You'll have to do better than that, son.'

'During these shows of strength, a group of younger members, more of the skinhead persuasion, shall we say, are going to use these demonstrations, for some out and out violence.'

'When isn't it out and out, am I right?'

'Fair point.'

'What's the goal?'

'Basically, provoke some sort of response.'

'Targeted?'

'Nah, it'll be random.'

Noble nods. 'And on the fringes of the march.'

'The march as cover. Our plod will be with the main group. The little hunting party will be off elsewhere.'

'But nearby.'

'Exactly.'

Noble thinks about this.

He knows why he's got Parker involved.

He knows the responsibilities he has.

He also knows there's a fragility here –

You can't compromise cover.

Noble says, 'I'll have a word with crowd control on the day. Tell them to keep a few plainclothes back and around.'

'All right.'

Noble knows, as he says this, that the wording is going to be very important.

'Brick Lane is the most heavily policed area in Britain, according to Chief Superintendent Wallis,' Noble says. 'That's a direct quote.'

Parker swallows the last of his sandwich. He wipes his mouth on his sleeve. He gulps down tea. 'There's one other thing,' Parker says.

'I'd hope so.'

'I don't know yet, and I'm not quite in a position to find out, but I reckon they've got one of theirs in ours.'

'Right. Go on.'

'A young bloke, I think. Someone with an ear upstairs.'

'You can't give me any more than that?'

'Not yet but I'm working on it.'

Noble signals to the blonde that they want their bill.

He says, 'Thing is, Parker, the only person who knows exactly what it is you're doing, is me.'

The bill arrives. Noble fishes notes out of his wallet. 'Have a bacon sandwich on us, love,' he says.

The blonde smiles. 'See you in here again, then.'

'You will.'

Parker's shaking his head. 'Jesus,' he smiles. 'Turn it in, eh, guv.'

Noble winks. 'What I mean to say,' he says, looking at Parker, 'is that it's nigh on impossible that brass, or anyone else, knows what you're up to. And if they do, well it ain't low level. You get my drift?'

'I think so.'

'Good.' Noble reaches into his jacket pocket and pulls an envelope. 'Per diem. Spend them wisely.'

'Ta.'

Noble stands. 'I get the go-ahead,' he says, 'we'll have someone in on the other side soon, someone in with the lefties and the hippies. Make sure you're a team player if we do.'

Parker closes his fists and makes a cross with his arms. 'I'm forever blowing bubbles, guv.'

'Good man.'

Suzi is in Keith's Sonic Bunker taking photos of a new punk band.

They're steaming through a version of Bob Marley's 'Johnny Was' and it's going on forever.

Suzi can see Keith in the control room nodding and twiddling.

The band look good, Suzi will give them that.

Boys from Belfast, Keith told Suzi, the band's called Stiff Little Fingers, they're just about to head off on a national jaunt with the Tom Robinson band.

They've been at it all night, the band and Keith, and they look a little worse for wear, which adds to the camera's sheen.

Suzi snaps, young punks pose and sneer.

The song ends. The boys grin. Suzi snaps more pics.

Keith pokes his head round the door. 'Nice one, lads. Now do one of your own, eh?' he says.

The boys laugh.

The Sonic Bunker is small. Part of an old forge just off Victoria Park.

Suzi says, 'After this number, we'll go outside. I'll shoot you in front of the original forge façade.'

The singer, a cocky little sod – of course – says, 'You shouldn't tell an Ulsterman you're about shooting him, lady.'

He's grinning.

Suzi pauses, she lowers her camera.

She smiles. 'Save your jokes for the interview, pal,' she says. 'Key thing is to get you outside. It stinks in here.'

The other boys roar.

Keith comes over the speaker. 'Stop flirting and get on with it.'

There's a one two three four and they launch into 'White Noise'.

Suzi's done her homework and these lads have some serious front coming over to play songs like this one.

The lyrics are something else.

Suzi hears: *nigger, thug, mugger, junky, horny monkey.*

She hears: *Paki, smelly, thieving, yids.*

She hears: *Paddy, moron, spud-thick Mick.*

She hears: *green wogs.*

Suzi thinks: This lot are something else.

Suzi snaps, Suzi scribbles.

'You're cutting it a bit fine, aren't you, mate?'

This is Gerard McMorrow. It's 2.45 p.m. Gerard stands at the public bar of the Jack the Ripper in Spitalfields and Jon Davies has, in fact, timed it just right.

On the way there, he's been to Companies House to check up on NF Properties.

Every single one of the company's shares are now in the possession of National Front members – for cash – or in the possession of National Front leaders as trustees for the members.

This is what Jon thinks he's sussed out and he's about ready for a drink. What Jon's sussed out doesn't help much at all.

The landlord is drying a glass with a dirty towel. He looks up at the clock, raises an eyebrow, says to Jon, 'What can I get you?'

Jon looks at Gerard who lifts his glass and nods.

'Two pints of ordinary, thanks.'

'And two packets of crisps,' Gerard adds.

'Flavour?'

'Beef and onion.'

Gerard gestures with his chin across the bar at the saloon. 'I'll wait in there, get us a table. Bit of privacy.'

The landlord snorts.

'All right,' Gerard sniffs. He throws back the rest of his pint. 'See you in there.'

Davies smiles to himself. 'Here, thanks.' He hands some notes over the bar. 'Take one for yourself.'

'Much obliged, I'm sure,' the landlord says. 'Time in a minute, yeah?'

Davies nods. He needs only fifteen of them.

He carries the two pints through the misted glass door into the saloon, the packets of beef and onion between his teeth. Gerard is an old associate – it's a stretch to call him a friend, but they've known each other a while and are now resolutely on each other's radars given that Gerard is chairman of the Hackney Trades Council. Jon's here to talk to Gerard about 73 Great Eastern Street, which is, of course, a stone's throw from where they now sit.

'Cheers,' Gerard says.

Jon nods at the door. 'You been over there yet?'

'I have. There's a bloke on the door. Called Gideon, I gather. A big lad.'

'Right.'

'He won't let you in.'

'No.'

'Point is,' Gerard says, 'if you lot at the council act, they will oppose, as they have certain reasons to remain on the premises. And there's enough of us to defeat that opposition and uphold the notices you serve. It'll be straightforward.'

'So that's what you think, is it? We serve them enforcement notices and see what happens.'

'Based on the Town and Country planning act of 1971. A planning issue. Use of property. That's how they got them out of their last place in Twickenham, on planning grounds.'

Jon thinks, It'll take some time. He says, 'And when they do oppose?'

'Public inquiry.' Gerard laughs. 'We'll tie them up in knots, mate.'

'Public inquiry. On what basis?'

Gerard shifts in his seat, places his pint on the small round table in front of him.

The dark wood of the place shines in the light that fights its way through the dull windows.

The saloon bar is empty.

Traffic coughs and splutters, lurches past, outside on Commercial Street.

Gerard leans forward. 'I'll argue, on behalf of the Hackney Trades Council, that the use of 73 Great Eastern Street by the National Front is, and I quote here, "contrary to the council's policy of encouraging employment opportunities".'

Jon's nodding. That might work, he thinks.

Gerard grins. 'It writes itself, old son. "The presence of the Front leads to political unrest, likely physical clashes, and this will act as a considerable disincentive to companies who might otherwise have set up shop in Hackney. Added to this, that the racist nature of the National Front will discourage black workers from seeking jobs in the area."' He pauses. 'People are frightened in Hackney South.'

'Sounds like you've been doing some thinking.'

'It pays,' says Gerard, tapping his nose, 'to do some thinking in this world, my friend.'

'How many have you had this lunchtime, Gerard?'

'On your bike,' Gerard says.

Jon leaves the pub and walks northwest up Commercial Street for a few hundred yards, walls covered in graffiti, train tracks humming. He turns and crosses Shoreditch High Street, avoids buses and cabs and scurrying hawkers, addicts and beggars in pairs, heads down, topless in the sun, muttering to each other, moving fast like rats. Jon notes a group of laughing City boys in shirtsleeves heading up from the Square Mile to the fifty-pence strip pubs on the Hackney Road, and then Jon is on Great Eastern Street.

He knows where number 73 is, of course, and he laughs at this thought: everyone does, it's at number 73.

There's not a lot to see on Great Eastern Street. A car wash, a textile workhouse, a couple of pubs, closed now.

Some roadworks happening just across from number 73. A ghetto blaster plays loud reggae. Jon thinks, I don't know this one. He nods at the Rastafarian labourer leaning on his shovel.

At the door of number 73, a man. Jon supposes this man must be Gideon.

Jon hasn't, Jon realises now, really thought this through –

He felt he needed to *see* the place, that's all.

Looking at Gideon, he suspects he's unlikely to see much more than Gideon.

Jon smiles at Gideon. Nodding, Jon says, 'I wonder if you can let me in?'

'I'm not a doorman,' Gideon says, 'so, no, I guess I can't.'

'OK,' Jon says. 'Do you mind if I—?'

Gideon takes a step forward. 'Oh, you can't come in.'

'You just told me that you're not a doorman.'

'No, I'm a chef.'

Jon smiles. 'You taking the piss?'

'Why would I?'

'Good question.'

Gideon lifts a plastic bag so Jon can see it. 'I'm bringing these leftover steaks for the boys.'

'For the boys.'

'Builders.' Gideon gestures with his head. 'Up on the roof.'

Jon's nodding. 'But you're not a doorman.'

'Which is why I can't let you in.'

'If you were a doorman,' Jon says, 'you could do, I suppose.'

Gideon taps his temple with a single finger. 'You'd have to get up early to catch you out.'

Jon thinks, Fuck it. 'I'm from the council. These builders, you tell them we're serving notice.'

'You got any credentials?'

Jon pulls his wallet, pulls his card, hands it to Gideon. 'You tell these builders I want a word, OK?'

'I'm just dropping off these steaks.'

'Give it a rest, Gideon, and do me this one favour. I'm asking you nicely.'

Jon notes Gideon's eyes narrow at the mention of his name.

'Jon Davies, eh, solicitor. I'll pass this on.' Gideon leans forward, looks left then right. 'All is not what it seems,' he says.

'You're telling me, mate,' Jon says. 'Be lucky.'

Jon crosses the road. He's remembered the name of the reggae artist.

The Rastafarian has watched Jon cross the road; he's watched all of Jon's conversation with Gideon, Jon thinks.

'Winston Rodney's all right.' Jon points at the stereo. 'Top group.'

The Rastafarian smiles. 'Not many white men know Burning Spear, let alone his real name.'

'Well, you know.' Jon looks back at number 73. 'What do you know about that building?'

'Wouldn't let you in?'

Jon shakes his head. 'I'm from the council. Some of us don't like who we think is in there, and we want them out.'

'We work here three weeks. Every morning,' he says, 'we clear out the rubbish and shit that's filled the hole during the night.' He spits. 'It's nasty, wet. It stinks of piss.'

Jon points at number 73, raises his eyebrows.

'Every night, men leave and call us dirty nigger bastards. Some nights, they throw stones.'

'What's your name?' Jon asks.

'Edward Shaw.'

'Mr Shaw,' Jon says, handing him a card, 'please give me a call. Tomorrow.'

Edward Shaw reads Jon Davies' card. 'Solicitor,' he says.

Jon nods. 'Someone has to do it.'

Whitechapel police station.

Noble's at it again with Maurice Young.

Maurice, sharing a surname with one of Britain's best-known breweries, is known as either 'Special' or 'Ordinary' depending on what you think of him at any given moment.

'Going for a pint' is a well-used phrase; Noble's having one now.

Old Maurice is having a bit of a 'Special' moment.

'My point, DC Noble,' he's saying, 'is that there has to be some sort of change in attitude and change in behaviour too. And perhaps the way to change attitudes – or beliefs, even – is to change behaviour first.'

'Yes, guv.'

'Let me give you an example of something I would change to affect behaviour which, over time, might affect beliefs in a positive way.'

'Please do, guv.'

'Language, for a start. The language of the streets, *racial* language, has to go. There is no difference, in my mind, between the relatively light sooty or satchy, and their heavier counterparts, coon or wog or the n-word, you understand?'

'I do, guv.'

'This language is, in my mind, and to quote the Yard's official position, a "cultivated rhetoric of abuse", in order to create the sort of us-and-them scenario that can assist police work in the minds of those using this language, meaning divide and conquer. Well, it's not on.'

'It's not, guv, no.'

'A better example,' Young goes on, 'is down in Brixton. Officers down there in the L Division Robbery Squad, I believe, have a tie, OK, a tie emblazoned with five playing cards, all spades, you understand, with the Ace of Spades at the top.'

'OK.'

'You're not an idiot, are you, DC Noble. You know what that means.'

'I think so, guv.'

'The claim, they say, is that this isn't racist, but in fact the motif is simply representing a five-card straight flush, which is known in card schools as a "fair deal to all". Well, you see where I'm going, I hope.'

'Yes, sir. They're being disingenuous.'

'Patrick, that is exactly what they're being.'

I know, Noble thinks. He glances at his watch. Get to the point, eh.

'The Met Race Crime Initiative is up against a lot,' Young says. 'Well, we're really up against it now, DC Noble.'

Noble says nothing.

'You'll remember that the body of a Shahid Akhtar was pulled out of the canal not too long ago.'

Noble thinks: you didn't want to talk about it before. 'I remember, guv.'

'And you'll remember that it was a suspicious death, at first, if not actually established as a criminal investigation. And that the killers of Altab Ali were to be questioned.'

Noble nods. 'The timeline, guv, it fit, something like that.'

Young looks thoughtful. 'You do remember rightly. But there's been new information, post-mortem, I mean.'

Noble shifts in his seat. His ears prick. He senses that this is why he's here.

'Misadventure, the coroner's post-mortem verdict, no need for an inquest. Full of booze and pills, he drowned in the canal as he couldn't face the shame of a pregnant white mistress.'

'But, guv, he was wrapped up in plastic—'

'*After* his death, is what they think.'

'I'm not sure I follow, guv.'

'Some scumbags find him floating in the canal and, well, use your imagination.'

'I'd rather not.'

'I don't blame you.'

Noble shakes his head. 'And the mistress?'

'She exists.'

'She's pregnant?'

'So she says. She threatens to blow the whistle, he's a community leader, a good old-fashioned mess – and he can't face it and gets off his face. Between us, it sounds like suicide. Either way, though.'

'And the family want it all to go away.'

'Misadventure. Easiest crowd control we've ever had. They didn't get all the details of the mistress. Tasteless.'

'Guv, why am I hearing this now?'

'Autopsy took a long time.'

Yeah, Noble thinks, it would have.

Young leans forward now. 'You meet our friend, did you?'

Noble nods. Noble tenses.

Parker's successful infiltration of the National Front infantry division is not what Young had in mind –

'It's working out?'

'So far.'

Young nods. 'Good.'

'I might need another one, guv, if you can swing it?'

Young nods, says nothing, clears his throat, stands,

'I'm talking to each member of the initiative individually, owing to the sensitivity of this,' he says. 'Leave the door open as you go out.'

Noble does as he's told.

Half an hour later and he's meeting Parker near Mile End tube.

They stand on the street, near the park.

'You've had a busy couple of Saturdays, haven't you, son?' Noble says.

Parker's twitching, not looking hugely happy. 'I'm not sure how much I'm helping here, guv, to be honest.'

Noble nods, softens. 'Patience, mate. In these situations, you don't always know what you're looking for.'

'I know what I saw,' Parker says. 'A fifty-five-year-old man beaten up by a gang of skinheads.'

Noble nods.

Parker says, 'I checked up on it. His name is Abdul Monan and he was knocked unconscious. He needed five stitches in his face. His face! You understand?'

Noble nods.

Parker says, 'There was no one around off the main drag, no one at all. The fucking uniforms took an age to do anything. They were laughing, most of them.'

'Yeah,' Noble says. 'I should think they were.'

'You told me you'd have some bodies about.'

'I did my best.'

'I have to see something like that again,' Parker says, 'and it's going to be hard not to break my cover, you understand?'

Noble nods. 'Old Bill Stewart told me you're a good lad. Don't let him down.'

'It's the same thing each weekend. I'm there and that's it.' Parker shakes his head. 'We're just *there*, know what I mean? It's all so meaningless. Like this is ours. Then some poor cunt gets done for walking by at the wrong moment.'

Noble says, 'It's a shame.'

'That business outside Bethnal Green nick, those protests. They're getting organised.'

'I know.'

Parker's talking about the Bengali youth mobbing up with the Anti-Nazi League and setting up self-defence groups. The Indian Workers' Association, the Standing Conference of Pakistani Organisations and the Federation of Bangladeshi Organisations, they're all in on it.

Eighteenth of July and there's an East End-wide strike, school walk-outs and a protest ending on Bethnal Green Road.

'The Bengali kids are tough fuckers,' Parker says. 'They're guarding the place. Brick Lane is like a fortress.'

'What does it mean for your lot?'

'Point is, we're a few hundred thugs. There are thousands of them,' Parker says, 'and then you've got your hippies and dopey lefties weighing in. It's just numbers.'

'And?'

'The Front are getting out, relocating.'

'Where to?'

'Chapel Market.'

'You're sure?'

'Looks that way.'

Noble nods. 'This lad you think they've got on ours. Anything?'

'Put it this way,' Parker says, 'there's never any uniforms about when it kicks off. There's one bloke, Gideon, he's called. Very pally with Day. I don't know what but there's something about him that's a bit off.'

'Gideon?'

'Yeah.'

Noble nods. He's thinking he should have a word with old Special Young about this but he doesn't know how he can, what with Parker supposed to be infiltrating persons of interest on the left.

And Parker doesn't know that either, of course.

'What about Shahid Akhtar?' Noble says.

'Who?'

'Pulled out the canal a couple of months ago.'

Parker shakes his head.

'Listen out for that name, right?'

Parker nods.

Noble hands Parker an envelope. Affectionately, he cuffs him, puts his arm round him. 'Hold tight, son,' he says. 'You're doing beautifully.'

'Yeah.'

'Stay stylish,' Noble says.

He watches Parker lope off down the street and thinks –

Thank fuck I'm not him.

Suzi's got the band against the forge wall round the side entrance and she's asking questions while snapping pics. Keith's set up a little recording device so she can multi-task. Clever fella.

The cocky lead singer turns out to be a thoughtful young man.

He's saying, 'Yeah, meeting Gordon was a defining moment in my life.'

This is Gordon Ogilvie, Suzi knows, a Scottish journo in Belfast and now lyricist for the band.

'We'd written "State of Emergency" and felt we'd dealt with the situation in Northern Ireland,' Jake Burns, the singer, is saying, 'but then Gordon was saying, Have you written anything about the Troubles? I said, We think that would be unfair exploiting people's unhappiness, you know? He said, You're wrong. If you're gonna write songs, they have to be about your life. Could you write a song called "Suspect Device"? And I said, Yeah, why not, and he gave me this little cassette box and in it was the lyric, and the design in the box, you know, the photo, was a newspaper picture of an IRA firebomb, and Gordon reckoned we could market it like that. Explosive, he said it'd be. Funny fella, yeah? It was like a light bulb turning on in my head.'

Suzi says, 'You must be excited to be here?'

'We are. I hope you're excited to have us.'

Suzi smiles. 'Not many people really know what's going on in Belfast. Do you think it's your job to educate them?'

'Music is about enlightenment, not education.'

Suzi raises an eyebrow at this. 'There are alleged links between the Ulster Defence Force and the National Front. What do you think about that?'

'I think it's very possible to be against all that without being pro-IRA. We are for peace, pure and simple. We are anti-violence.'

Suzi nods. 'Tell us what it's like to be young and in Belfast.'

Jake Burns grins. 'Listen to the songs, that'll tell you. It's a challenge being a teenager in Belfast. What's there to do? Sniff glue and get beaten up, is about it. It's a poor city and you're told, Shut up and be happy about it, the blacks down the road are a lot worse off than you are. But I hear it's a challenge to be an Irishman in London.'

'Listen to the songs,' Suzi says.

Jake Burns winks. 'Yeah, grand, do that.'

'I think we're about done here then, boys,' Suzi says.

One of the band says, 'What magazine is this even in then?'

Suzi smiles. 'You'll see it when you're on tour.'

Keith pokes his head out the door. 'Send them in, love,' he grins.

Jake Burns looks at Suzi. 'Thank you,' he says, 'for the opportunity, like.'

'You're grand,' Suzi says.

Jake Burns smiles and goes back into the Sonic Bunker.

Suzi takes down the lighting and recording equipment. She's fiddling with her camera when she feels him.

It's shadow, she sees, first. Then, a voice:

What you want to photograph a bunch of Paddy hoodlums for then, eh?

The tone, though, familiar.

Suzi turns. 'You,' she says.

In front of her, the man who cleared the stage at Victoria Park. The man who wouldn't let her photograph *him*.

'They let me,' says Suzi.

The man smiles. 'I might have changed my mind.'

Suzi crosses her arms. 'Is that right?'

'You weren't too hard to track down.'

'No?'

'No.'

'Well done, Sherlock.' Suzi nods at the heavyweight door to the Sonic Bunker. 'There's four Paddy hoodlums and my boyfriend just in there, so why don't you tell me what you want.'

'A word.'

'And why should I give you a word?'

The man hands Suzi what she thinks must be a warrant card.

His name and title: DC Noble.

Suzi gives it back. She takes a step towards the door, brings her hands up in front of her, says, 'Oh I don't know.'

Noble smiles. 'Trust me, love,' he says, 'it's nothing to do with you or your boyfriend – or the Irish hoodlums inside.'

'Well, what is it about then?' Suzi asks.

'I think we can help each other.'

'I'm not sure I need your help, DC Noble.'

'Squatters' rights aren't what they might be.'

'How do you know about that?'

Noble says, 'A man called Red Saunders gave me his card at the carnival. I figured you'd know each other. I called this Red Saunders and he lied. I called him again, though he didn't know it was me, and he told me about this place. I put two and two together.'

'Like I said, take a bow, Sherlock.'

'What have you got to lose? There's a pub on the roundabout. I'll be in there for half an hour or so. Get yourself sorted out and come and join me.'

Suzi, for the second time, snaps a shot of this man's back as he walks away.

She finishes packing up.

She waves at Keith through the tiny porthole window that looks out from the engineering room onto the street at the front of the building.

She heads over to the pub.

*

Noble nurses a pint in the pub on the roundabout on Victoria Park Road. Too much of my work, he's thinking, is sitting in pubs in the morning.

He's looking at the racing pages of the paper and keeping an eye on the door. It could be nice in here, he thinks. Big space like this, right next to the park. Families and so on. Food. Instead, there are half a dozen grumpy old men and a couple of wide boys using the place as an office.

The Inn on the Park down the road is trying it – families, that is.

There'd been some trouble in there on and off for years, a mixture of things.

Bit of a football firm pub, bit of a drug pub, bit of a punk pub –

It couldn't decide what kind of trouble it wanted on a regular basis.

It was, as can be the case, Noble thinks, a shooting that did it.

Broken glass and a bit of claret is one thing.

A regular shot dead sitting at the bar is a little bit naughtier.

He was a villain, the regular, there's no doubt about that.

Based in Essex, he'd come in to keep track every few days, use a few pubs to keep his books, see his associates and so on.

Essex semi-retirement didn't exactly work out.

So, they've gone all family down there at the Inn.

Which means they've filled a storage room with those little plastic balls kids love to mess about in and they've put a swing in the beer garden.

Noble smiles. He tips his empty glass at the barman, who pours him another, saying nothing.

Noble takes his new pint and his paper to a table.

He wonders if this Suzi will actually come.

His idea, admittedly, is a bit half-baked.

He needs someone in with the left, the RAR mob.

He needs someone he's found himself, as he's told Special Young that Parker is in a left-wing infiltration – and there won't be another Parker.

He needs to *appear* to be running an undercover in the RAR.

To achieve that, he needs something that looks like insider knowledge, which might as well be insider knowledge.

He just needs to convince this Suzi – the squat business should be enough.

And what he tells her and what he tells his superiors will be distinct –

Which is, after all, how you run any snout.

The difference here is that she needs to think that she isn't one.

The door opens and Suzi Scialfa walks into the dingy half-light of a pre-noon public bar.

A couple of the old drunks cheer. There's a round of applause from somewhere.

Noble, ignoring the clientele, stands, then escorts Suzi to the bar.

The barman says, 'Sorry about that. We don't get many women in here at this time of day.'

Suzi smiles. 'You don't say.'

'What are you having?' Noble asks her.

Suzi examines the bar, scans the occupants. 'I'll have a double gin and tonic, I think.'

Noble raises his eyebrows at the barman.

The barman winks:

Nice one, Cyril.

'Pickled egg?' Noble jokes.

'Maybe later,' Suzi says. 'I'll go and sit down.'

'Here.' The barman hands her a towel. 'You might want to give it a wipe.'

Noble, sitting down, hands Suzi her drink. 'Cheers,' he says.

'Cheers.'

'I'll get straight to the point.'

'Please do.'

Noble takes a sip of his pint. 'You've seen my warrant card but you don't know what it is that I do.'

'I don't, no.'

'I'm on the Met Race Crime Initiative. Normally I work out of Soho but these days I'm back east.'

'Back east?'

'I was born here. Hackney Mothers' on Lower Clapton Road.'

'Good for you.'

'You've got a bit of an accent – where's it from?'

'New York, via Chiswick. Born there, brought up here.'

Noble's nodding. 'Sort of insider outsider thing.'

'Something like that.'

'And I gather you're a photographer and a journalist?'

'Something like that.'

Noble nods. 'Fair enough.' He goes on. 'Part of what we're doing on this Race Crime Initiative is trying to break up the criminal element of the National Front.'

'So, there is a criminal element.'

'Well, there's definitely a *violent* element. We're starting with that.'

'And what's that got to do with me?'

Noble sips his pint. He rubs his hands together. 'I know that your lot don't trust my lot.'

'My lot?'

'Lefties, Rock Against Racism, right-on types.'

'If I didn't know you were a copper before, I do now.'

Noble laughs. 'Take it easy. I mean, quite rightly, we're not exactly top of the Christmas card list for the right-thinking.'

'That's true. But what's it got to do with me?'

'I need a favour.'

It's Suzi's turn to laugh.

'Just listen a moment,' Noble says. 'I've got a lad working inside with the other mob. To help this operation, knowing a bit more about what you lot might be doing can only help, right? You see that?'

Suzi nods.

'So, what I'm looking for is someone who will, innocently, be able to give me a little more insight into the RAR thing and how it connects to left-wing activism.'

Suzi says nothing.

'I'm not asking you to grass or inform, absolutely not. I just want to know a bit more about it all to help combat what is, basically, a common enemy.'

'Why me?'

'Because I remember you from Victoria Park.'

'Really?'

'You're a hard one to forget.'

Suzi narrows her eyes.

'It's the perfect cover,' Noble winks. 'I fancy you.'

Suzi's shaking her head.

'I mean if anyone were ever to ask, you tell them I'm sniffing around, that's all.'

Noble's thinking: that is one seriously thin cover but if she's not as street-smart as she thinks this might just work.

'Tell me what you can do for me,' Suzi says.

'Two things.' Noble leans back in his chair. 'Firstly, I can see to it that you're not evicted from your squat.'

'Right. How?'

'Don't worry how, love, just trust me.'

'All right.'

'And the other thing is that you'll get access to stories, access no one else will have.'

'What sort of stories?'

'The sort that mean politicians lose their jobs.'

'Be more specific.'

Noble's shaking his head now. 'You can't rush these things, you've got to trust me.'

'And all this because we once met?'

'Your colleague Red Saunders gave me a card at that carnival, right? Well, I did a bit of digging and I can't exactly use him.'

'Why not?'

Noble smiles. 'He takes up a lot of space, you know what I mean?'

'I suppose.'

'So, there you go.'

'I'm the only other person you can think of.'

'Basically, yeah.' Noble finishes his pint. 'There you are. You in?'

'Tell you what,' Suzi says, leaning forward, 'when those eviction notices come down, we can have a chat.'

'Beautiful,' Noble says. 'When they do, you give me a ring.'

He hands her a card.

'I suppose you don't want me telling anyone about this.'

Noble gestures with his hands. 'What I'm doing is no secret.' He's bluffing now. 'You're helping me with my enquiries, you could call it. I'd say that's up to you, darling.'

Suzi nods.

She's looking pensive but Noble can see the cogs are turning in there –

What she can get out of this, what a hero she can be –

'All right,' Suzi says.

Bingo, Noble thinks.

Suzi stands. 'Thanks for the drink.'

'I'll see you to the door,' Noble says.

He holds it open for her and off she goes into the sunlight.

Back in the pub, the drunks laugh, commiserate.

Noble's then straight back in the Britannia with another full Irish and he's got Old Bill Stewart in front of him. Noble says, 'So you think you can swing that?'

Stewart laughs. 'Hackney Council and Hackney police? It's what they're built on, son. It's a one-stop shop.'

'Will this do it?'

Noble hands Stewart an envelope.

Stewart weighs it in his hands.

'Leave it with me,' he says. 'I know just the palm to grease.'

Noble nods. 'Just make sure it happens soon. And once it's done, it's done.'

Stewart snorts. 'Grandma sucking eggs is the phrase, Chance. Don't take the piss.'

'All right.'

'Squatters are squatters,' Stewart says. 'No one gives a fuck where the quota lies, so long as there is one.'

Noble stands. 'Socialism is a great leveller.'

'Fuck off, Chance.'

Noble grins. 'Gladly.'

Jon Davies locks his office and walks down the long, echoing corridors of Hackney town hall. He takes the stairs; his heels click and echo as he spirals down them. The click and echo of institutions, of court, of power, of public baths, of head teachers' offices, of empty warehouses, of textile factories, of unfurnished council flats, of underground car parks –

He punches the code into the door that leads down into the underground car park. Here, he unlocks his bicycle. He straps his briefcase into the baby seat behind his own. He clips his suit trouser leg neatly back and he turns on his bicycle's two lights. It's late and it's getting dark.

He bicycles up the ramp from below Hackney town hall and turns left, past the Britannia pub, past Graham Road, past the old Woolworths, and then left again, past Hackney Central Station, past the disused toy warehouse, past the pet shops and knock-off white goods stores on his right, and he circles round towards Hackney Downs before turning right past the Pembury Tavern and up Pembury Road, the Pembury Estate flanking either side, looking ominous and vast and warren-like. He carries straight on past the Seven Sisters' pub, not far from where he and Jackie first lived together on Queensdown Road, down Cricketfield Road and past the Cricketers' pub, the West Indian takeaway to his left, and then out onto Lower Clapton Road, then left at the pond and down Mildenhall Road, all the way down, about three quarters of the way down, until he is opposite the small, low-rise estate and outside his own home, number ninety-nine.

It's then, as he dismounts his bicycle and is unstrapping his briefcase and unclipping his trouser leg, that he notices the police car glide quietly in behind him.

A uniformed policeman steps out of the passenger door.

'Evening, Jon,' he says.

He doesn't close the door, stands behind it like it's a sort of shield.

Jon thinks: has he still got one leg inside?

'Good evening,' Jon says. 'Can I help you at all, officer?'

The officer smiles very wide at this. 'Just checking you got home safely, that's all, Jon.'

'Got home safely?'

'You never know, Jon.'

Jon nods, confused. 'I suppose you don't.'

'Working for the council, it's worth having someone keep an eye out.'

'Right,' Jon says. 'Why do you say that exactly?'

'Anyway, here you are,' the officer says, 'and a very good night to you.'

'Same to you,' Jon says.

He unlocks his front door and goes inside. He hangs his coat and puts down his briefcase. He can smell cooking and can hear music.

He goes down the stairs and into the kitchen. Jackie is pushing things around a frying pan.

'Hello, love,' she says, leaning back and kissing Jon on his cheek.

'What's this, stir fry?' Jon says.

'It's Thai.'

'Very fancy. The boy all right?'

'Yeah,' Jackie says, 'he's just popped out for a drink.'

'Very funny.'

'He misses you.'

'I miss him. I'll just go and say good night.'

'Don't wake him up, Jon.'

Jon climbs two flights of stairs and puts his head into the boy's room.

There's a little blue night light and Jon sees him snug against his rabbit, his arms flung back, his breathing steady.

'Night, mate,' Jon whispers. 'See you in the morning, bright and early.' He laughs, quietly. 'We'll have the kettle on.'

Jon goes back downstairs and Jackie hands him a hefty glass of white wine.

'You all right, love?' she asks.

Jon nods. 'Fine, love, fine,' he says.

Jon Davies smiles at his wife.

He's not going to tell her he's got policemen following him home.

He's not sure who he *should* tell, to be fair.

It turns out that she, Thatcher, needs to go on a diet.

If her idea of power is to be achieved, then she needs to look a little different, sleeker, more *glamorous*. She thought a nice frock rather than skirt and jacket might do it. My father's a grocer, she said. I know what passes for glamour among my people.

It turns out that her people are more impressed by power and glamour than they are by humble origins and hard work.

If she's honest about it, she is too.

It's not so much the weight she has to lose, it's how she has to lose it.

If she looks *better* then she's a more viable alternative.

She wonders aloud in the meeting with this new advertising team Saatchi & Saatchi, if a man would have to do the same thing.

Oh, yes, she's told, Geoffrey Howe's having his hair cut and getting a new pair of specs next week.

He could lose a few pounds himself, to be fair, Michael Heseltine said, when she told him all about it.

Lipstick, Margaret, is all Denis says. You know I love you in it.

Watching the television the other night, he was howling about how she might be Margo from *The Good Life*'s twin.

'You ask the housewife,' is a line she's used more than once to comment on the pitiable state of the economy. 'Perhaps it takes a housewife to see that Britain's national housekeeping is appalling.'

Another Dennis, Potter, said she reminded him of Lassie: everyone's favourite celluloid bitch, he said.

There's something, she thinks: if her idea of power is about persuading every man and his wife that she's *better*, then shouldn't she look like she's chairing a WI meeting?

Saatchi & Saatchi say no: you're behind in the polls and we need to sell your brand in the most easily understandable terms. Glamour does that for you, she's told.

So, the diet. And here it is, on a tray, on her spartan desk –

Her lunch prepared for her by one of her aides. She is so casual about this diet; she doesn't even know which aide is in charge of making it.

One thing she said to the Saatchi brothers:

If I need to look better, if glamour is what this is about, then why is this new poster devoid of not only my face, say, my *person*, but also my values, my policies?

She remembers the brothers smiling at each other, glancing, almost a private joke, she thought, passing between them.

But the message is clear, Mrs Thatcher, they said. Unemployment under Labour has reached a point that we simply cannot take any more. Labour isn't working.

I understand that, she said, and the clever use of 'working', of course I do.

No, Mrs Thatcher, what I mean is the *implication*.

Go on.

That unemployment will be your government's priority and that you will do it better than it's being done now.

Without promising anything, she said.

The brothers, she remembers, looked at each other again, more openly, and in relief.

On the radio the other day, she said:

We'd have been drummed out of office if we'd had this level of unemployment.

Another thing, the brothers said. The nickname.

She knows that the research department call her 'Hilda', her middle name, and not in an affectionate way.

She called herself the Iron Lady a couple of years ago, talking to Finchley Conservatives. She thought that might stick.

We like 'Maggie', the brothers told her. We're talking to the *Sun*.

She addresses her lunch.

Her lunch, now, is also her dinner and, in part, her breakfast.

For two weeks, as a trial run, to make sure she can actually shed the weight, she, Thatcher, is on a diet of twenty-eight boiled eggs a week, with one or two bits on the side.

Today's lunch: two boiled eggs, spinach, and a glass of whisky.

While she eats, she examines a headline and smiles:

> *National Front thugs deface body of Asian man*
> *found dead in an east London canal*

Discredit the movement, she thinks, and hoover up the votes.

Saturday morning, and Jon Davies is on his front doorstep taking a little early summer sun.

He's sitting on a piece of foam and reading the paper. He's got a cold bottle of supermarket brand French lager on the go, and he's wearing a pair of denim shorts and nothing else.

It's a quiet, almost suburban scene, despite the fact that Hackney is about as inner London as you can get. Hedges are trimmed and cars washed. Kids play football on Chailey Street. Younger kids mooch about in the gardens of the estate. Families with prams and bikes roll past towards Millfields Park and the canal.

Harry and Lil next door totter by with their dog, Peppy.

'Wotcha, Jon,' Harry says, tipping an imaginary hat. 'How's tricks?'

'You know,' Jon says. 'Same old and then another day.'

Harry laughs. 'The boy all right?'

'Golden.'

'Glad to hear it.'

'How's Jackie, Jon?' Lil asks.

'Too good for me,' Jon jokes.

Harry snorts. 'Have a good day then, old son.'

Jon waves them off.

Harry, a builder, drinks in the public bar of the Prince of Wales and they see him in there from time to time with his boys.

A lunchtime break can be four pints, Jon's heard.

Imagine manual labour after that. Jon has a pull at his lager.

He's reading the football news.

It's a more pleasant experience than it was a few weeks ago when West Ham's descent into the second division was confirmed.

It always comes as a blessed relief when summer arrives and he can enjoy a little half-hearted interest in the county championship before a test series begins.

Time off for good behaviour, he thinks now. It's a mug's game, football.

He can hear Jackie and the boy inside. She's cooing over this or that and the boy's making that funny little laughing noise he does, and then squeaking in excitement.

His favourite thing, now, is being carried up the stairs, looking over Jackie's shoulder and watching Jon follow behind.

He laughs like a little drain; it's the most joyful thing that Jon's ever seen.

Jon turns the page, looks up. He sees Mrs Akhtar leaving the estate opposite.

Poor woman, he thinks.

He hasn't said much to her since it happened, but they sent flowers and Jackie gave her a hug in the street not long ago.

A terrible shame and they don't know even what's happened. Least, nothing's been said. Jon's asked around the town hall a little but everyone just shrugged.

Mrs Akhtar crosses the street and edges between the parked cars and then she's outside Jon's gate and saying, 'Hello, Mr Davies, do you have a minute?'

'Of course,' Jon says, suddenly very aware of what he's not wearing. 'Just let me, you know.'

He doesn't hang about to see Mrs Akhtar's expression – he nips inside and pulls on the T-shirt he'd been wearing earlier then nips back out again.

He goes to the gate and opens it, and they stand together in the small front garden.

'How are you, Mrs Akhtar?' Jon says.

He feels, despite being outside, the cramped space between them, the tang of the dustbins behind the hedge.

'It's a very difficult time, I'm sure you understand, Mr Davies.'

'Jon, please.'

'Thank you, Jon. I wonder if you can help me, Jon?' she says, trying out his name.

'Of course, anything I can do.'

'Thank you, Jon.'

Mrs Akhtar looks down.

She leans against the gate like she might keel over.

Jon worries that the gate, unlatched, will swing open under her weight and that she *will* keel over.

She says, 'They tell us it was misadventure, Jon. They didn't say it was suicide, but it might have been, I suppose.'

'I'm so sorry.'

'We don't believe it, Jon, we don't believe them, Jon. We …'

At this, Mrs Akhtar starts to sob. She composes herself. 'He wasn't stupid, Jon, my husband.'

Jon lays a hand on her shoulder. She pulls a tissue from her sleeve and dabs at her eyes.

'You're a solicitor, Jon. And you work for the council, too.'

'That's right.'

'I wonder, Jon, if you might be able to help, might be able to give us some advice?'

Jon nods. 'Of course I can,' he says. 'I'd be delighted to.'

'Thank you, Jon.'

Mrs Akhtar steps back onto the pavement. She straightens her clothes, straightens her scarf, straightens her posture. She composes herself.

Jon smiles. 'I'll see what I can find out for you on Monday,' he says. 'I'll come over one evening next week. Is that all right?'

Mrs Akhtar nods and thanks Jon.

She takes a step backwards, then turns to cross the road.

Her path, though, is blocked by a police car.

Jon steps out, out beyond his gate, onto the pavement, into the road –

A policeman leans out of the passenger window and says, 'Don't worry, Mrs Akhtar, we're just checking you're OK.'

She bows, says, 'Yes, yes, fine, sir, thank you.'

Jon, at the window, says, 'You heard her.' He looks at Mrs Akhtar. 'Go home, Mrs Akhtar, they're just doing a community visit, that's all.' He smiles.

The policeman says, 'I've something for you, in fact, Mr Davies.'

He hands Jon a card.

'See you, Jon,' he says. 'Have a good one.'

Jon studies the card.

It is his card, his details, but his name has been blacked out, a line through it, and, above his name, written in a thick black marker pen, are the words Excalibur House, with a rough sketch of a sword next to these words.

Jon pockets the card.

He turns, thinks, Fuck, feels dog shit between his toes –

He scrapes his foot on the pavement, swearing.

Jackie appears in the doorway, the boy wriggling in her arms.

'Bloody hell,' she says.

'Tell me about it,' Jon says. 'You couldn't pass me a cloth or something, love?'

Suzi takes the bus to Liverpool Street, gets on a train to Audley End.

An hour later and she's sitting quietly in her mum's car.

Her mum's saying, 'Your dad will be so pleased to see you.'

'And you're not?'

'That's not what I meant, Suzi.'

'I know.'

Suzi would like to come home more often but it's not really home, is it, if you've never lived there. And if you don't go for a while and the gaps grow longer and longer between each visit, then something else has crept up on you, something freighted with expectation and worry and disappointment. And then the silent car journeys, the silent meals. And then you stop visiting 'home' altogether.

She's not there yet.

'How's Keith, sweetheart?' are Suzi's dad's first words to her. 'Still working in the hit factory?'

'He's great.'

Suzi's dad is nodding. 'He reminds me of guys I knew in the Village back in the fifties, before you were born.'

'Yeah?'

'Yeah, his style, his scene, you know?' He's smiling benignly, Suzi's dad. 'Showbusiness,' he says. '*Jazz*.' He makes a face: hip cat.

Suzi misses her dad, her American heritage. His clinging to something that Suzi has no idea ever existed.

'He's a nice young man,' Suzi's mum adds. 'Polite.'

They're sitting at the dining-room table eating roast chicken and drinking red wine. The house, Suzi will admit, is tasteful, spacious, a nice place to relax in, to *be* in. They moved out there when Suzi left home – a burden lifted, perhaps – and they've retired, they're happy. Suzi's dad was a journalist, a foreign correspondent who settled in England with his English wife and now he's what passes for an exotic bohemian in Saffron Walden. His soft New York vowels, his battered suede jackets, his French cigarettes, his hair.

He chews thoughtfully.

Fork in the air, he asks, 'How's the old ...' and he seems to search for the right words among the food in his mouth, 'the old ... living situation?'

'We're still in the co-operative. It's good for us.'

'The squat, you mean.'

Suzi smiles. 'It's a co-operative living arrangement.'

'Legally speaking.'

'We're there and everyone knows it and everyone is happy.'

'You pay rates?'

'It's organised.'

'For now.'

'Yes.'

Suzi's dad chews harder and he's nodding in that way when you know he's thinking the opposite of agreeing with you.

'Be careful,' he decides. He smiles. 'Just be careful.'

Suzi's mum says, 'You and Keith should find somewhere of your own.' She smiles. 'When your dad and I, well, when you …' She puts her cutlery down. 'It's nice to be on your own, a little family.'

'We're not there yet, Mum.'

'Next time, bring him!' Suzi's dad yells. 'Tell him I say he works too hard!'

'I will.' Suzi drinks some wine. The food is lovely, she feels warmth. 'He's doing a lot of work with some political bands, protest shows, that kind of thing. So am I.'

Suzi's dad's nodding again. 'Round here –' his mouth full of food – 'they're talking a lot about this Thatcher lady.'

Suzi sees her mum's eyes dart.

'And they're saying,' her dad goes on, 'that she's the kick up the ass this country needs. And you know what? I might be inclined to agree.'

Suzi opens her mouth, says nothing for a moment.

'We don't know,' her mum says gently. 'It's just talking, dinner parties.'

Suzi nods. 'I know.'

'We'll see,' her dad says, deep into another mouthful. 'We'll see.'

'Tell your friends they'll regret voting for Thatcher, one day.'

Suzi's dad roars. 'I might leave you to do that yourself.'

Suzi smiles, thinks, Enough.

Later, sleepy from the wine on the train home, she's happy she went. She'll not leave it as long next time.

Suzi stands with the rest of the squat co-op and watches as the eviction notices are taken down.

There's a fair bit of clapping and whooping going on and someone yells, I bloody told you, and someone else, That's what happens when you stand up for your rights, and Yeah, fuck yeah. For he's a jolly good fellow starts up when Tiny Tony comes down, marches through the front door, triumphant, like he's about to lift a trophy and make a speech.

Suzi approaches one of the workmen. 'You don't know why this is happening, do you?'

'I don't, love, sorry.' He frowns. 'I'd be counting my blessings if I were you.'

'Happens a lot, I suppose.'

'First time I've ever done it.' He nods at the celebrations, at Tiny Tony peacocking. 'Must have a way with words,' he says. 'Or some influential friends.'

'Right.'

'Can you sign this for me?' the workman asks, handing her a clip-board with a council-stamped form on it. 'It's confirmation the notice has been retracted.' Again, he nods at Tony. 'I don't fancy asking him, the show he'll put on.'

Suzi smiles. She scribbles her name, takes a copy, pockets it.

'Cheers, love,' the workman says.

Suzi shakes her head to say, No problem.

She looks up the road at the billboard that greets visitors driving in from Walthamstow and Leyton and Essex and even further afield.

On it, a new advert she hasn't seen before –

There is, in red and white, the sign:

Unemployment Office

A queue, into the distance.

A cross section of Britain, Suzi thinks, in this queue.

Small letters at the bottom spell out:

BRITAIN'S BETTER OFF WITH THE CONSERVATIVES

Above, in much bigger letters:

LABOUR ISN'T WORKING

2

The English Civil War

September 1978

Gideon

You scatter, this hunting party, and spread out, and Little Derrick is saying, Anyone, it doesn't matter who, anyone who shouldn't be here, gets it, right? Anyone. And Phil's got a look to him that you haven't seen before, he's never really been one for fighting, he's a mate though, and he's a good lad, so if it comes to it, yeah, of course, he's got your back, but you suppose in the end that this isn't really fighting, is it, unless there's some about that want fighting, and you're running down Curtain Road and that's when you see him, an old bloke, Indian or Bengali or Bangladeshi, you don't know and you don't care, none of you care, and one of your mob runs over to this old bloke, this lad must be nearly sixty, carrying his shopping home, pulling one of those little old folk trolley things, and one of your mob runs over and kicks the trolley away from him and slaps him across the face, and then two more are over there and swinging, and one puts his forehead into this old bloke's face, and he goes down spilling blood and he takes a few kicks then he's spat on, once, twice, three times he's spat on and you're looking on, and Phil's looking on, and then Little Derrick gives the nod and you split up into groups of two and three and pile off back to the main march and you tell the line of uniforms that you were just off for a piss in the park and they let you back in and there you are again on Brick Lane, chanting and throwing salutes. Weekend after, you're watching as about four thousand are marching through Brick Lane and around from the Anti-Nazi League and there's mutterings and anger, so the weekend after that you're back down there and there's no march this time, no official demonstration, so there's no police, and Little Derrick gathers about two hundred and you pile down Brick Lane and you put in every window and you overturn anything that isn't bolted down, and they've all scarpered, the Pakis, doors are locked, the streets are empty, and someone sticks a brick through a window and yells, Brick Lane is fucking right! and there's laughter at that but you don't hang about, you're all back in the Blade Bone singing by the time the Old Bill turn up and one or two of the more senior members go outside and have a word with them, and they're laughing and you think, All right then, we're all right then. Then they get organised and the fighting starts. And it starts getting pretty interesting and it's not just Pakis, there's gangs of blacks too, and whites, and not just soppy cunts in corduroy but lads that fancy it, and each week there's more of them, and you're hearing rumours they're being paid by someone, and then a few weeks after that there's a blockade at the north end, and down the Whitechapel end too and you say to Phil, What's the point of all this, eh? And Phil says, Don't let any of the other lads hear you saying that, and you think, Fuck the other lads, you're getting a bit of a hammer-ing for free while the other side are on wages and there's more of them, it's a numbers thing in the end, and the mood in the pub ain't much fun either, and you're wondering what's the point, again, and you're signing on, there's no work, but you're not seeing a great deal of evidence that any-one's taking that work away from you, and you bring this up in a meeting, and Derrick Day Senior, old Fat Bastard, shouts you down, calls you a coward and a scum-lover, and the crowd in the pub all turn to see how you like that, and you say, simply, Amateurs, you lot, fucking amateurs, you lot ain't going nowhere, couldn't organise a piss-up in a brewery, and there's a few murmurings now, a few elders seem to agree with something of what you've said, so you push on a bit, Excalibur House, you say, You call our new building Excalibur House, and none of you ain't got a fucking clue what that means, Excalibur, eh? what, you think we're fucking Alfred Lord Tennyson, I'm off, and you walk out the door, but a few come after you, and you think, Here we go, and there's something brewing and then Derrick Day himself, Fat Bastard, says, You got a better idea then, and you say, Yeah, first thing we sack Brick Lane off and we get organised, we got money and an HQ, right? Day nods, and you say, Well then, let's find a better pitch to battle on, and Day's smiling now and Phil's smiling, and someone says, Where? and you say, North, Chapel Market, perfect place

*to give them the run around, and Day says, What's your name? and you
tell him, Gideon, and he says, You want a job, Gideon? Yeah, you think, I
do, and there's something you can do.*

Her spies tell her that all six of the big union bosses are going to Callaghan's farm for dinner. They're good, her spies, and they also tell her that five of these bosses – Len Murray, Dave Basnett, Moss Evans, Geoffrey Drain and Alfred Allen – intend to tell Callaghan that an autumn general election is the right move to ensure that the Labour Party remains in power. One of these six bosses – Hugh Scanlon – is set to tell Prime Minister Callaghan to wait until Spring 1979.

Upper Clayhill Farm in late summer is a lovely place to spend the evening, she knows this; Mrs Callaghan is an ebullient hostess.

'*She* can cook,' Denis mutters when she tells him what's going on.

She doesn't need her spies to know that Callaghan is sticking resolutely to the wage cap and that the unions are twitchy about this.

'He's got the national interest at heart,' Denis says helpfully. 'It'll sink him, of course.'

She knows this, or at least she hopes this.

One doesn't become – or remain – prime minister by doing anything other than serving one's own particular interest at any given moment.

Of course, if this aligns with the national interest, then one's power is being used for good, one can claim. Which then aligns, again, with one's own particular interest.

What the national interest really is, is a very good question. Callaghan, she thinks, is being awfully presumptuous.

She tap-taps at her first boiled egg of the day. The diet works and she's been adapting it for a while.

'It's the *smell*, Margaret, that I can't stand,' Denis tells her cheerfully. 'I'd rather you plump and wind-free, I'll be honest.'

He'd rather she gets a grip on this country and drags it behind her for the next decade, she thinks. His business interests – talking of interests – will be much enhanced, by association if nothing else.

So, to the dinner. If Len Murray, Dave Basnett, Moss Evans, Geoffrey Drain and Alfred Allen intend to tell Callaghan that an autumn general election is the right move to ensure that the Labour Party remains in power, and Hugh Scanlon intends to advise him to wait, the smart money is on Scanlon being ignored.

She's spotted the rub, she thinks, and she's not the only one. But she might be the only one who can do anything about it.

The unions will not accept Labour's social contract any longer; with the wage caps off, they are going to push for a lot more than a maximum 5 per cent pay rise. The shop stewards – a class of gent she understands – will lead them straight down to the local pub if they get anything less than 15 per cent, is her thinking.

Hoskyns thinks the number is irrelevant: it's not Callaghan's obsession with 5 per cent that's the problem, it's that there is any per cent at all.

The sensible time for an election is October, which doesn't give her very long. Lose the unions, and Labour lose the election. For the sheer number of votes they can pull in. However, the people – the national interest – are growing ever suspicious of the power these unions wield. There is no doubt in her mind that union influence exacerbates Britain's economic problems of unemployment and inflation.

She hates the unions and the fat, grubby, heavy-drinking, trouble-stirring Marxists that run them.

Equally, her spies know that Len Murray, Dave Basnett, Moss Evans, Geoffrey Drain and Alfred Allen won't guarantee their workforces will stay at work and off the picket lines beyond November. Autumn election means thanks awfully and now let's scrap the 5 per cent and have some free collective bargaining.

The country, she realises, must grind to a halt if she, Thatcher, is to be sure of victory.

No one votes for a government that can't get the bins emptied and the streets swept.

But there isn't time for all that.

There is, however, time to create the impression that the country is *about* to grind to a halt.

A Labour / TUC schism could last a long time.

She hesitates over her teaspoon, puts it down, picks up the phone.

She has an idea where maximum disruption can be caused with minimum fuss.

Len Murray, Dave Basnett, Moss Evans, Geoffrey Drain, Alfred Allen and Hugh Scanlon will wake up at Upper Clayhill farm to their cups of tea and their hangovers, their fried breakfasts and their newspapers, and they'll have no idea that they're about to help elect a Conservative Party that will do everything in its – in *her* – power to end their pernicious influence.

Denis says, 'I'd bloody ban trades unions altogether.' And then, 'Whatever you're doing, make sure it's favourably reported. I don't want you stitched up by bloody BBC poofs and Trots.'

On the phone, she says, 'Gordon, tell Larry Lamb to keep an eye on Dagenham.'

Gordon Reece, her media advisor, says, 'He'll want to know when.'

He, Larry Lamb, editor of the *Sun*.

She'll need her favourite chief inspector again. She smiles at the euphemism.

It won't do to rely on one of the big six; she understands that power can corrupt most efficiently *upwards* in certain situations.

And her spies tell her there's a certain high-up union stalwart, name of Dai Wyn, who has the ear of several of the big six, a man who has appetites, she gathers.

That's what she'll tell her favourite chief inspector; it'll be quite enough.

'End of the month, Gordon,' she says.

'Jolly good.'

She thinks, We'll get the bastards yet.

Noble's in with Maurice Young again –

'We appreciate these things take time and we're happy with the work you've done,' Young's saying. 'The Brick Lane and Chapel Market disturbances were a decent result, arrests-wise. And not just anarchists. Some National Front hooligans too.'

Noble nods.

'We gather end of this month is another big concert. Is that right?'

'South London,' Noble says. 'They're saying Brockwell Park.'

'You'll remember what I was talking about the other week, about that tie, Ace of Spades and whatnot.'

'I do remember, guv.'

Young swallows. 'Brixton plod might need some guidance on how to police an event like this.'

'They're going to walk there from Hyde Park.'

'To Brockwell Park? Bloody hell.'

Noble smiles.

'Look,' Young says, 'you asked a while ago for another one. Well.'

Young opens a desk drawer. He pulls out an envelope. He hands Noble this envelope. The envelope is unmarked.

'Same drill, DC Noble, you understand?'

'Crystal, guv.'

'Now listen, Patrick, you get this, but you do something in return with your man, OK?'

'Yes, guv.'

'Our friend will explain.'

'OK.'

'You just do what he says and your team will be left alone for as long as you need. Within reason.'

Noble nods. 'That's very generous, guv.'

'It is generous, yes.' Young smiles, runs his hands through his dark hair, his dark, thinning hair, hair that is slicked back and tidied behind his ears.

Noble says, 'Thank you, sir.'

'One other thing I need you to do for me, Patrick.'

Noble nods.

'Go and see DS Williams and find out what's going on with Shahid Akhtar's family, can you?'

'You mean—'

'I mean I want to know what it is I don't know. OK?'

Noble nods. 'Of course, guv.'

'Sometimes,' Young says, 'it's hard to know which side is which and which side we're on, you understand?'

'I think I do, sir.'

'Good man. I won't see you out.'

Noble's in the caff on Chatsworth Road, but he's not staying.

'Tonight,' he says to the blonde behind the counter, 'I'll take you up west.'

The blonde shrugs. 'I haven't seen you in here for a while.' She's drying a mug and looking a bit sniffy. 'You don't even know my name.'

'You don't know *my* name.'

'I'm not the one asking you out.'

Noble grins. 'I'm Patrick, nice to meet you. What's your name, darling?'

'Lea.'

'Lee? As in Marvin. Nice.'

'Ha, you're very funny. With an "a".'

'Like the canal.'

Lea makes a face. 'You wanna go out with me or what?'

'It's a pretty name, Lea.'

'Well then.'

'So, tonight. You fancy it?'

'Why not?'

'Beautiful,' Noble says. 'I'll pick you up here, shall I, around six?'

After champagne and a steak dinner, Noble says, 'Can I drop you anywhere?'

'Don't be cheeky.'

'It's not far,' he says, 'my gaff.'

Noble gives Lea the tour.

'You just moved in then?' she says.

'Eighteen months or so.'

'Right, OK.' Lea reddens.

'What?'

'Well, it's a bit … rudimentary, isn't it?'

Noble has his hands on her hips now. 'But you don't think I am – a bit rudimentary, I mean?'

Lea shakes her head and Noble leads her into the bedroom.

Later, as Lea sleeps, Noble sits up at the counter in his tiny kitchen overlooking Whitfield Street. He can see drunks and addicts gathering in the park round the back of Goodge Street tube.

He tells himself, It's good for work, it's not permanent.

And it was good for work when he was at West End Central every day.

The drive east is a bit of a cunt, to be honest, but he's doing *something*, even if no one else knows it.

He sits at the counter while Lea sleeps and he takes a piece of paper and pen and makes a list.

Eight names. Two dead. One murdered. One suicide or close to it. One knocked unconscious, five stiches to his face. One hospitalised: broken jaw, broken collarbone. One bleeding from a head wound caused by a broken bottle. One beaten unconscious, picked up by an Asian minicab driver, taken to hospital. One slashed down the neck with a razor, requiring seven stitches. Another hospitalised: fractured jaw, broken sternum.

Summer of hate, Noble thinks.

Poor old Parker –

He looks at this list by the light of the streetlamps outside and he thinks:

No one's bothered to consider what might connect these victims other than their skin colour, their race, their names and where they live.

It doesn't matter, really, who they are, is the point.

Except of course it fucking does, not least from a police work perspective.

He folds the piece of paper and puts it inside his jacket pocket.

Then he slips back into bed to Lea with an 'a' and nuzzles her neck, nudges his legs between hers, gives out a little groan –

'Pull the other one,' Lea says. 'If you're just waking up, I'm an Irishman.'

Noble laughs. 'Come here,' he says, turning her to face him. 'I am Irish, after all.'

The streetlamps fade, the sun settles —

In bed, later, Noble winks. 'Do us a bacon sandwich and a cuppa, would you?' he says.

Lea laughs. 'Drive me to work and I'll think about it.'

'You're on,' Noble says.

Jon Davies sits in the town hall canteen, yawning. He's tired, Jon is. It's a tiring business, life, especially when you have a nine-month-old boy in it. Is he that old already, the boy? Something like nine months, Jon's sure. Jon used to count it in weeks, which he preferred, the exactness of weeks. Months are fickle buggers, always different lengths and starting whenever they fancy it, very cavalier.

Jon likes the certainty of weeks.

He's trying to work out how many weeks old the boy is now when his colleague Kate plonks herself down in front of him.

'Morning, Jon,' she says. 'You look tired.'

Jon smiles. 'I've been avoiding you,' he says.

'That's honest.'

'I'm too tired to be anything but.'

'Go on then,' Kate says, 'tell me why you're tired.'

Jon makes a face. 'Teething and bad dreams, I think.'

'You look a bit old for that.'

'Very funny.'

Kate leans over and picks up half of the bacon and egg sandwich that sits on a plate in front of Jon.

'You eating this?'

'Not now.'

Kate takes a bite. 'Lovely.'

'Go on then,' Jon says, 'tell me why I've been avoiding you.'

'Pass the ketchup.'

Jon passes the ketchup and waits.

Her mouth full, wiping her fingers, Kate says, 'That hit the spot.'

Jon smiles.

Kate says, 'The squat in the old textile factory by the canal. What happened?'

'You should probably ask God, Kate,' Jon says.

Kate pulls a face. 'Fuck off, Jon,' she says.

Jon sighs. 'I don't know. We looked at the paperwork and I signed off on the decision.'

'I don't understand.'

'The squat petitioned Councillor Heaven and the original decision was reversed.'

Kate frowns. 'In all my time here, I've never seen one successful petition.'

'I can show it to you if you like.'

'That's not what I mean.'

Jon nods.

Kate says, 'They've closed down a squat in Arbour Square instead.'

'It's housing allocation, that's all.'

'The one by the canal is all white lefty types scrounging roll-ups.'

'And?'

'The one in Arbour Square was a group of poor, hardworking Bengali families who are now homeless.'

'Housing allocation, they'll be allocated.'

Kate snorts. 'Hackney Council is hardly known for its speedy processes, Jon.'

'Fair enough.'

'So, you don't know?'

'I don't, no.' Jon sighs, he rubs his eyes. 'But I can probably guess.'

'Well, go on then.'

Jon yawns. He's tired, after all, and the fact is, he *doesn't* know who told the committee to reverse the decision – it's not his remit to know.

He's tired – tired of all this, in fact.

Jon says, 'Someone's doing a favour for someone else. My guess is that ethnic integration and building communities weren't as important as keeping the old factory in squat-limbo.'

Kate's nodding. 'Bastards,' she says.

'It's just a guess.'

Kate pushes back in her chair, stands. 'I'll have a word with the kingdom of Heaven, see if he can shed any light.'

'That's funny.'

'I'll tell you a joke,' Kate says. 'What do you call a Bengali family living in a one-room doss house in Stepney, Jon?'

'I don't know,' Jon says. 'What *do* you call a Bengali family living in a one-room doss house in Stepney?'

Kate pauses. 'Homeless.'

At least they'll know the area, poor sods, Jon thinks.

Walking away, Kate says over her shoulder, '73 Great Eastern Street.'

Jon calls after her. 'What about it?'

She's laughing. 'They're calling it – wait for it – Excalibur House.'

I thought so, Jon thinks.

Ayeleen: My friend Lauren tells me that her dad told her that my uncle Ahmet owns 'every bloody thing on Chatsworth Road'.

I say to Lauren, 'So what? Someone has to.'

She laughs at that one.

We're walking to my uncle's café. 'Do they have kebabs?' Lauren asks. 'I've never seen any kebabs there.'

'No,' I tell her, 'it's a normal caff, it's not Turkish.'

'Turkish ain't normal, Leen?'

'I don't know,' I say. 'It is for me.'

We're laughing but not exactly sure why.

'One day,' Lauren says, 'I saw three Turkish men with a baseball bat and they had this black boy against the wall and you know what they did?'

I shake my head.

'They made this black boy eat a watch.'

'A watch?'

'Yeah. It was right by the café too.'

We both laugh about this.

Later, I tell my mother what Lauren said about my uncle and ask her if it's true.

'Your uncle has lots of businesses,' she tells me. 'He is important in the community, at the mosque, he's made many friends.'

'On Chatsworth Road?'

'And Stoke Newington and Brick Lane – he's done a lot to integrate us with the more established communities. Don't ever let your father hear you talking like this.'

'Why not?'

'Because it's not polite. It's disrespectful.'

I think about this. 'When can I work for him?'

'When you're older.'

'My cousins work for him now.'

'They're older. What's all this about your uncle anyway?'

'Well, it's just, he's different.'

My mother snorts. 'He is different, that's very true, Ayeleen.'

Some time passes after this conversation, and then one night, very late, my uncle Ahmet comes to our house and speaks to my father for a long time.

The next day, my father tells me that he has to go back to Turkey for a little while, to help Uncle Ahmet with his business, to look after family affairs. He leaves and it's strange for a while, but then Mother and me, we get used to it.

Every time I get good marks at school, Uncle Ahmet gives me a pound note. I keep the notes in a small box in the same drawer where I keep my socks. Sometimes I take one of the notes and me and Lauren buy sweets or ice cream and we walk down to the park and lie in the grass and eat and talk. Lauren's always on about her big brother, how he's at Hackney

Downs now, an all-boys school, and him and all his friends are always up to stuff.

'We'll go to Kingsland,' Lauren tells me. 'They take girls there,' she sniffs. 'It's nicer too, you'll see, we're going to love it.'

'We're only in the juniors,' I say.

The sun is hot and the grass is yellow. We can hear shouts from the estate, dogs barking. Someone's playing tennis. Across the road in the other park, there's Indians playing cricket.

'Anyway,' I say, 'I might not go to seniors. I'm going to work for my uncle.'

Lauren sits up. 'That's not even allowed, Leenie.'

I'm smiling when I tell her it doesn't matter what she thinks.

Suzi's in a meeting of the RAR Central Committee at the Prince of Wales pub again, and they're talking about who's going to do the next carnival set for later in the month in South London.

Red Saunders is yelling something about Paul McCartney being too much of a good boy. He's yelling how he wants John Lennon and Bob Marley.

Someone else is yelling something about the RAR logo, that it has to be bigger than the Anti-Nazi League arrow on the poster.

Someone else is yelling about Aswad headlining over Elvis Costello –

Suzi sits tight, drinks her drink, bides her time –

In a lull, she says, 'Jimmy Pursey's been getting death threats. If Sham 69 play, they're going to kill him, they're saying.'

This shuts everyone up and Suzi has the floor. 'Keith heard from their sound guy who heard from their manager who heard from Jimmy. He doesn't know what to do.'

Syd Shelton says, 'Well we can't have them, then. It'll ruin it, there'll be a punch-up.'

There are murmurs of agreement.

Red Saunders says, 'Jimmy's a good lad, he'll understand. I'll talk to him.'

Suzi says, 'You should ask Stiff Little Fingers.'

There's one or two nods to this, a chorus of *who*?

'Trust me,' Suzi says, 'they'll blow everyone else off the stage.'

Red Saunders and Syd Shelton exchange a look.

Red Saunders says, 'You've heard them then, at Keith's?'

Suzi nods.

Red Saunders says, 'He likes them, does he, Keith?'

'Yes, Red,' Suzi says. 'Keith likes them.'

Syd Shelton claps his hands together. 'They should open. "Alternative Ulster", all that, it's a statement.'

Red Saunders says, 'We'll square it with Jimmy.'

Suzi thinks, These men.

She wants some real excitement, she thinks.

Protest, she's beginning to think, changes precisely fuck all.

She's thinking, Suzi is – a lot.

Noble carries four polystyrene cups of tea and a paper bag with four bacon rolls up the stairs to a room at Panda's Chinese takeaway.

There's Bill Stewart and Parker and the new lad, Alan.

'Here.' Noble puts the teas and the bacon rolls on the table. He digs into his pockets and throws down sachets of white sugar. 'Tuck in.'

Parker and Alan are straight in gulping tea and tearing into their bacon rolls.

Bill Stewart looks at Noble and sniggers. 'Age before beauty, eh, boys?'

The lads look up, nonplussed.

'As you were,' Bill says.

Noble says, 'We'll get straight to the point. Bill here has a bit of extra muscle-work for us, very much off the books, for which you will both be paid handsomely.'

Parker nods. Alan nods.

'Count me in,' Parker says.

'It's not a fucking offer, son,' Bill Stewart says. 'It's an order, all right?'

'All right,' Parker mumbles. 'Keep your hair on.'

Noble shoots Parker a look. 'Enough. Bill?'

'Week of the fourth of September is the TUC conference in Brighton. Either of you clever clogs know what the TUC is?'

Parker shakes his head.

Alan says, 'Trades Union Congress. Like the federation of the lot of them.'

'Very good, Alan,' Bill Stewart says. 'We can see which side Chance has got you working on.'

Noble taps his temple. 'Homework.'

Alan nods, wipes his mouth.

Parker points at Alan. 'We got a union then, me and him?'

'I'm all the fucking union you need.'

Parker grins.

Bill Stewart says, 'Yesterday, all the big bosses were at the prime minister's Suffolk farmhouse for dinner to persuade him to call a general election next month.'

Noble nodding. Noble watching as both Parker and Alan are clearly puzzled as to what the fuck this might have to do with them.

'Tomorrow night,' Bill Stewart says, 'on their way to Brighton, these bosses will be staying at the Montague Hotel on Montague Street in Bloomsbury. Over dinner, they're having a secret meeting to discuss whether or not to *really* support the prime minister's election decision.'

'If it's secret,' Parker says, 'how do we know about it?'

'Who do you think's doing the security?' Noble says.

Parker nods. 'Fair play.'

'We'll be there to have a word with one of these bosses' associates. And that's where you come in.'

'Muscle,' Parker smiles.

'We need to be as persuasive as possible,' Bill Stewart says, 'so there's you two for starters.'

Noble leans forward in his chair. 'You'll be in a room at the hotel waiting to deliver a message.'

'Waiting for who?' Parker says.

'Dai Wyn.'

'Who the fuck's Dai Wyn?'

'A union man. We're going to persuade him to do something.'

Nodding.

Parker's smiling.

He says, 'So what, we're going to break into his room then?'

Noble shakes his head. 'No, we've got our own sorted out, thanks to our security contact. Someone's going to bring him to us.'

'Who?'

Bill Stewart smiles at Noble. 'Go on, son, it was your idea.'

'A woman,' Noble says. 'Mr Wyn is going to think he's quids in on a very attractive young woman.'

Parker laughs, looks at Alan, who laughs too.

'Oh, that is very persuasive,' Parker says. 'What's the message?'

Bill Stewart grins. 'Don't worry your pretty little head about that, my son.'

Alan says, 'This Chapel Market business, guv. Can I have a word about that?'

Noble nods. 'After, downstairs.'

'I need a word too, guv,' Parker says.

'All right.'

Bill Stewart stands. He says to Alan, 'Why don't we go and have a spring roll or something?'

'Yeah, course.'

Alone, Noble and Parker look at each other.

Parker says, 'They've found out the date of this next carnival, twenty-fourth of September.'

'Hardly kept it a secret, have they.'

'It's South London, right?'

'Looks that way.'

'They're going to turn up at Brick Lane, take it back.'

'Clever.'

'Victory parade from the new HQ on Great Eastern Street.'

Noble nods.

'What's he doing, Alan, exactly?'

'There's troublemakers on their side, too, son. Anarchists, you know.'

'I do know. I've seen a few of them on weekends down Chapel Market.' Parker pauses. 'I've seen Alan. That ain't exactly on, is it?'

'I know, son,' Noble says, 'but needs must. We're a team, there's a budget. You're both good lads, the very best, is what Bill says anyway.'

'Right.'

Noble leans forward. 'It's not for much longer.'

'But I ain't getting anywhere.'

'What I want to know is who chooses who gets done, that's all. Think you can figure that much out?'

'It's random, it's just violence.'

Noble shakes his head. 'No, son, it's never random. Nothing ever is.' Parker nods.

'We find that out,' Noble says, 'then we'll know which of theirs has got the ear of one of ours, you understand?'

'Yeah, I think so, guv.'

'Sweet. I'm off for a spring roll downstairs,' Noble says. 'Keep your chin up.'

Whitechapel.

Jon Davies sits in Abdul Noor's front room taking notes. Abdul Noor is an executive member of the Bangladesh Youth Movement for Equal Rights. Abdul Noor is telling Jon what happened the night he walked past Excalibur House on his way home from work. Four white skinheads exited Excalibur House and, as they stood outside, they saw Abdul Noor walking towards them. They began to shout and laugh, and Abdul Noor, seeing these four white skinheads, hearing these four white skinheads shout and laugh, Abdul Noor crossed the road and quickened his pace. He wasn't quick enough. Two of the white skinheads ran past Abdul Noor then turned to block his path. The four white skinheads began to abuse

Abdul Noor, verbally. Abdul Noor tried to run. Abdul Noor, who is not a small or timid young man, tried to elbow, to barge his way past the smaller of the two pairs of skinheads. But Abdul Noor could not. The white skinheads, Abdul Noor remembers now, took real exception to his attempting to barge past them and run away. As a result, these four white skinheads punched and kicked Abdul Noor until he lost consciousness. Abdul Noor does not know exactly what happened next but he gathers that a minicab driver based in a cab office near Old Street tube station, was driving past and saw Abdul Noor prone on the pavement. This minicab driver lifted Abdul Noor into the back of his minicab. He helped Abdul Noor drink water from a bottle. He drove Abdul Noor to the Royal London Hospital in Whitechapel where Abdul Noor received treatment.

'What did the police say?' Jon Davies asks Abdul Noor.

Abdul Noor smiles.

His face creases as he smiles, the scar that runs along the side of his head flashes in the light. When he smiles, the swelling around his eyes is purple and ripe.

'Did they say anything at all,' Jon asks, 'when you told them which building these four white skinheads came out of?'

Abdul Noor shakes his head.

'They laughed,' Abdul Noor says. 'They said nothing but they did laugh.'

'Why is that, do you think?'

'Because they knew exactly which building those men came out of and why.'

'What gave you that impression?' Jon asks.

'They told me,' Abdul Noor says. 'When they were leaving, after taking their report, they told me.'

Dalston.

Jon Davies sits in Edward Shaw's front room taking notes. Edward Shaw is telling Jon Davies what he told him before, about what it was like to work outside Excalibur House. Edward Shaw says, 'We worked there for six weeks. Every morning, we cleared out rubbish and shit, rubbish and shit that was dumped in the hole we were digging during the night.' Edward Shaw shakes his head. 'Every morning, this rubbish and this shit was nasty, it was wet, and it stank of piss.' Jon Davies nods. 'Every night, white men left that building and called us dirty nigger bastards. Some nights, they threw stones at us, some nights they threw bricks.'

Jon Davies says, 'This building these white men left. Can you tell me exactly which building you're referring to?'

Edward Shaw says, 'It was number 73 Great Eastern Street. Excalibur House.'

Jon Davies calls Gerard McMorrow and tells him, 'I'm taking statements.'

'The more the merrier,' Gerard says.

Excalibur House.

Jon Davies is standing outside 73 Great Eastern Street, looking at the same man on the door as the last time he was standing outside number 73 Great Eastern Street.

Jon holds up his defaced business card. He says, 'Did you do this, Gideon?'

Gideon nods. 'I did, yes.'

'And you gave it to a policeman to return it, did you?'

'Lost property. I handed it in.'

'Very thoughtful.'

'It was.'

Jon says, 'You going to let me in this time?'

Gideon shakes his head. 'Not a good idea.'

'But you *can* let me in this time?'

Gideon nods. 'I can now, yes, it's in my capacity.'

'You've got a way with words,' Jon says.

'I'm a real heartbreaker.'

Jon's nodding. 'Not long ago,' he says, 'four white skinheads left this building and beat unconscious an Asian man who happened to be walking past. He was picked up by a minicab driver and taken to hospital just in time. If that minicab driver hadn't been going past – well, you should see the state of the poor man. He doesn't look good.'

'I wouldn't know about that. I work shifts.'

Jon points to the plastic bag at Gideon's feet. 'Meat for the boys, is it?'

Gideon nods.

'That policeman who so kindly brought me back my property. He a mate of yours then?'

Gideon leans forward, looks right then left, says, 'Come back in a few months and I'll talk to you.'

'Come back in a few months. What does that mean?'

'It means exactly that. I got that card to you, didn't I?'

'So?'

'So trust me.'

Jon thinks, What choice do I have?

He says, 'If you're taking the piss, it's not funny.'

'We'll just have to see, won't we?'

'Gideon,' Jon says, 'how old are you?'

'I'm twenty-four.'

'I hope you sleep well at night.'

'I'm afraid I do, yes.'

Rushmore Infants' School, Rushmore Road.

Jon's been invited to an open evening at a local primary school. This is because the boy's in the playgroup round the corner. It's a bit early for him but Jon's curious about something he's heard and he wants to talk to the headmistress, Mrs Walkinshaw, whom he's met before and who Jackie knows a bit from playgroup jumble sales.

Mrs Walkinshaw, Jon knows, is a force of nature.

'They're setting up, Jon, all across the borough,' she tells him. 'They're calling it the Young National Front. They've reduced the minimum age for membership from sixteen to fourteen.'

Jon tries a joke, regrets it immediately. 'They'll have them in nappies soon.'

Mrs Walkinshaw's eye blaze. 'You didn't mean to make that joke, Jon, I know that. My teachers – even *my* teachers, teachers of five-year-olds, of six- and seven-year-olds – are accused of being "Red Teachers", and there are parents who are influenced by this, by this peddling of lies and hate.'

Jon's nodding. He says, 'You'll make a deposition to that effect?'

'Absolutely.'

'Thank you.'

'You know,' Mrs Walkinshaw says, 'I am the first black headmistress in this borough. The first. While I'm here, this school will be run my way. My children will grow up with empathy; prejudice is learned.'

Jon nods and puts the boy's name down.

'How old is he, Jon?'

'Nearly a year.'

Mrs Walkinshaw smiles. 'I bet you and Jackie haven't had a night out for a while.'

'We haven't, you're right.'

'Those two big teenagers over there –' Mrs Walkinshaw points at the gates – 'working the door.' She laughs. 'My boys. They babysit sometimes, for some pocket money.' She gestures. 'Go on, don't be shy, you've earned it.'

Jon does what he's told.

As he walks away smiling, he calls back to her, 'Which one would you recommend?'

Mrs Walkinshaw laughs. 'They're the best young men I know,' she says. 'Take your pick.'

Bloomsbury.

In the lift of the Montague Hotel, Suzi stands next to union man Dai Wyn.

'Hello, duck,' he says. 'You staying here too?'

Suzi smiles. 'I am.'

'We'll be in the bar later,' Dai Wyn tells her. 'You should join us.'

Suzi nods. 'I might do.'

The lift bell rings, ground floor.

Dai Wyn, joking, says, 'This is me, duck.'

He lets Suzi leave and she walks across the hotel foyer, looking back only once.

Later, in the bar, which is small, Suzi watches as Dai Wyn comes in with a group of men in suits. These men are red-faced and roaring. They order bottles of wine and bottles of ale.

Suzi sees Dai Wyn notice her and, quite deliberately, she holds his eye as she gets up from her seat and steps out onto the cigar terrace.

She's seated in the corner with a cigarette when Dai Wyn comes out with two glasses of wine and a cigar clamped between his teeth.

'Here you are, duck.' Dai Wyn hands Suzi a drink. 'Get your laughing gear around this,' he says.

Later, they discover their rooms are next door to each other.

Gallantly, Dai Wyn says, 'I'll see you get back to yours safe and sound.' He grins. 'This is London after all, the big city.'

Suzi laughs at that.

She sees Dai Wyn thinking, Right, we're on.

When Suzi unlocks her door, opens it and says, 'Nightcap?' Dai Wyn is through it quicker than a trap rabbit.

The flash of a camera is a real surprise.

'Oh, you bloody idiot, Wyn,' he says. 'You bloody idiot.'

Suzi hands Dai Wyn a sealed envelope. It is sealed and stamped in wax.

'Open this and read it,' she tells him.

Dai Wyn looks at the two large, young men either side of him. 'I don't think I've got much choice, have I?'

'No, duck,' Suzi says, 'I don't think you have.'

Dai Wyn reads the letter. Dai Wyn turns its single page over in his hand, examines it, as if he's expecting to see something more –

To Suzi, he says, 'The wax was a nice touch.'

*

Noble drives Suzi back home.

'This is for you.' One hand on the wheel, he reaches into his inside pocket with the other and gives her an envelope. She weighs it in her hands and raises her eyebrows. 'Yeah,' he says. 'Pays well, blackmail.'

Suzi says, 'And the other thing you promised?'

'Two things, actually,' Noble says. 'Number one, something you can tell your mob down the RAR, is that the Front intend to put on a show at Brick Lane while the little concert goes on in Brockwell Park.'

'Fuck,' Suzi says.

Noble laughs. 'It's hardly Sun Tzu-level strategy, love.'

'Very clever.'

'Anyway, there it is. God knows what uniforms will be there but there won't be many. You can pass that on, too.'

Suzi nods.

'And for your bonus,' Noble says, 'at least when I know myself, that is, I'll tell you what was in that very official-looking letter old devil Dai Wyn read before my lads burned it in the fireplace.'

'OK.' Suzi's pouting now. And sulking, Noble thinks.

'Give it a rest with the attitude,' he says. 'It'll be a story, Suzi, and by the time I do find out, it won't matter to me whether or not it breaks.'

Suzi makes a face. 'That's very generous of you.'

'Be nice, girl,' Noble says. He keeps his eyes on the road. 'Think about it. There's an election round the corner. My guess is this is something from high up.'

'And you don't care what it is? You just do what you're told?'

'In this instance,' Noble says, 'abso-fucking-lutely. It's quid pro quo.'

'You *are* clever.'

Noble looks at Suzi until she looks back.

Grinning, he says, 'I'm not just a pretty face, no.'

She's watching the television – *everyone's* watching the television – as

Callaghan speaks, makes his address to the nation. The difference is that she, Thatcher, has tuned in not to hear the expected announcement of an autumn general election, but to hear why there *isn't* to be an autumn general election. In short, what excuse this time, Sunny Jim, for ducking me?

Her ideas about the unions haven't changed, of course. If anything, the unions are more important than ever.

Callaghan looks so *comfortable*, she thinks. Those jowls sit so happily under his owlish glasses and those oddly pointed eyebrows. He, Callaghan, is a man more suited to a black-and-white television set, she thinks. More gravitas; colour pulls all the seriousness out of him and he looks *old*.

What she, Thatcher, feels for Callaghan, she realises now, is *contempt*. This happy disposition, this avuncular, kindly next-door-neighbour demeanour, this gentle, reluctant headmaster act, disguising his crippling social economic demands as a bedtime story in which the country is tucked up tight and told, Don't worry, I know it wasn't a great day today at school, but there will be plenty of hard days ahead and the important thing to remember when you go to sleep tonight and wake up tomorrow is that things are better now than they've ever been, and they will, with our forbearance and perseverance, get better still, good night sweet children, good night –

Contempt is what she feels.

She, Thatcher, listens. You only get one chance as a woman, she thinks, one chance to win and the same chance to lose. She *listens*.

Let us think for a moment, Callaghan is saying, of the great domestic issues that the country faces now and ask ourselves whether a general election now would make it any better this winter.

She thinks: *There*. You're not coming back from that, Lucky Jim.

Would a general election now prevent inflation rising once more? Would unemployment be any less severe this winter? Would a general election now solve the problem of how to deal with pay increases during the next few months? Would it bring about a sudden dramatic increase in productivity?

She thinks, Jimbo, you need a new speechwriter.

Because, of course, the answer to these questions is: NO.

The other answer to these questions is: Labour isn't working. Dagenham will be the start, the tip of the iceberg.

Let's see it through together, Callaghan says.

I don't think we've got much bloody choice, Jim, she thinks.

She will travel shortly to the West Midlands to begin her campaign and she knows what she will say.

She'll say that she's deeply disappointed by the news, that he has lost his majority, and when that happens, it means you lose the authority to govern.

She rehearses what she'll say:

He should now seek the verdict of the people.

This country belongs to the courageous and not to the timid.

In Lea's caff on Chatsworth Road, drinking tea and generally making a nuisance of himself, Noble's looking at the papers.

The *Mirror*'s headline screams:

JIM UNFIXES IT

He wonders about Mrs Thatcher, if she's got the bottle.

He remembers one of her MPs saying what a bird she is –

Something like:

She is so beautiful. Quite bewitching, as Eva Perón must have been.

What a cunt, Noble thinks, that MP must have been.

His name is Alan Clark, Noble remembers, and he *is* a cunt.

That's the thing with Mrs Thatcher, she's a Tory, which means she's a cunt, end of the day, bewitching or otherwise.

And Eva Perón's fascist ex-husband and his new missus kept the bewitching Eva's exhumed corpse on show in their dining room.

Takes all sorts.

There's no argument.

He turns the page, does a double take and smiles.

There's their friend Dai Wyn, just behind his associate Moss Evans.

Evans saying, 'There is no ambiguity at all and no qualification. The TGWU does not support pay restraint.'

Interesting, Noble thinks, that he's saying this in the press so quickly. There's a quote in the article which lays out Moss Evans' position. There is definitely no ambiguity.

He's saying Callaghan needs to 'back off and let the unions get on with the job of securing the best settlements they could'. He also says, and here Noble is not sure about the level of irony, that Callaghan needn't worry, the unions will 'behave responsibly'.

Well, well, Noble thinks. Nice to delve into politics from time to time.

Noble folds his tabloid. 'Lea, darling,' he says. 'What do you make of this Thatcher then?'

'*Mrs* Thatcher,' Lea says. 'She's a woman.'

So I've heard, Noble mutters. He says, 'I'm off then.'

'OK then,' Lea says.

She turns back to her customers.

'Right,' Noble says. 'OK then.'

3

Murderers

September 1978

Gideon

You tell Day you've done all sorts of work and he says, Big lad like you can work the door, and you say, Which Door? and he tells you, Excalibur House, son, you're the new head of security and you think, Yes, that is exactly what I want, exactly what I need. You have a good look around on your first day, there's nobody there, in fact you don't really understand why they need an HQ there's so little work that goes on. There's a security box by the front door, a small bench for security staff and a telephone with a list of numbers by it, including that of Centerprise, the radical bookshop in Hackney, the SWP, the Socialist Workers Party, including their print shop which you hear will get a visit sooner or later, 10 Downing Street, and various radio phone-in programmes. Stacked in the corner, under the window, there is a pile of weapons, including wooden clubs and iron bars. A wooden pickaxe handle has something written on it in ballpoint pen. It says Jew beater. You have a good shufty through the office of the Front secretary, Martin Webster. It's revealing: you find a letter from a National Front infiltrator in a left-wing caucus of the National Union of Mine-workers. Well, well, you think, everyone's at it. One day the Front lawyer Something Reed-Herbert comes in and sells you an Excalibur House tie, and you're a bit sniffy as really you should get your uniform for free, you reckon. That bloke from the council's back and this time you give him a little bit more, let him in, you'll pick your moment. It's pretty straight-forward, even now, in the inner sanctum, to keep everyone fooled, you just keep your mouth hanging open and polish your boots, it's all racist abuse, it ain't politics, and if you're honest you're still getting off on the rush of the thing, on the adrenalin, on the promise or threat of violence, of being a stormtrooper, that's how it feels, so there's some conflict, but not really, you know you're doing the right thing and going round to Fat

Bastard's house for a cuppa and delivering him a bit of meat is no fucking skin off your rosy red behind, no way, you're not falling for him even if hundreds do. End of the month and it's the second lefty concert down in South London somewhere, Bandit Country, and someone, well, you, has the bright idea of putting on a show at Brick Lane, taking it back after the Chapel Market distraction and celebrating the opening of the new HQ on the same day, as the ANL plonkers won't get their act together to stop you, they're more interested in the carnival, the wankers, when are they going to learn what causes change to happen and what doesn't. Day of, and there's been a London-wide Front mobilisation so there's hundreds, all milling about at the Whitechapel end of Brick Lane and you all pile down through, flags and placards, and you get to the end and you clock some of the anti-fascists, the tastier elements, dockers and right-on West Ham and Millwall fans, always a delight when those lot get together, but you see the route to Great Eastern Street is clear, and you see police, heavy police, gathering in vans round the back of Shoreditch Station, palling up, mobbing up, and you think, Hang about, and you look at Phil and he says, I think they ain't here for us.

Noble considers the modus operandi of the Met Race Crime Initiative. It is designed to be distinct in practice from the type of policing that is exercised by the Special Patrol Group. What this means is that the forms of policing that the Special Patrol Group undertake – saturation, stop and search, physical harassment of minority communities – are neither approved by, nor employed in, the Met Race Crime Initiative. The Special Patrol Group are troops; the state's army of bodies to prevent civil unrest and curb lawbreaking. In reality, this means state-sanctioned violence masquerading as an expression of government policy. Or, perhaps, it's simpler than that: it is a literal expression of government policy.

In 1973, two young Pakistani men were waving plastic toy guns around in a demonstration outside India House and they were both shot dead by the Special Patrol Group.

In Lewisham, in 1975, in response to the perceived threat of muggings, the Special Patrol Group stopped and search 65,628 people to arrest only 4,125.

In Notting Hill, the Special Patrol Group launched violent raids on the Mangrove restaurant and the Metro Club, raids which the local community believed were examples of targeted harassment.

In 1974, during an anti-fascist demonstration in Red Lion Square that was policed by the Special Patrol Group, a young man called Kevin Gately died in circumstances best described as questionable.

And these are only the examples Noble can remember off the top of his head.

Noble's heard that the Special Patrol Group have a real esprit de corps, he believes is the phrase. It's hardly a surprise; it's a chance for your average plod to go up in the world. You've got to be a stone-cold psycho to qualify.

So, they look out for each other and tell themselves they're the dog's bollocks.

Noble's also heard that the Special Patrol Group don't consider your standard issue Met truncheon to be quite sturdy enough, they think it's a bit flimsy.

Instead, they use pickaxe handles with the words Crime Squad burned into them.

Knives, iron bars, wooden staves –

Sledgehammers and jemmies to carry out search warrants.

All a bit different from the Met Race Crime Initiative, which, Noble's beginning to think, is a bit of a mess, focus-wise.

There was something of the Heavy Mob, the Sweeney, about its conception –

Operating across London without borough policing boundaries.

Bringing together specialists to do more than simply feel a few collars, to *effect social change*, is the theory.

Very unlike the old Sweeny Todd / Flying Squad in that sense.

Noble thinks, It's fucking 1978. Are we still using cockney rhyming slang?

No, the problem with the Met Race Crime Initiative is not the principle it was founded upon.

It's definitely not Detective Chief Inspector Maurice Young.

The problem might be Detective Sergeant Williams' lack of effective coordination.

One problem is that the mid-level boys like Noble and Gardiner and Caldwell seem to be pretty much ploughing their own furrows.

End of the day, Noble's not sure any of the others really gives a monkey's.

Hackney nick, to see Williams. Williams is not pleased to see him.

Noble says, 'Shahid Akhtar.'

Williams nods.

Noble raises his eyebrows.

Williams says, 'What do you want to know, Chance?'

'What the family's up to.'

'They've left us alone for a while.'

'Why do you think that is?'

Williams sighs. A big man, Williams. Noble notes yellowing stains creeping out from under his armpits.

The shirt is striped, scratchy-looking, a market stall knock-off, maybe.

Williams says, 'You've seen the report.'

'I have.'

'Well then.' Williams sighs again.

Noble is happy for them to sit in silence for a little while. It's golden, after all, silence. Battle of wills.

'If there's something specific, DC Noble, spit it out.'

'Name and address of the mistress,' Noble says.

'OK.'

Williams heaves himself up and opens his filing cabinet.

Noble studies the office. It's grey and unimpressive, smells of old smoke and Brut.

Williams pulls and opens a file.

He sits down heavily. He takes a pen and a notepad.

He scribbles messily on this notepad and tears off the top sheet with a flourish.

He holds out the sheet for Noble to take –

Elegantly, between thumb and forefinger, Noble plucks it, grinning.

'Cheers, guv,' he says. He has a gander at the address, grimaces.

Williams smiles. 'No need to send a postcard.'

'Wish you were her,' Noble winks.

'When you see the state of her,' Williams says, 'you bloody won't.'

Noble's double-parked outside Hackney Baths, a traffic warden lurking.

Noble shows his warrant card. 'You best leave off,' he says.

The traffic warden doesn't disagree.

Noble does a U-turn and heads past Clapton Square and bends right towards Hackney Downs.

The fringes of the Pembury Estate to his right, low-rise blocks and balconies flapping with washing.

Parched grass, all fag ends and dog shit, graffiti on the footpaths. A drunk sits on the wall, sunbathing.

To Noble's left, a row of boarded-up houses.

In the bus shelter, two pensioners with their shopping have a peer at him.

A rusting Ford Cortina growls up the road towards him, reggae flooding out of it, heavy bass making the doors shake, the exhaust choke. The air, for a moment, is weed-thick. Calmly, two Rastafarians eye Noble as the cars, next to each other, dawdle.

'You got a light?' Noble jokes through the window.

As he pulls away, he doesn't hear anyone laughing.

He's under the bridge at Hackney Downs and up onto Dalston Lane. He grew up round here; he's seen it change.

But he never misses a chance to look at Navarino Mansions. He's never understood it, they're *nice*.

When he was a kid, Noble was desperate to get out of East London. He never fitted in. His parents came over from Belfast after the war for work, simple as that. His dad was a builder, his mum was a nurse who cleaned houses on the side. They lived off the Hackney Road at the Bethnal Green end in an Irish tenement slum, at least that's what it felt like, what he remembers.

He never had an accent; he put as much distance from his parents as he could.

When he was fourteen his old man asked him to join him on a job.

He said no.

'It's a different life you're about then, is it?' his old man spat.

To that, Noble said yes.

His old man – his *Pa* – sniffed. 'On you go, boy.'

They didn't speak a lot after that.

Noble was spending his time in Soho mainly, by then anyway, out the house.

He liked the sharpness of the scene, the coffee bar clubs, the rhythm and blues, standing around shooting the breeze –

It was about as far from Hackney as he could get. And he could walk it in less than an hour.

He remembers Soho in the early sixties as a camera roll of images, especially in the mornings, as he left whatever club he was at, started the walk home –

A cleaning truck hosing down empty market stalls. Newspapers blowing about in the breeze. Pigeons flutter, then scatter. A series of restaurant façades: Asia Famous Curries, Choys, Chez Auguste, Isola Bella, Trattoria Toscana. A gas lamp, a brick workhouse, a modern high-rise towering above. Red phone boxes and empty alleyways. Lisle Street in Chinatown, the Doris Café. Delivery vans and film posters. The Swiss Hotel and its Toby Ale. The Heaven and Hell Coffee Lounge and the 2is Coffee Bar. The Cameo Moulin cinema showing *Naked as Nature Intended*, the Nosh Bar next door. The Lyric Theatre and the Windmill Revudeville. The Moulin Rouge Strip Tease Revue, Non-Stop Strip Tease, the Metro Revue Club. Metal dustbins spilling more newspapers. Empty milk bottles in clusters of twos and threes. Uniformed dustmen in caps and jackets smoking –

About the same time – 1963, he thinks – he started hearing about, and then reading about, Harold 'Tanky' Challenor, an SAS war hero and ferocious and controversial Detective Sergeant working out of West End Central in 1960s Soho. He once chased Reggie Kray on foot down Shaftesbury Avenue and halfway back to the East End. The twins offered a grand to anyone who'd help stitch him up.

Noble liked the sound of this Challenor.

Noble couldn't stand the way the twins ran his neck of the woods, the hypocrisy – the honour and code and decency among thieves was cobblers, in Noble's eyes.

So Challenor became something of a role model.

Fighting crime in Soho was, Challenor said, 'like trying to swim against a tide of sewage'.

Noble understood that and he liked this story in particular:

One evening, Challenor was called to investigate a disturbance in a nightclub on Dean Street: glass everywhere, tables and chairs over-turned. A young punter on a night out tended to a nasty wound in his eye. The proprietor, a known villain, sat at the bar.

'What happened?' Challenor asked him, nodding at the punter.

'Fell down the stairs.'

Challenor took the punter to hospital; he lost the sight in his wounded eye.

One of the proprietor's thugs was taken to West End Central police station in possession of a flick knife. After Challenor visited him in his cell, the thug claimed the knife was planted and that Challenor had given him 'a belting'.

The following night, Challenor returned to the nightclub.

'You've got porridge on your suit,' Challenor said to the proprietor, meaning, It's time you went to jail.

'Uncle Harry,' the proprietor said. 'Why not let us sort this out among ourselves, eh?'

It was a protection racket dispute, one gang muscling in on another's turf.

'Tell that to the lad with one eye,' Challenor said. 'You're coming with me, my old beauty.'

It's not clear what Challenor said or did to this known villain or his thug – no charges were pressed – but there was no more bother over protection money.

Noble stayed in school then joined the Metropolitan Police.

Just in time, he thinks now, to watch it all go up the spout again, this endless bloody civil war.

He's down Dalston Lane in a flash, past Ridley Road and across the junction onto Queensbridge Road, past the blacked-out drug pub on the corner, moody-looking black blokes sitting on the outside tables keeping their eyes peeled, and he slows down a touch and finds a spot and parks, and on the sign by the road that announces he's arrived at the Holly Street Estate, scrawled in cheap paint across the map of the towers and corridors, is the word –

Welcome home, Noble thinks.

Hackney police station.

Jon Davies is sitting in front of Detective Sergeant Williams. Two Welshmen, Jon thinks, but only one accent.

They've been talking about the Met Race Crime Initiative, how it might help Jon with the whole Excalibur House planning dispute. If there is a possibility that intelligence gathered by the initiative might be of use to Jon and his team, especially regarding the abuses that occurred outside Excalibur House that Jon knows about.

The answer is: not really.

'We can't share any intelligence in this sort of a capacity,' Williams says, 'you understand.'

Williams doesn't look like he'd be too happy if Jon were to press the point, so Jon doesn't.

Jon says, 'Shahid Akhtar's widow is a neighbour of mine, a friend.'

Williams nods.

'She feels,' Jon says, 'that she hasn't really had much closure. That you, that the police, haven't been as open as you might have been.'

Williams says, 'It wasn't a criminal investigation, Mr Davies. Coroner's verdict was misadventure.'

Jon says, 'Mrs Akhtar doesn't feel like she's been given the whole story, for want of a better expression.'

Williams leans forward and smiles. 'Well, she hasn't, Mr Davies.'

'OK.'

'The fact is, Mr Davies, Mr Akhtar had a bit on the side, a woman who is now pregnant with his bastard.'

Jon nods.

'She came forward, helped us with our enquiries. She told us he tried to blackmail her to get rid of it, and she told him she was going to tell your friend Mrs Akhtar.'

'I see,' Jon says.

Williams gives it the benevolent uncle, says, 'But I don't mind if you tell her that, boyo. We just didn't think she needed to hear it.'

Jon Davies nods. The meeting over, he says, 'I'll see myself out.'

Mid-September. Finsbury Park, RAR offices.

'Callaghan ducked it.'

This is Paul Holborow, founder of the Anti-Nazi League. 'He ducked it, end of story.'

Suzi's thinking that they might have called all this a bit late.

Red Saunders says, 'Who have you got speaking at the rally?'

Paul Holborow says, 'Tony Benn.'

'That's good,' says Syd Shelton.

'Good?' says Paul Holborow. 'It's a cabinet minister talking at a demonstration clearly outside the parameters of traditional British politics. It's unprecedented.'

'I said it's good,' Syd Shelton mutters. 'And it *is* fucking good.'

Suzi's watching the two groups feel each other out again.

This time there's a division of labour: RAR do the festival, ANL do the rally and the march.

Except that RAR are doing the music on the march.

And they're really going to town –

On the floats there will be Crisis, Charge, Eclipse, Inganda, RAS, The Derelicts, the Enchanters, The Members, The Ruts and The Straights.

At the mention of The Ruts, the focus of the room, for a moment, settles on Suzi.

'One thing,' she says, 'is Brick Lane. There'll be no one there.'

'What's your point, Suzi?' someone asks.

'There've been running battles all summer. The ANL, the Bengali Youth Movement Against Racism and IWA have secured the area and the Front have done one, we think. That's right, isn't it?'

There is some nodding at this.

'Well,' Suzi says, 'what's going to happen if everyone's in Brockwell Park and none of our lot are in Brick Lane?'

Silence for a moment, then voices saying things like:

'There's going to be a hundred thousand people, Suzi.'

'It's going to be huge.'

'Look, we'll get a hundred thousand there, *minimum*. Huge, Suzi, *huge*.'

'But what about Brick Lane?' Suzi insists.

'Like you said, it's safe.'

'OK.'

'We can always get some coaches and ship a few back, can't we?'

Everyone nodding now.

Suzi thinks: I hope you're right and it really is safe and you do know what you're doing.

At home, lying next to him on their mattress, Suzi says to Keith, 'Do you think this is worth it, love?'

Keith, startled, says, 'You what, love?'

'Oh, no, I mean this second carnival.' She laughs, kisses him. 'I think you're worth every penny, my darling.'

Keith smiles. 'It's a job, Suze, it's *my* job.' He puts his hands behind his head, stretches. 'I love it. I don't think much beyond that, to be honest.'

'That's OK.'

'Yeah, it is.' He props himself up on an elbow. 'I'm lucky that my job gets to make a difference.'

Suzi nods. 'I'm lucky too,' she says. 'Because I get to have you.'

She, Thatcher, is reading about Moss Evans. One of her spies has gathered a little dossier.

Denis Healey thinks Moss Evans has 'no leadership qualities and little loyalty to the Labour Party'.

Edward Pearce, one of her least favourite political journalists, thinks he lacks 'courage, mind and energy to work even for mitigation of the mood'.

Bernard Donoghue has written, she now reads, about Callaghan's pay restraint, this 5 per cent cap on *any* pay rise.

He concedes that politically it is problematic but that it's 'the only way of avoiding high inflation – and avoiding the monetary squeeze and high unemployment which would inevitably follow such inflation'.

She thinks that it is asking a lot of the British people to understand this. An enforced limit of 5 per cent for a pay rise does not a happy nation make.

Tom McNally, she reads, questioned Callaghan on this 5 per cent cap.

She reads that Callaghan responded to this by thumping the table and shouting at Tom McNally, 'Are you saying, Tom, that five per cent would not be best for the country?'

She thinks: It certainly won't be best for you, James.

Noble remembers when the Holly Street Estate was built, late sixties. It was supposed to be a *good thing*, with a real community vibe –

And a mile-long corridor right down the middle joining the high-rise blocks, the longest urban corridor of the sort in the whole of Europe.

Optimism and opportunity –

Community pride and spirit. A modern utopia in the East End –

There's not a lot of that about, Noble thinks.

That mile-long corridor is a mugger's paradise.

Dark passages, blind alleys, stairwells – no wonder the police never come in. What's the point? The decay is, in some cases, literally falling off the walls.

Noble thinks, It's only the graffiti that's keeping the whole thing standing.

The estate reeks of unemployment. It reeks of *dole*.

It reeks of betting shops and cash for cheques, of net curtains and readers' wives, of Special Brew and frozen dinners, of drug abuse and racial tension, of *glue* –

Noble knocks on Shahid Akhtar's former mistress's front door.

He thinks, I didn't know Hackney was going to come to this. And, Thank fuck I left when I did.

In a dressing gown, smoking a cigarette, a woman opens the door, and Noble shakes his head: could this get any more kitchen sink?

'Dawn Driscoll?' Discreetly, Noble shows her his warrant card.

'What can I do for you?'

'You sure you should be smoking in your condition?'

Dawn Driscoll sighs. 'You better come in.'

Inside it's poky and the carpet matches the wallpaper. Dawn Driscoll leads Noble into the living room and sits down. On the coffee table are two half-empty takeaway containers, Indian, judging by the smell. Bits of poppadom on the floor.

'Excuse the pong,' Dawn Driscoll says. 'It's a habit I learned off of him.'

'Curry lunch is a treat where I'm from.'

'Which is?'

'Up the road.'

'Lucky you.'

Noble clocks the mantelpiece: no photos. Noble clocks the television set: new. There's a half-decent stereo in the corner and a big old sofa with plastic wrapping still on it.

Dawn Driscoll puts out her cigarette in the emptier of the two take-away containers and plonks herself down on the easy chair.

She gestures at the new sofa. 'Have a seat. Put your feet up if you like. It won't get dirty.' She laughs.

'You not pregnant then?' Noble says.

Dawn Driscoll smiles. 'Why don't you tell me what you think you know and we'll go from there.'

Noble gives her the gist.

Dawn Driscoll laughs. 'That sounds about right.'

'Except.'

'Except I'm not in the family way, as you can probably see.'

'Right.'

Dawn Driscoll takes another cigarette from an open packet of Silk Cut and lights it. She offers Noble the open packet but he shakes his head.

'You're not the first to come round.'

'I'm not surprised to hear that. What did the other one want?'

'He wanted to know what I was going to do.'

'What did you tell him?'

Dawn Driscoll laughs. 'I told him there was nothing *to* do.'

'Why don't you tell me what you're going to do?'

'I'm not going to do anything.' She leans forward. 'This whole thing was a set-up. Do you think me and Mr Akhtar move in the same social circles? He fell in love with me, that's all. I was going to take his money the first time he offered it but I thought I'd get more if I held out, so I threatened to tell his wife. And then ...'

Dawn Driscoll sniffs.

'Who introduced you?'

Dawn Driscoll snorts. 'Introduced us?' She laughs. 'There's a pub on the Hackney Road, Ye Old Axe. You know it?'

Noble nods.

'Well then,' Dawn Driscoll says. 'You'll know how we met.'

Noble thinks fifty-pence pieces in a pint mug and a disco ball. Shahid Akhtar with a double whisky at the bar, gawping. Dawn Driscoll parading her wares, all the trimmings, punters cheering –

'But someone told you to threaten him.'

Dawn Driscoll nods.

'Who told you, Dawn?'

'One of yours.'

Noble leans forward. 'Who, Dawn?'

Dawn Driscoll shakes her head, bites her lip.

'Who, Dawn?'

Dawn Driscoll smokes her cigarette, plays with her fingernails.

'You don't know?'

'I don't know.'

'So why did you do it?'

Dawn Driscoll makes a face. 'Don't be naïve. Why do you think?'

Noble nods: easy enough to put a solicitation on a cheap afternoon stripper.

'I liked him,' Dawn Driscoll sniffs. 'Really. I didn't want to do it. It was just information, I was told. As in "we'll have one over him". A bloody shame.'

Noble stands. 'Not true though, is it?' he says, meaning the pregnancy. He gestures at the room with his chin. 'Expensive gear you've got here, Dawn.'

Dawn Driscoll nods. 'He was generous, Mr Akhtar, I'll give him that.'

Noble nods. 'I'll see myself out,' he tells her.

Panda's Chinese takeaway, 21 September.

Parker says to Noble, 'It's going to be a march from the Whitechapel end of Brick Lane, all the way to Bethnal Green Road, then straight across to Excalibur House. They're calling it a victory parade.'

'There going to be an open-top bus?' Noble jokes.

Parker gives Noble a look. 'Just tell me there'll be a presence, guv, please.'

Noble nods. 'I'll be there myself, son.'

Same place, next day.

Alan says to Noble, 'They've bottled it, there's no organisation at all. There's going to be a small number of militants and dockers, and that's it.'

Noble nods. 'And me,' he says. 'I'll be there.'

'Whose side will you be on, guv?' Alan jokes.

'Good question, son. That's a very good question.'

Later.

Noble tells Chief Inspector Maurice Young that one of his inside men has it on good authority that the heavier members of groups of anti-fascist organisations will be gathering on Sunday, 24 September to 'hold Brick Lane' in a show of strength.

Young says, 'We'd better be ready for them then, DC Noble.'

Noble's thinking it's the only way to ensure a police presence. He tells himself it doesn't matter, that protecting Parker and the work they're doing is the priority.

159

Later still, in bed, Lea with an 'a' says, 'I think there's something on your mind.'

Noble smiles. 'Only you, darling,' he lies.

'I wasn't sure you were boyfriend material at first.' Lea smiles. 'I might have been wrong.'

Noble grins, pulls her in close. 'For once, eh?'

Same day.

She knows that any pay rise set by Ford is considered a private industry benchmark. She knows that Ford are performing admirably and have the coffers to offer an impressive percentage. She also knows, of course, that Ford is a significant government contractor.

She, Thatcher, thinks: Go on then, make the pay offer within Callaghan's 5 per cent and see where that gets you.

She reads that the management at Ford have made this offer in line with their position as a significant government contractor.

She reads that from today, Friday, 22 September, 15,000 Ford workers, mostly from the TGWU, will strike in response to this offer.

The TGWU, she notes, is led by Moss Evans.

She allows herself a thin smile and slices the top off a boiled egg.

She says to Denis, 'We give them a chance to buy their council house, they'll vote for us in their thousands. They want that chance to buy their own home.'

'The buggers have obviously got jam on it,' Denis says. 'If one seriously thinks a few quid on the rent is going to hurt these sponging sods, you must all be mad.'

'That's not what I'm suggesting, Denis.'

'Still,' Denis says.

Saturday, 23 September, late afternoon.

Jon Davies sits in the front seat of his car listening to the football results come in. The boy is asleep in the back. Jackie's inside the house getting the oven on.

Jon is pleased to hear that West Ham have beaten Sheffield United 2–0 away from home. Both goals were scored by Pop Robson and both were penalties. There were 24,361 in attendance. This, Jon thinks, is a decent result.

He switches off the radio and closes his eyes for a moment.

There's a tapping on the window and he starts.

It's Mrs Akhtar.

Smiling, Jon opens the window, says, 'You scared me, Mrs Akhtar.'

'Did I, Jon? I'm sorry.'

Jon shakes his head. 'It's nothing at all.' He sits up in his seat. 'What can I do for you, Mrs Akhtar?'

She leans into the window. 'My sons and I,' she says, 'we'd like to go to the carnival in Brockwell Park tomorrow. We wondered if you will be attending?'

'I'll drive you,' Jon says. 'We can go together.'

'Really, Jon,' she says, 'I don't want to, you know, cramp your style.'

Jon laughs at this. 'It'll be my pleasure.'

The boy stirs. Mrs Akhtar nods at him. 'Thank you, Jon.'

Inside, Jon tells Jackie.

'That's good, Jon,' she says. 'That's really good.'

Same time, Finsbury Park, RAR offices.

There's a last-minute logistics meeting going on and Suzi's there as she's covering the whole event again for *Temporary Hoarding*.

Roger Huddle says, 'A few of us will stay at the SWP print shop, just in case. There've been threats by the Front to burn it down, as you know. We've got binoculars and baseball bats; we'll sit on the roof. It's a bit bloody toy town but better safe than sorry.'

Someone else says, 'We'll divert a group from the march at Hyde Park and that'll cover it.'

There are, Suzi hears, murmurings, mutterings.

They sound something like, Oh, OK then, you'll sort it out, nice one, thanks.

She phones Noble and tells him.

He tells her, 'It's covered. You go and have a nice time at your concert.'

Sunday, 24 September, Hyde Park.

It's a beautiful, sunny Sunday morning and people are streaming into Hyde Park from all entrances, and there's a joyous mood to the crowd, a real buzz, and as Suzi takes photos and looks around and sees all these smiling faces, all these smiling black, brown, white faces, for a moment she forgets about being worried and relaxes and smiles herself too, and remembers that she really is part of something big, bigger than her, bigger than any one individual, a crowd that is bigger and more significant than the sum of its parts, and the demo itself, the placards, the whistles, the badges, all of it really feels to Suzi like today it might actually *mean* something –

Paul Holborow takes the platform to set the march on its way, takes the stage to introduce Tony Benn. Paul Holborow tells the crowd not to worry about the East End, that the Anti-Nazi League has sent supporters to Brick Lane to make sure it's safe and it is safe! There is no Front presence now and if there was, it's been smashed!

There are cheers and lots of nodding, some fists raised.

What Suzi feels is a good deal of relief.

This is a victory parade.

Keith's on the float with The Ruts and Suzi walks with the crowd.

Brockwell Park, when they get there, is an oasis –

Suzi clambers up the stage steps and stands right as Stiff Little Fingers do their stuff, the same clothes, she thinks, as when she took their photograph. She's heard they've been staying on Syd Shelton's floor in his flat in Stamford Hill. Stamford Hell, as Syd Shelton's flat is known. They don't look any the worse for wear. 'Johnny Was', Suzi thinks, is magisterial.

As they bound off, triumphant, Jake Burns sees Suzi and winks.

'See you later?' Suzi says.

Jake Burns shakes his head. 'We're going straight to your station, Paddington, is it? Cardiff tonight. You know how it is.' He's grinning.

'And tomorrow the world,' Suzi says.

*

Same time, same day, Brick Lane.

In plainclothes and not officially involved in the policing of the semi-official National Front demo and march to their new headquarters, Noble is skulking around the back streets of Brick Lane trying to look inconspicuous.

What he wants to know is exactly where and when Alan and his mob are going to pitch up.

He's also wondering about the police vans circling Shoreditch with decent numbers of officers in the back. This sort of crowd control is in no way part of the Met Race Crime Initiative remit, but Special Young will have passed on the info Noble gave him and Noble wonders how much of what he's seeing is in direct response to that info.

Jon Davies, Mrs Akhtar and her sons are enjoying Aswad's set. It's very loud, Jon thinks, exactly as a reggae sound system should be, in his experience, which, live events-wise, is limited. He does love his reggae though, Jon, and he does have Aswad's first LP –

'It's very loud, Jon,' Mrs Akhtar says. 'But beautiful.'

It *is* beautiful. Aswad are immense, such style and grace, Jon is quite lost in it.

The opening to 'Natural Progression' merges in and out, that mournful harmonica glancing off the soft edge of the bass, the scratchy guitar solo cutting through the wah-wah rhythm of the other guitar, Brinsley Forde like a dub warrior-poet, or something heroic anyway –

The song drops down into the bass and drums and Brinsley is speaking –

'What's he saying, Jon?' Mrs Akhtar asks.

'He's saying,' Jon says, 'that this is ire, ire there are so many people here today, I think.'

'Ire, Jon?'

'Good, I think, you know, it's a really good thing.'

'It is,' Mrs Akhtar says.

Later in the set Brinsley Forde brings on his newly born baby and lifts his newly born baby to the skies, the sun, in celebration.

Misty are playing a monumental set, and at the side of the stage David Widgery turns to Suzi and says, 'This is joyous! Misty are joyous, lilting and weaving into the rhythms so evocatively it's like Brockwell Park has been transferred to the Jamaican mountains by their open, rural, spiritual magic!'

Suzi likes David Widgery, respects him, and she smiles and says, 'I'm going to write that in my notebook, David, if that's OK?'

'Joyous!' David Widgery says again.

Misty finish up and there's a bit of confusion on the backstage steps and then Jimmy Pursey is running on and he's got the mic and he's speaking and Suzi's scribbling it down and he's saying:

'All week you've probably read a lot of things about me and Sham 69. We've been dictated to. Last night I wasn't going to come. But this morning I met this kid who said, "You ain't doing it 'cos all your fans are National Front." They said I ain't got no bottle. But I'm here. Nobody's going to tell me what I should or should not do. I'm here because I support Rock Against Racism.'

There are cheers and you've got to admire Jimmy's front, as it were, his face, his fucking bottle is the chorus at the side of the stage, what a lad, this is a staunch show of faith, Suzi hears. And then Jimmy turns and Suzi's got her camera up and –

The sky is blue. There's not a cloud in it. There isn't a cloud in the blue sky.

The sea of faces stretching back and on and on.

The trees at the far end of the park lean one way and then the other in the breeze, sway and swing like lovers dancing.

Ayeleen: Then one day my mother tells me we're not going to live in Clapton anymore and in fact we're going to live in a little house in

Dalston, just the two of us, and we should be very grateful to Uncle Ahmet, and, yes, one day he's promised me that you will definitely work for him, if you stay in school and keep doing as well as you are, he'll definitely give you a job, he can't wait to teach you everything he knows about business –

And I wonder if I'll see my father in the holidays in this new house or in Turkey or maybe everyone else has just forgotten about that promise.

Jon Davies is a long way from the stage but he hears the announcement correctly and he realises that he is now listening to Ernie Roberts of the engineers' union, a sometime acquaintance of Jon's, giving a passionate speech.

'What's he saying, Jon?' asks Mrs Akhtar.

Jon doesn't catch every word, but he gets the gist and he understands the conclusion all right. He says to Mrs Akhtar, 'The Front was at Brick Lane but so were anti-fascists, in their thousands. Something like that, I think.'

Jon squints and holds a finger to his left ear.

'He's saying that the NF's feeble attempt to disrupt the carnival and invade Brick Lane was completely defeated.'

'Oh, that is very good news,' Mrs Akhtar says.

After Elvis Costello comes off, there's a fight backstage between his road crew and some of the council workers who put up the stage –

Suzi hears a nasty racial epithet but she's not sure who's said it to who. The fight calms down, big Red Saunders and a bunch of others breaking it up.

About five minutes earlier, Suzi's seen Nick Lowe with tears in his eyes as Elvis Costello and the Attractions tear through his song, 'What's So Funny About Peace, Love, and Understanding?'

Suzi thinks of Keith, smiles.

Brick Lane.

Noble's round by Bethnal Green Road examining the uniforms that have gathered in considerable numbers and he thinks:

Special Patrol Group.

By six o'clock the Front march is over and what some people are calling a 'rally' is happening on Curtain Road just by the new Front HQ at 73 Great Eastern Street, but when Noble goes to have a quick look at this rally, it is basically a few dozen skinheads drinking cans and being anti-social. He clocks Parker in the mix and thinks, again, Thank fuck I'm not you.

Back over by Bethnal Green Road, under the arches that lead to Commercial Street, the uniforms have contained about forty anti-fascists. The mood is tense. Noble noticed some aggro between different groups of lefties earlier, sectarian nastiness, but those that are left look pretty united and there's a grim determination on a lot of weathered, lined and experienced faces –

Some younger faces too, kids with scars, kids with badges.

Older lads calling out *stick together, stick together,* bottles in hands, bricks half-hidden in other hands, but they look, Noble thinks, on the defensive.

They look, Noble thinks, surprised by what is unfolding, surprised and unprepared.

This doesn't look quite right to Noble. There's a look about this group, a hooligan-look now, a caged-animal look, a look of fear –

Stick together, Noble hears, *it's going to go off, it's going to go off.*

This is new, *this*: the police, fighting. Noble sees it; Noble sees their faces –

They're waiting, they're pushing, they're jostling, they're positioning themselves, waiting for the crowd, wanting the crowd, this tightly contained crowd, the caged animal of the crowd, waiting for the crowd to become a violent crowd, and it won't take much, it never takes much, Noble thinks, to push the crowd, to transgress, to move into something irrevocable, something violent that can never be undone –

And then Noble sees it. In the second or third row of the police line, a bottle flies above, to the left, away from the crowd, as though thrown by the crowd, and the bottle smashes, the glass like water on a hot fire, and then another bottle, also from the police side, also landing as if thrown by the crowd, and then a bigger smash as a car window cracks, and that's it, that's the incitement they need –

Stick together, stick together.

The line of police moves forward –

The anti-fascists hold their ground –

More bottles now, from the crowd, half-bricks.

There's a rising, ugly hubbub of swearing and threats –

Noble spots Alan in the middle –

Noble spots Alan encouraging sense into some of this crowd or trying to –

A group of anti-fascists splinters off and makes a run for the thinnest part of the blue line under the arches, breaks through and away –

Others – individually, in pairs – try to slip the line.

The police charge, batons out, and a melee –

Noble skirts the edges, looks on –

In the dusk, in the cooling dusk, the police set about this splinter group –

There are fists flying, there are boots flying –

A few anti-fascists get away and keep running –

There is noise and there are commands, there is dust and there is the thump of bats on slabs of meat, the crunch of deadened limb, of nose and cheek, of broken glass.

Noble sees blood, Noble sees truncheons and sticks, bottles and bricks –

Noble sees Alan raising his hands, Alan ducking his head, Alan shouting, Alan screaming –

Noble sees blood, Noble sees bodies –

Noble sees Alan turn and run, Alan trip, Alan stumble –

Noble sees blood, Noble sees bodies –

Noble sees a Special Patrol Group officer raise his cosh, raise his club –

Noble sees a second Special Patrol Group officer raise his hand, in his hand a heavy, weighted sock –

Noble sees a third Special Patrol Group officer raise his fist, his knuckles glinting gold, gold and heavy –

Noble sees one body, prone, blood leaking –

Noble sees Alan.

Noble turns –

Noble gasps, he pushes through the line, he gets down on his knees, a body prone and leaking, alone now, still, and Noble bends down and holds Alan in his hands, he slaps Alan's face, he cleans Alan's face, his own tears damp, dripping, Alan still, unmoving, and Noble shouts for an ambulance, Noble waving his warrant card, shouting, and he's surrounded, and he's pulled up and Alan is lifted, and Noble stands, he shakes, dazed and dirty –

Noble thinks –

What have I done?

It's when they're halfway down Mildenhall Road that Jon Davies notices the blue flash of a siren light, the bustle of bodies, the crackle of radios –

He turns to Mrs Akhtar, says, 'It's nothing to worry about, I'm sure.'

They stop the car and get out. They walk briskly down the road, and then Jon Davies understands, and he's running, sees the police van and the ambulance, and he's grabbed and held, and a policeman is saying to him, It's OK, it's OK, and Jon – confused, panicky – asks, It's OK?

And there's Jackie and the boy and they're OK, and they're holding Jon and he asks, What, what is it? And Jackie points and Jon sees it, their front windows smashed, a smouldering wet mess, a dark stain, and a policeman is saying, A brick and a lit firework, could have been really dangerous, kids round here, right?

And Jon turns, Jon says, Kids?

The policeman says, Yeah, kids. He points across the road, he points at the estate. Kids, he says, kids mucking around, and then Jon – confused, panicky – sees this policeman, he's sure he sees this policeman, he sees this policeman look at him and smile, smile and wink, smile and wink as he says, again, Kids, Mr Davies, kids messing around, that's all. It's OK now, everyone's OK.

And Jon shakes his head, and Jon holds his family, and Jon – shaky, relieved – breathes out and Jon thinks:

Enough.

Monday, 25 September, Dagenham.

STRIKE.

She thinks, This is the first blow. It's going to be a long, cold winter –

A winter of discontent –

A victory parade, she thinks.

PART THREE

Inglan is a Bitch

1983

1

Wild East

January 1983

For Hackney is a sump for the disadvantaged of every kind, a place to which those with the fewest resources sink, and from which those who gain any freedom of choice escape. It is a place of deprivation, of poverty, of toil and struggle and isolation, a knacker's yard for society's casualties, a breaker's yard where the pressure of need grinds people against each other and wears them down.

From *Inside the Inner City: Life Under the Cutting Edge*
by Paul Harrison, 1983

Parker

You know that the best way to get onside with any mob is to prove your-
self when it gets lively, so you're there in the thick of it when the uniforms
pile out of Stoke Newington nick and start laying into your new friends
with their sticks and their belts and their shields. You wonder how many
of them you may have crossed paths with over the years, how close you
were to being one of them, and you still are, to a point, but you're not
one of them, you're not, and that's one thing you've learned through all
this, through all this work you've done over the years. There's a lot of hate
pouring from these uniforms. You remember what they used to do, what
you saw yourself on Brick Lane and Chapel Market whenever they did
turn up, they'd grab dustbin lids from front gardens and use them, milk
bottles and any old iron, whatever came to hand. For a lot of new recruits,
it was an eye-opener seeing so much in the streets at all, paved with gold
they'd tell you given half a moment, northern Ernies and provincial hicks,
no understanding of how it is on the streets of the smoke. You think that
George Howlett the G-Division Hackney Metropolitan Police Commander
has got no real plan to widen recruitment, that George Howlett thinks
that bringing in boys from the estates, boys who know the score, bringing
in black lads and Asian lads, lads who could really help the community,
you know he thinks that would be lowering the standards, so you're faced
instead with these, thinking they're here to stick one in the eye of the arro-
gant southern Nancy, not knowing that the poor cunt they're braining
with their homemade cosh has got even less than their friends at home on
the dole and up the dog track, their two up two downs and their fat wives
and three angry kids, even less as they've got the whole system on their

backs, spat on every day, working all hours at shit jobs and told to thank their lucky stars for the privilege, no wonder they look for other ways to make a quid here and there, and now you see the uniforms pinning men on their backs, twisting arms and battering legs, and you're right there, right in the thick of it, but you realise they're not bothered about you, a white man, a white man dressed like a trendy do-gooder, they're not after the likes of you at all.

A scream –

    Noble sweating –

    He shudders awake –

    Telephone shrieking.

    'Hello?'

    'DC Noble.'

    It's not a question. 'What time is it?'

    'Five twenty-five, son.'

    Noble sits up, rubs his eyes. 'Chief Inspector?'

    'The very same.'

    'But I thought—'

    'I'm not sure thinking is your strongest suit.'

    'Fair enough.'

    Lea with an 'a' stirs, moans, rolls over.

    Noble's up and out of bed –

    'Get yourself over to Stoke Newington nick, sharpish.'

    'I thought—'

    Looking out the bedroom window, the sun trailing pink –

    'What did I tell you about thinking, DC Noble.'

    'What's going on, guv?'

    Scratching at his stubble, rubbing at his eyes –

    'Get yourself over to Stoke Newington nick and report to DS Williams.'

    'Williams? I don't know, guv.'

    Into his kitchen –

    'You tell him I sent you and you're to have access.'

    'OK.'

    Phone lodged between his ear and shoulder –

    'You find out what's going on and you report back to me, today. You know the number.'

    Kettle filled with water, kettle on –

    'What about West End Central?'

'It's taken care of. For the moment, you're mine and mine alone, old son.'

'OK.'

'You know your nickname has changed, don't you, son?'

'I didn't know that, no.'

Kettle boils, water poured into a dirty mug –

A laugh barked in Noble's ear. 'They're calling you *Last* Chance now, son. Last Chance Saloon.'

'Beats Paddy,' Noble says.

Teabag squeezed with a dirty spoon –

'Good to see your sense of humour's intact.'

'I'm a hoot these days, guv.'

Milk on the turn –

'Now get a move on, Chance. And when you get there, go in the back entrance.'

'Right.'

Tea slurped, lips burned –

'Why?'

'Because there's a dead black man in the foyer, that's why.'

Into the shower –

The water scalding, the water freezing –

Noble scrubbing at himself, his head down, his eyes closed.

Bedroom: clothes on the floor, pulled on –

Kitchen counter: jacket, keys, wallet –

'I have to go,' he says to Lea.

She rubs her face, she clears her throat. 'Now?'

'Now.'

She props herself up, she tries a smile.

'Stay as long as you like. Just close the door behind you.'

She nods.

'I really have to go, I'm sorry.'

Noble tries a smile.

Lea, smiling, says, 'That was a one-off, you know. Old times' sake.'

Noble smiles. 'OK,' he says. 'Help yourself to whatever you need.'

Noble opens the front door, hears, 'I won't be here when you get back!'

Car –

Keys in the ignition, engine on, Eddy Grant on the radio –

'I Don't Wanna Dance.'

Tell me about it, Noble thinks.

Car steaming, windscreen spray and scrape –

Lark-time quiet, Noble goes east on the Euston Road then north through Barnsbury, east again past Highbury Fields then north through Newington Green.

Backstreets around Kingsland Road waking up or going to bed –

Badlands to the east, squats and dens –

The Stoke Newington plod have a reputation for extracurricular earnings, shakedowns and backhanders, but Noble can't be sure what's what and he's got no allies this far north.

He didn't think he had any allies at all.

Special Young wants him for something.

13 January 1983 –

Cold as ice and dark as hell and Noble in at the deep end –

He thinks, You've got to start somewhere.

The car park is jammed even though it's only six-thirty. Noble leaves the car on the street and his warrant card gets him inside –

Most of the downstairs is taped off –

Crime scene.

Uniforms everywhere. Noble says to one of them, 'Where's the war room?'

The uniform nods up the stairs. 'Second floor.'

'What happened?'

The uniform sniffs. 'Some half-crazed darkie nearly took his own head off with a shotgun.'

'In the foyer?'

'Well, that's where he is now, guv,' the uniform says. He snorts. 'Most of him, at least.'

'Surgeon?'

'Been and gone.'

'Right,' Noble says. 'Any word?'

'Looks like a suicide, guv, that's all I can tell you.'

Noble nods. 'Next of kin?'

'No idea.'

'Who was on the front desk, you know that?'

The uniform shifts from foot to foot. 'You'll want DS Williams. Second floor.'

'Cheers.'

Noble climbs the stairs, keeps his head down –

There's a buzz about the place, an aftershock.

On the second floor, a meeting room –

In the meeting room, Williams and two other men look at statements, examine documents, a timeline on a blackboard –

Williams sees Noble at the door and says, 'Jesus fucking Christ.'

Noble smiles.

'What do you want, Noble?'

'Can I come in?'

'No.'

Noble steps into the meeting room. 'Detective Chief Inspector Young has sent me to find out what's what.'

Williams looks at the other men. 'I won't be a minute,' he says.

In the corridor, Noble says, 'I'm going to need access.'

With both hands, Williams grabs Noble by the neck and pushes him against the wall.

'You're going to do exactly what I tell you, DC Noble,' Williams spits. 'You've got a fucking nerve coming anywhere near me, boyo.'

Noble lifts his neck, keeps his hands down. He gestures with his eyes at the meeting room. 'This won't look too good if anyone comes out.' He pauses. 'Given our previous.'

Williams loosens his grip –

Williams steps back, his breath heavy and wet –

Noble says, 'You've been in better shape.'

'Listen, Noble,' Williams says. 'Whatever it was we did together was a long time ago and long disbanded. You understand?'

'Funny place to do yourself in, a nick.'

Williams is nodding.

'Just walk into the foyer with a shotgun, it's unbelievable.'

Williams says, 'It's a fucking nightmare is what it is.'

'What was the lad's name? You can give me that, at least.'

Williams smiles. 'Press release went out hours ago. One-thirty in the morning, see. You can read about it in the papers.'

'Press release, already? You must be desperate.'

Williams turns. 'Not as desperate as you must be, showing your face here.'

Noble straightens up.

At the door to the meeting room, Williams turns back. 'You'll need paperwork to get anywhere *near* any of this.'

Noble thinks, OK, here we go.

Out the front, crime-scene tape and uniforms –

One or two gawpers hanging about, in tracksuits and hats, camel coats, shuffling, blowing into their hands, trying to keep warm.

Noble nods at one of them, offers a smoke, which is accepted.

Noble says, 'You know who it was then, in there?'

The gawper draws on his cigarette. 'It was a young brother.'

'You know his name?'

Noble hands over the packet of cigarettes.

The gawper pockets the cigarettes.

'Colin Roach,' he says, and he arrows away into the dust and into the fog, into the damp grey morning.

Noble nods.

Noble circles the station.

He unlocks his car, he starts his car, he heads south to find a cup of tea and a payphone.

Noble drives all the way down Stoke Newington Road, Kingsland High Street, Kingsland Road to Haggerston, then wriggles left through to Hackney Road –

He avoids Queensbridge Road, avoids the Holly Street Estate –

He finds a spot for some breakfast and gets on the phone in the back.

Hackney Road: his childhood home, pissing distance –

He dials West End Central and asks to speak to records. 'It's Noble. Run me a name? Colin Roach. He currently on anyone's list?'

'Ring back in half an hour.'

Noble hangs up.

He sees a bacon sandwich and cup of tea being placed at his table.

His mouth dry, his head thumping –

Last night: a reunion of sorts. Four years it had been. Noble doesn't know what to think about it. They'd had fun; when they fucked, her eyes were screwed shut and she moaned –

Her legs around him –

Sweat beading between them –

Noble gasping –

The sheer relief of it all, the joy –

To touch and be touched –

On hard muscle and soft skin –

Her hands in his hair –

Noble felt something all right and he wonders now if she was joking about not being there when he got back.

Noble dials Special Young's number and waits.

'Go on,' Young says.

'They were not pleased to see me, guv.'

Young snorts. 'I expect they weren't.'

'Suicide, they're saying. Mental health case. Police surgeon been and gone. Uniforms keeping the foyer and front desk clear. Williams and two DCs upstairs.'

'That'll be DC Rice and DC Cole.'

'OK.'

'You want to keep an eye on them.'

'Right, I will.'

'Starting today.' Young pauses. 'Listen, DC Noble, by Monday you'll have access. Come and see me first thing and I'll explain. Until then, you keep an eye on Stoke Newington nick for me, got it?'

'Yes, guv.'

Noble sits down. He wolfs his sandwich, slurps his tea –

His head settles, his head clears –

Flashbacks of Lea with an 'a' –

Her smell, her taste, her cunt –

Her mouth, her smile.

Yeah, he's missed her. It's been four years and she didn't even ask.

She *knew* –

Noble's been in exile and then in hiding.

His face lined, his hair greying.

His heart heavy when he thinks about Alan, that gasp and sob.

So, he doesn't think about Alan.

The Met Race Crime Initiative immediately disbanded, Noble signed off for two years, a gradual way back in –

And Noble knows why he's being let back in now:

That favour he did for Young with Old Bill Stewart, heady stuff, high up, corridors and echelons –

Dai Wyn. Winter of discontent. Thatcher. The *landscape*.

He wipes his mouth, he finishes his tea, he gets on the phone in the back –

'No.'

'Nothing doing?'

'No one currently on the lookout for a Mr Colin Roach.'

Noble nods.

On the phone, he dials his home number.

A pause, a sleepy-soft hello –

'Hello,' Noble says back.

Same day, some hours later, studio at Stanhope House, near Marble Arch.

It's not started too badly for Suzi, 1983.

Just the week before, she's been to see this new band everyone's banging on about called Everything but the Girl at the ICA Rock Week, and Paul Weller joins them and sings along on 'The Girl from Ipanema' dressed in a polka dot shirt and white socks.

'Told you,' Keith winks, afterwards.

Paul Weller looks pretty good, thinks Suzi, stylish. The times they are a changing and all that.

Suzi likes the look of Tracey Thorn – the singer – and especially her big black earrings and her slim gold wristwatch. Her hairstyle too: it is a bit of a mess but it's obviously been washed.

Perhaps, Suzi thinks now, looking at Tracey across the studio, surreptitiously trying to capture that sexy aloofness, I'm just getting older.

Keith's behind the desk and looking thoroughly happy.

He's been happy, really happy, fulfilled, Suzi realises, ever since he started working with Paul Weller.

'It's the professionalism, girl,' Keith says, often. 'The man's got that drive, that seriousness. And he's got that pop sensibility to go with it.'

Keith was hit very hard when Malcolm Owen of The Ruts died of a heroin overdose, in his mum's bathroom for crying out loud, in 1980.

So, Suzi was thrilled to see him back working again.

They both felt it was time to move away from that punk scene too. Put a bit of distance. It only goes so far; the underground is called that for a reason.

'Maybe we're Thatcherites?' she says to Keith one night. 'Upwardly mobile and all that.'

Keith laughs. 'I don't think paying rent on a flat in Stoke Newington and filing your taxes on time makes you a Tory, love.'

Suzi's heard that their old squat was sold by the council on the sly to a private developer, that the factory is being made into canal-side apartments. It all sounds very New York to her, and not a project with any legs, surely. A river view when the river's full of rats and piss, rotting barges and waste, the odd dead body, is hardly aspirational.

'It does in some people's eyes,' Suzi says. 'To some people, we're class traitors, you and me.'

'Yeah, well,' Keith says, 'the middle class is the fucking problem. It's easy to be anti-materialist when you've got everything you need. Nah –' and Keith makes a face here as if to say *end of story* – 'what we're part of is working class, right? It's about hard work and shining a light on inequality and looking good while you're about it.'

Suzi kisses him.

'It's defiance,' Keith says. 'We're about Europe, about inclusivity. There are too many grim-faced lefties. Let's be proud of what we are and celebrate it.'

So that's what they're doing, and on the thirteenth of January in Paul Weller's new studio, Suzi is hearing for the first time what his new band, his new *collective*, is working on.

Keith is now an Honorary Councillor, meaning he's part of Weller's extended inner circle. Hearing the song they've just recorded this very day, 'A Solid Bond in Your Heart', Suzi hopes her photos might make her an Honorary Councillor too.

It's all piano and sax, and sounds a bit like what you might get if Dexys' songs were played by Aretha's backing band.

But with lyrics that Suzi hasn't heard since, well, since The Jam, she thinks.

There's a sofa in the corner of the studio and Tracey Thorn's sitting there alone, so Suzi angles over and snaps away while Tracey Thorn pretends not to notice –

Suzi raises her eyebrows at the speakers. 'What do you think?'

Tracey Thorn smiles, adjusts her pose. 'Paul's songs were always very complicated,' she says. Tracey Thorn, joking, pouts. 'Writing a song like

"The Eton Rifles" with that lyric *and* making it catchy? Clever boy, our Paul.'

With her camera in front of her face, Suzi asks, 'What about this song?'

'If punk wasn't dead before,' Tracey Thorn says, 'it is now.'

'They think it's all over,' Suzi says.

Tracey Thorn laughs. There's a pause.

Suzi says, 'I thought you were wonderful last week at the ICA.'

Modestly, Tracey Thorn smiles. 'Your review was pretty wonderful, thanks.'

The song stops. The microphones in the booths are still on, and Suzi and Tracey Thorn listen to Paul Weller talk to Mick Talbot and Keith.

'It's this or "Speak Like a Child" for the first single. And I've got a dynamite quote to stick on the album sleeve. Tony Benn,' Paul Weller is saying. 'He says History teaches us that it's not enough to compose songs about freedom if there are not enough people dedicated to making it all come true, right?'

Tracey Thorn flicks Suzi a look. 'Sounds like something he might have written himself.'

Then Keith cuts the sound.

Hackney town hall.

Jon Davies still thinks about Gideon the doorman from time to time.

Gerard McMorrow – Jon's colleague from the Hackney Trades Council – was exactly right about how it would pan out with the National Front and Excalibur House: the serving of enforcement notices by Hackney Borough Council to NF Properties, of which Jon in his role as council solicitor was a major part; an appeal against said enforcement notices; a public inquiry contesting this appeal.

It was a planning issue under the Town and Country Planning Act: the enforcement notices were served on the basis that NF Properties claimed the premises were used solely for printing and business purposes, whereas, in fact, there was evidence to show that the premises were used as the national HQ of the National Front.

The point being that it was all about this planning issue: there was no question of ideology involved in the inquiry.

This wasn't about removing the National Front from Hackney due to their politics, officially speaking; it was a planning issue, end of.

Result: Excalibur House no longer occupied by NF Properties.

Jon remembers Gerard McMorrow repeating his line about people being frightened in South Hackney.

'And they're frightened of being mugged too, by blacks, if you want to bring politics into it,' shouted Derrick Day, Jon remembers.

A real charmer, Derrick Day, sitting in a pervert's mackintosh coat, dirty, brown and creased. Jon doesn't like to think too much about him and he doesn't have to now.

Jon recalls Gideon's performance at the inquiry:

'My political beliefs are that I am an anarchist and I am not formally a member of any political party other than the National Front.'

That threw the room a little. Derrick Day was furious, Jon recalls. He didn't have a clue.

That lawyer Reed-Herbert talking how the second and third floors of the 'appeal premises' at Excalibur House were used by a subsidiary of NF Properties for storing ties and shirts. Old Gideon's response to that was golden.

'That's absolute rubbish. They never stored anything there. If there had've been ties there, I'd have nicked them ... Actually, I'm wearing an Excalibur House tie, which you yourself sold to me, if you remember.'

Jon laughs at this.

Thing is, Jon thinks, he *was* one of them for a bit, he did what he did. He's not sure it's right, regardless.

And there were those threats, that murkiness, that mystery –

The official message from the Hackney police was that it was the National Front mucking about, not real intimidation.

A brick and a firework, his *family*, for crying out loud. That wasn't exactly mysterious. It was very much *there*: a broken window and a smouldering carpet –

Naughty children, police on the estate, a couple came forward but – Jon didn't believe a word, course he didn't.

And Gideon? Jon's not sure.

The Hackney police told Jon, told the inquiry, that they were investigating, but so far had been unable to identify the policemen involved, the policemen who had followed Jon home, and Gideon the doorman wasn't about to do so.

He doesn't have much faith in this process, Jon. It might well have been a couple of chancers on the ground that gave him the eye, but the National Front–Hackney police relationship feels murky at best –

Bygones is perhaps the only way forward.

Jon Davies has a new role now, regardless. He's involved with the council's Police Committee and looking at the paperwork for the Hackney Black People's Association and their request for an independent inquiry into the behaviour of the Hackney police. Jon is part of the committee that's putting together a report which they're tentatively calling, Policing Hackney.

What the Hackney Black People's Association are concerned about is corruption and violence against black people.

Jon reads a statement from Detective Constable Declan Costello:

'The community hated us and we hated them. It wasn't a black thing. It wasn't as complex as that. If you went out in uniform or plainclothes you could feel the hatred.'

Jon reads a statement from Hugh Prince, a young man claiming to be a victim of the Hackney police:

'The officers involved in these atrocities can do this because they are not accountable to anybody. They cover up their crimes by picking on the weak – unemployed and uneducated people who do not have any knowledge of the law. There are no rights for black people, and if you are poor it's worse: as far as the law is concerned you have no place in society. You are a dog; when they kick you, you move.'

Jon thinks, Here we go.

The following night, Friday 14 September.

Noble's standing outside Stoke Newington nick watching uniforms threaten the friends and family of Colin Roach who are, quite reasonably, asking what the fuck happened the other night –

The uniforms are not in a very understanding mood.

This isn't a planned protest – no barriers, no organisation, no march –

Just around fifty or so, mainly young men, black and white, flocking round the front entrance of the nick.

To the left, around the corner, Noble sees a blue-green police bus, and behind that the light blue Metropolitan Police Control van –

Heavy mob.

The crowd is peaceful enough: they're standing there, defiant, arms crossed –

There's a refrain, not quite a chant, more than a murmur, not quite a song –

Who killed Colin Roach?

Who killed Colin Roach?

Who killed Colin Roach?

The uniforms fan out and another line appears behind them.

The crowd is heaviest at the left of this line, they've blocked the traffic and that's a charge straight off the bat, Noble thinks.

Kebab-shop neon and off-licence glow –

Twenty-four-hour mini-markets changing shifts, rearranging fruit and veg displays –

Minicabs and buses, shift workers and night lurkers –

Pubs still open, which, Noble thinks, will suit the uniforms.

Last thing they need is a bunch of pissed-up white blokes prowling.

Noble sees two uniforms sent off down Stoke Newington Road towards the nearest pubs to deliver, he expects, an unlikely, police-approved, Friday-night lock-in.

A handful of the biggest, youngest black men at the front of the crowd are jabbing their fingers and yelling, getting angrier.

No answer is forthcoming.

Noble edges along the back, towards the end of the uniform fan –

There's a ripple at the door of the nick, the two plainclothes DCs Noble saw with Williams –

DC Rice and DC Cole.

They're giving instructions and pointing, shouting into the ear of the uniform lead –

A phalanx shuffles into a semicircle, partly containing the front line of the crowd. There's word from the second line and half a dozen uniforms pile straight in, truncheons up, pinning down three black lads –

The crowd surges back, then another five or six lads – black and white – come forward to help their friends, pushing and kicking –

Another unit of uniforms and another group of lads pinned to the ground, hands yanked behind them, feet on their necks, boots on their necks –

Yells of, You're nicked and Stay down and Don't fucking move –

Noble's got his warrant card out and his collar up and he shields his face from the crowd and gets around the side of the uniform line.

Noble sees Rice and Cole duck back in –

He elbows his way up the steps, he shoulders his way through the second line, his warrant card in the air, his head down –

He gets right up in the face of the uniform giving orders, warrant card out, hard stare.

He nods down the steps at the men on the ground, hands behind their heads, hands behind their backs, hands cuffed, knees in their backs and necks –

He says, 'What's the charge, officer?'

The uniform's hat is low, his eyes narrow, his bearing squat, his thick moustache and big nose –

Noble looks down on him.

'Officer?'

'Who the fuck are you?' the officer says.

Noble looks at the officer's stripes, looks at the officer's number, reads out this number, says, 'Detective Constable Noble on assignment from

Detective Chief Inspector Maurice Young.' Noble jabs his finger, nods down the steps. 'Now what's the fucking charge?'

'Threatening behaviour, carrying offensive weapons, breach of the peace, obstruction, you name it.' The senior uniform smiles, he winks.

Noble shakes his head, goes, 'OK then.'

The crowd is edging back, shouting, the front line in an arms-out, palms-down, stay-calm pose –

The uniforms have the loudhailer out now, Disperse, disperse –

The arrested men – Noble counts eight – are dragged and pushed inside –

Noble skirts the arrested men, eyes peeled for Rice and Cole.

The uniforms are bundling the arrested men down the stairs, in head-locks and half-nelsons, down to the holding cells.

Noble sees Rice and Cole slip out the side door –

He follows, slips out the same side door.

Noble sees Rice and Cole go down the steps and into the side road where the blue-green police bus is parked.

Noble sees two uniforms sitting inside, near the front of this police bus, flanking a young black man who looks scared, panicked –

Noble hangs back in the shadows of the side road, the shadows of the tree, the shadows of the smashed streetlamp –

Rice and Cole board the blue-green police bus.

The two uniforms give them some room.

The young black man is slapped round the face, cuffed round the back of the head, kneed in the stomach, kneed in the balls –

Fingers are jabbed at him, threats, Noble thinks, are being made, words being had –

The young black man is pulled by the collar to the front of the police bus, he is kicked off the police bus, his backside kicked, his back kicked, his neck kicked –

And he staggers and he runs, this young black man runs for his life, and Noble looks both ways, sees the police bus lights go off, the engine start, and Noble turns, head down, collar up, runs after him –

Noble runs down Victorian Road, the road dark, the trees stark, follows the young man left and down Victorian Grove for fifty metres, moonlight and terraced housing, then left again onto Beatty Road heading back towards Stoke Newington Road, cats howling and snaking between parked cars, and the kid is fast, but Noble can see him and he's not giving up yet –

The kid flashes across Stoke Newington Road, straight out into traffic, weaving between cars beeping their horns, dodging a bus, a motorbike screaming and skidding, and the kid's out on the other side.

Noble's got his hands up and he's slapping the bonnets of parked cars and he waits for a moment as the kid passes the church on the corner, its small spire lit in a thundery yellow light, and Noble gets across the road, and he's lead-footing it down Amhurst Road after the kid, and he remembers the estates just this side of Hackney Downs, or just north, and if he doesn't get him before then, he'll be away.

Amhurst Road is quiet and straight, and Noble can see the kid tearing along, pace eased a touch, looking over his shoulder. Noble keeps to the shadows, keeps to the trees –

There are skips in the road spilling rubbish and white goods, there is broken furniture and bin bags spilling clothes, there are houses with boards and cars with no wheels –

The kid's slowing down now. Noble's far enough back and Noble thinks, *Gamble*.

He's headed north of Hackney Downs, got to be –

Noble leaves Amhurst Road, watches the kid bend double for a moment, and then does a left onto Foulden Road and legs it, really rockets down it, and then a right, and he's guessing the kid's going to take the next left and if Noble's lucky he'll catch him where Rectory Road meets Downs Road –

Noble's gasping, his legs heavy, his stomach tight, his chest tight, his chest sharp with pain –

And there's the kid, yes, there he is, and he's walking now, and he's bending over again, breathing deep, hard, heavy breaths, and it's a quiet corner, patches of burnt grass at each point of the crossroads, no one around, and Noble slows down, Noble walks, and the kid hasn't clocked him and the kid turns right onto Downs Road, and Noble, at a sprint, a last push, catches him, grabs his collar, spins him round and says –

'Easy, son, I'm here to help.'

And the look in the kid's eyes is pure fear, pure panic and Noble says –

'I just want to know what those policemen said to you in the bus.'

The kid's eyes wide, his breath short, his head shaking –

'I don't know,' the kid says, 'no, I don't know, nothing.'

Noble shows his warrant card, he looks into this kid's eyes and he says –

'Trust me, son.'

The kid needs to, Noble can see that, he needs something to hold on to, something to give him some relief, some *respite*.

'Come on,' Noble says, breathing hard, smiling now. 'Trust me, yeah. After all, you ain't got a lot of choice now, have you, Carl Lewis?'

And Noble sees a flicker of something in the kid's eyes.

'What did those policemen say to you?'

The kid, breathing shorter, says, 'They told me to keep my mouth shut.'

'About what?'

The kid shakes his head, looks down. 'Nothing, it's nothing.'

Noble insists. 'About what?'

The kid shudders, sobs, starts to cry –

'About what, son? Tell me.'

The kid struggles to get the words out. 'Colin Roach was my friend,' he says, 'that's all. That's all, please.'

Noble nods, thinks, Take your time, do this right.

He takes his notebook and a pen from his inside pocket, gives them to the kid.

Noble says, 'Write down your name and an address where I can find you tomorrow morning, and your phone number, all right?'

The kid hesitates, turns as if to run –

Noble says, 'You don't do what I tell you and I'll make sure those policemen know right now that you haven't kept your mouth shut, you understand?'

The kid sobs, he bites his lip, his eyes water.

He writes in the notebook. He shows Noble what he has written. Noble nods.

Noble offers his hand. The kid shakes it, limply –

'I'll see you tomorrow, son,' Noble says. 'Get home safe.'

The kid turns and runs.

Noble looks at his notebook: estates just north of the park.

Great, he thinks, It's a fucking labyrinth up there.

His sweat cooling, Noble has a think about where he is exactly.

Well, he knows where he *is*, but in terms of the likelihood of a drink.

Truth is, he's parched.

His car is up near the nick, just off Kingsland High Street. He heads back in that direction along Farleigh Road and he thinks –

There's that Turkish drinking club underneath the betting shop, next door to the new mosque, opposite the old BP garage, that'll do nicely.

He keeps his head down, his collar up, his eyes skinned –

Friday night's all right for something, he thinks.

One thing that's changed in the last few years, Suzi thinks, one thing that might be a bit more Thatcherite, is the *drugs* –

There's four of them in the back of a taxi, yakking.

Gone is the weed and the speed, it's all about what Keith likes to call 'the bugle'.

Paul Weller and Mick Talbot and Tracey Thorn all go home after the studio drink-up that finishes the two-day recording session with the Honorary Councillors. (Suzi is now an Honorary Councillor.) Paul Weller is on Radio One in the morning to talk about his new project and what might be the first single, so he doesn't fancy a 'big one'. It's been a good couple of days. As well as finishing 'A Solid Bond in Your Heart', Paul Weller gets a vocal he is happy with on 'Party Chambers', a song Suzi really likes, a lovely mix of longing and sadness, heartbreak and positivity, with a bonkers synth line that doesn't sound like anything, really –

Well, it sounds like a band who have found their own bonkers synth sound and want to use it.

When Suzi offers this theory to Paul Weller, he gets the hump.

He tells her later that, Yeah, maybe, but so what? It sounds bonkers.

He also tells her that taking photos at the same time as delivering a theory means she can get away with constructive criticism like that.

He uses his fingers to make air quotes around the words *constructive criticism*.

Suzi smiles at that.

Making her own air quotes she mouths, 'You're welcome.'

They're shooting along the Euston Road, piling back up towards Stoke Newington for some afters.

Keith, another sound engineer called Monster, and his girlfriend who goes by The Child, and is, apparently, twenty-eight years old.

Suzi likes them but she's not sure –

The *names*, after all; she's not sure she gets it.

Keith loves them.

Suzi can see him falling in love with the pair of them right in front of her.

Monster's a sort of multi-instrumentalist, a sonic gnostic, who is well-versed in Jung's *Red Book* and the basic tenets of Buddhism, which he's explaining now.

'It's *easier* than jogging,' he says, 'Buddhism. You just sit there and *think*. You sit there and *be*.'

'Seems pretty straightforward,' Keith offers.

The Child says nothing. She is outrageously hot, Suzi thinks, The Child.

She says nothing, *ever*.

'It might be news to you both,' The Child suggests, 'but the pair of you are high on cocaine, that's all this is.'

Suzi's on one of the back-facing seats and is looking out the window and she can feel The Child's foot halfway up her leg, but she reckons it's just likely female solidarity.

They're too right-on, surely, for an orgy.

'Where are you taking us, Keith?' Monster sniffs.

The Child rolls her eyes and smiles at Suzi.

'Oh, this great drinking club,' Keith says. 'We know the owners.'

'Yeah?'

'Oh yeah.'

'That's good, Keith,' decides Monster. 'That's really good.'

Suzi's smiling to herself, and she leans her forehead against the window, feels the cold of it, feels it tingle against her skin, her buzzing skin –

She'll need a top-up of Keith's bugle when they get there.

Monster and Keith are discussing some new piece of equipment that makes everything sound twice the volume it really is.

'Why on earth,' The Child points out, 'don't you just turn it up twice as loud?'

It's a reasonable question, Suzi thinks, but Keith and Monster are laughing –

Suzi drifts.

It's cold. It's really fucking cold.

It hasn't been this cold since, well, since 1979, since *that* winter, the winter of Suzi's dip into politics.

It didn't end well, her dip into politics. She kept an eye out for that charmer Dai Wyn in the papers after the honey trap.

But it was Moss Evans who was on holiday the day of the TUC vote to negotiate around the 5 per cent cap, which would have likely settled things with the Callaghan government and averted the strikes. All it needed was consensus.

But Moss Evans was in Malta and it was a tied vote 14–14, and the casting vote couldn't be used, partisanship, or something like it, Suzi thinks.

What the fuck was Moss Evans doing in Malta on the day of the vote?

The whole thing is bewildering, Suzi thinks, what exactly happened, how it finished almost as soon as it had begun –

It's one of those things that burrows into her mind, vexes her. She gives a little shake of the head and it's gone again.

'Take my photo,' The Child says, nudging Suzi's leg with her foot.

'Now?'

The Child nods.

Suzi opens her bag, takes out her camera. 'Just lean towards the window, will you?'

The Child – compliant, slow – leans towards the window, smiling.

Suzi frames the shot. The taxi is on Holloway Road, near Highbury Corner.

Suzi smiles. The traffic slows, the lights change –

Suzi snaps. 'Perfect,' she says.

The Child wriggles in her seat, peers out –

'Oh, perfect,' she says.

Keith and Monster are snorting bumps of cocaine from a train ticket, oblivious.

Suzi develops the shot in her mind:

Nightscape, London. The Child, sullen, punkish attitude, New Romantic garb, lolling on the back seat of a starkly lit cab as it passes the Garage club, a faceless queue in the drizzle, a pink neon lightning bolt like the synth sound on 'Party Chambers' –

And then they're climbing out the taxi on Kingsland High Street and bustling down the stairs to the basement drinking club, and Keith, showing off, shouts at the proprietor, 'All right, Turkish?' and Turkish beams back up at Keith and says, 'Keith, my friend, how's the weather?' and they both laugh and they're quickly at a table with bottles of Turkish lager and some aniseed spirit shots.

Suzi and The Child visit the facilities and whoosh –

Monster's laying out the problem when they come back.

The Child winks at Suzi, who finds she's enjoying herself and grins.

'Too much has happened,' Monster's saying, 'there's your problem. Since Thatcher won, too much has happened, it's that simple. We can't process it. Think about it.'

Keith considers this.

'That winter, the strikes, the Iranian embassy palaver, the riots, the fucking Falklands. I mean,' says Monster, 'it's a lot. No wonder the Tories are so popular. Things happen with the Tories.' Monster takes a pull on his cigarette, leans back. 'I mean, Keith, what's next?'

'I don't know, Monster,' Keith admits. 'I don't know.'

Suzi sips at her lager and sniffs at her aniseed shot. She looks around at tables of small groups laughing. It's civilised, it's fun. She looks at Keith, his warmth and passion, the way he's hanging on to every single one of Monster's words –

It's lovely, really, his enthusiasm. It's innocent –

'We've just come back from New York,' Monster tells them. 'It's wild, Keith, what they're doing with the noise. Industrial. Massive sound systems, ghetto parties. Yeah?'

'Right, yeah,' Keith agrees.

'The drugs, Keith, will be the end though, yeah? It's dirty what they're doing over there. To this.' Monster taps his nose. 'It's coming in here too, already. You don't touch that shit, all right?'

Keith, certain in his resolve not to touch that shit, whatever *that shit* is, nods.

Suzi raises her eyebrows at The Child.

'Called crack cocaine,' The Child tells her. 'Cheap.' She raises her own eyebrows. 'And very addictive. Best avoided, he's right there.'

Suzi smiles. She peels the label off her bottle. There's an agreeable silence for a moment as they drink and look about them and smile.

The stereo's playing Mediterranean pop music.

'Hang about,' Keith says, 'I've got an idea.'

He jumps up and waves at Turkish, has a word in his ear, and then Suzi watches Keith pull something out of his bag and bend down to where the stereo is, the Turkish pop cuts out, and then –

The whole bar is getting a very private, very naughty, very loud, very early taster of The Style Council.

Keith's standing behind the counter gurning, air-playing all the instruments, and all the tables in the place are looking at him and laughing, not just the trendies, but the old Turks too, and Suzi can see a few puzzled looks on the faces of the trendies, like, Who *is* this? and Keith's singing along and then so is Monster and The Child, and Suzi gets up to dance, and she goes over to Keith and puts her arms around his neck and they sing the chorus at each other, 'A Solid Bond in Your Heart', and Suzi, again, feels that love for Keith deep down and bubbling up, and they kiss, and the room spins, and Turkish, delighted, is pouring a round for the house, and then the power cuts, the lights go out for a moment, and when they come back on –

Friday night at the Labour Club, Dalston Lane.

Family night –

There's a steel band playing and a bonfire.

A barbecue –

The air is crisp, the smoke threads through its damp chill and Jon Davies can see his own breath –

Jon watches his son, for the third time, kick a football over the fence and into the garden next door as the bonfire crackles and kids shriek and the steel drums roll.

A very patient old couple, who are leaning over their fence to enjoy the calypso and the fire, fetch the ball and throw it back.

Jon sees Gerard McMorrow eating jerk chicken with his hands and swigging Red Stripe, his family laughing at him.

It's been a while. Since the Excalibur House business, he thinks.

The steel band take a break.

Culture Club's 'Do You Really Want to Hurt Me?' comes on over the sound system. Jon watches families dance –

All the kids wearing GLC and I Love Inner London Education Authority jumpers and hats.

He's glad it's dark tonight; he can have a couple of cans in peace.

Jackie's chatting to Rushmore mums and laughing a lot.

The boy's tearing about the place –

Friday night, family night.

'Come on Eileen', then Phil Collins.

There's Mrs Akhtar, Jon thinks, and one of her sons.

Jon waves –

He couldn't help with what she wanted, closure after her husband's death, a better sense of what happened, but Jon's doing the next best thing.

Last year, he helped set up the Police Committee within Hackney Council, and within *that* a support unit is in place to keep an eye on crime and policing and to make public documents that might be critical of police powers.

It's not very popular with the thin blue line.

Gerard McMorrow comes over and gives Jon Davies a can of lager.

'Cheers, Jon,' Gerard says.

'Cheers, Gerard,' Jon says.

They watch the fire. The steel band starts up again. Kids make light-shapes with sparklers –

Gerard says, 'You heard about what happened in Stoke Newington?'

Jon shakes his head.

'Put it this way,' Gerard says, 'that Police Committee of yours might have a busy few months.'

The boy runs over, eating a hot dog. Jon wipes ketchup off his face.

'Go on,' he says, pushing his son towards the other kids.

'There was a demonstration up there today,' Gerard says. 'Eight arrested.'

'Demonstration?'

Gerard nods. 'A young black man called Colin Roach died of a shotgun wound in the foyer of Stoke Newington nick.'

'Jesus.'

'Verdict: suicide.'

Jon thinks, It *will* be a busy few months.

'Monday, there's another demo, a meeting,' Gerard says. 'Hackney Black People's Association. You should come.'

'I will.'

Gerard fishes inside his coat pocket for more lager.

'One for the road?'

Jon nods. 'Why not?'

On the sound system, 'Reggae fi Peach' by Linton Kwesi Johnson.

Jon and Gerard look at each other.

'Coincidence?' Gerard says.

Jon thinks, Unlikely.

Blair Peach, a peaceful anti-fascist protestor, killed by an unidentified police officer in the Special Patrol Group, 23 April 1979, in Southall, west London.

Linton Kwesi Johnson speak-sings the word *murderers* again and again –

Noble gets a funny look from the bloke on the door but ducks down the stairs anyway, and when he ships up in the basement bar he sees why –

DC Rice and DC Cole have got the Turkish owner cornered while some dopey, frightened-looking hippy looks down at the floor.

Noble hangs back.

The room silent, the tables of drinkers silent, examining their hands, examining the walls.

Behind the counter, Noble sees the owner nodding, the owner's hands up –

Noble sees the owner opening the till, rifling through the till –

Pulling an envelope, handing the envelope to DC Rice who discreetly pockets it, who now smiles, a nasty smile, and thanks the owner with a little cuff to the cheek –

Noble sees DC Cole put his face very close to the face of this dopey hippy –

And Noble steps in, steps over to DC Cole, puts his hand on his shoulder and says, quietly, 'Easy on, Detective Constable Cole. What's the charge?'

Rice and Cole take a moment to register who it is.

Cole shakes his head. Brushes imaginary dust from the hippy's shoulders. Steps back, hands out and smiling in an only-joking sort of pose.

He and Rice exchange a look. Rice nods up the stairs. They sniff, they look back at the owner, they smile and they leave.

There's a moment, Noble feels it, where the room waits, waits to see if this is really over, this little ordeal, waits and holds its breath, and when it's clear that it *is* over, that the ordeal is over and everyone is OK, the room exhales.

The owner smiles at Noble.

The hippy-type claps Noble on the back and says, 'Let me get you a drink.'

'Finally.' Noble grins.

The hippy nods at the owner who hands Noble a bottle of lager and pours him a shot. Noble pulls at the lager, which is cold and slakes his thirst. Christ, what an evening –

And the hippy says, 'Come and join my friends,' and he's pushing Noble to a small table in the corner, and Noble's smiling as he sees the three people sitting at this small table, in this dark corner, and it takes a moment, a quick double take, but then he sees her, he sees it's her, and there she is, looking at him, and Noble goes, Nice to meet you all, and sits down –

He's struggling a bit, Noble, struggling up the high street –

He staggers and he struggles, he wrestles himself forwards, he falls back –

He spins and he staggers, he breathes and he coughs –

He coughs and he groans –

He thinks, I'm pissed.

His car: another hundred or so yards up the road.

It's Hannibal across the fucking Alps, he thinks, and snorts with laughter.

His head lurching, his stomach slopping lager, churning aniseed liquor –

He sniffs and hacks, coughs and spits.

He takes a deep breath. You're fine, mate, he's muttering now, you're grand.

The old Irish talking-to.

Up ahead, a phone box.

He digs in his pockets for change. He finds some notes, he drops some notes –

He clutches the coins he manages to find deep inside his jeans and he thinks –

Why not?

He pulls open the phone box door and praises the saints it might be the only working phone box in Hackney.

The glass needs a little work. Shattered on the floor, it crunches under his shoes. It stinks of piss in there too – that's par for the course – but there's a dial tone.

He still remembers the number and he punches it in with his knuckles.

It rings and rings. Noble hums and shakes his head, shakes a little sense into it –

That soft-sleepy, 'Hello?'

Noble says nothing for a moment, breathes.

Again, more urgent, 'Hello?'

'Oh, hello, it's me.'

'Oh yeah?'

'Yeah, course.'

'Come on, who is it?'

Noble thinks, Bollocks. 'It's Patrick.'

A short, soft laugh. 'I know who it is, you wally.' A pause. 'Are you OK?'

'I'm drunk.'

Another laugh, louder this one. 'Well, you ain't coming round.'

Noble smiles. 'I know. I just felt like saying hello.'

'Hello.'

'Yeah, hello.' A pause, Noble sniffs, crunches glass underfoot. 'Listen,' he says, 'Sunday, you busy?'

'Are you asking me out?' says Lea.

'I am.'

'Call me tomorrow when you've sobered up.'

But there is a lightness to this instruction.

Noble smiles. 'Is that a yes?'

'It is if you call me tomorrow.'

Noble grins. 'Beautiful.'

'Go to bed, Patrick, all right?'

'Yeah, all right, I will. Goodnight, Lea.'

'Goodnight moon, goodnight cow jumping over the moon.'

'You what?'

'Never mind. I'm going now.'

'OK.'

'OK?'

Noble nods. 'Beautiful,' he says, and he hangs up the phone –

He thinks: Perhaps I better sleep in my car.

Ayeleen: Lauren's got her feet up on one of the tables and I shoo her off it and wipe it down.

'That one?'

She's pointing at a building, the old cinema, not far up Stoke Newington Road. It's mid-afternoon and no one in, and we're bunking off our after-school games.

'Yeah, that one.'

'And your uncle bought it?'

I shake my head. 'No. He *helped* buy it.'

'Helped who?'

'The Turkish Islamic Association.'

Lauren's chewing gum, picking at her nails. 'Never heard of it.'

'I don't suppose you would have.'

'So what, it's a church now, is it?'

'A mosque. Or it will be.'

Lauren tries out the word in her mouth, says it slowly. 'Mosque.'

'It's our church,' I tell her. 'Well, for some of us.'

'What that word mean on the banner in front?'

'Aziziye is a place in Turkey, Laur, I don't think it means anything.'

'Big man your uncle, ain't he?'

'I don't know.'

'Flash though. Money.'

I smile.

'When's he going to let you work in that drinking club, Leen? Be more fun to hang out there.'

'We might have to wait a few years for that,' I tell her. 'He'll have me in the New Country Off-Licence and Foodstore first.'

Lauren laughs at this; it's a joke we have, full titles. The shop's just down on Kingsland Road and he'll put me to work there if I don't behave myself, is the threat.

'Well,' she says, 'if you prove yourself at the Gorki House Café and Restaurant-bar, then you might have a chance.'

'When are you going to get a job, eh?'

'From your uncle?'

'Might as well.'

'I don't fancy it,' she says, 'hospitality.'

'What about retail, babe?'

We're laughing again. 'He's got retail?'

'Yeah, factories, you know textiles. He's selling up though.' I make a serious face. 'The bottom's gone out of it, apparently.'

'Just as well, I don't fancy that either.'

'His was one of the first. Textile factories, I mean. Not that many Turks here in the seventies, not from the mainland anyway, and he set up before anyone else.'

'Why'd he come?'

'They all did – my mum and dad, I mean – because of the government, the military.'

Lauren's nodding. 'You've told me that before.'

'Then why'd you ask?'

'Polite, I am, Leen.'

I snort.

'What about your dad?' Lauren asks. 'When's he around again?'

I think of my father, his letters, wonder where he is, when I'll see him next.

I say, 'Family stuff, he's needed back home, that's all.'

Lauren nods, but I can see she's not convinced. She doesn't ask me very often, knows me well enough not to, I suppose.

The door rings as it opens and my cousin Mesut comes in. He nods at Lauren.

'All right, Lauren,' he says.

Lauren doesn't look up from her nails. 'All right, Mesut.'

I watch Mesut stare at Lauren for a little bit too long.

I clear my throat.

'Sorry,' Mesut says.

'You should be. We're only fourteen, you perv.'

'I'm only nineteen.'

'Well, she ain't going to marry you, are you, Laur?'

'No, I bloody ain't.'

Mesut grins. 'That's a shame.'

'What do you want, Mesut?'

He takes an envelope out of his inside pocket. 'Those two guys will be along later. You've seen them with me before.'

I narrow my eyes. 'I don't deal with them,' I say, 'you know that. My uncle has explained that to you, Mesut, more than once.'

'Yeah, well, I've got something on, haven't I.' He looks at Lauren, then gets on one knee. 'Do me a favour, Leen, please.'

Lauren's laughing. 'Well, I bloody ain't now, if that's how you go about it!'

'What do you want me to do?'

'Just give them this, that's all.'

He hands me the envelope.

'That's all?'

'Yeah.' He's smiling again at Lauren, not looking at me. 'And if they give you something for me, just stick it behind the counter.'

'What are they going to give me, Mesut?'

'Steady on, I'm not asking you to do the business with them, Leen,' he jokes.

'That ain't funny,' Lauren says.

'It's really not,' I add.

Mesut nods. 'Sorry, bad joke.'

'What are they going to give me, Mesut?'

'A bag, that's all. A small bag. You just store it for me, that's all.'

'Right.'

'OK?'

'Not really.' I cross my arms. 'I got much choice?'

Mesut leans forward, kisses me on the forehead. 'Love you, Leen!'

He opens the door to leave, looks at Lauren. 'Love you too, Lauren!' He winks.

I put the envelope into the till.

'You should go, Laur,' I say.

It's her turn to snort. 'Don't be dopey, I'm not leaving you on your own.'

'It's all right,' I say, but I'm pleased.

Later, the men come, they take the envelope, they leave a small bag like Mesut said they would, and then after that, he comes back and takes the bag, and everything is fine.

2

European Female

January 1983

Parker

You know about other spycops, others from SDS, the Special Demonstration Squad, your covert, undercover unit, people you don't meet, people you don't know. You've heard about the ones who infiltrated Greenpeace and the South London Animal Movement and the like, the ones who got married to the perps, sometimes even got them pregnant, carried on like they were family men – and sometimes they were, sometimes they had another family tucked away in the real world. You know about those buried in the Socialist Workers Party, the Anti-Nazi League, in the Revolutionary Communist Group, the Revolutionary Communist Party, the Revolutionary Communist Party of Britain, the Friends of Freedom Press Ltd, in the Direct Action Movement, the Campaign for Nuclear Disarmament, going back a little further they were there in the Vietnam Solidarity Campaign, in the Irish Civil Rights Solidarity Campaign, the Northern Ireland Civil Rights Association, in Sinn Féin – any movement and one of your lot is likely in there somewhere, not doing a great deal, watching and listening, it's about information, the transfer of information, that's what you've learned over the years, your job is to watch and listen and then pass it on and not worry too much about what is done with this information when it is passed on. It was a baptism all right in the Front, and Noble was clever pulling that stunt, but it worked out all right for you and you went from being Stewart's prodigy to fully fledged SDS and you've been out of London long enough to come back and do a job here, but this job now is murky – bloody would be with Stewart on board – and you're not sure whose side you're on, which is not always a bad thing in this line of work – first thing's first and first thing is figuring exactly where you need to be, the landscape, and you've figured it sharpish, and there are three overlapping movements in which you need to insinuate yourself:

the Roach Family Support Committee, the Stoke Newington and Hackney Defence Campaign, and the Hackney Campaign Against the Police Bill. But Noble's done it again and you might just be a plant and he's running you so in the end it's the same business as before, you glean the information and you pass it on, just like you've learned, and you're a bit older now, a bit more respectable, a bit more about you, and you were in there right at the beginning, so you're quickly one of the inner circle, or at least what counts for one with this bunch of lefties – cleverest thing you can do is get in there with the black lads, get in there and get stuck in. And it turns out that being black and living in Hackney, living in Stoke Newington is no fucking picnic, and given what you know about London recruits, given what you know about the SPG knocking about and banging heads unlicensed and unlimited in the borough since 1980, you're not surprised. You've seen them arrested ahead of you – you've seen them stopped and searched while you're left alone – you've seen the looks they get and the looks they give – and the looks they want to give, the looks they can't give. And as far as you can see, these lads are decent lads, they're not slinging dope or sticking up petrol stations, they're just friends with the poor dead kid and they want some answers, which is fair enough – but they ain't getting any and the vans full of uniforms circling the streets and pulling over to pick on any group of young blacks are treating this like an affront, like a direct confrontation, like the young black man is picking a fight with Old Bill and Old Bill is going to make sure the young black man loses.

Mrs Thatcher is about to telephone Willie Whitelaw, her home secretary. She imagines him at home, his physical bulk, his large, 'big-boned' frame folded inelegantly into his armchair. A cup of tea and a plate of biscuits on the coffee table. A newspaper folded to the racing results. His weekend, she thinks, doesn't normally find her, Mrs Thatcher, at the other end of his telephone line.

'Staunch Willie Whitelaw?' Denis mutters when she tells him who she's calling. 'You'd think he'd pulled the bloody trigger himself at the Iranian embassy the way he carried on.'

'What was that, Denis?'

'You heard,' Denis grumbles.

She did hear and she smiles.

Staunch Willie Whitelaw is right, she reflects. He's a big man in character, she's always said, not just physically. He only wants success in my government, she thinks, and he knows that it's mine, that it's guided by my philosophy.

'He's as loyal as a Bull Terrier,' she calls out now to Denis.

'Shits like one too, I'll bet,' Denis says.

She pretends she doesn't hear this.

She's fingering a memo sent by one of her spies. The minutes of a recent Monday Club meeting. They're not subtle, these backbenchers. She reads their restated immigration policy:

An end to New Commonwealth and Pakistani immigration, a properly financed scheme of voluntary repatriation, the repeal of the Race Relations Act, and the abolition of the Commission for Racial Equality; particular emphasis on repatriation.

Her spy is the committee secretary – for now.

She thinks she's going to arrange for this policy to be leaked, which was her spy's idea, somewhere like *Private Eye*, which was hers, and when she does, she'll make sure that, first, they leave the Monday

Club quietly, on the basis of it having racist members.

He'll be useful, this spy, one day, she thinks. And this is another way of securing the support of the extremists. She makes a note.

Now, she dials Willie Whitelaw's number and she waits.

'Hello?'

It's Celia, Willie Whitelaw's wife, who answers, no doubt ruddy-cheeked in gardening gloves and headscarf.

Mrs Thatcher makes herself known.

'I'll fetch him just now,' says Mrs Whitelaw, who bustles off to find Big Willie.

She, the prime minister, laughs at this thought.

'Good morning, Prime Minister,' Willie says. 'Your most humble and so on.'

She smiles. 'Quite. I'll be quick.'

Willie, doing as he's told, says nothing.

'Election year, Willie, and I want no news, you understand? Squash *everything*. We did the right thing repealing the sus law, which was undeniably draconian.'

'Agreed, ma'am.'

'But your short, sharp shock approach to law and to lawbreakers remains ever so popular with a large number of our supporters, understandably.'

'Understandably,' Willie says.

'So, you see, the hard line is the right line. Police pay continues to rise, which is good. Our ethnic communities continue to need policing. It's a clear relationship.'

'Yes, ma'am.'

'No mistakes, Willie, a firm hand.'

'I understand, Prime Minister.'

'Brixton,' she says, 'the Midlands, Liverpool. Need I go on?'

'No, ma'am. A new police bill, I think. We have the plans in place.'

Mrs Thatcher dawdles a moment, waits to see if Willie can handle the silence.

It transpires that he can.

He is, after all, the man who, when telephoned in the middle of the night by Merseyside's Chief Constable Ken Oxford seeking permission to use CS gas on rioters in Toxteth, gave his consent, rolled over and quickly began snoring again.

Willie Whitelaw says, 'Power to hold people for up to ninety-six hours without charge, to set up random roadblocks around any specific area, the power to conduct forcible intimate body searches, the use of force where necessary to take fingerprints, access to confidential information, doctors, lawyers and so on. There's some fine-tuning but these are the headlines.'

'Good,' Mrs Thatcher says, and hangs up.

Sometimes, Mrs Thatcher thinks, all one needs is a large Scotch Presbyterian in one's corner getting his hands dirty on one's behalf.

Denis wanders past, wiping *his* hands on his trousers. 'How's the fat controller?'

'Busy as a bee,' she says.

Denis shakes his head. 'Well,' he scowls, 'he'll have his fat paw in the honey jar, that's for damn mustard.'

Only when I tell him he can lick it, she thinks.

Suzi sits on her sofa under her duvet, a cup of tea propped up by pillows, happy to be at home with Keith. Monster and The Child finally left when they realised that they were shutting the curtains to stop the morning light getting in, and there's something a little dirty about that, Monster pointed out, so they wrapped up in their coats and their scarves, took a can of Red Stripe each for the journey and went to look for a bus to get home.

Keith, in leather waistcoat and vest, barefooted, is messing about with an unwieldy cassette machine and listening to a recording he made of Paul Weller gassing between takes.

Suzi, in her daze of half-sleep, is lulled by Paul Weller's voice, its intimacy, the closeness of Keith's recording, its purity:

... the Tories are trying to dismantle the communities of the working classes: attacks on the trade unions, small businesses disappearing and so many aspects of English life being closed down to people, yeah? There's this illusion ...

The tape stops.

Keith mutters something through the cigarette wedged in his gob, through its smoke, through the smoke drifting out of his gob, he grunts, there's a clank, a whirr and –

Suzi nods along, she can hear the hiss and crack, the echo of the studio –

... a phony pretence that we suddenly can be middle class because we're allowed to buy our own houses, get a mortgage, great, be in debt for the rest of our fucking lives. If you've got any kind of compassion at all and you see other people suffering, unless you're a complete nonce then I can't see how you can feel, not exactly how these people feel, but you must be able to see that it's wrong and this whole situation is wrong ...

Keith stops the tape, says, Huh, makes sense.

Suzi thinks about something David Widgery said to her the last time she saw him.

We didn't stop racial attacks, far less racism.

But they did help a lot of young white kids see that racism is really not cool, didn't they? And that's *something*.

Suzi thinks Paul Weller and The Style Council might fare a little better.

The songs, for a start.

Then she drifts to last night:

A jab of worry, a twist in her gut, her blood freezing –

He said, *Patrick* said, smiling, 'Don't worry, you won't see me again.'

She believes him; he looked *happy*. Then drunk –

Keith twiddles with something, unknots a cable and a version of 'Party Chambers' comes over the speakers.

'Turn it down, love, will you?' Suzi says. 'I'm going to bed.'

'Groovy,' Keith grins.

Saturday morning.

Jon Davies with the de-icer out, the motor running, the car stereo on, and he's scraping his windscreen.

The boy, wrapped up in duffle coat and West Ham scarf, looks on.

Jon's playing a cassette he's made, a compilation of a few tracks from a few new albums he fancies. There's Echo and the Bunnymen, Joe Jackson on there, and right now it's a newish single by The Stranglers he's taped off the radio –

'European Female', from the album *Feline*.

They're not subtle, the lyrics.

Jon quite likes the new direction The Stranglers have taken with this LP; very chic, very *now*, like they've listened to Spandau Ballet and the other Blitz Kids and decided they can do it a bit better –

The boy's shivering, huffing and puffing, and Jon really should get him back inside, knowing Jackie's feelings about the cold weather.

'Dad,' he says, 'what do you think of Van der Elf?'

'Elf?' Jon laughs.

The boy frowns, pouts. He insists, 'That's his name.'

'Van der *Elst*, son. His name's Elst. He's Belgian.'

'Where's Belgian?'

'Belgium.' Jon's scratching and scraping away. His hands, in heavy gloves, are sweating now, and he pulls one off and wipes his forehead. 'Belgium's in Europe. Over the water.'

The boy's nodding. 'So, what do you think of him, Van der Elst then, Dad?'

'I think he's good,' Jon declares. 'He brings us a bit of glamour too. Bit of style.'

'Right, style.'

'It's important, style,' Jon says. 'It's like a philosophy.'

The boy nods, says *philosophy* slowly.

'Hear this.' Jon points towards the stereo. 'This song's about Europe. Can you tell? The style, you see.'

The boy's mouthing the word *Europe*. Jon smiles to himself.

He says, 'Well Van der Elf had better bloody score tomorrow, hadn't he?'

'Dad,' the boy says, 'it's Elst, you said.'

Jon grins. 'You're right, come here.' He adjusts the boy's coat and scarf, keep him warm, but it's an excuse, really, to give him a cuddle.

On the stereo, 'The Cutter' by Echo and the Bunnymen.

Jon Davies says to his son, 'Pop in the driver's seat and turn it up, will you? You'll like this one.'

The boy does as he's told. His legs, in wellington boots, hang out the door and, watching them twitch, Jon can tell he's struggling a bit with the dial. Jon feels an overwhelming surge of something, which can happen, from time to time.

The song booms out.

'Hear that?' Jon says, meaning the distinctive synth line, almost Middle Eastern. 'What do you think that is?'

The boy thinks for a minute. 'Is it from Belgium?'

Jon laughs. 'Can you turn on the wipers, son?'

It's when the boy is sitting on the front seat watching the windscreen clearing that Jon sees Mrs Akhtar crossing the road towards them.

Jon waves. 'Lovely day, Mrs Akhtar!'

She laughs. 'Football today, Jon?'

'Tomorrow.' He points inside the car. 'He's making me take him to Nottingham Forest. On a Sunday, no less.'

The boy waves.

'He's making you.' Mrs Akhtar smiles. 'Of course, he is.'

She's wrapped up warm and off out, it seems. 'You enjoy the Labour Club last night?' Jon asks.

'We did! That band. The food, though, well.'

'Bloody awful.'

'Anything you need?' Mrs Akhtar points at her car. 'From the shops?'

Jon shakes his head. 'We're fine, thanks, Mrs Akhtar.'

She smiles.

Jon says, 'This Police Committee thing I'm doing, I told you about. We might be able to get a few answers, if that's what you'd like, I mean.'

Mrs Akhtar gives a tight little nod. 'Yes, we'd like that, Jon.'

'I mean, we might be able to, you understand.'

'I do.'

Jon smiles. 'I'll, you know, when or if, OK?'

Mrs Akhtar smiles, she turns to her car. 'You should get him inside, Jon.'

Jon nods at the upstairs window where Jackie stands, waving. 'You're not the only one who thinks that, Mrs Akhtar.'

There are days when Jon Davies thinks about Shahid Akhtar and he wonders what happened to that woman. He never said anything, of course he didn't. This committee might … Well, he'll have to use his discretion.

Jackie appears in the front door in her dressing gown. 'Kettle's on, Jon.'

The lad on his bike delivering papers skids to a halt and hands Jon his *Guardian* and his *Hackney Gazette*.

'Perfect timing,' Jon says. 'Come on, Billy Bonds,' he says to the boy. 'How about a fry-up?'

The boy scrambles out from the front seat.

'With chips from the pan?'

Jon wonders, sometimes, if his love for his son has in fact deepened, since trying and so far failing to produce a brother or sister for him.

He grins, winks at Jackie.

Under his breath, he says, 'If your mother will let me.'

Noble shudders awake –

His teeth chatter, his eyes sting, his head hums –

Jesus, he thinks. *Jesus fucking Christ* –

Car, steaming and freezing –

He starts the engine, he turns the heat up to full, he rubs his hands together, he licks at chapped lips, he holds his head in cold hands –

Jesus fucking Christ –

He laughs at himself quite loudly.

The windscreen frost melts –

He teases the motor into gear and heads east.

Twenty minutes later in a caff near Hackney Downs, Noble shovels egg and chips and gulps coffee. His plate is heavy with yolk and brown sauce. He cleans his plate with bread and butter. He wipes his mouth on a tatty napkin. He waves at the bird for more coffee.

In the bog, he examines his face. His eyes red, his cheeks rough, his hair greasy, his face greasy –

He runs the cold tap and washes his greasy face, water to the back of his neck, dispenser soap like toilet cleaner –

He sniffs and coughs, studies his reflection, gives himself a thorough going-over.

He says to his reflection, You're fine, you've done this before, you've been here before, you've got through this before, you're fine, you're *grand* –

He leaves the bog, takes his fresh mug of coffee from the bird with a cheers darlin' and a wink and asks her if there's a phone he can use.

There is. He pours sugar into his drink and takes it with him.

He dials the number the kid gave him. The kid's mum answers. Noble adopts a younger man's patter, tells her it's a mate.

The mum bustles off, yelling the kid's name.

'Yeah?'

'All right, Lloyd Manley,' Noble says. 'About last night—'

In the caff, at a table by the door, two blokes look alarmed as the kid Lloyd Manley pushes inside –

'He's with me,' Noble reassures.

'What, he your fucking babysitter?' the heavier of the blokes says.

A joker, then. Maybe now's not the time.

Noble stands, gestures for Lloyd to sit down. 'I'm his manager.' Noble winks. 'Featherweight. You should see him.'

The bloke looks appeased by this, holds up a hand to say, Cheers, my mistake, didn't mean to start a row.

Noble says to the bird, 'Get the boy a milkshake or something.'

Theatrically, she sighs.

They watch as she takes a pint of red top milk from the fridge, turns it sharply a few times this way and that, opens it and pours a belt of it into a half-pint glass that looks like it was recently lifted from a pub. She dumps this sorry-looking glass on the table.

'Milkshake,' she says.

The blokes wheezing with laughter.

'Yeah, good one,' Noble says. He looks at Lloyd. 'Well, drink up then.'

Noble sips coffee, watches Lloyd slurp his milk.

Noble points a finger. 'Suits you.'

'Eh?' Lloyd's confused.

'Wipe your top lip, son.'

Noble hands Lloyd a napkin and he does as he's told.

Noble takes out his notebook, fishes in his pocket for a pen.

'Now,' he says, 'you're going to tell me everything you know about Colin Roach and his sad demise, all right?'

Lloyd Manley nods.

'How long have you known Colin Roach?'

'Since school, infants.'

'When did you last see him?'

'On the night.'

'What time?'

'Just after ten.'

'Where?'

Lloyd's got a bit of a sullen bottom lip going but Noble thinks he might just be upset.

'On the street.'

'OK. Where?'

Lloyd points at Hackney Downs.

'Listen, kid,' Noble says, 'give the attitude the heave ho, all right? I'm on your side, so shape up.'

'What does that mean?'

Noble smiles. He nods, he softens. 'I don't believe for one moment that your mate killed himself in the foyer of Stoke Newington police station the other night.'

'No?'

'No. And the only way to prove he didn't is to find out who did. Yeah?'

Lloyd Manley nods, his eyes dart. 'He was in a car with a friend of ours, a guy called Keith Scully. They were driving around. Colin was saying something about being in trouble, about people out to get him.'

'He said those words, out to get him?'

'Yeah, like that, you know?'

'OK. What else?'

'Keith wanted to take him home. Colin said it was too dangerous, they'd be waiting for him. He was saying to Keith that they need to keep moving, telling him to drive fast and take him somewhere nobody knows him.'

'Did he say why?'

'No.'

Noble gives Lloyd Manley the look.

'He didn't, I swear. He said he couldn't tell us.'

'He couldn't tell you?'

Lloyd Manley shakes his head.

'Why not?'

'He said we were all going to die and if he told us, they'd get us.'

'They'd get you?'

Lloyd Manley, looking down, leaning back on his chair, the chair legs lifting slightly from the floor, nods.

'But you don't know who they might be.'

Lloyd Manley shakes his head.

Noble clears his throat. 'Who else was there?'

'In the car?'

Noble nods.

'Another friend, Jim Joseph. They were looking for his brother, Joe.'

'Where?'

'I don't know but Denise Carlow might.'

'Who's she?'

'Another friend.'

Noble nods. 'Anything else?'

'That's it. I went home after that.'

'Your mum there, was she?'

'Yeah.'

'Anyone else?'

Lloyd Manley shakes his head.

Noble nods. 'Tell me, Lloyd. Was this normal behaviour from Colin?'

'No.'

'He was panicked, was he, spooked?'

'He was worried, you know. He wasn't acting crazy if that's what you mean.'

Noble gives it the six of one, half a dozen of the other.

'These friends of yours,' Noble says, 'any bother with the police at all?'

Lloyd Manley shakes his head.

'I can check, Lloyd.' Noble points towards the phone at the back. 'I can check that right now.'

'No bother, no.' Lloyd pauses. 'Well, you know, they bother *us*.'

'Go on.'

'You know, sus us, push us about. Happens all the time.'

'I'm sure it does.'

'I'm black and I'm young and I'm male. They take the piss.'

'Tell me about it,' Noble says.

'Well then.'

Noble nods, satisfied. 'You're sure Colin Roach wasn't wanted by the police and wasn't involved in anything else?'

Lloyd Manley, more confident now, nods. 'I'm sure.'

Noble leans back, breathes in, gives his head a little shake.

'If you beg my pardon,' Lloyd Manley says, 'you seem a bit out of sorts, detective.'

'Long night, son.'

Lloyd Manley smiles.

Noble pulls his wallet. 'You want anything else?'

'Nah, cheers.'

Noble waves the money at the bird, leaves it on the table under an ashtray. 'Have a bacon sandwich on me, darling,' he says.

Lloyd smiles at this, goes to stand up.

'Hang about,' Noble says.

He grips Lloyd Manley's wrist; his eyes tell Lloyd Manley *don't fucking move.*

He says, 'What I want to know then, Lloyd, is why the fuck you were pulled into that van last night and what the fuck those two detective constables said to you.'

Lloyd Manley says nothing, he trembles –

'Why you, Lloyd?'

Lloyd Manley shakes his head.

He says, 'I don't know.'

'Yes, you do, Lloyd.'

Lloyd Manley's eyes dart. 'Not here, yeah.'

Noble nods. 'We'll go to my car.' He lets go of Lloyd Manley's wrist. 'Easy now, son.'

The blokes by the door make fists. 'Be lucky, champ,' they say.

Noble winks.

In the car, heading towards Stoke Newington.

'Where we going?' Lloyd Manley asks.

His eyes dart, his black cap pulled down low, his hands twitching.

'You've got until the nick to tell me.'

Lloyd Manley looks scared. 'OK, OK, just pull over.'

Noble eases down a gear, does a left off Amhurst Road, finds a spot on Farleigh Road and pulls in.

Saturday-morning quiet, streets frosty.

Milk bottles and empty bins –

Paper boy winging tabloids into front gardens –

A pair of pensioners battle the elements, their shopping trolleys slipping on the ice.

Boys with football boots hanging around their necks by the laces skid along to the downs, pushing each other and laughing.

Noble kills the engine.

'I'm waiting, Lloyd.'

Lloyd Manley breathes out. 'It might be nothing.'

'You'd be surprised, Lloyd,' Noble says, 'how often I hear that.'

Lloyd Manley nods. He says, 'I've seen the men in the van before. Once.'

Noble nods. 'When?'

'About two weeks ago. I was leaving the estate where I live and there was a car parked I didn't recognise.'

'OK. Colour? Make?'

Lloyd Manley shrugs. 'I don't know what it was. Blue, maybe.'

Noble raises his eyebrows, makes a note. 'Go on.'

'I was messing about, the windows were steamed up, you know, it looked like, you know, so I went and had a closer look, just messing about, I swear.'

'All right, Lloyd, you're not in trouble. Go on.'

'They were in the car, in the front seats. A woman was in the back.'

'The same men.'

'Yeah.'

'Can you describe the woman?'

'She was white, sort of pretty, bit old.'

'You're a real charmer, Lloyd. What was she wearing?'

'Didn't look like much,' Lloyd mumbles.

'And the men saw you?'

'Yeah, one of them opened the door and told me to fuck off.'

'And did you?'

'I did. I stood where I was for a minute, looking, then I ran.'

'And you haven't seen them again since?'

Lloyd shakes his head.

'Did something like this ever happen to Colin?'

'I don't know.'

'You tell me the truth or you'll see these men again today, you understand?'

'It's the truth, I swear, I don't know.'

'He never said anything like that?'

'Not to me.'

Noble nods. 'And what did these men say to you in the van, Lloyd?'

'They said they'd seen me and that I know what that means.'

'What do you think that means, Lloyd?'

'It means I should keep well out of their way.'

'It does mean that, Lloyd. It means that if they want to, they can fit you up.'

Lloyd Manley nods.

Noble pats Lloyd Manley on the back. 'Well done, son,' he says. 'You've done the right thing.'

Noble takes out his notebook, his pen. 'Lloyd, I want the names and addresses of all the friends of yours you've mentioned. And I want Colin Roach's home address, his parents' gaff.'

Lloyd Manley nods.

Lying in bed, legs threaded round the duvet, Suzi's awake.

She's had a patchy hour or two. Keith came in for a cuddle around eight but conked out before they could really rock themselves off to sleep, and she's not ready to relax –

She's hungry, restless.

She whispers into Keith's ear, 'I'm just going for a walk, love. I'll pick us up some breakfast.'

'Beautiful,' Keith grunts.

Suzi slips out of bed, pulls jogging bottoms over her pyjamas, finds thick woollen socks and a jumper, and wraps her coat and scarf around her. She picks up camera, keys and purse, goes quietly down the stairs – she wants to avoid the neighbours, just in case they've kept them awake – and lets herself out the front door.

There's a mid-morning mist, the sun up but too weak to shift it. Suzi blows on her hands, her breath icy damp, visible. She takes the wet chill deep into her lungs and it feels prickly, cleansing.

She wanders up to Kingsland High Street and turns right, not exactly sure where she's heading, but with a vague sense that Ridley Road market might have something worth looking at.

When she takes these walks, she doesn't know what she'll photograph until she does; if she's looking for something, she never seems to find it.

Her camera is what's given her the opportunities she's had over the last few years; without that in her locker, she wouldn't have had the writing work, if she's honest with herself. There aren't many women music journalists and even fewer with any credibility. Credibility, of course, meaning grudging respect from the men, both artists and media. She can't remember how many times she's pitched up to interview a band or singer and the basic assumption on their side has been that she's game.

The camera is a decent shield. More than that, it's why she gets so much work: she'll do the photoshoot and the interview as a package deal, good value for everyone.

Which is how she's graduated from *Temporary Hoarding* to *NME* and *Melody Maker* to freelancing for the Sunday supplements and more upmarket glossy magazines.

Her unique selling point, she calls it.

Julie Burchill told her she was a Jackie of all trades, mistress of none.

Suzi agreed. 'I'm no mistress, Julie.'

She likes Julie Burchill but she's not sure about that fella of hers.

Kingsland High Street is all hustle.

Newspapers and cardboard, fast food wrappers and broken plastic crates filling the gutters, blowing about between illegally parked cars.

Outside the Rio Cinema, hawkers have set up on the pavement selling cheap linen and felt, moody sports gear. To the left, a group of skinny two-tone kids laughing and mucking about.

Suzi looks up at the cinema's crumbling, dirty, black-and-white striped art deco façade, the word Rio in a flash font, 'modern', she supposes, set against a dynamic arrow. Behind the cinema, John Campbell Motors painted on the side of a brick terraced house, a finger pointing to MOT, a row of red Ford estates –

She click-clicks away.

Keith likes the Rio. They always sit in the front row; it's very comfortable, the front row: the seats are broken, they're like retractable armchairs, the velvet worn and rough, and there's always an atmosphere in there.

When Darth Vader let the cat out the bag during *Empire Strikes Back*, there was a chorus of 'No!' One bloke yelled, 'I knew it!' and another, from the other side of the cinema, 'No, you fucking didn't.'

At the end, some joker in a stormtrooper outfit jumped out from behind the curtains.

She passes Dalston Kingsland station, three black lads perched on the railings outside, in leisure wear and jeans, bright caps with huge rims.

Suzi shows the camera. 'OK?' she asks.

'Yeah, lady, it's your lucky day,' and they pose, arms folded, smoking ostentatiously, big grins beneath their thin moustaches.

Behind them, on the station concourse, shady figures shuffle around shoppers and day-trippers headed for Kew Gardens or the river by Richmond. There's nothing in the other direction –

The North London line trains are to be avoided during the week, Suzi thinks, with their smoking carriage nooks purpose-built for addicts and muggers, door handles jamming whenever Suzi's leaned out the window to open one.

She knows women who refuse to use the line, even during the day.

Especially during the day: there's *only* rapists and perverts and junkies outside peak hours.

Across the road, the market bustling –

Suzi thinks, I'm at this market too often, I don't need batteries or a pensioner's shopping trolley, Keith won't want waking with flowers any time soon, so she pushes on, past the Woolworth's, past the Centerprise bookshop, past the *Hackney Gazette* offices and down to the junction, has a look to see if they've started work yet on this peace mural she's heard about near the Four Aces on Dalston Lane – they haven't – so on she goes, past the international telephone exchanges with their WE WILL TYPE FOR YOU offers, the electronic and white goods fronts, the carpet-sellers and domestic stores, fishing tackle and outsize fashion, snooker clubs and corner pubs, handwritten signs taped in their windows, NO TRAVELLERS, safe repairs and keys cut, the newsagents and the caffs, the pound shops and the Turkish grills, the sweatshops and the post offices, Travis Perkins and the community centre, and then across the canal at Haggerston, to the left, on the railway bridge, graffiti spells out ACT NOW SUPPORT BRITISH NATIONAL PARTY BNP FOREVER, and, on the other side, a demonstration in progress outside the mosque, so Suzi stops –

Suzi takes photos.

Grizzled men in flat caps and unfashionable leather jackets and grim-faced women in woollen checked skirts and headscarves make up most of the participants. Homemade signs in English and Turkish: NO MORE DEPORTATIONS, NO WORKERS ARE ILLEGAL. A couple of trendies in denim and roll-neck sailing jumpers, yellow badges pinned to their lapels –

Suzi knows that colour. Anti-Nazi League.

She smiles.

It gives her a thought –

She remembers a job a few years ago, taking photos for the *Gazette* at the opening of the Britannia leisure centre, which she can see now, just beyond the Pitfield Street estates. She got the nod through the Labour councillor, Joannie Andrews, who oversaw the development, using it as a direct response to complaints from Derrick Day who claimed Shoreditch was never developed, left behind by the council. Joannie Andrews liked Suzi's RAR credentials.

It was a funny day, she remembers now, snapping it through the trees against its Shoreditch Park backdrop, Hoxton estates in the distance.

Prince Philip did the honours, ribbons and scissors-wise. He was given a judo lesson by an Olympic medallist but what Suzi remembers best of all was what the Duke of Edinburgh said to Grace Ellis, a young recreation assistant who worked there, maybe still does. He, Prince Philip, HRH Duke of Edinburgh, asked Grace Ellis if she ever used the facilities for 'chest development'.

'He was a nice man,' Grace said afterwards, 'but I was very surprised.'

Suzi feels, suddenly, weary.

She's walked too far, she's *really* hungry now and thirsty too.

She heads back the way she came, stops in a Jet garage and buys black coffee, a bottle of water, a breakfast bar –

She'll pick up bacon and eggs and orange juice nearer home, the papers maybe, *Hackney Gazette*, why not, for old times' sake –

She gets on a bus, sits downstairs, places her head against the cold glass. The conductor takes her coins, winds his machine, hands her a ticket.

She sips her drinks, chews on her snack. I really wanted to be taken seriously, she thinks. That's why I did it, I thought it was a short cut to some sort of success.

She smiles now at her naïvety.

The bus is smooth, green lights all the way, they're through Dalston Junction, and then, for no reason Suzi can see, it stops, idles and the driver cuts the engine.

The conductor skips down the aisle telling everyone, Sit tight and we'll be moving again shortly.

Passengers crane necks. Suzi's behind the driver –

She switches seats to the left-hand side of the bus and sees the obstruction.

A police van, lights flashing, parked messily in front of Dalston Kingsland station.

Suzi lifts her camera –

She sees four uniformed police officers surround three young men, corral them against the wall. She watches these police officers, using truncheons and sticks, elbows and fists, spread the legs of the three young men, rifle their pockets, their wrists secured with temporary handcuffs behind their backs.

One of the young men, Suzi sees, wears a bright red cap with a wide rim –

He turns and says something to one of the uniformed police officers.

Suzi watches the uniformed police officer jab the young man in the kidneys with his truncheon, slap the young man in the backs of his knees with his truncheon –

The young man's legs buckle.

Suzi takes photos through the window of the bus. The same three young men –

Suzi sees more police, more police vans further up the road.

The van blocking the bus pulls round and the bus moves off.

Suzi looks back, takes more photos, the young men prone –

She lowers her camera, pulls the cord, rings the bell for the next stop.

She jumps off the bus as it slows down and walk-runs back to the station.

She puts her camera in her bag.

She pulls her notebook from her bag –

She arrives as the young men are being slowly uncuffed, free to go.

They mooch off, scowling, angry, defiant –

Suzi asks one of the uniformed police officers what was going on –

Stop and search, he tells her. They're all at it, one way or another, you can't be too careful, love.

Suzi nods. She follows the three young men up the road. They turn left and Suzi follows. She calls out, Hey, slow down.

They turn and see her. She's waving her notebook, her camera –

Can I talk to you? she asks.

The three young men exchange looks, their eyes dart –

You saw that? Red Cap asks.

Suzi nods.

And you did nothing.

Suzi hesitates –

The young men suck their teeth, turn, lope off.

Suzi thinks, He's right.

She feels weary, she feels sad –

Fifteen minutes later, bacon frying, kettle whistling, Suzi's looking at the papers, *Hackney Gazette*, reading about Colin Roach.

Keith comes into the kitchen in open dressing gown, grinning and scratching himself.

He kisses Suzi, says, 'You're an angel.'

Over his fried breakfast, Jon Davies reads about the death of Colin Roach.

'It's unbelievable,' he's muttering.

'What is, love?'

Jon points at the article in the *Gazette*. 'This,' he says. Jon looks up the stairs, hears the television on, is sure the boy really did scarper after wolfing down his sausage and chips. 'Have a read,' he says. 'They're saying a young black man committed suicide in the foyer of Stoke Newington nick.'

'That's unbelievable,' Jackie agrees.

Jon pushes the paper, open at the correct page, across the table.

'That's what I said,' he says.

Noble sits in Mr and Mrs Roach's front room.

There's a pot of tea on the table, but no one's touching it.

Mr Roach is a serious-looking man who is, quite understandably, on the verge of some terrible rage. Noble thinks he'd be an affable type in other circs.

They were not pleased to see Detective Constable Patrick Noble when they opened the door, the Roaches.

Noble told them, I'm not here to investigate you, Mr and Mrs Roach, or your son. I'm here to talk about the police. He showed them his credentials. I'm part of something called the Met Race Crime Initiative, he lied.

That got the door open.

Noble takes out his notebook and pen. 'I'd like to ask you some questions,' he says, 'to establish what happened exactly at Stoke Newington police station on the night of the twelfth of January this year.'

Mr Roach nods. He says, 'I'll tell you what happened, detective, if that's quite all right.'

Noble nods. 'Please.'

Mr James Roach begins. 'I went to Stoke Newington police station a little after midnight to look for my son.' Noble opens his mouth and James Roach holds up a finger. 'I went there as Colin's friend Keith Scully telephoned us here at Colin's home to tell us that he had dropped Colin off at Stoke Newington police station at Colin's request. I was worried, so I went.'

Noble nods.

'When I arrived, the front door of the police station was taped off, no access. I was taken to the rear of the building and upstairs to a room. Once in this room, I was questioned until two forty-five in the morning. Then, only then, I was told my son was dead.'

Noble thinks, The press release went out before that.

He says, 'What did they ask you?'

'I was asked what my son was involved in, criminal activity, you understand. I was asked how come I came looking for him here, if he weren't a criminal. I was asked about Colin's mental health: did I know that he was suffering from clinical depression and delusional behaviour.'

'Was he?'

'He was not.'

'What happened next?'

'What happened next is that I was held at Stoke Newington police station until four forty-five and I was not allowed to see my son's body. What happened after that is police officers brought me home and then they searched my son's bedroom. My wife, Pamela, was in a state of shock, her son dead and the police turning his room upside down. She stood, she was upset, alarmed, and a lady officer forced her back into her seat, gripping her round the neck.'

Noble looks down. There must be a lot of them in on it, he thinks.

He says, 'Did they take anything from your son's room?'

James Roach shakes his head. 'The next day,' he goes on, 'I returned to Stoke Newington police station with a Tower Hamlets councillor to try to get some answers.'

'But you didn't get any.'

'No, we didn't get any answers and in the evening, well, some people asking the same questions were arrested.'

Noble nods. 'I know this is difficult but you're absolutely sure that Colin could not have killed himself?'

'My son did not commit suicide,' says James Roach. 'He had too much to live for.'

Keith Scully's dad sniffs when he opens the front door. 'You better be on the level,' he tells Noble.

In the front room, Keith Scully sits quietly. It looks like he's been crying.

Noble takes out his notebook, he takes out his pen, he says, 'Why don't you tell me what happened.'

Keith Scully nods. 'I picked Colin up with our friend Jim Joseph at about ten fifteen. He was agitated. He told me to drive around, fast, and to take him somewhere where no one knew him.'

Noble nods. 'Go on.'

'I said I thought I should take him home. He said: "No, don't take me there, they will be waiting for me."'

'Did he say who?'

'No.'

'OK. Then what happened?'

'I asked Colin if he was in some sort of trouble and he said he was and that we were all going to die.'

'Those were his words?'

Keith Scully nods.

'Go on.'

'He said that if he told me what was going on, they'd get me. I asked him who and he said he couldn't tell me.'

'OK.'

'While we were driving around, Colin said that Joe Joseph – a friend of ours and Jim's twin brother – was dead. So, I dropped off Jim who went to look for Joe. He went round our friend Denise Carlow's flat and she told me later that Jim had said to her that Colin was cracking up, thinking someone was going to kill him.'

'Then what happened?'

'Colin was asking me to take him to Bethnal Green police station and I thought it was a bad idea, so I agreed to take him to his brother's place. I dropped him off near Stoke Newington police station, where he lives. Colin got out, told me not to worry, he'd be safe here, but instead of going down a side street he went on up the road and into the police station by the front entrance.'

'You saw him go in?'

Keith Scully nods. 'I drove past, slowly, to check on him, you know, and I saw someone in there on their own but against the light, I couldn't be sure it was Colin.'

'Then what happened?'

'I drove home. I phoned Colin's dad. And then—'

Keith Scully's voice cracks.

'You've done nothing wrong, son,' Noble says.

Keith Scully quietly sobs.

'How did Colin seem to *you*, Keith?' Noble asks. 'You were mates. Was it all a put-on or was he really scared?'

'He was upset but I don't know – I suppose that's how I'd put it, upset.'

'Not cracking up? Not hysterical?'

Keith Scully sniffs, breathes in. 'Upset,' he confirms.

'He get upset a lot, did he?' Noble asks. 'Would you say he was often upset, depressed?'

Keith Scully shakes his head. 'No. Colin wasn't like that.'

'Did Colin, as far as you know, have any reason to think someone was after him?'

Keith Scully shakes his head. 'Not that I know of.'

'There's nothing you can tell me, nothing you lot—'

Keith Scully, adamantly, shakes his head. 'No.'

Noble nods. 'I believe you, Keith. One last thing: was Colin carrying anything when you picked him up?'

Keith Scully nods. 'Yeah, a bag, a holdall.'

'How big was it, Keith?'

Keith Scully places his hands a foot or so apart horizontally, then a little further apart vertically. 'Like a gym bag but a small one.'

Noble nods. 'He tell you what was in it?'

Keith Scully shakes his head.

'Any reason, Keith, that there might have been a shotgun in there?'

Keith Scully shakes his head. 'It was too small, anyway.'

Noble nods, smiles. 'How long have you known Colin, Keith?'

'Since school.'

'Do you think he could have committed suicide, Keith? Did he ever talk about that sort of thing?'

Keith Scully shakes his head. 'Never, no way.'

Keith Scully's dad comes into the front room. He gestures with his thumb. 'I think that's enough for now, Detective Constable Noble.'

Noble nods.

Mrs Thatcher's thinking it's about bloody time she got rid of the GLC.

It's a total façade, a quango, a drain of resources, everyone who knows, knows this, but not enough people *know* this.

Livingstone, she thinks, should have done for it already. *Fares Fair*, his multi-million-pound revamp of public transport was a disaster.

The GLC council houses sold to private buyers. That made him look pretty stupid.

But he's like Lazarus, with worse skin and less hair, she thinks.

She wonders, sometimes, about this idea that men of the left are sexy. Livingstone, Benn, Kinnock – they're not exactly Spandau Ballet, are they?

She laughs at her little joke.

Livingstone isn't best pleased with Conservative Central Office, she thinks. He claims they've been touting certain stories contending his enjoyment of schoolgirls, and his pitching up at an orgy where, and she can remember the wording, 'he was buggered by six men in succession'.

'Not true, of course,' Denis said, reading the article. 'It was seven.'

He's only rattled her once, Livingstone.

After the riots, after Toxteth and Brixton and Southall and Moss Side, Livingstone blamed her, Mrs Thatcher, and her 'press allies pumping out a daily diet of filth and making racism respectable'.

And not just Mrs Thatcher and the press, the Metropolitan Police Commissioner too, calling his views 'racist', which 'set the scene for a worsening of police–black relations'.

And not just the police but unemployment too, and appalling housing.

The GLC, the suggestion went, should be keeping a close eye on the Metropolitan Police, overseeing it, really.

'Tugging on its bloody purse strings, he means,' Denis said.

'Thanks, Denis,' she replied. 'Where would I be without you?'

'In a bloody grocer's shop, minding the till,' Denis muttered.

She ignored that. Everyone knows about her father, the grocer. Too easy.

She's looking at a memo from the end of the year before.

One of her aides is being clever about Red Ken. Second, behind the Pope, in the annual BBC Man of the Year poll, he was. *Second*.

The joke is, her clever aide writes, that Red Ken's popularity goes up with every incompetent stunt: he's more showman than politician. He certainly can't run the capital and enjoys County Hall more for its stature and suggestion of power than as a base for any attempt to improve the services that the GLC is responsible for: better to harp on about what they *should* be responsible for.

Classic deflection.

Her aide identifies one topic that Red Ken can't bluster through –

The two most boring words in the English language, as the joke goes: *Northern Ireland*.

She, Mrs Thatcher, has already made public the letter that Livingstone wrote in December to Sinn Féin on behalf of the GLC inviting them to London for 'fraternal' talks to facilitate 'British withdrawal and a united Ireland'.

Second to the Pope, of course.

She wonders if the BBC poll had a high Ulster turnout in certain communities.

The press was brutal, Red Ken took a hiding.

His comments on British involvement in Ireland and the comparison with Hitler and the Jews was pretty silly, she thinks, sixth-form stuff, but the papers loved it and so did the big boys across the house –

Foot, Hattersley, Shore all jumped on their high horses to condemn him.

But Red Ken remains.

And it's his remarks about those riots that bother her, the idea that she's making racism respectable.

It bothers her as she knows it's true – to a point.

It's true in that she drew the more respectable *voters* from the National Front and the BNP to her side. And that was a *strategy*, a political strategy.

The other angle is this worsening of police–black relations that he detects.

Another strategy, she thinks, might be a way to reverse this worsening.

And keep Red Ken harping on about Sinn Féin.

With a few months until the election, time to sow a few seeds –

While making sure Staunch Willie shuts up shop.
She, Mrs Thatcher, will of course be minding the till.
All's fare in love, et cetera, she jokes.

3

White European Dance Music

January 1983

Parker

Course there are some streetwise kids on the firm, and though they're not naughty boys themselves they've got cousins or brothers or uncles or fucking nephews who are, or who know someone who is, and they all know who's who and what's what in that sense and the big thing they're hearing is there is going to be a switch-up in the drug trade, that heroin is too cheap and too readily available now, supply and demand ain't doing the business and the customers are all thieving junkies, and there's something coming over from New York which is cheap but doesn't last long, effects-wise, and it's got the fun of cocaine but without the glamour and the price and the nightclub necessity of it all, without the scene. You watch, they're telling you, Stoke Newington police station is going to be first in on the action, and this is something you feel you should pass on even if it's beyond your remit, so you do, and Noble tells you that it's the first he's heard and nice one. And they're telling you about how plainclothes boys are cornering their women, their sisters and aunties and mums and their mates, their school friends and their girlfriends, and offering easy money and a bit of protection on the estates if they'll just turn a few tricks every now and again, just for the lads, no one they won't vet first, no violence or funny business, just an easy weekly salary and pocket money, too, if the lads like them. And you tell Noble this and he says he knows, it's an old-school set-up for dirty bastards, been around a while, but he didn't know they were harassing young black women, and you're hearing that the more elderly churchgoing community is blaming the youngsters themselves, and you're hearing that part of that is the goal, divide and conquer, and then you're hearing, Why is it only because of the white media that we've any coverage at all? and Why are our problems only reported through the lens of white politicians in this white media? and you think these are very good questions to which you don't actually need the answers right now, so you just keep on.

Suzi doesn't tell Keith what happened on Kingsland High Street on Saturday morning, puts it behind her.

She's got work to do: a commission for the *Face* for a big piece on Thatcher and music.

She's going back to Steve Strange and Billy's in Soho, the Blitz Kids and St Martin's College, the Kemp brothers, speed pills and Yamaha synths –

She's got some good quotes.

She was there for some of it, after all.

That now famous phone call, January 1980, to tastemakers and night shakers:

'My name's Steve Strange and I run a club called the Blitz on Tuesdays and I'm starting a cabaret night on Thursdays with a really great new band ... they combine synthesised dance music for the future with vocals akin to Sinatra, they're called Spandau Ballet and they're going to be really big ...'

Suzi went along.

It was a hoot, she recalls, mannequin-chic and pretty-boy quiffs.

'Elektro Diskow' they called the music.

The door policy – which Suzi remembers as being more important than the music – was a Bowie reference, *Heroes*, a *just one day* philosophy, for 'people who created unique identities'.

Bowie again, Suzi eye-rolls.

She thinks of the fashion student, Chris Sullivan, a regular at the Blitz.

Punk, he told her, was over.

'Young people are no longer prepared to be sold clothes they don't like or go to clubs playing records they don't want to hear, being run by grunters three times their age, and having to pay for the privilege. When the Blitz opened, for a start it was cheap, but it was also extraordinary to have someone aged nineteen vetting the door.'

A few people have lumped the New Romantics in with Thatcher, slick sound, pure disco sensibility, jazz and soul-lite, with style that looks expensive and substance that sounds cheap.

Suzi disagrees.

She likes Spandau Ballet.

The songs have something about them, they're pop stars.

They're also working-class boys whose families have trade union connections, who grew up in the terraced council houses of Angel, Islington.

Terrific haircuts, too.

There's a reductive element to this criticism of them, a bit of rock/punk establishment sneering, she thinks, and this might be her angle –

Spandau Ballet aren't the only people not voting for Thatcher; unemployment, at least, is pretty democratic.

Suzi was there taking photos when Ken Livingstone hung that '3 MILLION' banner from the roof of County Hall. He said he'd liked to have an electronic one, like a scoreboard that could be updated hourly, but they couldn't afford it.

And a third of that 3 million are under twenty-five now, she thinks.

In her article, it is Suzi's contention that by setting up their own nightclubs and secret gigs, the New Wave excluded the establishment – the labels, the A&R men – to entice that same establishment into giving them lucrative recording contracts.

And Spandau Ballet hit the jackpot, record deal-wise.

Very clever, the Angel Boys.

'The sound of Thatcherism on vinyl' feels a little snide as an evaluation of pop music. Suzi won't have that.

Keith tells her that Spandau Ballet's next album is going to be massive.

Gary Kemp says that they're 'making the most contemporary statement in fashion and music'. And there's the class war at its heart.

'A cultural identity is a great outlet for people's frustrations. Kids have always spent what little they have on records and haircuts. They've never spent it on books by Karl Marx.'

He also says, of Suzi's profession:

'They don't understand style in working-class terms: they think it means money. Well, it doesn't. One of the most difficult things is explaining what style is to middle-class journalists because they always connect style with being bourgeois and they spend their whole lives trying to escape it. I don't feel guilty because I've made enough money to own my own home. It's only the middle classes who feel that kind of guilt.'

Eddy Grant on the radio, 'Electric Avenue'.

Suzi looks up from her notes and listens. It's a protest song with a cracking chorus. Electric Avenue: Brixton market. Violence on the streets. Not enough space. Not enough money. Not enough food.

Keith comes in, whistling. He dumps papers on the table next to Suzi.

'All right, gorgeous,' he says. He cocks an ear, theatrically. 'You still working on that Spandau piece, love?' He nods at the music. 'This ain't exactly White European Dance Music,' he grins.

'But it comes from the same city,' Suzi says. She notes down the phrase, which she'd forgotten, Spandau's description of their early sound.

'Very clever, love. Tea?'

Suzi nods. She looks at the papers. She picks up what looks like a flyer. She holds it up. 'Where did you get this, love?'

'Some kid on the high street was giving them out. That lad last week, you know, terrible business.'

Suzi nods. The flyer advertises a meeting of the Hackney Black People's Association, a picture of a smiling young man called Colin Roach –

Suzi says. 'I think I'll go to this meeting. Do you want to?'

Keith's back is turned as he tends to teabag and milk. 'Working!' he calls out.

Suzi nods.

'Weller's going to call the first single "Speak Like a Child",' Keith laughs, his head in the fridge. 'Monster's delighted!'

Suzi, her mind elsewhere, smiles.

Town hall.

Godfrey Heaven pops his head round Jon Davies' office door and asks Jon if he has time for a quick word.

'For you, Godfrey –' Jon smiles – 'I've got time for two.'

Jon Davies is not unhappy that Godfrey Heaven is the chair of the Police Committee. Their work together on the squatter situation was straightforward and Jon likes Heaven's approach, it turns out.

Most of all, Jon Davies is pleased that *he's* not chair of the Police Committee.

'Very funny,' says Godfrey Heaven.

Jon leans back, puts his hands behind his head. 'You don't have to be mad to work here, Godfrey, but it doesn't half help.'

'OK.'

'What can I do for you?'

Godfrey Heaven sits down. 'You're aware, Jon, that this whole thing is a bit of a gamble, a bit of a punt.'

'I am.'

'We – and by "we" I mean the Police Committee – don't have any actual power or any real mandate.'

Jon nods. 'It's a beautiful thing,' he says.

He enjoys playing this character with Godfrey Heaven, he brings it out in him.

'Really, there's no precedent and no grounds for a committee such as this one and all we're likely to do is put people's noses out of joint.'

'It's a dirty job but someone's got to do it,' Jon says.

'I didn't know you were such a wag, Jon.'

Jon Davies smiles. 'You will, Godfrey.'

Godfrey Heaven gives Jon a look. 'I've heard something, Jon, that I want to share.'

'I'm all ears.'

'Ernie Roberts, our honourable member for Hackney North,' Godfrey Heaven says, 'is set to make a statement on public concern regarding the breakdown of community and police relations, as well as pledging his support for a public inquiry into the death of Colin Roach. Additionally, the Greater London Council, I hear, is planning to fund the Roach campaign to the tune of fifteen hundred pounds shortly after Ernie Roberts makes this statement.'

Jon nods. 'That *is* interesting.'

'There is, of course,' Godfrey Heaven suggests, 'the potential for outrage in the press at such a use of public money. It might look like a donation of cash to undermine the police. It might look like the GLC is looking to, quote unquote, foster discontent amongst the black communities.'

'You're absolutely right, Godfrey.'

'Forewarned is forearmed and all that.'

'Now who's being a wag, Godfrey.'

Godfrey Heaven smiles. 'All worth keeping in mind.'

Godfrey Heaven stands. 'And I won't keep *you* any longer, Jon.'

'There's a meeting later,' Jon says. 'Hackney Black People's Association have called it. About Colin Roach, about that campaign you mentioned. I'm going.'

'Good plan,' Godfrey Heaven says, 'like your mind.'

Jon nods. 'I'll see you there?'

'You betcha.'

'One last thing,' Jon says. 'I'm going to propose that we request all police files pertaining to the death of Shahid Akhtar in 1978. Using that non-existent power that we might or might not have.'

'Right you are.'

'It's about the timing,' Jon says, 'forewarned and all that.'

'You plucked the words right out, Jon.'

Jon smiles.

Scotland Yard, first thing Monday.

Noble's in with Detective Chief Inspector Maurice Young.

'Have a seat, Chance.'

'Nice office, guv.'

'It's temporary.'

Noble nods. He's feeling wired, excited, and Sunday was a glorious day –

Early night on Saturday, pub lunch in Soho with Lea, afternoon walk through posh Marylebone, winding back to his flat, a light supper and a bottle of wine, she's still there, day off today, he can't wait –

Noble's buzzing.

Detective Chief Inspector Maurice Young rubs his hands together. 'Well then,' he says. 'Let's have it.'

Noble nods. 'The deceased is a young black man, twenty-one years old, no proper form. His family and friends say no way he committed suicide. His father went looking for him at the station and was questioned for over two hours before they informed him of his son's death. They sent the press release out beforehand, in fact. Very classy. Turned over the family home after that, intimidating the mother. Friends say the boy was worried someone was going to get to him, but they don't know why. No suggestion he was involved in anything heavy, or anything at all, in fact. Circumstantially, one of the friends says he was poking about a vehicle on the estate a week or so ago, though no sense that the deceased was with the friend when this happened. Inside were two plainclothes in the front and an underdressed woman in the back. So, you can imagine what might have been going on.'

In his mouth, he tastes Lea.

'Spell it out.'

'It sounds to me like a classic prostitution kickback scheme: protection and premises for a decent share of the profit.'

'You ever come across this before?'

Noble nods. 'West End Central was the model, what with Soho and Mayfair access, guv. Franchise situation across jurisdictions. And not always protection and premises: they run the girls themselves, it's been known.'

'What else?'

'On the night of the fourteenth of January, during an impromptu protest outside Stoke Newington police station, I witnessed DCs Cole and Rice physically and verbally threaten a young man who was attending the protest. I followed the young man. He told me about the plainclothes and the woman in the vehicle on the estate.'

'Very good. Keep a hold of him.'

In his mouth, on his tongue, he tastes Lea.

'Same night, I witnessed evidence of extortion by DCs Cole and Rice – protection, most likely – at a drinking club close to the station.'

'They get around then, these two. Anything else?'

'On the night itself, DS Williams denied me access to any witnesses or reports. The police surgeon had been and gone by the time I arrived. Frankly, guv, there are only two certainties in my mind. One, this lad didn't choose a police station as a scene for suicide. Two, Stoke Newington is dirty.'

Detective Chief Inspector Maurice Young nods.

'Patrick, you'll remember your work with the UCOs.'

Noble nods.

'A recap, I think. When we were involved in the Met Race Crime Initiative debacle, you were running two undercovers. One of whom, thanks to injuries sustained at the hands of the Special Patrol Group, now lives out his days on a police pension in rural Gloucestershire cared for by his family.'

Noble looks down. He swallows.

His heart heavy, his face lined, his greying hair.

In his mouth, on his tongue, in his nose, he tastes Lea.

'The other lad distinguished himself, as you know. As you also know, he wasn't supposed to be infiltrating the group in which you placed him. He wasn't to know that, of course, so he's been treated well and deservedly so.'

Noble nods. Noble thinks, *Here we go.*

'I arranged your two-year leave of absence on the basis that the complex undercover work you were doing necessitated a rest period. You were doing a good job – the SPG incident was out of your hands – and I wanted you back working for me.'

Noble nods. 'Yes, guv.'

'The Met Race Crime Initiative was folded, quietly, after Brick Lane. Your undercover, Parker, was a helpful foil. Remember Blair Peach? It could have been worse. That the investigation was squashed cleared the path a little for you to come back.'

'Yes, guv.'

'I'm telling you this so that you are in no doubt that you're in my debt.'

'Yes, guv.'

'And because your particular brand of deception will be useful to me.'

Noble nods.

In his mouth, on his tongue, in his nose, in his throat, he tastes Lea.

'You know, of course, that spycops are UCOs placed in activist groups to root out sedition and subversive activity. I'm giving you your old friend Parker. You will place him as a spycop in any group or movement or campaign that springs up from the tragic death of Colin Roach.'

'Guv?'

'I'm giving you access. You'll have a free hand at Stoke Newington thanks to this. You understand?'

'I think I do, guv.'

'Your other old friend Bill Stewart's got Parker at the usual spot. I suggest you get over there as quickly as possible.'

'Yes, guv.' Noble stands –

In his mouth, on his tongue, in his nose, in his throat, he tastes Lea.

'I won't see you out.'

Noble nods. He leaves.

Forty-five minutes later.

Noble parks the car, opens the gate to Clapton Pond, walks through Clapton Pond, the water filthy and shallow, the shrubbery tired and sad, the ducks wading in mud –

Noble crosses the roundabout, sees Dan's Island Chinese Takeaway is still going strong, smoke from the chimney, sign half missing, MSG wafting across the road –

Noble nips down the side alley, the alley stinks of piss, knocks on the back door, the paint peeling, the wood knackered, climbs the stairs, the carpets threadbare, the walls greasy, knocks on the door –

Opens the door –

'Look what the cat dragged in,' says Old Bill Stewart.

'You didn't bring us any breakfast, guv?' says Parker.

Jesus, Noble thinks. He says, 'The state of you two.'

Noble sits down. 'I gather you're both aware of what's what.'

Nodding, hands rubbed together, fixed, determined looks –

'That mob up Stoke Newington are iffy,' Stewart says. 'It's the fucking wild east, you understand?'

'I do now,' Noble says. 'I've got access, thanks to you.' He points at Parker. 'You got any black mates that don't know you're Old Bill, son?'

Parker nods. 'One or two.'

'Give them a call,' Noble says. 'You're going to a meeting today.'

In his mouth, on his tongue, in his nose, in his throat, he tastes Lea.

Outside Panda's, Parker says, 'Is this a wind-up?'

Noble smiles. 'Clever boy.'

'You're using me again.'

'Not just me, son.'

'I'm not sure I follow.'

Noble puts a hand on Parker's shoulder. 'We're robbing Peter to pay Paul, that's what it's all about.'

'What the fuck does that mean?'

'It means you get yourself and your mates to this meeting and get in there with the protestors, OK, starting today.' Noble brushes Parker's shoulders. 'You look the part, all grown up.'

Parker shakes his head but he's smiling. 'Yeah, well.'

'All you've got to do, son, is what you're very good at doing.'

Parker rolls his eyes.

'Listen,' Noble says, 'it's a good cause, trust me. You're going through the motions but you've still got to do it right, *right*?'

'Yeah, crystal.'

'Good lad. We'll meet in that caff on Chatsworth Road tomorrow.'

A slow smile, then Parker's quickly grinning. 'That blonde, bloody hell, I remember.' He claps his hands. 'Dark horse, guv.'

'It's safe, is what it is.'

Parker laughs. 'Well, well,' he says.

'You get yourself tarted up and off to work, all right?'

Parker nods. 'I grew my hair out especially.'

'Very nice. Corduroy or leather, right-on badges, decent pair of boots. Rainbow jumper, elbow patches, that kind of thing.'

Parker nods.

'Good man.'

Noble gets straight up the road to Stoke Newington nick, parks round the side, in the front entrance, up the stairs, down the corridor, and into a smoke-filled room, a room that reeks of stale booze and coffee, of takeaway curry, of body odour and grease, a tired, strip-lit room where Williams and Cole and Rice are having a powwow –

'Morning, lads,' Noble announces. 'Where's my desk?'

Williams looks up. His hair unwashed, in clumps. Tufts peeking through his worn-out shirt, a visible string vest, a thick, sheep-shagger, valley-boy moustache –

'We've been wondering when you'd show up,' he says.

Rice and Cole don't meet Noble's eye. Williams hands Noble a piece of paper.

'Gist is, boyo,' Williams explains, 'you want any access at all, you need a written, countersigned request.'

Noble folds it and pockets it. 'Understood.'

'It's a suicide, Noble. It'll be treated as such.'

'I know.'

'The facts are the facts.'

Noble nods. 'I know.'

'Whatever it is you're doing—'

'Best you don't know, DS Williams.'

Williams nods. He glances at Rice and Cole. 'Anything you need, DC Noble –' he points a finger – 'you have the protocol.'

Noble taps his chest. 'I do.'

Noble gets on the blower and leaves word for Special Young.

What he needs –

Police Surgeon. Evidence room. Officers on duty –

In that order.

Next, he dials Gardiner's new number, moved across from Whitechapel and now resident Detective Sergeant at Hackney nick.

'Bloody hell, Chance, been a while,' Gardiner says.

'We can catch up over high tea another time, mate.'

'What can I do you for?'

'I need a list of names, women. Solicitation, known police associates, grasses, that kind of thing.'

Gardiner whistles. 'Nice and specific. Area?'

'Hackney. From your old place up to Stoke Newington.'

'Jesus, that might take a while. Be a few weeks, Chance.'

'No problem, mate,' Noble says. 'No one's going anywhere.'

He hangs up.

In his mouth, on his tongue, in his nose, in his throat, he tastes Lea.

Suzi's in her bedroom, a red light in the dark, developing the photos she took earlier at the Hackney Black People's Association meeting and the protest – the second in four days – outside Stoke Newington police station.

The meeting was electric but respectful. There were a few simple pieces of business. The Roach Family Support Committee was formed and a written resolution was drafted demanding an independent public inquiry into the death of Colin Roach.

Suzi shot in black and white.

As she dips and hangs, the faces of the hundred and fifty attendees look back at her, pinned on a washing line above her bed.

In their coats and their scarves, in their hats and their gloves, Suzi sees men and women frown and squint, glare and hold back tears, bite their

254

bottom lips. She sees ashen faces, angry faces, confused and despairing faces –

It's got the look of a memorial service about it, a state funeral.

After the meeting they took to the streets – an impromptu, as far as Suzi could tell, demand for an independent public inquiry.

Suzi had her notebook; she wasn't the only press there. She watched as uniformed police manhandled a man in leather flat cap and leather jacket with a camera around his neck. Roy Cornwall, she found out later is his name. Now she sees the image come to life. A uniform, not looking at Roy Cornwall directly, has his hand out, reaching for the camera. Next to him, a man with a fierce expression looks on, and next to him, a man with a video camera.

Behind, uniforms in and around the crowd.

The next photo develops –

Suzi saw uniforms swarm around the group nearest the police station. *Truncheons out, shields out.* She saw them identify the most vocal group. *They were chanting, Who Killed Colin Roach?* She saw the uniforms pointing, nodding, picking out a handful of young black men. *The men pinned on the ground, the uniforms kneeling two or three on each of the young black men.* She saw some of these men dragged, marched, pulled into the police station. *Arms behind their backs, fists in their sides.*

Suzi flips through her notebook. She spoke to a young black man, Delroy Thompson, who told her:

'I knew Colin Roach. I don't believe that he would go into a police station to kill himself as the police would have us believe. I took part in the first demonstration because I support the demand for an independent public inquiry. I know the truth will never come out at an inquest.'

The inquest is scheduled to start tomorrow but it was made clear in the meeting that it will be postponed immediately, until April at the earliest.

Suzi spoke to a uniform who told her:

'No comment. This is an unplanned, unorganised, illegal gathering of people and we are upholding the law by making sure they disperse in a timely and peaceful fashion.'

Another photograph is ready, this one from the meeting.

It's of the crowd, their faces, taken from near the stage –

She examines it, examines the faces.

There's one at the back that stands out.

A young white man, arms crossed, his look curious, his face open, observant –

She studies this face; she knows this face –

Jesus fucking Christ, she thinks.

The last time she saw this face was in the Bloomsbury hotel room she shared briefly with Dai Wyn.

One of the young lads.

Looking a bit older, a bit trendier, but it's definitely him.

Town hall.

Jon Davies sits in his office in the late-evening gloom with a single desk light on and lists the major flashpoints between the community and the police that he can remember over the last few years.

December 1978, Stoke Newington again, and a young black man called Michael Ferreira is stabbed in a street fight with some white youths. His friends carry him – bleeding, prone – to the police station where they would rather interrogate Michael and his friends than help them. Michael dies of his wounds before he arrives at the hospital.

April 1979, St George's Day, and the death of Blair Peach. Blair Peach lived in Hackney and was protesting the National Front in Southall when he was hit on the head by a member of the Special Patrol Group. Blair Peach dies of his injuries later that evening. As part of the internal investigation, the lockers of the SPG were searched and all sorts of things were found: non-police issue truncheons, sticks, knives, crowbars, a whip, a three-foot wooden stave, a lead-weighted leather cosh and various bits of Nazi-themed regalia. No police officer has been identified as the culprit, despite – at this point, anyway – the fourteen witnesses on record who saw the fatal blow being struck.

In February 1980, five units of the Special Patrol Group are at large in Hackney. There is no consultation in this decision. Commander Mitchell is quoted as saying, 'I don't feel obliged to tell anyone about my policing activities'.

In December 1981, a black man, Newton Rose, is convicted and imprisoned for the murder of a white man from Clapton, Anthony Donnelly, who is a known associate of prominent National Front members. The following year, Newton Rose is released due to, quote unquote, 'grave material irregularity' during the trial. Or, what they call a framing or a stitch-up.

In April 1982, a black couple, pensioners David and Lucille White, are awarded £51,000 in damages for, quote unquote, 'a catalogue of violent and inhuman treatment' from, you've guessed it, Stoke Newington police.

It's a fucking walk of shame, Jon thinks, and this is just what makes the news.

He thinks, What can we do?

He picks up his phone and dials Godfrey Heaven's home number.

He wonders what on earth Godfrey gets up to at home of an evening.

Noble's walking in his front door, the phone ringing –

'Guv?'

'Parker.'

'Just one thing I thought you should know now.'

'Go on.'

'That ginger bird from the thing at that hotel a few years ago.'

'What about her?'

'She was there today, taking photos and snooping about.'

'She on the inside?'

'Don't think so.'

'She clock you?'

'No way.'

'Have a word with the committee, vouch for her, on the sly. Reckon you can swing that?'

'Yes, guv.'

Noble nods to himself. 'See you in the morning, son,' he says.

In his mouth, on his tongue, in his nose, in his throat, he tastes Lea.

And here she is, smiling.

Lea, glass in hand, warm coat and scarf, big smile, looking up at the moon, bathed in the light of the bloody thing, eyes all over the place, glinting –

'You bring all your girls up here, do you?'

'All my girls,' Noble says, slowly. 'All my girls.' He smiles. 'Yeah, all one of them.'

Lea cosying up. 'The view's amazing. What's that, Nelson's Column?'

'Clever girl, aren't you?'

The pair of them sitting on a bench on the roof of Noble's building, drinking red wine and keeping warm by a fire in a metal bucket.

Noble poking at it, adding wood.

'No one else ever comes up here,' he's saying, 'far as I can tell.'

'Good view of that,' Lea pointing at the Post Office Tower looming above, 'tallest building in London. That why you live here?'

'Not anymore, it isn't,' Noble smiling. 'Wrong again, love.'

'Cheeky sod.'

'There's one in the city that's bigger, NatWest.'

'National Westminster. Makes sense.'

'Why's that?'

'Mrs Thatcher.'

'I suppose. You still a fan then?'

'I was never a bloody fan. She's a woman, that's all it was.'

'Didn't vote for her then?'

'Course I bloody didn't.'

Noble nodding. 'Not that it made any difference.'

'Nah, it didn't.'

'It was time for a change, the seventies were bloody awful.'

'The strikes did it.'

'Maybe.'

Noble thinking about Dai Wyn, pointing at the tower. 'You know about the bomb there about ten years ago, went off in the gents.'

Lea shaking her head.

'They keep this building very secretive. National communications, all that.'

'So how do you know about it?'

'I don't.'

Lea sniffing, sipping wine.

Noble stoking embers, teasing out a few flames from the bucket. He's shifting in his seat.

'It was some anarchist mob. The Angry Brigade was their name.'

'What was?'

'The bomb, blondie.'

'I told you not to be cheeky. I never heard of them, anyway.'

Noble smiling, his hands round Lea's face. Noble kissing her –

'They were tried, right, the "Stoke Newington Eight", they were called. Four of them got ten years.'

'What happened to the other four?'

'They calmed down.'

Lea laughing. 'Very funny.'

'Point is,' Noble's saying, 'at least one of the four didn't do it, maybe two of them. But they *had* been involved in other bombings.'

'So, what, it's OK then?'

'That's what they say. Framing a guilty man is a clever play.'

'Sounds dodgy.'

'It's complicated, is the point.'

Lea turning, eyes flashing, smile widening –

'Why are you telling me this?'

Noble turning, face opening, hands tingling –

'Because it's illustrative of what I did, what I've done, but not what I do. It's all changed, for the better.'

Lea nodding, drawing herself in –

Noble pouring wine, traffic crunching, aeroplanes humming –

'That why you went away?' Lea earnest, nodding.

Noble laughing. 'I wasn't inside, darling.'

'I know.'

'But yeah, it was.' Noble nodding now, Noble's lips wet, his eyes wet. 'I made a mistake, but I've learned from it and they've given me another chance.'

'Yeah?'

'Yeah.' Noble leaning, Noble smiling. 'Just like you have.'

'You needed it, did you, this chance?'

'I did.'

The pair of them, thinking.

PART FOUR
Doublethink

1

Buffalo Gals

February 1983

Even by Inner London standards, Hackney is an unusually underprivileged place. It has by far the highest proportion of dwellings unfit for human habitation – one in five – and by far the lowest educational attainments in London. Incomes in Hackney are the lowest in London, and well below the national averages despite much higher-than-average housing and transport costs.

From *Inside the Inner City: Life Under the Cutting Edge*
by Paul Harrison, 1983

Parker

Key thing is to use your copper nous without giving yourself away. What you can do is offer an insight, you see, you can show them things they don't know and make yourself invaluable as a result. Take this example: protest number three is the first organised by the Roach Family Support Committee and so the first where the numbers are a little better-looking but also the first when the police know what to expect and can get themselves organised and treat it like a march, a rally, which means they can control it, which means that they can arrest anyone for whatever the fuck they like. So, it's no surprise that the number of collars goes up, again, to twenty-five, from seventeen week before, and a handful week before that. Point is that the campaign is legit now, taken over by the committee and not just family and friends, it's organised, and it's intended as peaceful and it's pushing for an independent public inquiry. But the police don't like it, in their eyes there is no need for one, no right to one, so they criminalise all involvement wherever they can. One lad you've been seeing around, Delroy, is charged with threatening behaviour and carrying an offensive weapon. You're sure he ain't carrying nothing at all, but no one's going to prove that at this point: the collar's made based on an assumption, ratchet up the sheet and the kid's in more trouble – before he gets his brief. So you tell Delroy to appeal, and to stress the offensive weapon part is especially heinous, and that'll make the uniform who booked him a little nervous and suddenly there's a chance it'll get thrown out. Same for this student, an activist-type, Chas Holmes, who gets pulled and charged with obstruction. You see young Chas, who ain't especially naughty, you see him with your own eyes as he intervenes as another lad is collared. His intervention: asking for the lad's name and address. Not an illegal act. You tell Chas to watch the evidence, the copper's *claiming young Chas put him in a headlock, and you tell Chas that'd be assault not obstruction, so keep your eyes and ears about you. Noble has a good idea then, which is all about getting yourself in there further by helping with strategy. And this is achieved by suggesting to the committee the sorts of questions that need to be asked, questions that Noble feeds you based on what he's finding out, but he doesn't tell you why, or what the answers are. Questions like: what position was Colin Roach's body lying in when he was discovered? How many officers were present when he was discovered? What objects, if any, were in contact with his body and where exactly were they when he was discovered? Where is the bag Colin was carrying and how big is it? Was Colin wearing gloves or not? These questions get you a little further up in the considerations of the committee, and so when they identify a need for an official photographer, and someone mentions a redhead, you're able to vouch for her and help her get the nod ahead of some other blokes. And then when the Stoke Newington and Hackney Defence Campaign gets to work as more people are arrested with each week that goes by, your nous, your copper savvy, is employed to good effect, and you keep your head down but you dole out little bits and bobs, and you're trusted, but you keep well away from the redhead and you're grooming a few lads for some other bits and bobs, hanging around parks and caffs together, pub arcade machines and kebab shops, playing football, the odd drink, the odd mosey-about down by the canal of a weekend, up by the marshes watching Sunday League, and that's when one of these lads tells you about a lad who knows a lad who knows a certain Dalston Yardie who is very unhappy about certain new markets being taken over by certain dirty coppers, and that if you need to know where to buy your crack cocaine you need to start by looking up in Stoke Newington. Same day, someone tells you the Roach Family Support Committee has written to the home secretary, so let's see, and there's a bit of optimism about the place, and you like that, it feels good, like you're on the winning team, the moral victory anyway.*

Mrs Thatcher is on the telephone again to Willie Whitelaw. Willie's doing a lot of talking and she, Mrs Thatcher, really wants to get on –

'I'll stop you there, Willie, if I may?' she says.

Willie's silence is gratifying.

'You know where we stand on this issue, it's an election year. What we say, Willie, is that we, and this is the wording I want you to use, "we accept that there is a need for a full independent and public inquiry into the matter" and we explain that this need is fully satisfied by the inquest procedure, by an inquest itself.'

'I understand, Prime Minister, but—'

'Yes, Willie, an inquest is an inquiry to be held in public and not a public inquiry, I know, we all know the difference, but there are to be no buts, no exceptions, I leave it with you, yours in all good, et cetera. OK?'

And she, Mrs Thatcher, hangs up.

She thinks, MPs can think what they like, sign what they like. It takes time, of course.

There's no honour in hedging, Willie, she thinks, cooking up the new Police Bill at the same time as dithering over public inquiries –

'You'd think he's gone soft.' Denis shuffles past, muttering. 'Flabby, more like.'

Quite.

Of course, what the new Police Bill will do is punish people on the streets for the kind of criminal or anti-social behaviour that other government bills and acts have created the conditions for, that *explain* this behaviour, in fact: poor housing, unemployment and so on.

No point being Janus-faced about this, at least in private.

Thatcherism, she thinks, is a term she's beginning to hear a lot more often.

She, Mrs Thatcher, is rather pleased.

It's a little after five in the morning and Suzi is standing on the top deck of an open-air London Routemaster bus looking through a pair of binoculars at the sun rise over Paul Weller, who is sitting on a rocking chair on top of a hill in Malvern, Worcestershire.

They're in Malvern to shoot the video for The Style Council's first single, 'Speak Like a Child'. The premise is: pratting about in the countryside.

Suzi and Keith are there to make up the numbers, for the beano, as Keith put it.

Paul Weller and Mick Talbot and Tracie Young, who sings backing vocals on the single, and Nicky Weller and a few others are all going to be in the video.

Suzi said yes as she wanted out of London for a bit, and she's never been on a video shoot –

Turns out it's a very budget-driven business.

Tim Pope is the director and to achieve his vision, to get that sunrise moment, the £15,000 budget is spent on a hotel for everyone, the Routemaster and the rocking chair.

Suzi's got permission to take photographs and notes and she's thinking of pitching the experience as a piece; someone will have a couple of thousand words and half a dozen images on anything Paul Weller's up to at the minute, so shrouded in secrecy it is ever since he broke up The Jam. Clever boy.

It's a very beautiful morning. There is snow on the hills, ice on the trees, crisp sunny air –

A couple of the girls – including Suzi's old friend The Child – and one of the boys are dressed as hippies in pink kaftans and hats, white thigh boots and short skirts, that kind of thing. Tim Pope shoots them in the mist on a hill dancing and playing plastic trumpets.

Then they're on the bus and Paul Weller's wearing a sharp raincoat and a checked scarf and his hair's been cut, and he's miming along, ducking branches as the bus careens around, wry smile, trying not to lose balance. Tracie Young is in a black dress, black coat, black hat and looks very cool sitting at the back of the bus miming her bits.

Then they've got the rocking chair and Mick Talbot's organ into an icy, muddy field, Paul Weller's taken his raincoat off, he's wearing a natty block-colour jumper, blue, green, white, the dancers circling, twirling umbrellas, Suzi up the hill with Tim Pope to get the side of the Route-master, on which is daubed in child-like handwriting:

really free ← aren't we!?!

There's a ridge in the mist, the sun creeping through, and Paul Weller and Tracie Young and Mick Talbot shiver and smile their way through the number again.

Tim Pope goes, That'll do, guys. I'm going to fill it with trippy colours like graffiti and whatnot and it'll be the business.

Then it's back to the hotel bar –

And they're playing the game where they pretend to interview Paul Weller, with Mick Talbot being Timmy Mallet, and Paul Weller gets stuck in for fun and they're all laughing –

I hate all the wimp, pop music we get over here, like Duran Duran and all these creeps.

Kajagoogoo?

Same thing.

Eddy Grant?

No, he's useless, though quite a good songwriter.

Keith nudges Suzi and she makes a face, *What*?

She does like Eddy Grant, though.

Well, is there anything currently out in Britain that you like?

Oh yeah! Culture Club are great! George has got a brilliant voice. Fun Boy Three are brilliant.

Favourite record in the charts at the moment?

Orange Juice with 'Rip it Up', the 12-inch version especially.

Paul Weller then sits down next to Suzi, and he's holding a folder and he wants her opinion on a couple of promo photographs for the single, taken in Boulogne a couple of weeks before.

'Course, Paul,' Suzi says. 'Let's have a look then.'

Paul Weller takes out the photographs. Suzi examines them –

'Who took them?'

Paul Weller tells her that Peter Anderson took the photographs.

Suzi nods. She looks at them and then holds one up, says, 'This one.'

Paul Weller nods.

It's a shot of Paul Weller and Mick Talbot beside a wall which has been spray-painted with the slogan, YANK BASES OUT and, in smaller writing, WHOSE CONTINENT IS THIS? OURS OR THE USA?

Paul Weller tells Suzi they want to put 'a record by new Europeans' on the image and translate it into a load of languages.

Suzi nods. 'Clever boy,' she says.

Paul Weller grins.

On the hotel bar stereo a very odd song comes on, weird screaming, records scratched, samples, repetitive synths –

'What the fuck is this?' someone asks.

Suzi thinks it's some sort of avant-garde performance.

Keith yells out, 'All that scratching is making me itch!' and everyone laughs.

'See?' Keith is saying. 'Punk is dead, and Mr Weller here worked that out long ago.'

'Who *is* this?' someone asks.

'Malcolm McLaren,' Keith declares. 'The godfather of punk. Song's called "Buffalo Gals". They go round the outside, you see,' he adds, thoughtfully.

'It's a bloody racket.'

'Mark my words,' Keith says, 'he's onto something.'

'*On* something more like,' someone says and, again, everyone laughs.

'Brooklyn, Harlem, Queens, the projects, you know,' Keith proposes. He nods at the ceiling. 'They're all at it, dance parties like this. It's political, innovation through necessity.'

Paul Weller puts the photographs away, thanks Suzi, stands –

*

Back home, listening to Eddy Grant, Suzi's looking at her notes for the Roach Family Support Committee bulletin.

There's a disconnect concerning perceived relations between the black community and the police. The reality is that there is a fracturing of those making the law and those enforcing it.

She'd been reading the *Hackney Gazette* and the name Godfrey Heaven kept cropping up, chair of the new Police Committee on the council.

She telephoned him and got some lovely soundbites.

'Sir Kenneth Newman. The Metropolitan Police Commissioner. He has absorbed seriously large amounts of Management Theory of the less immediately helpful kind, which inflects his every pronouncement. Ploughing through his written output is unrewarding; the local bobbies roll their eyes. He doesn't understand what loosely might be called the sociology of black London families, highlighting the law-abiding religiously observant mothers of the young black men who are not getting on with his officers.'

Suzi likes his style.

'The Hackney Council Police Committee is statutory only in the sense that it has the local authority's administrative machine behind it and that the members are elected representatives of the people and a few co-options from relevant organisations like the Community Relations Council. The actual police authority for London is the home secretary. Make of that what you will.'

Suzi told Godfrey Heaven he sounded like a trendy. What were his credentials?

'Do I know of what I speak so volubly and which causes such obvious pain to the Thatcherites? As it happens, yes, I am well equipped, having lived in John Campbell Road and seen the riots of 1981 up close. The police stole our dustbin lids to use as shields. And the next year walking to the town hall along Sandringham Road, part of which was then known as the front line. I may come across to many as a young whippersnapper who has swallowed a dictionary but I live in and know well this borough. One of the most striking and damning traits of the police is their often-reported informal advice to middle-class householders to get out while you can.

'No doubt there is a strong canteen culture of hostility to black men, in particular, at this time from the police on the street. The faltering attempts to deal with it include lines of senior police officers down at Roots Pool in Montague Road on familiarisation courses. The vogue phrase is "Inner City". We are becoming a sink borough.'

Suzi thinks, What's the first thing that upsets the committee, the family?

The white politician lens.

She writes:

Who can blame them when cause and effect is so blatantly reversed?

She thinks, A piece on the breakdown of community and police relations.

Jon Davies sits on his bicycle and watches the boy run across the playground of Rushmore Infants' School to his friends, Shaun, Wally, Shuhel and Simeon. He seems happy, very happy and relaxed, his son.

It's been a difficult couple of weeks for him.

One afternoon after school, waiting for Jackie to pick him up, he was pushed into the narrow corridor where they hang their coats and his face scratched from temple to chin with a signet ring by an older boy from the Junior school over the road.

The scratch didn't look too clever, but it was only a scratch, so they weren't too worried about his physical state.

He came out into the main corridor looking a bit shaken, and his teacher, Mrs Wilson, saw him and she got hold of Mrs Walkinshaw, and while the boy recovered in her office, her secretary feeding him biscuits and juice, Mrs Walkinshaw got hold of the older boy.

Jon doesn't know exactly what happened, what Mrs Walkinshaw said or did, but that boy – that *young man*, he was fourteen, for fuck's sake – would never set foot in the Infants' school again.

What was he doing there at all? Jackie asked, reasonably.

He didn't know, apparently.

Why my son, what did he do to deserve this? Jackie in tears now.

There was no reason at all, it was random.

What do I tell my boy? Jackie asked.

And this is what Mrs Walkinshaw said:

He's a clever boy, your son. You tell him the truth: a big boy with serious mental health problems did it because he wanted to hurt someone, anyone, because he is unwell, and he wanted to feel something. He will get the help he needs, and in the meantime, he will be punished, and my pupils will be told that bullying is wrong, whatever the reason for it.

Fair play, Jon thinks, it worked.

Mrs Walkinshaw knows their son, he'll give her that.

He doesn't seem hugely traumatised, seems to have understood it was nothing to do with *him*, which is the point.

Mrs Walkinshaw bustles towards Jon, waving hello.

He smiles back.

She says, nodding over at the boy and his friends, 'He's doing very well, Jon, he's a good kid.'

Jon smiles. 'Takes after his mother.'

Mrs Walkinshaw punches Jon playfully on the shoulder, quite hard. 'You're all right, Jon,' she says.

They stand together quietly for a moment, looking out at the school, its matching halves, its stock and red brick, its slate roofs and brick chimney stacks, its gables at east and west, its large rectangular windows, its red roof tiles –

'That older boy,' Mrs Walkinshaw says, 'he's been taken into care.'

Jon nods.

'His family situation is undesirable. His father is absent and his mother is having problems.'

'That's sad,' Jon says.

'It is. These young black boys without male role models, they can struggle.'

'I understand.'

Mrs Walkinshaw nods over, again, at the boy and his friends. 'He lived on the same estate as Shaun – Pembury.'

Jon nods.

He's been there a few times to pick the boy up after some sports team or other.

They're decent footballers, these kids, better than he was at their age.

More organised, more focused –

'It has its problems,' Mrs Walkinshaw says, 'but it's a community too. Like us, we're a community.'

'We are, Mrs Walkinshaw,' Jon says, though he's not exactly sure how figurative she's being.

'Just remember we're all part of a community,' she adds, smiling.

Jon nods. 'We are.'

Mrs Walkinshaw breathes noisily, smiles. 'You're a good man, Jon Davies.'

'It's a dirty job,' Jon jokes, 'but someone's got to do it.'

They both laugh at that, loudly enough that there's some shaking of heads in the playground, some mutterings of embarrassment –

Town hall.

Jon Davies and Godfrey Heaven stand over Jon's desk and look again at the wording of their proposed motion:

'That the council take whatever steps are open to it to withhold the payment of the police precept both as an expression of anger at the state of policing in Hackney and with a view to bringing home to the Government the community demands for an independent inquiry into policing in Hackney.'

'Four million quid, isn't it, this precept?' Jon asks.

Godfrey Heaven nods.

'They'll want to know what we intend to do with it instead,' Jon says.

Godfrey Heaven nods again.

'Any thoughts, Godfrey?' Jon asks.

Godfrey Heaven smiles. 'To that question, Jon, another question: are there not, in fact, better ways to spend this money that will reduce crime?'

'You'll say there are better ways of reducing crime than funding the police.'

'No, not exactly. Defunding the police frees up the budget to tackle the *roots* of crime, the inequality caused by the Thatcher government's utter lack of interest in the working class and the underprivileged.'

'But how, exactly? You're going to buy some playgrounds or what?'

'It doesn't matter, Jon, the conversation is what matters.'

'And if we win?'

'We won't win.'

Jon scratches his cheek. 'I don't follow, Godfrey, I have to say.'

'Oh, we'll pass the motion at committee, no bother whatsoever. We're the ascendant party. But it's a gesture, Jon, that's all, a vote of no confidence in the police. We can't withhold the money; it would be illegal, and the council is not going to break the law.'

'OK.'

'And there's more to the gesture than that too, Jon.'

'I expect you're about to tell me what it is, Godfrey.'

Godfrey Heaven smiles. 'By making the gesture, Jon, we are demonstrating that we are paying up under protest: we hand over our ratepayers' money every year to the police, and yet, Jon, London is unique in this country in not having an elected police authority. This is the point, Jon, and this is what we'll tell the press. London boroughs are all coming to the same conclusion.'

'They'll have a bloody field day,' Jon sighs, 'the press will.'

'As our esteemed colleague Patrick Kodikara said to me only yesterday, Jon: "Thirty per cent of the ratepayers of Hackney are black. Why should the council pay the police to practise repression on us?"'

'It's a good question,' Jon says.

*

Noble's had a busy couple of weeks. He's interviewed the duty officers, he's interviewed the police surgeon, he's read the transcripts, he's read the reports, he's read the witness statements.

He's gathered what appears to be the correct version of events, a version that establishes a very murky timeline, a confusing and contradictory set of circumstances.

Old Special Young has asked for an update, a report, a bald and simple statement of Noble's findings, but, crucially, no names, no dates, no references –

Noble's got the feeling that Young wants deniability. He reckons Young might be passing this little document up the food chain; he doesn't know to who or why or what purpose that'd serve, but there you go.

Noble thinks, I'm just like Parker.

He sits at his kitchen counter, blank page and biro. He sips his tea, chews on his toast. He thinks, Clear and simple.

He writes:

It is the view of the police that the victim died of a self-inflicted shotgun wound to the head in the foyer of a London police station.

The victim entered the police station of their own free will.

The victim's friends confirm that the victim believed that "someone was out to get them" and sought refuge in the police station.

The victim was carrying a sports bag; it is the view of the police that the shotgun was inside this sports bag.

Said sports bag is not big enough to hold a weapon of this size.

The position of the victim's body and the position of the shotgun are not consistent with a self-inflicted shotgun wound owing to the recoil of a weapon of that nature.

Two officers were on duty; their accounts are contradictory.

According to their accounts, other officers were first on the scene, and the body and the objects around it were in different positions.

Shotgun cartridges were first discovered in the victim's jacket pocket by, it is claimed, two different officers.

No fingerprints were found on these cartridges.

No fingerprints were found on the shotgun.

The victim was not wearing gloves.

Both accounts state that the body and the objects around it were not touched until a forensic team arrived.

The precise time of death is unknown, given between 11.30 p.m. and 12 a.m.; this is inconsistent with the nature of logging activity in a police station.

It is unclear as to whether there was an officer present on the front desk when the victim entered the foyer.

Noble folds the page, no longer blank, puts the folded page into an envelope, licks the envelope, seals the envelope, puts the sealed envelope into his inside jacket pocket, puts his jacket on, calls out to Lea, 'I'm off then!' and waits, a moment, to hear her soft groan of assent, of goodbye, and he smiles and he leaves –

Godfrey Heaven puts Suzi onto a very interesting bit of research carried out by John Fernandes, a black sociologist who teaches at the Hendon Police Cadet School.

Suzi's studying it now.

Fernandes has taught at Hendon since the mid-seventies, and now heads up a multicultural studies course, thanks to Lord Scarman's recommendation that there needs to be improved race relations within the Metropolitan Police.

Suzi thinks, Too right there does.

As part of the course, Fernandes asks new cadets to write essays on black people in Britain, sixty-two students, sixteen-year-olds many of them, straight out of school, training to police the streets of London, the diverse, multicultural streets of London, streets filled with black, brown, Asian faces –

Fernandes published his findings, disclosed his results –

There was quite an uproar.

At best, it was believed that the questions were somehow set to prompt a desired response, loaded.

At worst, it was believed that some responses were a joke, or even false responses, fakes.

An internal inquiry establishes neither of these is true.

The essays were anonymised, no names, no way of identifying which cadet wrote what.

Two examples from these essays:

Blacks in Britain are a pest. They never seem to work at a legal job (except as doctors) but seem to exist off sponging off the welfare state to which decent tax-paying, white, law-abiding citizens like myself contribute.

The black people in Britain claim they are British ... This is just a load of junk ... If the blacks were deported back to Africa or wherever they came from there would be less unemployment ... Putting it bluntly: 'Kick them Out'.

There were, Suzi reads, a dozen essays with similar comments.

Over half the respondents, Fernandes writes, showed hostility to black people in offensive terms. The other half were a mix of neutral or positive.

She thinks of something Godfrey Heaven said to her when she spoke to him on the telephone:

'Personally, dealing with ordinary beat cops, I am struck by how poorly educated and slightly adrift some of them are.'

Suzi reads about Les Curtis, the chairman of the Police Federation, which represents approximately 120,000 police officers. He is asked if an officer should be dismissed if he were to use a racially charged epithet to address a citizen or a suspect, to use racial invective or offensive language.

Les Curtis' response is that it's like calling an Australian a Pommie or a Londoner a Cockney.

'It's a common phrase that is used throughout the land,' Les Curtis is quoted as saying. 'And what about the colour nigger brown? Are we to change those sorts of things?'

Suzi thinks that Colin Roach dying on the police's doorstep – literally, *on their doorstep* – is shocking enough, but it's the little regard the police have for it that might be even worse.

The treatment: they're giving the whole community the treatment.

Suzi writes, Whose lives matter?

Keith comes out of the bedroom rubbing his eyes and scratching his chest.

'Tea, love?' he says.

'Kettle's on, love.'

'So it is.'

Keith leans over Suzi's papers. ''Allo, 'allo, 'allo, what's all this then?'

'Work, Keith,' Suzi says.

Keith makes a noise. 'When's the next march?' he asks.

'Saturday, love.'

Keith pouts, nods. 'That's the twelfth, right?'

Suzi nods.

'I'm coming with, then,' Keith declares. 'Do what's right.'

Suzi smiles.

Jon Davies and Godfrey Heaven have the conservative tabloid newspapers spread out in front of them on Jon's desk, the *Mail*, the *Express*, the other two –

Valentine's Day, 1983, Monday morning, and Jon thinks poor old Godfrey Heaven has been proper stitched up.

Godfrey's having a bit of a rant.

'So the *Mail* and the *Express* have both done hatchet jobs on me employing the not very subtle, and, by the way, Jon, wholly untrue, suggestion that this is all being got up by white lefties, of whom I am supposed to be some sort of lead agitator. They have gone to an enormous amount of trouble. On Saturday at the Colin Roach march, I modestly hung back from the front rank. They joined the interior of the march, furnished me in my innocence with a standard placard, then got their photo of me holding it.'

'I can see the photos, Godfrey.'

'It's outrageous. In fact, as we both know, Jon, the critical accelerator in the Colin Roach publicity has little to do with me, but in fact is all about the extraordinary number of arrests outside Stoke Newington police station, which have alerted the national media, who have come to me, and then Ernie Roberts, MP for Hackney North, in the first instance.'

'I don't disagree, Godfrey.'

'It's a stitch-up, Jon.'

'It is.'

'A Valentine's Day massacre.'

'I said you were becoming a wag, Godfrey.'

'At least I wasn't arrested.'

'It might have been better if you had been.'

Godfrey Heaven nods. 'Only nine this week, but it's nine more than it should be,' he says.

18 February.

Over three hundred people attend the funeral of Colin Roach.

In the days that follow, the Roach Family Support Committee writes to all Hackney councillors asking them to vote to withhold the police precept payment, to hold a vote of no confidence in the Stoke Newington police, and to 'break links' with the police until an independent public inquiry into the death of Colin Roach is held.

Godfrey Heaven shows Jon his copy of the letter.

Jon says, 'Break links is a good phrase.'

'It'll be more than that, Jon, if the national campaign against the Police Bill gets going.'

Jon nods. 'Based in Stoke Newington.'

'Fifty Rectory Road.'

'I've heard the GLC have kicked in thirty-eight thousand pounds. Do you know if that's true?'

Godfrey Heaven winks. 'I couldn't tell you, Jon.'

23 February, town hall.

Jon signs off on the motion to withhold the police precept of £4 million. An easy win, as Godfrey Heaven predicted: all Labour and Liberal councillors voted for, all Conservatives against.

The Loony Left, according to the tabloids. Cut their funding, is the cry.

In parliament, Hackney Central MP Clinton Davis: My own local authority may be very frustrated – sometimes with justification – by some of the actions, or the inaction, of the local police. The suggestion of the withdrawal of the police precept is, however, an empty but unacceptable gesture which increases the anxiety of many of my constituents – particularly the elderly – that the police are suddenly to be withdrawn. But, of course, that will not happen. When I spoke to Councillor Heaven, the chairman of the Police Liaison Committee, he readily agreed that it would not happen. It is a gesture – a vote of no confidence in the police – but I do not believe that such a gesture is justified by the circumstances. If we are to make constructive criticisms about the police, as sometimes we must and as I do today, it does not add to the authority of those who support such criticism to join in every meaningless gesture and every attack on the police.

In The Times *newspaper, 24 February 1983:* Tower Hamlets Council is to be asked on Tuesday to follow the Hackney Council example and consider withholding the Metropolitan Police rate precept. The Newham Monitoring Project is to call upon the local council to do the same unless an independent inquiry into Forest Gate police station in Newham is set up. Mr Unmesh Desair, the project's full-time worker, yesterday described the station as a 'torture chamber'.

*

Noble goes over to the Turkish drinking club to have a chinwag with the manager.

The manager shrugs. He gestures at the empty room –

'Protection and slot machines. They collect. Sometimes in person, sometimes someone else.'

'Who else?'

'Sometimes younger men, sometimes a woman.'

'A woman?'

'Yeah, pretty woman, bit old, yeah, but you know, you would do, given half a chance.'

He's laughing now, the manager. Noble isn't.

'What else?'

'Here, nothing. Up the road, well –'

'Where up the road?'

The manager sniffs. 'You didn't hear it from me, right, but have a look at the first fashion retailer past the mosque. Downstairs, OK. Tell them you want to see the new imports.'

He's laughing again. 'Subtle like a brick in the face!'

Noble says, 'This conversation never happened.'

'Suits me, boss,' the manager says. 'Come by for a drink sometime, I make special price for you.'

'You're not kidding,' Noble says.

Up the stairs, out the door, turn left, past the mosque, past the luminous pink-and-orange handwritten signs announcing sales and closures, all sizes and all fashions, into the shop-front door, past the piles of coats, the piles of hats, the piles of shoes, down the stairs, the damp stairs, threadbare carpets, walls peeling, a smell of rough cigarettes and herbal tea –

'What the fuck do you want?'

A man behind a counter scowling.

'I'm after some new imports,' Noble says.

The man – four-day stubble, red eyes, sweat on his neck – sniffs. 'White or brown?'

Noble's had something in mind for a while, something Parker told him –

'I've heard there's something new.'

The man runs his tongue over his teeth, hacks, swallows.

'We don't do that here.'

'No?'

The man shakes his head. He spits on the floor.

'Why's that then?'

The man shrugs.

Noble sees two other men further back behind the counter, sitting at a table, smoking, drinking tea.

He nods in their direction. 'This is a social club, is it?'

The man puts his hands on the counter. 'Fashion emporium,' he says. 'White or brown.'

The man smiles.

Noble says, 'Second thoughts, I'm all right.'

The man raises an eyebrow, smiles again –

He ain't bothered, Noble thinks. Which means Stoke Newington's finest likely have an interest.

'I'll see myself out,' Noble says, cheerfully.

The man points at the stairs, the door.

Noble finds a little Turkish café across the road and orders herbal tea and a kebab.

The tea tastes like piss.

He waves his teacup at a waitress. 'Be a good girl and get us a lager, darling.'

He uses the phone and calls West End Central to check his messages. There's one from Gardiner.

He dials Hackney nick and Gardiner's extension.

'About time,' Noble says. 'Shall I come and pick it up or do you fancy a pint?'

'Does the Pope wear a silly hat?'

'Easy, I'm Irish, mate.'

Gardiner laughs. 'But without the luck.'

In the public bar of the Crown on Mare Street, top of the Narrow Way, winter sun fighting to get through the stained glass, blowing on his hands, cold in his bones, stamping his feet, Noble spots Gardiner and nods and points to say, I'll have what you're having.

Noble finds a table through the glass door.

Gardiner dumps two pints and two packets of Beef and Onion.

He raises a glass. 'In honour of the Met Race Crime Initiative,' he says.

Noble gulps beer, laughs. 'Pint of Special, is it?'

Gardiner winks. He takes a piece of paper from his inside pocket, pushes it across the table.

Noble nods. 'Ta,' he says. He has a look –

Names, names, names, women's names –

Gardiner half-sings, 'Oh East London, is wonderful, oh East London is wonderful—'

Noble looks up, shakes his head.

Gardiner ups the volume. 'It's full of tits, fanny and West Ham.'

Noble says, 'Give it a rest, eh.'

Gardiner raises his eyebrows. He gestures at the list. 'Anyone you like?'

'Yeah, three-thirty at Chepstow, number six.'

'Very good, Chance. Seriously.'

Noble scans the page –

A name jumps out, screams out –

'Yeah,' he says, pocketing the paper. 'She's not a dead cert—'

'But I'll have her each way!' Gardiner pissing himself laughing at the joke.

'I need to use the telephone,' Noble says.

He dials Parker's number. Parker sounds half-asleep.

'Wake up, you dozy cunt,' Noble tells him. 'And get yourself to Queensbridge Road in half an hour.'

'I've got workers' rights, you know,' Parker grumbles.

'Union of one, son. Get a move on.'

Three-quarters of an hour later, in Dawn Driscoll's council flat on the Holly Street Estate, Noble and Parker stand over a bath, a bath half full of dirty water.

The water is warm, putrid, a layer of scum, thick, clotted –

The bathroom window smashed.

Syringes on the floor, pipes on the floor, foil burnt and crumpled –

The grey sky visible. The damp, white, freezing sky –

The council estate grey, cold. Windows slammed shut, steam.

Voices and coughing, sniffing and hacking –

Kettles whistle, kids shout, television sets crackle and shriek.

Radios play Dionne Warwick singing about all the love in the world.

Parker says to Noble, 'She's not in then.'

Noble gestures at the floor. 'It doesn't look too clever in here, does it?'

February 1983, another day in paradise.

'Get your glad rags ready,' Noble says. 'We'll have a gander at her former work establishment.'

Parker nods at the room, ironic. 'Nice place then, is it?'

'Put it this way,' Noble says, 'we'll need a few fifty-pence pieces.'

Parker snorts. 'Bleating about workers' rights and now look at me.'

Noble shakes his head, mutters, 'You youngsters don't know you're born.'

Parker grins.

2

Total Eclipse of the Heart

March 1983

Parker

So you say to one of the lads who seems to have the knowhow that you're interested in a little draw and does he know anyone who can sort you out? Yeah, sure, I know someone. How much you want? Just a ten-draw, something like that, a little bit. Yeah, that's easy, mate. Tell you what, meet me this afternoon on Hackney Downs and I'll have it for you. Yeah? Yeah, course. You give him a tenner, he goes, Beautiful, and grins, and you think, All right, step by step, easy does it. Don't fuck this up. You spend the rest of the morning at the RFSC office on Rectory Road, and you're having a nose-around as there's no one there and the place is trebling up as the home of the RFSC and also the Stoke Newington and Hackney Defence Campaign, and the Hackney Campaign Against the Police Bill, so you're having a butcher's about the place to see where there is any overlap and whether the people running it all are in any way competent, as you ain't sure, you think so, but in the end what can you do but pester the home secretary and organise marches? In the back office, the door half-jammed and unlocked for once, behind frosted glass, you find what you're looking for: a ledger. Where's the money coming from and why is always a good question. You open it up and look for the bigger numbers. It's a bit of a mess and the donations and pledges for the three campaigns seem blurred – you're looking for repeat amounts or names and you've got to be quick as you're expecting a few others to arrive soon, and then you see 1,500 – GLC, and then 38,000 – GLC and you think, Hello. You leave the ledger where you found it and slip back out the door and leave that as it was, someone was in a rush last night, and back to photocopying flyers and stacking leaflets. After lunch you wander over to Hackney Downs and some of the lads are kicking a football about, a couple of others chatting, and your mate gives you the nod and you sit down under a tree and he palms a clingfilm-wrapped brown rectangle into your jacket pocket and says, Have a nice trip, and laughs. Next day you find him again and tell him, Fuck me, mate, that was good stuff, any chance of any more, a fair bit more in fact, I've got a couple of mates interested, and he goes, I'll have a word with the guy I know and we'll see, yeah? You nod, you understand, you know the score with this kind of thing, so yeah, relaxed, whenever, yeah. And in the meantime, he says, and winks, pulling out a spliff. Nice one, you tell him, and you smoke it on the Downs and lie back and watch the grey sky crack and dissolve in the cold, watch your breath float up and you're quiet and it's cold on the ground – Come on, you say, I've got the fucking munchies, let's get something to eat, and your mate laughs at this, Again! You're on it, mate, and he laughs all the way to the Jamaican place Granny's, just before Lower Clapton Road, and you get in there and have some rice and peas and chicken, and you ain't ever been in there before, never quite had the bottle, a big young white cunt in boots is not your normal clientele in Granny's, but your mate here vouches for you and Granny herself gives you a big grin and tells you you're welcome any time. Two days after this and your mate has some news for you – Yeah, answer's yes, in principle, but he wants to meet you, that all right? And you say, that's fine, mate, not a problem, and your mate says, Look, it's not the friend I told you about, yeah, it's the next one up. OK, you say. Yeah, he says, but it's easy, it's the same thing, they just wanna know if you're on the level, and anyway, I vouched for you. On the level? you bristle, playing up, Course I'm on the fucking level. Calm down, big boy, it's more that there might be an opportunity, you're white, you've got mates, some mutual benefit. That all, is it? Yeah, swear, relax. Fine yeah, that's fine, just tell me where and when, yeah.

Mrs Thatcher sighs. Denis has just reminded her of Sir Ronald Bell, arch right-wing agitator and member of the Monday Club. His key line quoted in *The Times* in 1980, something about how immigrants were resolutely *not* forming a polite queue to be paid to leave the country, and how that was a bad thing. Repatriation as a policy has been a dead duck for some time.

Sir Ronald, of course, is no longer a problem, also being a dead duck.

Last year, in his Commons office, right in the middle of having sex with a woman who was not his wife.

'Died smiling then,' Denis consoles.

Things have changed since 1980, Mrs Thatcher knows this. She's not entirely unaware that things have changed.

The issue is no longer about immigration; the issue is about race.

All this send them back, taking our jobs –

It's simply not true. Over the last decade or so, more people have emigrated than have been allowed in, and despite a rising birth rate, the population has more or less plateaued.

So why is immigration still a problem?

She, Mrs Thatcher, remembers 1979, a time when one could say things that now, in 1983, one can't.

The Vietnamese refugee crisis, the UN appeal to Britain to take on 10,000 'boat people', the GLC – Tory-run in those days, unlike now, of course, led by that 'IRA-loving, poof-loving Marxist' to quote the *Sunday Express* – offering four hundred homes for the families, staunch Willie Whitelaw telling her how the public is moved by the footage played on the television, boats and boats fit to bursting with teeming families, foreign secretary Lord Carrington telling her we must, it's good form, they're all pouring into Hong Kong, and that's ours after all, and the government there needs our help, the Home Office telling her there's a bulging bag of letters telling us we should offer help –

'All those who wrote letters,' Mrs Thatcher said, 'should be invited to accept a refugee in their homes.'

See how they like that.

She, Mrs Thatcher, told the GLC that 'it's quite wrong that immigrants should be given council housing whereas white citizens were not'.

In 1980, this would not have been called racism; it was about national identity.

So, what's changed?

It's about race, not immigration. It's about perception.

In February 1981, unemployment rose by two-thirds, but for black people the figure was 82 per cent.

It's no longer about them coming here and taking our jobs; it's about them being here and not pulling their weight, scrounging and thieving.

One, she thinks, should know one's place.

3 March.

The home secretary Willie Whitelaw writes to the Roach Family Support Committee to explain that he agrees that a full and public inquiry is necessary but that this will be provided by the inquest.

There is a discussion going on about how to counter this obviously flawed position most effectively, and, for now, Suzi isn't offering any advice. Instead, she's volunteered to go through the mail, catalogue it. The vast majority are overwhelmingly supportive and Suzi is moved when she reads the letters, the sentiments, the offers, the pledges, the love –

Letters from Sister Asher, from the Radical Black Students Society of Sunderland Polytechnic, from SPEAR, the Solidarity of Pupils in Education Against Racism, from the General Secretary of the Students' Union at Warwick University, from the Tameside Immigration Campaigns Support Group, from the Reverend Robin Millwood of the Methodist Church and Stoke Newington Mission Circuit, from the National Convention of Black Teachers, from the Hackney branch of the Confederation of Health Service Employees, from *For Musique*, a west country-based community magazine –

Suzi scans, Suzi skims, Suzi reads:

My previous experience with the police ... my brother was being arrested ten minutes after leaving home for allegedly committing a mugging on the Narrow Way ... They abused me verbally, used violence to arrest me, then charged me with assault, criminal damage and obstruction. My brother was released without charge ... We must not give up! ... We would further like to show our support by marching with you in solidarity ... In recent years too many people, white as well as black, have died in similar mysterious circumstances in police custody. It can no longer be ignored that black youth in many of our cities are continually harassed and intimidated by police officers ... wish to extend our condolences ... we will write to the home secretary ... I was particularly impressed with the measure of codification and discipline ... my personal conviction, commitment and dedication to the total and whole liberation of oppressed and indigent people ... May the eternal light of love, i.e. concrete human love and brotherhood keep you and your committee contiguously ... peace, justice, love, brotherhood and manumission ... full support in the fight against systematic attempts on the part of the police to cover up and to obstruct any investigation ... we wish to extend our sympathy ... May I offer our support ...

She spends the morning transcribing the letters for the next RFSC bulletin.

A good typist, it doesn't take her as long as it would others, so she's happy to do it.

She finishes and thinks about lunch.

She stands, she gathers the letters, she files them neatly into a hanging file, she takes the file to the filing cabinet, she feels for the little key that is tacked against the back of the filing cabinet, she opens the filing cabinet, she finds the correct main file, she neatly slots this new file inside it, she turns –

Going into the photocopy and print room, she sees her friend again.

It's definitely him.

He hasn't seen her; his head is now bent over the copier.

Suzi hesitates –

Jon Davies decides the time is right to exploit the media coverage that the council has been receiving over the Police Committee's decision to withhold the £4 million precept, to try and find out a little more about what happened to Shahid Akhtar, or, at least, access the police files that pertain to his death. His thinking is that he'll get an audience, given the situation, and that he might be able to use it to help Mrs Akhtar.

He makes some calls.

Hackney Council, he discovers quite quickly, is not very high up the Metropolitan Police's Christmas card list.

Jon leaves the town hall, walks down Mare Street, up the Narrow Way, and into Hackney police station.

He smiles at the officer at the front desk.

'Jon Davies. I'm here from the council to see DS Williams,' Jon says. 'It's about the Met Race Crime Initiative.'

'The what?'

'The Met Race Crime Initiative.'

Jon thinks that's what it was called the last time he came here. And he *knows* the DS's name was Williams as he was Welsher than Nye Bevan –

Less of an egalitarian outlook, however.

The officer screws up his face. 'DS Williams?'

'Big old Welsh fella, you couldn't miss him.'

'I'm not sure I know what you're talking about, sir.'

Jon nods. 'Well, it was a few years ago, I suppose.' He smiles. 'You don't look much past eighteen, son. You new, are you?'

The officer nods.

'Where you from, officer?'

The boy straightens, juts his chin. 'Stevenage.'

'Right, Stevenage. So, you likely wouldn't know what was going on here five or so years ago.'

'I was in school.'

'Course you were, does you credit.'

Jon smiles. Makes a face: *come on then, you know it makes sense.*

'I'll just ring upstairs. Jon Davies, your name?'

Jon smiles yes. 'From the council's solicitors' office.'

The officer picks up the desk telephone and turns away from Jon, and Jon half-hears one side of what, for both parties, is a clearly confusing conversation.

'Follow me,' the officer says.

Up the stairs, two flights, down a corridor, into a damp grey room –

A man behind a desk says, 'Sit down, Mr Davies.'

Jon sits. 'Thank you. Detective—'

'Detective Sergeant Gardiner.'

Jon extends a hand. 'Nice to meet you, Detective Sergeant.'

Gardiner gives a weak smile and leaves Jon's hand where it is.

'What can I do for you?' he says.

'The Met Race Crime Initiative—'

'Was disbanded at the beginning of 1979.'

'Because?'

Gardiner shakes his head. 'Internal inquiry.'

'OK.'

'Again,' Gardiner says, 'what can I do for you?'

Jon leans forward. 'When the Met Race Crime Initiative was in operation, I came here to speak to a DS Williams about the death of Shahid Akhtar, who was pulled out of the canal by the Lea Bridge Road in 1978.'

'Williams has been at Stoke Newington since 1980.'

'OK.'

'Shahid Akhtar. Misadventure. Coroner's post-mortem verdict is public.' Gardiner shrugs. 'Nothing doing there. I was on the Initiative and I remember it well.'

Jon changes tack. 'Do you know about Hackney Council's Police Committee, DS Gardiner?'

'I know you don't fancy paying our wages.'

Jon nods, gives it the fair enough. 'Bit awkward, that, what with us talking now.'

'I'm not feeling awkward.'

Jon nods. 'Point is, I suppose, you'll be aware of the media attention.'

Gardiner points at the wall.

On it, tabloid cut-outs, a grainy picture of Godfrey Heaven –

'We're flattered,' Jon says.

'Why don't you get to the point, Mr Davies?'

'Acting on behalf of the Akhtar family, I formally request access to any police files pertaining to Shahid Akhtar's death and the coroner's verdict of misadventure. Our intention is to petition the home secretary for an inquest based on the content of these files.'

This is, Jon concedes privately, about half true.

'You know that I can't just hand these files over, Mr Davies, regardless.'

'So, usual protocols, is it?'

'You do know why Shahid Akhtar fell in the canal?'

'Misadventure, I suppose.'

'He had another woman up the stick. Couldn't handle the shame.'

'It's all in the file?'

'We're not a library service here.'

Jon smiles. 'Yeah, I don't see many books.'

'I suggest you leave, Mr Davies.'

Jon stands. 'I'd prepare your superiors. We don't get to look at those files, we'll have a chat with the media.'

Gardiner snorts, points again at the wall. 'They really seem to like your mob.'

Jon smiles. 'Don't be naïve, Detective Sergeant, it doesn't matter either way.'

Jon turns to leave, opens the door, turns back. 'If we're in the papers,' Jon says, 'then so are you.'

On the stairs, skipping down two at a time, Jon's heart races.

*

Noble to Parker: 'West end of Hackney Road, by the church, just before midday.'

Noble waiting in an illegally parked car on Austin Street by St Leonard's churchyard.

Parker bouncing down the road –

Noble opens the door, Parker bends and stretches, folds –

Noble pulls out, does a right round the back of the church, a left, pulls into a space by Boundary Gardens in Arnold Circus.

Parker points at the old bandstand. 'London's first housing estate.'

Noble, putting on handbrake, turning the key, pulling warrant card from glove compartment –

'You what?'

'End of the nineteenth century, guv, this was a notorious slum. The Old Nichol.'

'Thanks, professor.'

Parker hand-flourishes, quotes, '"It is but one painful and monotonous round of vice, filth and poverty."'

'Jesus.'

'Local history, guv. School, you ever been?'

Noble smiles.

'They built the estate, the park.' Parker nods. 'The bandstand.'

'Who's they?'

'Fuck knows, some cunt.'

Noble raises his eyebrows. 'You're not kidding.'

Parker opens the passenger door. 'I'm not, guv.'

Noble gets out the other side.

Across the roof, he says, 'I grew up down the road, mate. The only thing I remember about the Boundary Estate is Mick builders and Polish Jews.' He nods at an Asian family, trundling along with their shopping. 'And it's changed again.'

'London, innit.'

'Bangladeshis here.' Noble nods east. 'Bengalis in Whitechapel. You remember Altab Ali?'

'I do.'

'Well then.'

They set off, shape up. Parker lights a fag –

'Let's go and have a look at another London, shall we?' Noble says.

Parker laughs –

Five minutes later, they're at the front of Ye Olde Axe on Hackney Road and the doorman's establishing club rules –

'... no touching, no singing, no shouting, no wanking, fifty-pence a round in the glass the girl's carrying, drinks at the bar, cash up front, any nonsense and you're out.'

Noble nods. He pushes a five-pound note into the doorman's top pocket. 'Nice one,' he adds.

'Much obliged,' the doorman confirms. 'This way, gents.'

He points at the door. Parker pushes it open and gestures at Noble –

'Age before beauty.'

The doorman laughs. 'You've got both in there, son.'

Noble nudges Parker, points up at the angular clock tower, the colour of the brick, the latticework –

'Look familiar?'

Parker ushers him inside. 'Social housing.'

Noble laughs.

Inside, Noble hands Parker a tenner. 'Get us a couple of pints and some change.' He nods at the booths. 'I'll get us a table.'

The carpet, rose-patterned, smudged with stains and cigarette burns, sneaks all the way down the long, narrow room, mounts the little stage in the corner.

White-and-black checked lino floor by the bar. A couple of regulars on stools.

A pool table that's seen better days. Or not, Noble thinks, depending on what it's used for.

Corniced ceiling, dividing mirrors, faux gas lamps –

Another, cleaner, more salubrious use of this place and you're calling it a historic relic.

The seats firm, red-tinted, brown leather, wipe-clean –

The booths wide, plenty of leg room –

The banquettes wrap around the sides of each booth where they join, a prime seat at the edge of the action.

All but two of the booths, empty.

These two accommodate two men on their own, both eating packets of crisps, newspapers open, sipping slowly at their first pints of the day –

One bloke at the fruit machine, face set in grim determination, cigarette hanging from his cracked lips.

Noble settles in.

He counts three, four thin pillars roughly spaced down the corridor between the booths and the bar, green paint scratched and rubbed off where the dancers have twirled and swung, bent and spun –

Parker slides round and pushes drinks across the table. He points at the wraparound banquette. 'Called the "perv seats", apparently.' He nods at the bar, at the barmaid. 'She reckons we might want to bag one soon.'

Noble smiles. 'Getting busy, is it?'

'Friday lunchtime, mate. They do a sandwich.'

Parker makes two piles of coins in front of them. He flicks a look over Noble's shoulder. 'Oi, oi, look lively.'

A blonde in knickers carrying a pint mug smiles at them and they drop their coins into her glass. There's an echo; the early shift.

The lights dip, the disco ball shimmers –

Music starts. Bonnie bloody Tyler.

Parker grins, nods at the blonde. 'Turn around, bright eyes,' he says.

She does turn around. She turns around and around and around –

'Not her, is it?' Parker asks.

Noble shakes his head. He thinks, Where is she then?

Dawn Driscoll, Shahid Akhtar strolling in to see her, big toothy smile, wide-boy lapel, pocket watch and handkerchief, braces and belt, flashing his cash, buying her flowers –

'Total Eclipse of the Heart.'

The song grinds to a halt, the glittering stops, the lamps back on –

The blonde picks up her knickers off the floor, counts her money on the pool table.

She comes round again with her glass.

Noble picks up a fist of fifties, starts feeding them in. 'How long you been here, darling?'

She screws up her mouth. 'Three years now. It's all right. The charge ain't too bad and you keep the rest.'

'The charge?' Parker says. He nods at the bar, appalled. 'Don't tell me you pay *them*?'

'What of it?' she says. 'You pay me.'

Parker makes a face: *fair enough*. 'When you put it that way,' he says.

Noble says, 'Dawn on later, is she?'

'Dawn? That a stage name?'

'You never work with a girl called Dawn?'

'I never.' She nods at the barmaid. 'She might know her. She's been here donkeys.'

'Right.' Noble stands. He smiles at the blonde. 'Can I get you a drink, love?'

'Babycham,' she winks.

'Nothing sparkles like one,' Parker says, doing the advert.

'I'll leave you two to get to know each other.'

At the bar, post-pleasantries, Noble says, 'I'm looking for someone, an ex-employee of yours.'

'Oh yeah?' The barmaid pulling pints, feigning indifference.

'Yeah, a dancer.'

The barmaid snorts. 'Well, fella, I didn't think you were after the chef.'

Noble smiles. 'Dawn, her name. Dawn Driscoll.'

'Dawn, you say.' She's nodding now, the barmaid.

'Dawn Driscoll.'

The barmaid snags the attention of one of the regulars. He's turned back to face the bar now the dance is over, nursing a whisky with his lager.

'When was the last time you saw Cracker in here?' she asks him.

He's the picture of deep thought for a moment, this regular. 'Cracker Dawn? I'd say four years.'

'Cracker Dawn?' Noble says.

The barmaid rolls her eyes. 'Get it?'

The regular's cackling with laughter. 'Crack o' Dawn. Best cheeks east of Belfast.'

The barmaid, tutting, 'Away with you.'

Noble starts. 'She's Irish?'

'Don't hold it against her,' the regular coughs, 'I never could.' Laughing again, hacking and coughing and laughing right to the punchline: 'She wouldn't let me!'

'Jesus,' Noble says, 'these lunchtimes must fly by.'

The barmaid hands Noble the blonde's Babycham. 'Her daddy was Irish.'

'Why did she leave?'

'Why does anyone?'

Noble looks around, says, 'I haven't the foggiest idea.' He hands over a fiver. 'Take one for yourself, love.'

'Big spender.'

Noble winks. 'Plenty more where that came from.'

Back in the booth, Noble distributes drinks. 'You two behaving yourselves, I hope.'

Parker grinning, the blonde all demure, 'Billie Jean' on the stereo –

Noble doesn't sit down.

The blonde says, 'You not staying?' She nods at the ceiling. 'This is one of my warm-up numbers.'

Noble looks at Parker. 'I've got to use the phone. We'll be off after, all right?'

Parker says to the blonde, 'You better give me your number then.'

She's giggling, and shrieks as Noble crosses the dark, patchy, damp carpet, end of the bar, picks up the phone –

Message from Gardiner. Again.

He dials Hackney nick, he waits.

'There was a bloke in from the council, asking about Shahid Akhtar, wanting the files.'

'Oh yeah?'

'Might be nothing, thought you should know.'

'What was his name?'

'Jon Davies. Said he spoke to Williams during the Initiative.'

Noble mouths, 'Jon Davies', commits the name to memory. 'You tell anyone else?'

'Only Williams.'

Noble nods. 'Cheers,' he says, and hangs up.

Back across the corridor, narrowly avoiding the blonde, who's spinning around to Michael Jackson, lunchtime punters piling through the door –

'Get your coat on,' he tells Parker. 'You've pulled.'

In the car, Parker says, 'About that bird—'

Noble snorts. 'I don't wanna know, son, tell you the truth.'

'I mean the redhead.'

'Right.' Noble's been letting this information marinate, hasn't quite worked out the best path. 'You're sure she hasn't clocked you?'

'Pretty sure.'

Noble weighs it, Parker's spycop report in his inside pocket, knowing that he's out on a limb –

'Make yourself known but say nothing. You know each other. That's it. You're on the level.'

'Yes, guv.'

'And the other thing you're up to –' Noble taps his jacket – 'keep it out of these, yeah?'

Parker nods. 'Course.'

'Groovy,' Noble jokes.

'There's a big demo, Saturday,' Parker says. 'Town hall, a march right up to Stoke Newington. The redhead will be taking photographs. I'll do it then.'

'Good man.'

12 March: third Roach Family Support Committee Demonstration for an Independent Public Inquiry.

Crowds chant 'No Cover Up', then 'Leave Us Alone', Suzi takes photographs, Suzi makes notes. A banner unfurled, white letters on black – ROACH FAMILY SUPPORT COMMITTEE. Placards with Colin's face, his young face, placards demanding an Independent Public Inquiry. More chanting, call and response: 'Colin Roach, No Cover Up, Colin Roach, No Cover Up.' Police barricades line the route. Police on one side of the barricade, police on the other side. Police in uniform line the route, laughing and smiling, Hurry along now, please, there's a good fellow, police laughing and chatting in light blue vans – Metropolitan Police Control – in dark green vans – Police – reading the newspapers, laughing and winking, in white police vehicles, in unmarked blue vans, police on motorbikes, police flanking the marchers, marching side by side, police marking off traffic lanes, police diverting traffic, diverting buses, laughing and smiling, joking with the passers-by –

Suzi feels a tap on her shoulder, wheels round –

'I thought it was you.'

Suzi, nervous, smiles.

'We're on the same team, yeah.'

Suzi nods. 'What's your name?'

The young man winks. 'What's yours?'

'I asked first,' Suzi says.

The young man says, 'You wanna decent snap, follow me.'

He pushes off through the crowd, makes space for her, a mix of firmness and kindness, he has a manner, she thinks, as he eases their way around the police, edges slowly towards the front of the march.

His presence seems to relax both the marchers and the police; black boys nodding at him, white officers giving him a grudging look, but appreciative of his courtesy. There's something about his size and his confidence that breeds further confidence, something about his straightforward manner that exudes authority, something about him that the crowd defers to –

He leads her past the stray uniforms into the inner circle –

There, Suzi photographs Mr James Roach and Councillor Dennis Twomey.

There, Suzi photographs Mr James Roach and Councillor Dennis Twomey as they are arrested.

As Suzi takes the photographs, a police officer confronts her, arms spread, he moves left and right to block her shot, her frame –

Suzi ducks, feints, clicks –

The police officer moves closer.

The young man now steps in front of Suzi, looks the police officer in the eye, smiles, his hands out in front of him.

The police officer stops.

The young man leans in, whispers something –

The police officer nods, turns, walks away.

'What did you say to him?' Suzi asks. 'And how did you know?' She points at the scene of the arrests.

The young man shrugs. 'Instinct, I guess.'

Suzi looks at him. She takes him in. This tall, muscular young man in donkey jacket and scarf, in denim and leather –

She shakes her head in disbelief. 'Who are you?' she asks.

'What I told him was we know the difference between obstruction and assault.'

'What does that mean?'

'It means he wasn't going to risk nicking your camera.'

'Thank you.'

The young man smiles. 'Be lucky,' he says.

Suzi, now deep in thought, watches him weave his way calmly back through the crowd.

Hackney town hall.

Jon Davies and Godfrey Heaven look at arrest statistics and charge sheets from the Roach Family Support Committee demonstrations.

Godfrey Heaven says, 'They made a mistake, last time, arresting Mr James Roach and Councillor Dennis Twomey? Hardly. They can't have known who they were.'

Jon Davies says, 'Twenty-four arrests in total, like an attack it was.'

'I'll leave it with you,' Godfrey Heaven says. 'For now.'

Jon says, 'Police Liaison Officer, get him in.'

Godfrey Heaven agrees. 'I'll investigate.'

Godfrey Heaven tiptoes out the door –

Jon Davies reads about Mr Merville Bishop, who, while acting as a steward on the 12 March demonstration, was physically assaulted by police officers and then arrested.

Mr Merville Bishop has subsequently been sentenced to twenty-eight days' imprisonment.

Jon Davies reads about Mr Fred Chitole, a man who did not attend the demonstration, but had, in fact, been shopping, to Woolworths to buy batteries, to Rumbelows to buy a cassette, and was on his way to Boots to buy shampoo when he was arrested.

Mr Fred Chitole has subsequently been sentenced to six weeks' imprisonment.

Jon checks court schedules:

May 17	Highbury Juvenile Court
May 17	Old Street M.C.
May 18	Highbury Corner M.C.
May 19	Highbury Juvenile Court
May 19	Highbury Corner M.C.
May 23	Highbury Corner M.C.
May 24	Highbury Corner M.C.
May 25	Highbury Corner M.C.
May 26	Highbury Corner M.C.
May 27	Highbury Corner M.C.
May 31	Highbury Corner M.C.

June 1	Old Street M.C.
June 1	Highbury Corner M.C.
June 2	Old Street M.C.
June 14	Seymore Place J.C.
June 20	Old Street M.C.

Mr Merville Bishop and Mr Fred Chitole came up against Magistrate Mr Johnson, who sits in session at Highbury Corner Magistrates Court.

How to best pursue the campaign for an independent inquiry in the context of the arrests when it's the opponents of the independent inquiry who are making the arrests?

The council solicitors, in collaboration with the Police Committee, are offering legal advice to the Roach Family Support Committee. Jon is gathering thoughts on the inquest vs public inquiry fobbing-off from the home secretary.

And not just the government, but the pro-government media, the pro-government media with enormous reach –

The *Sun* newspaper, 16 February 1983, from so-called expert Professor Vincent:

'The final decision will lie with the jury – twelve good men and true. If that is not a full and open inquiry, it is hard to know what is. The press will be there, the public will be there, and anyone will be able to give evidence.'

Jon knows that this comment from Professor Vincent amounts to the peddling of lies –

LIES. LIES. LIES. LIES. LIES. LIES. LIES. LIES.

Somebody must have the ear of the *Sun*.

A coroner's jury, in the first place, does not consist of 'twelve good men and true' but of between seven and eleven 'good and lawful' men. These good and lawful men, however, are chosen by the Coroner's Officer. The Coroner's Officer is a policeman.

The final decision in an inquest, of course, might well lie with the jury in theory, but the jury is guided by 'the coroner's summing up, definition of available verdicts and interpretation of evidence'. In other words, a jury is told what to do. A jury going against a coroner's recommendation is a very rare instance indeed.

The Roach family solicitor will not be able to address the jury. This is another key difference.

Jon drinks tea. Jon makes notes –

Other key areas where this inquest is absolutely not a public inquiry:

The scope of the inquest is limited to discovering 'how, where, when' Colin Roach died. There will be no consideration of the treatment of his family or the treatment of the black community in Stoke Newington more generally.

Jon swallows two aspirin with his tea, he underlines, annotates –

The inquest jury has three possible verdicts:

1. that Colin Roach killed himself;
2. that Colin Roach was 'unlawfully killed';
3. an open verdict.

If the jury finds verdict two, it cannot make any judgement as to who killed Colin Roach; this is outside the scope of an inquest.

If the jury finds verdict two, and it becomes clear throughout the inquest who did in fact kill Colin Roach, there is no legal guarantee of prosecution and this decision lies with the Director of Public Prosecution.

Jon breathes, Jon scratches his neck. Jon pours himself another mug of tea from the metallic pot burning a ring on his cheap desk –

The final, and perhaps most significant aspect, in Jon's eyes at least, is that the police report into the investigation of the death of Colin Roach is not submitted as open, public evidence.

What this means is that the police lawyers can discredit a witness if anything the witness states contradicts evidence given to the police by the witness at another time.

Anything at all.

Equally, as the Roach family solicitor is not granted the right to access witness statements given to – or, let's face it – *acquired by* the police, then the Roach family solicitor has no way of ascertaining if police witnesses have changed, or change in court, the content of their statements.

These are the headlines, anyway.

Jon rubs his eyes, Jon yawns, Jon scratches his neck. Jon feels fatigue crawling into his arms, into his legs, into his back –

Jon's desk telephone rings. It's Jackie.

'You'll never guess,' she says. 'I've got some news.'

Jon's heart thumps –

'Oh, yeah?' He grins. 'Who's the father?'

'Oh, Jon!' She's laughing.

Jon says, 'I'm coming home right now.'

3

We Are Detective

April–May 1983

Parker

Your mate delivers you to an address in Dalston, nods at the Rasta that opens the door, says, This is him, and then turns. You're on your own, now, mate, he tells you. I've vouched for you so be good. He's laughing, See you soooon, doing a ghoulish voice to scare you or something, and you just wink at the geezer that's opened the door and go, Pleasure's all mine, son, and he pulls a face like, Here we go, a wide white boy, but it's not a hostile look and he points at the car in front of this boarded-up terraced two-up two-down and you aim for the passenger door but there's another fella in there and he nods at the back seat and you hop in and there's a black balaclava in there but without any eye holes, and you say, What are you lot, the fucking IRA? but you're grinning and they look relaxed enough and tell you, When we give you the word, on goes the hood, and you say, Abso-fucking-lutely. You sit back in your seat and think about which topics of conversation you might broach as the car heads north, back the way you've come, and while you're thinking about it, hang about, these Yardies, they must have some interest, so you say, World Cup year, eh, bet you fancy a few quid on your mob, don't you? And Driver's Seat snorts, sucks his teeth, Man, not even worth it, odds-wise, you know? They taking money, is all there is to it. He's wearing a badge which declares 'Serious Business' across red, gold and green and you go, You know what, I quite fancy the Indians, they're decent this year, no word of a lie. The two men laugh. The West Indian cricket team, says Passenger Seat, is the finest example of the black man's brilliance currently on show in the sporting world, and you say, No argument, Winston, I'm just saying, this year, yeah, might be tricky. More laughter from both front seats. Passenger Seat says, Gordon Greenidge, Desmond Haynes, King Vivian Richards, Gus Logie, Clive Lloyd, Larry Gomes, Jeff Dujon, Malcolm Marshall, Andy

Roberts, Michael Holding and Joel 'Big Bird' Garner, he snaps his fingers,
high-fives Driver's Seat, howls, You know what I'm talking about. You
say, Respect is due to that fine side, no argument, and I've heard there's a
young kid coming up who might be even better than Isaac Vivian Alex-
ander Richards, goes by the name Richie Richardson. The two in the front
hoot and howl now, Man knows his stuff, they're saying, clapping their
hands, Richie Rich, next year when we come over here, you know what it's
going to be? and you say, Why don't you tell me? and they say, in unison,
in a lovely little chorus, Blackwash, it's going to be a Blackwash. You like
that, Blackwash, and tell them, and then, just as you're up around Stoke
Newington, guess what, jollity over, and Passenger Seat tells you, Hood
on, white boy.

Election, Election, Election.

Will they, won't they –

Radio's on and on and on about it, about why now or why wait –

Noble kills the engine; the radio jabbers on.

He thinks, This is what they're saying's going to happen, but it doesn't mean it will.

Manifesto this, Falklands that –

Unemployment and nationalisation, privatisation and union reorganisation; time to relax state control of the economy –

British Telecom, British Airways, British Steel, British Shipbuilders, Rolls Royce.

The Greater London Council and six other metropolitan authorities to be abolished; more power at borough and district level.

Rate-capping: lessen the ratepayer burden and, consequently, lessen the local authorities' responsibility for their own actions.

Which doesn't seem too clever.

Ten reasons to vote Conservative. Reason number ten:

Margaret Thatcher.

Noble's looking for another kind of woman –

He's had a thought, based on the list Gardiner's given him, that Cracker Dawn may have moved from stripping into brass work.

Her last pick-up was at Stoke Newington – surprise, surprise – on a solicitation, not pursued, same old address where she doesn't live, so he's been stripping himself: pulling down cards from telephone boxes and ringing the numbers, trying to figure out if any of these are working from a council flat, if there's a network or management scheme, but there's been no luck so far.

His forefinger numb from the dialling, his voice hoarse from the questions, his mind heavy with the names and the promises, the pictures and words –

Tits and telephone numbers, tongues and money-back guarantees –

It takes it out of you, imagining yourself in this place.

He hasn't told Gardiner who he's looking for, there's no central file.

Gardiner and Williams still friendly, so he's staying solo.

He likes Gardiner, but Gardiner likes Williams –

It's tiring, disheartening work –

Tart cards:

Tina, Debbie, Becky, Miss Whiplash, The Lovely Young Charlotte in Rubber, Heel Boy, Come on Eileen, New Young Delight for Watersports and Hardsports, Hot and Willing Blonde, New Stunning Oriental Beauty, Brunette Model, Naughty Schoolgirl, Elegant Brunette, Yuko Your Favourite Japanese Mistress, At My Command, Mature Lady Gives French Tuition, Lady Madonna, Roxanne, Breast Relief with Sexy Blonde, A&O Specialist, DUNGEON, Lisa's Back, New English Rose –

But not a single one of them giving anything away about where they work and who takes the money, not over the phone, and Noble's tired, and heavy, and his head aches with it all.

Maybe Dawn Driscoll doesn't want to be found.

Basing it all on a kid seeing a blonde in a car with a couple of plainclothes.

The other bit of work is that he's given Parker a list of names of young men taken into custody at Stoke Newington over the last twelve months.

'You know anyone on this?'

Parker studied it. 'Maybe.'

'Ask around,' Noble told him. 'I want anyone who'll talk about any kind of mistreatment.'

Parker barked a sarky little laugh. 'Shouldn't be too hard, guv.'

'Why's that then?'

'Come on.'

'I want you to tell me.'

'Heavy hands and light fingers, is the word.'

'So I've heard.'

Waiting for Parker and not getting anywhere tracking Cracker Dawn, Noble decides it's time to take things into his own hands.

He's had a word with Turkish at the drinking club and learned that DCs Rice and Cole have altered their schedule over the last couple of months. Picking up less often, and more friendly about it. Low profile, which makes sense given the heat at the nick.

He's parked off the main road with a view of Turkish's place. It's late afternoon.

Sports news on the radio –

'More goals there for Luther Blisset. Liverpool have dropped two points as Coventry City hold them to a goalless draw at Highfield Road. Time is running out for Birmingham City in their fight to avoid the drop as they lose 3–1 to Luton Town in a relegation six-pointer at Kenilworth Road. On the show later, we have Jenny Pitman, the first female trainer to train a Grand National winner, who tells us about life with Corbiere, the eight-year-old ridden by Ben De Haan who won by three-quarters of a length over Greasepaint with Yer Man in third last weekend …'

Noble had Greasepaint each-way, a tidy result. Listening out for any word on young Tony Cottee, but nothing –

He turns the radio off, stretches his neck, waits.

He's got a thin, black, autofocus Kodak Disc camera that fits neatly in his inside pocket and he checks that now. Some sort of new gadget, the tech guy at West End Central told him.

'It's small, is the point,' was the conclusion. 'And it'll get a nice close-up.'

Noble takes it out now and inspects it; it's set up to go off with no flash.

Where's the safety, he jokes.

He opens the glove compartment, pulls out a pair of leather gloves, a black, flat leather hat, a small pair of black binoculars.

He checks his watch –

He sees DC Rice and DC Cole crossing Kingsland High Street. He lifts the Kodak, snaps three, four times as they go into the Turkish drinking club, looking left and right.

He waits. He checks his watch. He pulls his coat up and his hat down.

Three and a half minutes later the door opens and, looking left and right, DC Rice and DC Cole step into the street. Noble snaps another three or four times, the camera zooming in, their faces clear –

They've got a narrow-eyed, mean set to their faces.

Stubble, neat haircuts, collars and leather bomber jackets, white pumps and gold watches –

Noble tracks them down the road, past the mosque, into the first retail unit, through the door –

He takes more photographs as they look right then left.

Snap, snap, snap.

He checks his watch.

Four minutes later, he photographs them leaving the retail unit, walking out between the signs declaring EVERYTHING MUST GO, ALL SIZES, watching as DC Rice swears, stops, checks his shoes for dog shit, rubbish blowing down the street, the sky heavy and damp, distant voices intimate in the wet air, warming up, springtime –

Noble starts his car and pulls onto Kingsland High Street. On the Jet garage forecourt he sees DC Rice and DC Cole climb into a blue Ford Escort with a bit of space in the back and head north.

Noble follows, three cars back.

They're not exactly testing the Escort's gear box, and Noble keeps pace easily.

The Escort pulls over by the Rochester Castle pub, double parks, and Noble drifts past and pulls in.

He turns in time to snap two or three more photographs as they go into the pub, looking right and left, hands inside their leather bomber jackets –

Noble studies the pub. Punk pub, it was. He saw The Jam here once upon a time, 1976, he thinks. Ian Dury, The Stranglers. *The Police.* He laughs at this.

He wonders what Paul Weller's up to now, he's not been keeping tabs.

Pub's been taken over, he's heard, a new brewery chain called Wetherspoons. Not doing any music.

Everything used to be something else.

Everything used to be something better.

He checks his watch.

In his rear-view mirror, he sees DC Rice and DC Cole leave the pub and turn left. He sinks into his seat as they walk past.

Noble snaps photographs as, looking right and left, DC Rice and DC Cole go into a Turkish café.

Noble checks his watch.

Two and a half minutes later, Noble photographs them leaving the Turkish café, DC Rice carrying a holdall now.

They walk on three, four, five doors down and go into another Turkish café.

Noble snaps photographs, DC Rice and DC Cole looking right and left.

Noble checks his watch.

Three and a half minutes later, Noble photographs them leaving the second Turkish café, DC Cole carrying a different holdall.

They continue north.

Noble eases into gear, drifts along the kerb, stops thirty yards further along.

DC Rice and DC Cole cross the road.

Noble photographs them – snap, snap, snap – looking right and looking left as they go into the Coach and Horses, carrying their holdalls.

Noble thinks: interesting.

The Coach is an old villain pub. The Kray Firm used to meet up there when John Dickson's mate, old Blondy Bill, was the landlord. It still hosts a few of the chaps, the reliable members of the profession, moody gear and hooky business transactions.

Noble checks his watch.

He writes names and addresses in his notebook.

Seventeen and a half minutes later, Noble photographs DC Rice and DC Cole leaving the pub, wiping their mouths, looking left then right, no longer carrying their holdalls.

Snap, snap, snap.

DC Rice and DC Cole walk south down Stoke Newington High Street across the road from Noble's car. Noble sinks into his seat. In his rear-view mirror, Noble watches DC Rice and DC Cole go into another Turkish café. Through the window, he sees them sit down at a table, sees the proprietor, all smiles and jokes, bring them two bottles of Turkish lager.

Noble sees a young black man in a maroon hooded sweatshirt and blue jogging bottoms, black hat and black shoes go into the Coach and Horses.

Noble checks his watch.

Less than a minute later, the same young black man leaves the Coach and Horses carrying the same two holdalls that DC Rice and DC Cole brought in.

Snap, snap, snap.

Noble checks the Turkish café. DC Rice and DC Cole are drinking and laughing.

Noble thinks: *gamble*.

The young black man crosses the road and down onto Church Street. Noble eases the car out and turns left, following.

At the fire station, the young black man crosses Church Street and heads down Kersley Road, and Noble turns left, following.

The young black man walks, six, seven, eight doors down, then –

He stops, opens a gate, goes down shallow steps to a basement flat. Number Seven, Flat A, Kersley Road.

Noble drifts by, pulls in.

Snap, snap, snap.

Noble checks his watch.

Twelve and a half minutes later, the young black man leaves, his hands empty.

He heads towards Church Street, turns right, Noble following –

He walks quickly south down Stoke Newington Hight Street, crosses the road –

Noble slows down, Noble sees a parking space in front of the Turkish café –

Noble passes the young black man, pulls in, pulls his coat up and hat down, his camera out –

The young black man goes into the Turkish café and hands DC Rice and DC Cole two separate, thick envelopes.

Snap, snap, snap.

DC Rice and DC Cole open their envelopes. Their envelopes are full of notes.

Snap, snap.

The young black man leaves the Turkish café.

Noble pulls out, drives slowly down the road, the traffic eases, he does a U-turn, parking a dozen or so yards behind DC Rice and DC Cole's blue Ford Escort.

Noble checks his watch.

Nearly six o'clock.

The traffic heavier, the streets bustling with shoppers and workers going home.

Noble waits.

Six minutes later and DC Rice and DC Cole leave the Turkish café, DC Rice carrying a black holdall. They cross Stoke Newington High Street, get into their blue Ford Escort.

Noble follows them north to Stamford Hill, then east towards Clapton –

The traffic heavy now, buses queuing and shunting, exhaust sharp and oily through the open window, kids on the railings by the park, kids playing football in the park, pensioners struggling to the big supermarket –

Down towards Clapton, past the estates, past the curry houses and electrical goods superstores, past the train station and the mosque, round the Lea Bridge Roundabout, Panda's open and doing an after-school-club trade, MSG and fried rice stink, past the junction and the West Indian takeaway on the right, past the pond and left by the off-licence, left by the public toilets, the piss and stale booze, the middle street of three, Noble holding back, watching DC Rice and DC Cole ghost down Mildenhall Road –

Until they stop, about three-quarters of the way down, just past Fletching Road, headlights on, engine running, car in the middle of the road –

Noble on Chailey Street, camera out.

Snap, snap, snap.

Number ninety-nine Mildenhall Road –

DC Rice and DC Cole talking to a man on the doorstep, a white man in a suit, a man Noble doesn't recognise.

Nodding and notebooks, the man's woman holding a little boy's hand, her other straying over her stomach.

DC Rice and DC Cole smiling, turning to leave, the man watching them –

The car revved, tyres squeal, a fist out the window –

And they're off.

Noble thinks, Where to first?

Suzi, sitting at a desk at 50 Rectory Road, transcribes another Godfrey Heaven nugget.

'And then there is the Police Community Liaison Officer, whose province has traditionally been vicars and youth clubs, who took my fingerprints by stealth (what he thought was stealth; I thought the balance of advantage was not to call him out, to see what else he was capable of … quite a lot as it happened, a useful source of information) by offering me a card which had been treated and then putting it gingerly back into a protected top pocket.'

She smiles – this Godfrey Heaven is a goldmine.

She doesn't need to do this now. She's waiting for that young man to come in; he usually does at some point in the morning.

Suzi doesn't know exactly what it was they worked on together. She doesn't want to know, exactly, either. But the young man was enlisted for his part by someone, and it might well have been Patrick Noble, which means the young man might well be a police officer.

Which would, at the very least, Suzi thinks, be a conflict of interest.

But there's also every chance that he had nothing to do with Noble, was just a bit of outside muscle is what they'd probably call it, and he's just a righteous geezer, albeit a fairly big one.

She sits at the desk she uses and keeps an eye on the front door, and then the young man comes in. Suzi spins round in her chair so she's looking out the window, breathes, thinks about what to say, prepares herself to follow him into the copy room, spins back round when –

'All right?' he says to her. 'Can you do me a favour?'

'Of course.' Suzi smiles.

'Groovy,' he says.

Suzi thinks, Keith says that too.

'Fire away.'

He's perched on the edge of her desk now. He's rummaging in his pockets, he pulls a folded and creased envelope, he pulls out of that a folded and creased list, a list of names, Suzi thinks –

'Do you recognise any of these names?'

Suzi thinks, Copper.

'Why do you ask?'

The young man smiles. 'Wrongful arrest, mistreatment, witness intimidation, you name it.'

Suzi nods.

'We're putting together a report for the Defence Committee, a dossier on Stoke Newington.' He nods in the direction of the police station. 'Last year or so, yeah?'

'OK,' Suzi says. 'Leave it with me.'

'Hang about, I'll make a copy.'

He jumps up, crosses the office. Suzi watches him go into, and then come out of, the copy room.

It gives her the moment she needs to make up her mind.

'Here.' He hands her a crisp, warm Xerox, the names clear, the reasons for arrest clear –

'I'll have a look later.'

'Beautiful.'

Suzi smiles. 'You in tomorrow?'

He nods.

'Good,' Suzi winks. 'Cos I'm going to need a favour from you.'

'Course.' He smiles, gestures it's no problem.

'Great,' Suzi says. 'See you tomorrow then.'

'No doubt about it.'

Suzi thinks, This boy is either clever or reckless. Or –

Well, fact is, she doesn't know.

Later, Suzi's mum calls her on the telephone at the Rectory Road office and it's then that Suzi realises she has to go and see her dad, that it's serious.

Back home: Keith, vest and roll-up, music on –

'What *is* this bollocks?' Keith asks, gesturing.

'Sorry, love?'

'I'll tell you what it is,' Keith decides. 'It's the Thompson Twins' new single.'

'Is it, love?'

Suzi hears pantomime, French-sounding melodies, cartoon lyrics about being detectives –

'They've really thought, you know what, singles-buyers are pretty stupid, haven't they, Suze?'

'I don't know, Keith.'

'Well, they have. I thought they fancied themselves as –' Keith makes a face here – 'as avant-garde.'

Keith's laughing. 'Cup of tea?'

'Please.'

He pours tea from the pot, bends into the fridge, Y-fronts straining, the smell of cheese and onion, of banana and veg pouring past him, he pulls the half-empty bottle of red top, sides streaked with cream, he adds milk to Suzi's mug, he hands her this mug, he smiles –

Suzi thinks, This is what love is, isn't it? *Time*. Being there, day in day out, making you tea and making you smile –

Home.

'Fancy a Spam sandwich, love?' Keith asks.

Suzi smiles.

Spreading white bread with margarine, Keith informs her: 'Mrs Thatcher describes it as a wartime delicacy, you know.'

Suzi laughs. 'In that case.'

'You can have a bite of mine, love.'

Home.

Early morning, red-streaked skies.

Jon Davies answers the front door and thinks –

Not another one.

'Jon Davies?'

'What can I do for you?' Jon says.

'I'm Detective Constable Patrick Noble.' Warrant card held out for Jon to study. 'I believe two of my colleagues were here to see you yesterday afternoon.'

'That's right.'

The bloke's nodding –

'I'm following up,' Detective Constable Patrick Noble says.

'Following up?'

More nodding.

Jon thinks this is odd. It wouldn't be the first time –

He says, 'False alarm. They'd had a report of a break-in, a brick through a window. I told them it was someone else's house, someone else's brick, as it were.'

'OK.'

'Which you know.'

'That's right.'

There's something fishy here, Jon thinks.

He says, 'They had a look to them.'

'What kind of a look?'

'Like they were sizing me up.'

This Noble smiles. 'Right pair, those two.'

'Anything else?' Jon asks.

'The Met Race Crime Initiative.'

'I'm listening,' Jon says.

'Just hold off on those files.'

Jon thinks, There's a look to this fella –

Detective Constable Patrick Noble nods over the road, over the road at the former residence of Shahid Akhtar.

'Give it a little while,' he says. 'OK?'

He hands Jon a card. 'Keep in touch,' he says.

'You got a family?' Jon asks.

'Thinking about it.'

'Good for you.'

Detective Constable Patrick Noble shrugs.

'It does one thing for you, family,' Jon says.

'Oh yeah?'

'It makes up for the barrenness of a political life.'

'What's that then?'

'Understanding that there's not a lot anyone can do.'

Detective Constable Patrick Noble nods.

Jon watches him leave. He goes back upstairs and gets ready for court.

St Pancras Coroner's Court, 18 April, 9 a.m. Resumption of the inquest into the death of Colin Roach.

Jon Davies and Godfrey Heaven exchange bewildered and exasperated looks as the coroner announces that the inquest will be immediately adjourned until the following Monday, 25 April, at the same venue, St Pancras Coroner's Court.

'Fix-up,' Godfrey Heaven says to Jon Davies.

Jon thinks, Not far off.

The Roach family solicitor petitions against the adjournment; the coroner ignores this petition.

Jon Davies confers with the Roach family solicitor.

They request that the inquest be transferred to Hackney town hall to enable everyone who wishes to attend the inquest to do so.

The police solicitors confer. They oppose this transfer request.

'Surprise, surprise,' Godfrey Heaven says.

The police solicitors refuse to explain publicly their reasons for opposing this request. They will explain their reasons by affidavits which will be offered to the coroner forthwith.

'Let's see how quickly they appear, these affidavits,' Godfrey Heaven murmurs. 'My guess is they're sitting in an envelope on that table.' He points at the lawyers' desk. 'Knowing the bloody liaison officer as we now do.'

Jon thinks, If that's true, then –

The coroner rules that the inquest will not be transferred.

So, no affidavits then, Jon thinks. Shame. He was curious as to just how clever Godfrey Heaven really is.

Later, same day, Hackney town hall.

Jon Davies and Godfrey Heaven open envelopes that contain summonses explaining that the coroner intends to approach the High Court to seek a Declaration that the GLC cannot legally require him to transfer the inquest proceedings. Jon notes that the Roach family solicitors, the Hackney Black People's Association and the GLC have also received these documents. The coroner, the documents state, will use the police affidavits as evidence to support the proposal.

Jon telephones the Roach family solicitors.

'We were just going to ring you. What do you think of this?' they ask him.

They read Jon a list of questions raised by the day's events.

'They'll be in the next Roach family bulletin,' they say.

Jon listens.

They're essentially asking how all this could have happened and whether there is some establishment plot to keep the inquest away from Hackney.

Either way, it's working.

Noble checks his messages at West End Central, one of these messages screaming at him –

From Suzi Scialfa: 'Fifty Rectory Road, tomorrow, eleven a.m.'

Noble calls Parker, tells him.

Parker says, 'Clever girl.'

Noble says, 'I'll do the talking.'

He cuts the call, waits for the tone, dials again.

He's tired, Noble. Feels it deep in his bones. He shakes his head and sniffs.

50 Rectory Road, next day, 11 a.m.

Suzi smiles at Patrick Noble and her new young friend, Parker, as she now knows he's called. Or at least *otherwise known as.*

'So, you do know each other,' she says.

'Indirectly.' Noble's smiling at her. 'Just about the same way the two of you know each other.'

'Indirectly.' Suzi nods. 'Right.'

She sits at her usual desk, Noble and Parker stand –

'That list he gave you,' Noble says. 'Anything?'

'He told me it was for the Defence Committee.'

'It will be.'

'What does that mean?'

'It means we'll give it to the Defence Committee when the time is right.'

Suzi breathes, nods at the door. 'That closed properly?'

Parker opens it, closes it. It clicks.

'You're telling me he's a police officer?'

Noble nods. 'Of a sort.'

'And I'm supposed to just keep my mouth shut?'

'We're on the same team.'

Nodding at Parker, Suzi snorts. 'That's what he said.'

'What about the list, Suzi?'

'I don't know.'

'What do you mean you don't know?'

'I need a bit more time.'

Noble nods. He puts his hand inside his jacket and hands Suzi an envelope –

'This'll help you understand,' he tells her.

In the envelope, a letter. Official-looking, something familiar about it –

Suzi raises her eyebrows. 'No wax? Cheapskate.'

Noble laughs.

Suzi reads the letter.

It's from Detective Chief Inspector Maurice Young.

The gist: thanking her for her contribution to the cause, back in 1978, of course, and once again, now in 1983.

Official involvement in an associate capacity.

Meaning: you ain't got much choice, duck.

Noble says, softly. 'We're on the same team.'

Suzi folds the letter. 'We better be,' she says. She looks at Parker. 'I'll have another look at that list.'

'Good girl,' Noble says.

Suzi shrugs. She feels a strange relief, a sort of inevitability –

Noble puts his hand in his jacket again and pulls out a thin, black, autofocus Kodak Disc camera. He places it on Suzi's desk.

'You know about these?'

Suzi nods.

'Good girl. I need you to develop the film and give the set and the negatives to young Parker here, quick as you can.'

Suzi nods. 'I'll go home and do it now.'

Noble smiles at her. 'Thank you.' He looks around the room, around the office. 'I best do one,' he says. 'I'll see myself out.'

Suzi, her hands shaking, her mind clear, puts the camera in her bag.

Parker says, 'Trust me, we're doing the right thing.'

'Meet me in the Amhurst Arms in two hours,' Suzi tells him.

As it happens, next week doesn't come, the adjournment rolls on and it's not until 30 April that the High Court rules that while neither Hackney Council nor the GLC has the power to insist the coroner change the venue, a bigger venue would be a good idea. It's a suggestion, but one everybody decides to follow, and kick-off is set for 6 June at Clerkenwell County Court.

6 June, Jon thinks, *D-Day*.

In Parliament, May 1983, Hackney South and Shoreditch MP Ronald Brown: Since 10 January, the new police commander has tried desperately to establish contact between the police and that organisation [Hackney Council for Racial Equality]. Recognising the complaints about the police in London, particularly in Hackney, as well as the difficulties in Hackney because of the tragedy that occurred, he has endeavoured to re-establish a relationship with the community. He has approached every group in an attempt to get a dialogue going. What kind of response did he get from the Council for Racial Equality? In a letter of 21 February, it said: 'I am writing on behalf of Hackney Council for Racial Equality Executive ' – not the council, but the executive – 'who have asked that you give instructions that the local home beat officers covering the HCRE Mare Street office, the HCRE Family Centre, Rectory Road, no longer call' – that phrase is underlined – 'at either of these offices unless HCRE gives a specific call to the police. I trust this will be acted on with dispatch.' This was signed by the community relations officer. It destroyed the relationship between the beat policemen and the community in the two areas. By common consent, that relationship had proved valuable. One letter wiped it out.

Ayeleen: I'm in the café, Lauren spread over a couple of chairs and a table, Mesut in the back doing something when Uncle Ahmet comes in and says: 'Come on, Ayeleen, I want to show you something.'

He sees Lauren. 'You can come too, Lauren. If you're not too busy falling asleep in the corner.'

Lauren sits up straight and smiles like she's impressing a teacher. 'I'd love to, Mr Ahmet.'

I roll my eyes and laugh.

Uncle Ahmet points at the back and tells Mesut to look after things for half an hour.

We walk down the road and then stop outside the old cinema, the new mosque.

'Here it is,' Uncle Ahmet says. 'Our future.'

'Our future?' I ask.

'It's a bit dirty, isn't it?' Lauren decides. 'Look at all those old posters stuck to the walls.' She breathes in sharply, shakes her head. 'I don't know, state of those towers, Mr Ahmet, we might have to knock them down.'

I'm smiling at her.

'It'll cost you,' she adds.

We both laugh.

'Girls,' Uncle Ahmet tells us, 'follow me.'

We climb the steps and go in through the one door that isn't boarded up, underneath the homemade banner that says AZIZIYE MOSQUE in red paint on a big white sheet.

Inside it's damp and empty.

'Bit of a pong, Mr Ahmet,' Lauren says. 'We might—'

'Yes, very funny, Lauren,' Uncle Ahmet interrupts. 'How about we pause the jokes for a few minutes.'

'Yeah, Lauren,' I say.

'You too, Ayeleen, OK?'

We turn circles in the large main room, which must have been the foyer and the ticket office when it was a cinema.

'My first question is History,' Uncle Ahmet begins. 'Construction date of the building. Answers, please.'

I'm looking at the ceiling and Uncle Ahmet is looking at me and we both hear Lauren saying: '"Originally built as a cinema, it first opened in 1913 as the Apollo Picture House, was reopened in 1933 as the Ambassador Cinema, and from 1974 played martial arts films and softcore sex films as the Astra Cinema, before closing in 1983. It is among Hackney Council's locally listed buildings."'

I start giggling. 'Softcore sex films in a mosque, eh.'

Uncle Ahmet is shaking his head. 'Where did you find that?'

Lauren hands over a dirty piece of paper. 'There's a bunch of them in the corner, information stand.'

Uncle Ahmet mutters that they'll need to clear that up then.

'What you have to do is imagine,' he begins. 'Close your eyes.'

We both start giggling again.

'I'm serious, close your eyes.'

We do.

'Breathe it in, the space. Now, imagine an Ottoman-style mosque for two thousand people, a Halal butcher, a weekend school for good Turkish, Muslim children, a restaurant, a wedding hall, all in a beautiful building restored and converted by our own people.'

Lauren elbows me. 'Beautiful building?'

'It will be,' Uncle Ahmet says. 'We keep the art deco details, the façade will be decorated Ottoman-style with patterned ceramic tiling, blue, turquoise and white, OK? Gold towers at the top, imagine them. Mosaic columns at the bottom. Bronze windows and mirrored glass. A dark green dome. Magnificent!'

I've never seen Uncle Ahmet so excited, so sincere. I like it.

He turns to me. 'We helped buy this building, our family, because Turkish people don't like to go to a non-Turkish mosque, you understand? Round here, you get half a dozen people praying together in a dirty flat, it's not right. The services will be in Turkish, not Arabic, and not English, certainly. But we will be an English business and we will have a stake in all of these businesses inside.'

'What about the factories, Mr Ahmet?' Lauren asks.

'The textile industry is collapsing. I knew it would.' He grins. 'And sold just in time.'

'And the caffs and the shops and the bars?'

Uncle Ahmet looks at me. 'Some we'll keep, some we won't. This –' he gestures at the empty room – 'is our future.' He smiles. 'This, OK?'

I nod. 'That's great, Uncle Ahmet,' I say.

'A cultural centre and a place of worship. I'm an entrepreneur!'

Lauren giggles. 'Softcore porn and kung-fu films. Just like Mrs Thatcher wants.'

Uncle Ahmet laughs. 'You're funny!' he tells her. 'Funny girl!'

Lauren does a little curtsey and I clap.

Later, in the café on my own, I think about how long it will take to do the work on the building and if I'll still be here when it's ready and if it means my father will come back.

10 May 1983: Margaret Thatcher calls a general election for 9 June.

D+3. Election, Election, Election –

4

Let's Dance

May–June 1983

Parker

Hood off now and you're in a basement flat and someone's put Bowie's new one on and you're going, Best thing Bowie ever done, and some big Rasta goes, Yeah man, and you go, No, I mean best thing Bowie ever done is introduce Stevie Ray Vaughan to the world, and someone else goes, Who? and you go, Guitar, mate, listen to the guitar and the Rasta goes, Fair, that's fair, and you go, I fucking know it is, son. There's a bit of laughter and the big man says, Business, now, yeah, serious business, and you say, What, the guitar? and the big man smiles and says, This is what we're going to do. I'm going to give you this, and here he holds up a package about the size of a hefty hardback book, and you're going to give me what's in your pocket and then you do what you do with this, he holds up the package again, and then we'll talk more, make sense? You say, Crystal, and you take an envelope from inside your jacket and hand it over. Passenger Seat, grinning at you, opens the envelope and counts it. We good? We're good. The big man tosses you the package. You make a neat catch. Passenger Seat says, Slip fielder! and everyone laughs and you go, Nah, spin bowler, and there's more laughter at that, they're calling you names, but it's in good fun and so you do it, you ask the question, I've heard there's something new about, something to smoke, yeah? You know where I can find some of that? There's a moment of silence, everyone in the room deferring to the big man here and his judgement. He gestures at one of the younger brethren, who hands him pencil and pad. He scribbles something. He tosses the pad and you take another sharp catch. Slip fielder, you wink, and there's low-level chuckling at your wit, your style, and you tear the page he's scribbled on off the pad and pocket it, toss the pad back, and the big man takes it one-handed and smiles and goes, Not for business, you hear, pleasure, that place a pleasure-only deal, yeah? And you go, Mate, understood, curiosity is what it's all about. Killed the cat, hip cat, says Passenger Seat, and this gets a murmur of appreciation. And you stand, and the big man says, My man here will see you to the door, sir, but he can't drive you home, and you go, Cool man, I'll get my bearings and we'll be in touch, and you bump fists and you're shown the door, and you're out the door, and you turn and clock the number of the house, the number of the flat, and you look right and left, turn left, walk towards the busier road, and you know where you are, that's Church Street, you can see the fire station, and you know where you've been, Number Seven, Flat A, Kersley Road, and you look at the address on the paper and you think, There's a very good reason these geezers didn't mind giving it up. Because it's safe.

Jon Davies reads about The New Hope for Britain.

The Labour manifesto promises unilateral nuclear disarmament and Britain's withdrawal from Europe. Siege economy mentality to weather the storm. The restriction of market forces. Quotas and tariffs to limit imports. Exchange controls and threats of public ownership to uncooperative financial institutions. State planning and widespread nationalisation. Thatcher tells Cardiff that if you put your savings in your socks, then Labour will nationalise socks. Nationalisation of any sector considered part of the national interest, as and when. Goodbye to private health and private schools. Trade Unions restored to former glories.

The title of the Labour manifesto:

The New Hope for Britain.

Jon Davies looks up. Godfrey Heaven says to him, 'It's a start, Jon.'

Broadsheets spread out on Jon's desk –

Bernard Levin in *The Times* on Michael Foot: 'Lurching between disaster and calamity with all the skill and aplomb of a one-legged tight-rope walker ... unable to make his own shadow cabinet appointments or indeed blow his own nose in public without his trousers falling down.'

Tabloid press all over Jon's desk –

The *Sun*, beneath an unflattering photograph of Michael Foot having a walk:

'DO YOU SERIOUSLY WANT THIS OLD MAN TO RUN BRITAIN?'

Left-wing press on Jon's desk –

Clive James in the *Observer* on Michael Foot: 'A floppy toy on Benzedrine.'

Right-wing press on Jon's desk –

The *Sunday Telegraph* on Michael Foot: 'An elderly, ranting pamphleteer waving a stick in Hampstead.'

'The centrists and left-leaners will regret this, this Foot-bashing, one day,' Godfrey Heaven says, wisely.

Jon's inclined to agree.

They're putting together publicity and information pamphlets for the Kill the Bill conference, which is happening on 15 May at the town hall.

The Police Bill, meaning stop and search and all sorts of draconian bother.

'We keep it anonymous,' Godfrey Heaven is saying. 'What we're doing is showing a case study and showing how that kind of thing will happen a lot more often if the Police Bill passes.'

'Anonymity for the family, but we're naming Mars-Jones, surely.'

'We are. Have a read, Jon.'

Jon has a read:

Monstrous, wicked and shameful conduct in the name of justice.

They [the police] assaulted this defenceless man in his own home with a weapon, and beat him up in a brutal inhuman way with the object of inflicting pain and injury on him.

Five-year cover-up of their brutal, savage and sustained assaults.

I regret to say I am forced to the conclusion there has been an orchestrated attempt to mislead the court in order to cover up illegality and unjustified use of force.

'This is Mr Justice Mars-Jones, High Court judge,' Godfrey Heaven says, 'awarding damages to a black couple after their home was invaded by the police.'

Jon nods.

'If the Police Bill does pass, they'll be entitled to do a lot worse than that.'

Jon nods again. 'Print on yellow and red, what do you think?'

'We're not designing it, Jon!' laughs Godfrey Heaven. 'It's a Coercion publication, sponsored by the GLC, or it will be at least. Calling it *Policing London* with handcuffs running through each letter o.'

'Very militant.'

'It's the final RFSC demo the day before. You've got to wonder,'

Godfrey Heaven says, 'with this on the *next* day, how many arrests there are likely to be.'

'We should run a book,' mutters Jon.

'Now, now.'

'You know that over a hundred MPs have signed a petition for an independent public inquiry.'

'I did know that, Jon.'

'So, it's encouraging.'

Godfrey Heaven smiles. 'I think Whitelaw and Thatcher might have better things to do than read petitions at this precise point in time.'

Jon nods.

'Whitelaw's been fobbing us off, Jon, as if they win, he's in line for a promotion.'

'And it won't be his problem any longer.'

Godfrey Heaven winks. 'I'm all right, Jack.'

'True blue, mate.'

'We'll be the ones with the blues, Jon.'

Noble on his way to meet Parker, driving north, the traffic light and the air clear, blue skies and dawn chorus –

Radio's on, another bloody political talk show.

Election, Election, Election –

Cecil Parkinson, Conservative Party Chairman: 'The Conservative Party has definitively *not* been infiltrated by the National Front or the League of St George, nor by any of the far-right, rogue members of these political groups.'

Noble thinks, Parker *will* be pleased.

Parker telling him late, late last night: 'I know the young black lad in those photographs.'

Parker telling him: 'Number Seven, Flat A, Kersley Road.'

Parker telling him: 'I've got another address you'll want.'

The talk show bunny goes on –

Rabbit rabbit rabbit rabbit rabbit rabbit –

Noble listening to the 'charming' Conservative MP Alan Clark, known for his 'flamboyance, wit and irreverence', according to the talk show host.

Alan Clark is telling the listeners that black British people are worried about being 'sent back to Bongo Bongo Land'.

How bloody irreverent of him, Noble thinks.

Not quite seven-thirty and Hackney yawning, rubbing its eyes.

Market stalls on Ridley Road filling up, street sweepers and traffic wardens, the clack and chatter of the North London line, bus conductors hanging off the back platform, laughing and waving, groups of kids dragging and kicking PE bags, homeless men and women packing their sleeping bags, shuffling down towards Shoreditch, the City, that gold-paved promise –

Noble jams the car into a tight spot and into the caff on Amhurst Road where he met Lloyd Manley.

Parker's already there, chewing on a bacon sandwich, flicking through a tabloid.

Noble sits down, waves at the waitress, points at Parker's mug.

Without looking up, Parker reads from the tabloid:

'From a Westminster gossip column. Privately, it is rumoured that Cecil Parkinson, Conservative Party Chairman, is expecting a "love child" with his secretary, Sara Keays. Mrs Thatcher has, we hear, Mr Parkinson in mind for foreign secretary; we suspect that if it proves that he has not remained foreign enough to his own secretary, she might well change her mind. Either way, it all sounds a bit French to us.'

Parker folds the newspapers, brushes imaginary dirt from his hands –

'Dirty bastard.'

'*Mirror* then?' Noble asks.

Parker nods. He slurps at his tea. The waitress brings another one.

'Cheers, darling,' Noble winks. 'Remember me?'

The waitress rolls her eyes, nods at Parker. 'He a bit big for a milkshake, is he?'

Noble hoots, slaps his thigh. 'We'll have the bill when you're ready, love.'

Parker folds his arms, leans forward. 'It's all set.'

'Ten?'

'Just as you asked.'

'Where?'

Parker nods over his shoulder. 'By the Downs.'

'Beautiful. He'll be on his own?'

Parker nods.

'Let's have that address in full then.'

Parker pulls a crumpled piece of paper from his pocket, hands it over.

Noble studies it. An estate, the Nightingale, north-west side of the Downs, about a ten-minute drive east-south-east from Stoke Newington nick.

'What do you think?' Noble asks.

Parker pouts, considers. 'I reckon it's run by our mob.'

'Why?'

'The Rastas have their own network, right? And I'm guessing there's an arrangement in place, up round here anyway.'

'Makes sense.'

'Point is, they were happy as pie to give me the address, but on one condition.'

'Go on.'

'I'm looking to buy and use, nothing more, no intent, yeah?'

Noble nodding –

'Why would they be so quick if it weren't safe?'

Noble nodding –

'Seems to me it was like a referral.'

Noble nodding –

'Partners or something. So—'

Noble nodding, smiling –

Noble says, 'Let's get over there now.'

He leaves coins on the table. His legs ache, his tongue thick.

The Nightingale Estate, Downs Road, Lower Clapton:

Six twenty-two-storey towers, each sixty-five metres high –

Seaton Point

Embley Point

Farnell Point

Rachel Point

Rathbone Point

Southerland Point

Built by the GLC in 1968; housing for London by London.

Concrete blocks and tiny windows –

Boxed in like rats in a drain.

Noble remembers this like he remembers Holly Street –

Scrapping to get to the top.

A utopian solution, a community of workers, streets in the sky –

Communal areas dark and empty.

The usual problems of anti-social behaviour, the lack of a police presence –

Nothing to do but sniff glue and nick car stereos.

Facilities broken, council funds never there to fix them, never there to empty the bins –

The bins full of rats and maggots. The lifts stink of piss.

A law unto itself –

The streetlamps smashed.

The walkways dirty and clogged.

Shivering in your cold front room in winter.

Outsiders' cars keyed and punctured –

Sweating in your broiling front room in summer.

Pensioners hobbling back from the post office on pension day, waiting for the muggers to break in –

Noble says, 'I think we'll walk.'

Crossing the Downs, he remarks, 'A couple I know did their wedding photos here, back in the late seventies.'

Parker goes, 'Oh yeah?'

'Looked good, the towers, rearing up behind them, the wind and the frost.'

'Brutal beauty.'

'That's right.'

'White wedding, was it?'

Noble laughs. Inside, he feels nothing.

Noble and Parker stare up at Rachel Point.

It is not yet eight-thirty –

'The trick here, then,' Noble says, 'is that for once we *want* to look like Old Bill.'

Parker doesn't laugh.

Noble pushes him forwards. 'Come on.'

The lift stinks of piss, but it works.

Fourteenth floor –

Noble and Parker looking right and left, eyeing the floorplan –

Noble nods. 'This way.'

Down the narrow path, front doors peeling, the odd pot plant dying, rusting bicycles with one or no wheels, threadbare mats insisting Wipe Your Bloody Feet, housewives twitching net curtains, shouts of kids on the ground drifting up, washing hanging in the arches –

Noble nods. 'This one.'

He stands to one side, gestures for Parker to ring the bell.

Ding-dong.

Sound of slippers shuffling and sliding –

The door opens. Parker sniffs –

A woman pokes her head round the door, Noble smiles –

'I've been wondering when I'd see you again,' says Dawn Driscoll. 'You best come in.'

'What you doing here, Dawn?'

They sit in a neatly furnished room, the coffee table clean and polished, a pot of tea and an ashtray, three cups, three saucers.

'You remember Shahid Akhtar?' Dawn asks.

'Of course.'

'He gave me something, something to use if I ever got in any serious trouble.'

'Why didn't you tell me this last time we met?'

'I wasn't in any serious trouble.'

'I've got to say,' Noble declares, 'this place looks better than your last one.'

'Slicker operation. Don't mean I'm not in trouble.'

'That's not a euphemism, is it? You were supposed to be "in trouble" the last time we met.'

'Good memory.'

Noble shrugs.

'My old place, Holly Street. There's a panel behind the television set. It's in there.'

'What is it?'

'You'll see.'

'I'm still not clear what you're doing here, Dawn.'

'Best you don't know.'

She readies herself to stand.

'Busy day, is it?'

'They'll be here soon, and then it starts, yeah.'

'Who's they, Dawn?'

She shakes her head.

'Dawn.'

'Go and find what's behind my old television set, and we'll talk.'

Noble nods.

'They miss you down the old Axe, you know,' he says. 'Let's dance, eh?' he winks.

'I bet they do.'

'This doesn't feel like something a girl like you would choose, Dawn, tell the truth.'

Dawn stands, folds her cigarette into the ashtray, swallows down the

344

end of her tea, smacks her lips, informs them, 'I'm going to have a quick bath.'

Outside the front door, Noble checks his watch.

'We've got time if we crack on.'

Parker nods. 'Nice turn of phrase.'

Noble agrees. His legs cave.

14 May.

Suzi attends the fourth demonstration organised by the Roach Family Support Committee.

Keith says, as they walk, 'It feels a bit subdued, doesn't it, love?'

'How do you want it to feel, Keith?' Suzi snaps. 'It's not a bloody carnival.'

Chastened, Keith acknowledges, 'You're right.'

The next day, Suzi attends the Kill the Bill Conference at Hackney town hall. Keith does not join her.

The conference, Suzi thinks, is a bit subdued.

There's something odd about the fact that there were no arrests the previous day, something disquieting.

They should be celebrating this fact, but they're not.

Saffron Walden.

Suzi hasn't seen her dad for a long time, and he looks frail, empty, deflated, like all that life in him, all that *energy*, has seeped out –

And she knows now, of course, how unwell he is. The sickness fills the room like the smell of sour meat.

He tells her, 'There'll be some money for you, sweetheart. Use it wisely.'

His grey hand feels brittle, cold like bone. His neck is yellow.

'Dad.'

'Location, location, location, am I right?'

'*Dad.*'

'I'm serious, sweetheart.'

He's coughing now; it sounds like it comes from somewhere very deep, somewhere rotten, somewhere barren –

Suzi nods. 'I know.'

'Just promise me, OK?' He clutches her fingers in his and Suzi thinks how easily it would be to snap one. 'Promise me you'll use it, buy somewhere for yourselves, you and Keith, and, well, you know, for yourselves.'

'I promise,' Suzi says. She nods, feels a swelling in her chest, a lightness behind the eyes. 'I promise.'

Her dad winks. 'Good girl.' He gives her hand a pat. 'Now fetch me the evening paper and go and help your mother in the kitchen.'

Suzi feels the tears come as she leaves the room.

She looks back and sees him looking up at her.

'I've really missed you, Dad,' she says, but she's not sure if he hears her.

Godfrey Heaven spills into Jon Davies' office brandishing a broadsheet newspaper.

'Easy there, Godfrey,' Jon says. 'You'll do yourself a mischief.'

'You seen this?'

He thrusts the newspaper at Jon with two hands, like he's shooing away a wasp.

Jon takes it, smooths it out –

A smartly dressed man, a headline beneath:

LABOUR SAY HE'S BLACK
TORIES SAY HE'S BRITISH

Jon tuts, his expression downcast.

He mutters, 'The same people who make jokes about a black man in a suit.'

'It's shameless,' Godfrey Heaven insists. 'Shameless!'

5

I Guess That's Why They Call It the Blues

May–June 1983

Parker

You edge the front door open, go in. The corridor is tight, the floor and walls covered in the same dull carpet. You check the living room – rubbish and broken furniture. In the bathroom, the same bath half full of the same dirty water. The same dirty water is warm, putrid, the same layer of scum, thick, clotted – the same bathroom window smashed, the same syringes on the floor, pipes on the floor, the same foil burnt and crumpled – the same sky visible. A bright, blue sky – the same council-estate grey, warm, breezy. The same windows slammed shut and steamed. The same voices and coughing, sniffing and hacking – the same kettles whistle, the same kids shout, the same television sets crackle and shriek. The same radios play Elton John singing about the blues. Back in the living room, you find the television, its screen put in, you get down on your hands and knees, you watch for broken glass, for live wires, you find the panel, you brush the dirt and the dust from its corners, you edge it out, bit by bit – behind, in a clear plastic folder, pristine, what looks like a leather ledger. Bingo. Not long after and you're at a pre-arranged meet-up with your mate Trevor who put you in touch with the Big Men and who's now sobbing, Trevor who you've just informed is in real trouble, Trevor who you've just told you can help. Trevor sobbing, Trevor shouting, you're saying, Trust me, Trev, we're on the same side, I'm not looking to stitch you up, quite the opposite. Trevor angry, wiping his eyes, Trust you, you fucking snake, and you're nodding going, Yeah, fair enough, but listen, they came to me to help you, I ain't one of them and look at these, and you show Trevor the photographs, you point out exactly who is in these photographs and you tell Trevor, It's not you lot they're after, and Trevor, sobbing, shuddering, wiping his eyes on his tracksuit sleeve, starts to nod, he starts to see it, he starts to understand and he says, I ain't got much choice, do I? and you tell him, *This is a chance, mate, an opportunity, you're going to get out of this and some, you understand?* and Trevor stops sobbing and he looks at you and you see it in his eye, determination, you see it in his eye, injustice, and he goes, *OK, yeah, OK.*

Queensbridge Road, outside the Holly Street Estate.

Noble's got the radio on as he waits for Parker. Another talk show, speculating.

'The positions, and the polarised nature of these positions, that the two main parties are taking are likely to squeeze the life out of the traditionally more extremist parties, the National Front, the British National Party, the Workers' Revolutionary Party – they all stand to lose votes, lose deposits, lose, lose, lose. You might ask: is this a bad thing? Well, perhaps what you should ask is: when did our mainstream politics become so extreme?'

He thinks, What's changed?

Parker gets in the passenger side, says, 'I wish they'd all give it a rest.'

Noble clicks the radio off.

'Let's have it then.'

Parker hands him a clear plastic folder.

Noble, gloves on, opens it –

A ledger. Sums, numbers, names –

Names of policemen, names of businessmen, names of known associates, names of families well known around Whitechapel, Bethnal Green –

Shahid Akhtar's ledger.

'I don't think the Inland Revenue have had a copy of this,' Parker says.

Noble flicks pages. He's looking for a specific date, to satisfy his curiosity, to indicate *something*, something he knows.

He goes through the years: '75, '76, '77 –

1978.

Months, now: January, February, March –

April.

He turns pages, end of the month:

30 April 1978, the Carnival against Racism.

A Sunday. The ledger weekend page is tight. Pencil marks and eraser marks, ink smudges –

A column suggesting money received: a list of initials, six pairs, ending with SH, suggesting the man himself has contributed.

A second column, a figure, quite high, a total amount.

A third column, a name: *Williams*. Suggesting money outgoing. Money from Shahid Akhtar, and others, to Detective Sergeant Williams.

It's something, it's a start.

Noble checks his watch. 'We better go and meet your mate,' he tells Parker.

Noble watches Parker lay it out for his mate.

He hasn't got a great deal of choice, Parker's mate, what with the photos, and Parker's giving him the options, the lay of the land.

Noble's on a bench on Downs Road, Parker and his mate in the car, making sure he times it just right.

The Nightingale Estate looms overhead, firmly punctuating the cloudless sky.

Beyond, the pylon buzz and dry crackle of Millfields and the marshes, grass yellowing, the terminal pollution of the canal heavy and slimy, wafting rotting sludge.

Where they found Shahid Akhtar, waterlogged and bloated, full of booze and pills.

Misadventure.

Dawn Driscoll said, *He gave me something, something to use if I ever got in any serious trouble.*

Noble can see why. The ledger suggests serious collusion. The ledger suggests Mr Akhtar was paying off Whitechapel plod as well as into the old villains for a fair wallop. The figures suggest there was plenty of movement between these parties.

One name crops up that Noble is not unhappy to see: Williams.

If this ledger is going to help Dawn Driscoll, it needs to be in the right person's hands, it needs to be leverage.

Why hasn't she used it before?

Noble knows she was under a charge threat and there's likely more where that came from. And of course –

Shahid Akhtar, under false pretences, is led to believe that his mistress is pregnant. *Extortion.*

Shahid Akhtar never knew that his mistress, a woman who claimed to love him, was an Old Bill set-up from the off. *Deception.* A means to get to him, which worked.

Shahid Akhtar in financial cahoots with police and thieves, and here they are, those records of corrupt practices. *Protection, evasion, money-lending.* It's no wonder he kept this ledger in such detail, no wonder he gave it to Dawn. His own insurance, Noble supposes.

Shahid Akhtar full of booze and pills to drown his sorrows, which he literally does. *Misadventure.* A bird on the side who was not, it turns out, very pregnant at all.

Cover-up.

Noble picks his moment, jumps into the back seat –

'Hello, boys.'

Parker says to his mate, 'This is Detective Constable Patrick Noble. He's got a few questions for you. If you answer them to his satisfaction, he'll be your liaison, OK?'

Parker's mate nods.

In the rear-view mirror, he looks beaten, resigned, Parker's mate, but practical, too, Noble thinks.

Bingo.

'What's your name, son?'

'Trevor.'

'OK, Trevor, I'm delighted to meet you.'

'I can't say the feeling's mutual,' says Trevor.

Noble enjoys this. 'Oh, you will, son, you will. I'm the best friend you've ever had.'

Trevor says nothing. His eyes forwards, his hands in his lap.

'You've become acquainted with my associate Parker through, ostensibly, the campaign for a public inquiry into the death of Colin Roach. That's not why you're here. You're here as I have photographic evidence of illegal activity in which you feature. You've seen the photos, I assume.'

Trevor nods.

'I wouldn't normally be interested in your low-level dealings, Trevor, except I couldn't help but notice your business partners.'

Trevor nods. He fidgets –

Parker passes Noble a photograph. 'This is you,' Noble says, 'and this here is Detective Constable Rice and this here is Detective Constable Cole, both based in Stoke Newington.'

Trevor nods.

'How did this business relationship begin, Trevor? We'll start there.'

Trevor glances at Parker, who nods. Noble watches the back of Trevor's head.

'About six months ago, I was picked up on a sus.'

'Sus laws are banned, Trevor.'

'You know what I mean, a stop and search.'

'Who by?'

'A couple of uniforms.'

'You were on your own?'

'Yeah.'

'Where?'

Trevor points. 'Back of the school, this side of Kingsland Road.'

Noble nods. 'Go on.'

'The uniforms said they found something on me. I didn't have anything on me, yeah. I told them. They called a car. They took me in.'

'What next?'

'They booked me into Stoke Newington on a possession. They left me in a cell for three hours, no water, no phone call, no brief, nothing.'

'Go on.'

'Rice and Cole come in after that and tell me there's a way I can avoid a charge for the possession. I tell them I wasn't holding anything. They hold up two bags, one small, one big. They say if I carry on with this line, they'll put the big bag on me and it's possession with intent. If I don't, they can make the little bag go away and I'll be working for them. And if

I don't take this new line of work they're offering, they'll put one on my little sister and bring her into another bit of their business.'

'So, you choose the little bag.'

'What else was I supposed to do?'

Noble nods. 'Fair enough. Tell me about the work.'

'Deliveries and pick-ups, that's all. Like in the photos.'

'You ever see what's in the bags, in the packages?'

Trevor shakes his head. His hands in his lap –

Noble nods. 'We've got you at Kersley Road, at the Coach, that Turkish café. Where else?'

Trevor points across the road. 'A flat in there.' He's pointing at the Nightingale Estate. 'A woman lives there.'

'What goes on up there?'

'I don't know, I just deliver.'

'What do you *think* goes on up there?'

Trevor shakes his head.

Noble nods. 'You think it might be the kind of business they wanted to involve your little sister in?'

Trevor shakes his head.

Noble nods. 'OK, Trevor.'

'What happens next?' Trevor asks.

'You keep me informed, through Parker, of exactly what it is you're up to. The first thing you do is get a look in one of those bags – we know what's in the envelopes. We also know what's going on at Kersley Road. I want to know what's going on over there.' He nods at the estate. 'Yeah?'

Trevor nods.

'If you want all of this to go away, and I mean all of it, you do what me and Parker here tell you.' Noble makes a face in the rear-view mirror: *come on, son.* 'You're going to have to trust us.'

Trevor looks at Parker, who nods. 'Yeah, I know,' Trevor agrees.

'And you keep your mouth shut.'

'Course.'

'One more thing, Trevor. You ever hear of Colin Roach in this kind of a context?'

Trevor shakes his head. He fidgets, his hands in his lap –

'You're sure?'

Trevor nods.

Noble nods. 'OK, Trevor, you're a good boy.' Across the front seat Noble tousles his hair. 'We're going to get you out of this very soon, mate.'

Parker adds, 'We will.'

Noble says, 'Play it cool, son. I can see you will.'

Trevor nods. There's a hopeful look in his eye. Noble smiles at him in the rear-view mirror –

'On your bike then.'

Trevor jumps out, jogs across Hackney Downs towards Clapton, doesn't look back.

Noble checks his watch.

He leans forward, a hand on Parker's shoulder –

'Come on, let's get ourselves over to Cracker Dawn's.'

He hands Parker the ledger –

'Stick this under the seat for me, there's a good lad.'

Out the car, over the roof, Noble admits, 'You done well there, son.'

Noble climbs back in, heart heaving, trying to compose himself.

Suzi's looking again at the list of names Noble gave her, the list of names and the list of crimes, thinking about how to contact these young men, how to tell their stories, whether she *can* tell their stories, whether she should, whether these stories are her stories to tell, even, to what end would she tell them, to what *purpose*, when Keith crashes through the door and into their kitchen –

'Babe,' he says. 'Have I got some good news for you.'

'You been to bed yet, Keith?'

'I haven't.'

Suzi's smiling.

'A long night, I grant you, but quality.'

'Really.'

'Top quality night.'

Suzi's shaking her head.

'What was I saying?'

'News, you've got some good news.'

Keith grins. 'Oh yeah! The *news*.' Gleefully, he rubs his hands together. 'Suzi Sweetheart, I am taking you to Paris.'

Suzi looks doubtful.

'I swear, God's honest.'

'Keith.'

'Most romantic city in the world, Suze. Who knows what'll happen, eh?'

He twirls a meaningful finger in the air.

'Keith!'

'The good news is it's work, all paid for, love,' Keith reasons. 'Weller and Talbot are going over to do some promo shots for the new single, all European, you know how they are, week or so after the election.' Keith pauses here, turns his hands into pistols, extends forefinger and thumb. 'And they want *you* to do the job. And as for me –' he points his thumbs at his chest – 'I'll be poncing.'

Suzi smiles. Week or so after the election, meaning week or so after the inquest, meaning, Yes, yes, yes.

Suzi kisses Keith, holds him. 'Who knows what'll happen.'

Hackney Mothers' Hospital.

Jon Davies holds Jackie's hand.

They're looking at a machine, wobbly lines and boom-boom, boom-boom.

A woman moves equipment over Jackie's tummy.

Jon's trying to follow what he's looking at, but it's pretty hopeless. It's taken a while to find everything they're looking for, but they've managed it. Jackie had to wriggle around, go for a walk – twice! – before the little bugger showed itself proper.

Tense, all that, Jon thinks, never quite knowing what's happening, the nurse implacable, the technician making noises like a car mechanic, Ooh I don't know about that, and do they mean the bloody machine or the baby –

'And that,' the woman is saying, 'means you're going to have a – wait, did you want to know?'

Jon squeezes Jackie's hand.

Jackie says, 'Yes, we did, if that's OK.'

The woman smiles. 'A little girl,' she says, 'you're having a girl.'

Jon claps, grins, he kisses Jackie. 'That's wonderful.'

Jackie nods. 'It really is.'

Holding hands, they thank the woman.

'Your second, I think,' she says.

'Yes,' Jon says.

Jackie adds, 'A baby sister for our son.'

'Lucky boy.'

'A very lucky boy.'

The lift stinks of piss.

Fourteenth floor –

Down the narrow path again, front doors still peeling, the odd pot plant still dying, rusting bicycles still with one or no wheels, threadbare mats still insisting Wipe Your Bloody Feet, housewives still twitching net curtains, shouts of kids on the ground still drifting up, washing still hanging in the arches –

Noble stops. He turns to Parker. He points down the corridor –

'What the fuck?'

Outside Dawn Driscoll's front door, a uniformed officer.

The front door off its hinges, blue-and-white tape across the space, neighbours gawping, hands wrapped round mugs of tea –

'Jesus,' Parker adds, unnecessarily.

Noble pulls his warrant card. The uniform inspects it.

The uniform sniffs.

'Well?' Noble demands.

'I was told you'd show up. I was told you'd need written authority. You got some then?'

Noble glares. Noble steps back –

Parker, who's been examining the window, leans in close to him.

'Guv,' he says, 'there's no one else in there. We could, you know.'

He nods at the uniform, raises an eyebrow.

Noble shakes his head. He turns back to the uniform. 'Cole and Rice.'

There's a flicker –

'Written authority.'

Noble nods. 'You stay here,' he tells Parker. 'Keep an eye.'

Noble leaves –

Noble, again, gets straight up the road to Stoke Newington nick, again he parks round the side, again he's in the front entrance, again he's up the stairs, again he's down the corridor, again he's into a smoke-filled room, a room that still reeks of stale booze and coffee, of takeaway curry, of body odour and grease, a tired, strip-lit room where Williams and Cole and Rice are having another powwow –

Noble shouts, 'She was mine.'

Williams and Cole and Rice turn.

Noble, again, 'You've compromised me.'

Williams and Cole and Rice, laughing now –

Williams shaking his head. 'Word came this morning. Open and shut. Possession with intent to supply. A shit-tonne of the stuff.'

Noble shaking his head –

'No—'

Williams saying, 'New stuff too, called crack cocaine, very addictive, very destructive, boyo.' Nodding at Rice and Cole. 'Decorated for this, these two will be.'

'I want to talk to her,' Noble says.

Rice and Cole shaking their heads.

Williams smiles. 'I don't see the harm in that.'

Noble turns, out the door, down the steps, into the basement, into the interview room where they've got Dawn Driscoll –

'Hello again,' she says.

'I'd say you're in real trouble now, Dawn.'

'I'd say I brought it on myself.'

'That's very fatalistic.'

Dawn Driscoll smirks. 'Rather more literally, I mean.'

'You tipped them off yourself.'

'Not exactly, no.'

'Why, Dawn?'

'A long and distinguished list of police officers I've had relationships with, one way or another. Has to end sometime.'

'You know how cases like these go, don't you?'

'I can guess.'

Noble shakes his head. 'No, you can't. You plead guilty, first off, is the only chance you've got. And you state that your co-conspirators were police officers and that you were compelled by them to commit this crime.'

Dawn Driscoll snorts.

Noble raises a finger. 'You state your belief that the raid was coordinated by your co-conspirators when you refused to continue to conspire.' Noble sits back, leans forward. 'Then what happens is the judge will take this into consideration *when sentencing*. And what he'll say is that his sentence is made on the basis that your crime stemmed from a corrupt officer, but this does not mean that he accepts the allegations.'

'Sounds a bit pongy to me.'

'It should.'

'Well then.'

'Point is, Dawn, the judge accepts your statement as true and sentences you with it in mind, and the statement and its contents have no consequences beyond your sentencing.'

'If I plead guilty.'

'His other option is to hold a trial within a trial to ascertain the truth of the part of your statement regarding your co-conspirators.'

Again, Dawn Driscoll snorts.

'And that ain't going to happen,' Noble concludes.

Again, Dawn Driscoll says, 'If I plead guilty.'

'This insistence, Dawn.'

'You find it?'

Noble nods.

'Well then.'

Noble bites his lip. 'Who turned you on to him in the first place, Dawn?'

Dawn Driscoll shakes her head.

'Without that, I'm not sure what I've got.'

Dawn Driscoll nods. 'You'll figure it out.'

She signals the uniform on duty.

'Look, you'll have to excuse me,' she tells Noble. 'I need to spend a penny.'

Noble nods, leaves –

D-Day, 6 June, Clerkenwell County Court.

Jon Davies and Godfrey Heaven sit down as the inquest into the death of Colin Roach begins.

'You may think on the facts you heard that this is the only possible verdict,' the coroner says.

'Or not,' Godfrey Heaven says.

Jon says nothing.

Godfrey Heaven leans over.

Jon can smell coffee and garlic on his breath –

'Professor Stuart Hall was speaking outside,' Godfrey Heaven is saying in a rapid whisper. 'A good line, he said: "It is open to doubt whether any home secretary in his right mind would calmly and quietly acquiesce in such an implausible story as an adequate explanation of the death of his own son in similar circumstances." Spot on, I think, don't you, Jon?'

Jon nods.

The county court is warm, close with all the bodies, stifling, that weight, the expectation.

Jon's already sizing up the players, wondering who'll perform.

In Parliament, June 1983, formerly Bedwellty, now Islwyn, MP Neil Kinnock: If Mrs Thatcher wins on Thursday, I warn you not to be ordinary. I warn you not to be young. I warn you not to fall ill. I warn you not to get old.

Scotland Yard.

Noble's in with Detective Chief Inspector Maurice 'Special' Young.

He's laid out his report, his findings, his recommendations, the evidence –

'What you've got here, DC Noble,' Young says, 'is a good start.'

'Sorry, guv?'

'All this –' Young gestures at the paperwork, the photographs, the statements – 'all this is a good start.'

'I'm not sure I follow, guv.'

Young smiles patiently. He points at pieces of paper, at photographs.

'Circumstantial, hearsay, collusion, entrapment, witness intimidation.' He smiles again. 'Key word is circumstantial.'

Noble nods.

'You've done sterling work, Chance.'

'What next?'

'You carry on. This is an excellent start.'

'I don't understand, guv, you asked me—'

'I asked you to look into Stoke Newington and you have done. It was not an internal police investigation or inquiry.'

'So, we do nothing with it?'

'It's a good start.'

Noble shakes his head. 'If it's machines as well as protection, then it's Inland Revenue.'

'You've got one spycop infiltrated nicely. You've worked a double

362

grass, which is no mean feat. You've got an associate, also on the inside.'

'The fabrication, the blackmail, conspiracy to pervert the course of justice—'

'Anything drastic pulls the rug under all that work. You sit tight, you carry on.'

'What about Colin Roach, guv?' Noble asks. 'What about his family?'

'This is a good start, DC Noble.' Young's nodding. 'You're doing what you can.'

Noble stands, legs wobble, arms shake, offers his hand. 'Thank you, guv.'

Young smiles, shakes. 'Have a word with my secretary on your way out. Bonus check, tax-free,' he winks. 'Take the old lady to Lanzarote, some island. You've earned it.'

Noble nods, staggers out –

Lea tells him: *I love you.*

Look after yourself for once, he decides. *You've earned it.*

He's not sure *how* though.

He thinks about Jon Davies: *the barrenness of a political existence.*

10 June, the news, everywhere: Mrs Thatcher and the Conservative Party win the general election in spectacular fashion. It is a particular personal triumph for the Iron Lady as she becomes the first twentieth-century Conservative prime minister to win successive working majorities.

It is rumoured that when victory was confirmed late into last night, early this morning, she turned to her husband Denis and whispered: *They won't be calling me Hilda anymore.*

Denis Thatcher is said to have replied: *You'll be called a lot more than that.*

The love birds shared a quick kiss and a cuddle and went straight back into Number Ten to sort this country out once and for all.

17 June, Clerkenwell County Court.

Jurors return a majority (8–2) verdict of suicide in the inquest into the death of Colin Roach.

Suzi shakes her head. Suzi thinks – two of you didn't.

Doesn't that mean anything at all?

Suzi looks around the court, the family in tears, the solicitors in tears, friends and supporters shaking their heads, shaking their fists, shouting –

At home, the inquest over, the verdict given, Suzi writes down three questions:

Who was Colin Roach?
Who is Colin Roach?
Who killed Colin Roach?

Some people know the answer to the first question, she thinks.

More people know the answer to the second.

As for the third, whoever it was that killed Colin Roach – and it wasn't Colin Roach, she's sure of that – has got away with it.

Benjamin Zephaniah, Who Killed Colin Roach?
Murder, murder, some a shout,
some of you might have your doubts
but what about our democracy,
we want public inquiry

20 June.

The jurors write a letter to Mrs Thatcher's new home secretary, Leon Brittan. The letter explicitly criticises the police handling of the case, and specifically police treatment of the Roach family, especially Mr and Mrs Roach.

Professor Stuart Hall: Coroner's inquests were never designed or intended to be, and cannot function as, a substitute for an independent public inquiry into matters of this kind which affect public confidence in the expectation of justice under the rule of law from the courts and the police. Nor in such circumstances can the police continue to investigate and 'clear' themselves when it is their own practices and procedures which are in question. The practice of a succession of home secretaries to refuse public inquiries on the grounds that the inquest was, in effect, such an inquiry is, to put it frankly, a dodge and a deceit which convinces no one, least of all the families and individuals involved.

28 June.

Home Secretary Leon Brittan – the youngest home secretary since Winston Churchill – replies to the letter indicating that it will be referred to the Police Complaints Board.

End of Book One

Acknowledgements

White Riot is a work of fiction based on, and woven around, fact. Much of this fact is recognisable in terms of certain names, places, statistics, institutions, events, laws and policy, which have been adapted and, in some cases, changed for dramatic purposes. I grew up in Hackney; this experience accounts for much of the information, and many of the anecdotes, in the novel. Friends, family, colleagues, associates and contemporary media outlets all informed the writing of the novel, both directly and indirectly. Most of all, I want to thank the people who were there for their accounts of what they did. I hope the novel shines light on the unjust deaths – and tragically short lives – of Altab Ali and Colin Roach.

Much has been written about this period; I am grateful to the writers who have gone before. I made extensive use of the exhaustive online archives of the wonderful Radical History of Hackney; the *Hackney Gazette*, too, was an invaluable resource; where documents from these resources are quoted, it is listed in the Notes section that follows. The Undercover Policing Inquiry hosts an archive of documents relating to the spycops scandal at ucpi.org.uk that is important, fascinating, and terrifying. Internet resources are cited in the Notes section where appropriate. Far less righteous, but no less useful in this context, was the online archive of the Margaret Thatcher Foundation, at margaretthatcher.org, which catalogues everything she ever uttered in public, as well as private papers and declassified documents. I came across this thanks to the author's note in Sandbrook, *Who Dares Wins*. During the writing of the novel, I consulted a number of sources to clarify certain facts and timelines; in general, these sources are news media, notably, the BBC, *Guardian*, *The Times*, *Telegraph*, among others. An edited version of the Soho/Challenor story appeared in *The Social Gathering* as 'Soho Mornings', 28 May 2020. Where fiction appears listed in the Bibliography, it has informed this novel in a broad sense, though specific quotation is included in the Notes section.

The plotline featuring my character Shahid Akhtar is fictional.

The police officers in the novel and their actions are entirely fictional.

Noble's interviews with a suspect in the murder of Altab Ali, and with Ali's friend in real life, Shams Uddin, are fictional, though based on a BBC report detailed in the Bibliography and Notes sections. Shams Uddin's words are quoted from this source, though the interaction with Noble is imagined.

The evidence that my fictional character Gideon gives to the planning dispute inquiry over 73 Great Eastern Street is based on the actual evidence of an infiltrator, referenced in the Notes, but otherwise the character is entirely imagined. 'Little Derrick' and other associates of Gideon's are fictional characters.

Moss Evans really was on holiday in Malta when the key union vote took place, as corroborated by a number of the sources in the Bibliography; the repercussions of his failure to cast what would likely have been a decisive vote is explored here. The plot featuring my character Dai Wyn is fictional.

Jon Davies and Godfrey Heaven are fictional characters, though the planning dispute at 73 Great Eastern Street was real. Jon Davies is, as my dad was, a solicitor working for Hackney Council in the late '70s and '80s. Certain stories have been inspirational and informed the writing of the novel. Brynley Heaven is the model for my character Godfrey Heaven; a special thank you for sharing memories of the Police Committee in Hackney in 1983. Gerard McMorrow was a real-life figure heavily involved in the planning dispute as Chairman of Hackney Trades Council. His testimony at the planning dispute – rehearsed in a fictional scene with Jon Davies in the Jack the Ripper pub – is based on sources in the Bibliography and quotes are referenced in the Notes. All interactions with Jon Davies, as well as actions within the novel, are wholly imagined.

Parker is a fictional character; the Undercover Policing Inquiry has demonstrated that spycops were placed in activist groups in Hackney.

Whilst the bands, the music and the magazines in the text are real, my characters Suzi and Keith are fictional and therefore the portrayal of their work and their interactions with those real people and groups is wholly imagined.

The Rock Against Racism and Anti-Nazi League movements are a true and lasting inspiration. In this novel, I quote the words of the real-life figures in those movements from a number of sources cited in the Bibliography and Notes sections. The situations in which they interact with my fictional characters are wholly imagined. Of particular help here was Daniel Rachel's masterful oral history, *Walls Come Tumbling Down*, and I thank Daniel for the depth and rigour of his research and writing; it is a glorious book, covering far more ground than my novel. David Renton's *Never Again* was invaluable here too; a work of academic and political focus that is also hugely entertaining and compelling. All quotes are attributed in the Notes section. Special thanks to Red Saunders, the late David Widgery and Syd Shelton for their accounts and heroics.

In the novel, Jon Davies interviews real-life victims of horrific racial violence and abuse, Abdul Noor and Edward Shaw. Their testimonies are based on statements made as part of the planning dispute inquiry as cited in the *New Society* article and in my Bibliography and specifically in the Notes section. I quote their words in these interviews with my fictional council solicitor; I assume that their statements were given as depositions, but this situation is fictional. In both cases, the facts of the interviews are established, and were part of the inquiry, but their interactions with my character, Jon Davies, are imagined.

I was a fan of Paul Weller, The Style Council and The Jam before beginning the work on this novel; the research and writing of it – and its follow-up – have filled me with further, deeper admiration for the musician and the man. There were 'Honorary Councillors' and Paul Weller's generosity and benevolence to fellow musicians is clear; Suzi and Keith's interactions with him and members of The Style Council and associates are wholly imagined.

In the novel, Noble interviews friends and family of Colin Roach. With the exception of Lloyd Manley, who is a fictional character, these interviews are based on media reports of the inquest – and build-up to it – into Colin Roach's death, as well as reports in the Roach Family Support Committee Bulletins published in 1983. I quote their words faithfully and in good faith; the situations where I do so are fictional. After the inquest into Colin Roach's death delivered an 8–2 verdict of suicide, the Roach Family Support Committee set up an Independent Committee of Inquiry, which led to the publication of their book *Policing in Hackney 1945–1984* (Karia Press, 1989), which informed much of the writing of the second half of this novel, specifically the established narrative of Colin Roach's death and the protests that followed, and key elements of the inquest process. I discovered this text via John Eden's illuminating article for *Datacide* magazine, which is essential reading and was, in hindsight, an inspiration for much of this novel.

I refer to a number of real people who were wrongfully arrested during protests in 1983; the reports of these instances are documented and cited in the Notes section.

Mrs Iris Walkinshaw was head teacher at Rushmore Infants' School when I attended in the 1980s. She is a figure of inspiration and I hoped to capture something of that in the novel. Her interactions with Jon Davies are wholly imagined, though certain aspects – including the incident where 'Joe' is attacked by an older pupil – are based on personal experience.

Please see the Bibliography and Notes sections for further detail.

Bibliography

Non-Fiction

Beckett, Andy, *Promised You a Miracle: Why 1980–1982 Made Modern Britain* (Allen Lane, 2015)

Beckett, Andy, *When the Lights Went Out: Britain in the Seventies* (Faber & Faber, 2009)

Blackman, Rick, *Babylon's Burning: Music, Subcultures and Anti-Fascism in Britain 1958–2020* (Bookmarks Publications, 2021)

Bloom, Clive, *Violent London: 2000 Years of Riots, Rebels, and Revolts* (Palgrave Macmillan, 2010)

Buford, Bill, *Among the Thugs* (Martin Secker & Warburg, 1991)

Burn, Gordon, *Pocket Money* (Faber & Faber, 2008)

Harrison, Paul, *Inside the Inner City: Life Under the Cutting Edge* (Penguin, 1983)

Huddle, R., and Saunders, R. (eds), *Reminiscences of RAR* (Redwords, 2016)

Independent Committee of Inquiry, *Policing in Hackney 1945–1984* (Karia Press, 1989)

McLean, Donna, *Small Town Girl* (Hodder & Stoughton, 2021)

McSmith, Andy, *No Such Thing as Society: Britain in the Turmoil of the 1980s* (Constable, 2010)

Morton, James, *Bent Coppers: A Survey of Police Corruption* (Warner Books, 1994)

Munn, Iain, *Mr Cool's Dream: A Complete History of The Style Council* (A Wholepoint Publication, 2011)

Rachel, Daniel, *Walls Come Tumbling Down: The Music and Politics of Rock Against Racism, 2 Tone and Red Wedge* (Picador, 2016)

Renton, David, *Never Again: Rock Against Racism and the Anti-Nazi League 1976–1982* (Routledge, 2019)

Sandbrook, Dominic, *Seasons in the Sun: The Battle for Britain 1974–1979* (Penguin, 2013)

Sandbrook, Dominic, *Who Dares Wins, Britain, 1979–1982* (Penguin, 2019)

Shelton, Syd, *Rock Against Racism* (Autograph, 2015)

Sinclair, Iain, *Lights Out for the Territory* (Penguin, 2003)

Sinclair, Iain, *Hackney, That Rose-Red Empire* (Penguin, 2009)

Stewart, Graham, *Bang! A History of Britain in 1980s* (Atlantic Books, 2013)

Thorn, Tracey, *Bedsit Disco Queen* (Virago, reprint edition, 2013)

Turner, Alwyn W., *Crisis? What Crisis? Britain in the 1970s* (Aurum Press, 2008)

Turner, Alwyn W., *Rejoice! Rejoice! Britain in the 1980s* (Aurum Press, 2008)

Walker, Martin, *The National Front* (Fontana, 1977)

Weller, Paul, *Suburban 100: Selected Lyrics* (Arrow, 2010)

Widgery, David, *Beating Time: Riot 'n' Race 'n' Rock and Roll* (Chatto & Windus, 1986)

Woodyatt, Andrew et al., *The Rio Tape/Slide Archive* (Isola Press, 2020)

Journalism

'"They Hate Us, We Hate Them" – Resisting Police Corruption and Violence in Hackney in the 1980s and 1990s' by John Eden, *Datacide* magazine, 12 June, 2015

'Back to Front' by Mike Goulden, Charles Ashleigh and Doris Archer, *Marxism Today*, March 1980

'Altab Ali: The Racist Murder that Mobilised the East End' by Catrin Nye and Sam Bright, *BBC News*, 3 May 2016

'Who Killed Altab Ali?' by David Widgery, *CARF 6* (autumn 1978)

'Rock Against Racism: The Syd Shelton Images that Define an Era' by Killiian Fox, *Observer*, 6 September 2015

'Spandau Ballet: The Sound of Thatcherism' by Michael Hann, *Guardian*, 25 March 2009

'Spandau Ballet, The Blitz Kids and the New Romantics' by David Johnson, *Guardian*, 4 October 2009

'Stand Down, Margaret!' by John Lewis, *Uncut*, 12 April 2013

'Blair Peach Killed by Police at 1979 Protest, Met Report Finds' by Paul Lewis, *Guardian*, 27 April 2010

'Police Use Unauthorised Weapons, Peach Jury Told' by David Pallister and Nick Davies, *Guardian*, 7 May 1980

'Simon Says' by Ian Walker, *New Society*, January 1980

'The Year Rock Found the Power to Unite' by Sarfraz Manzoor, *The Observer*, 8 April 2008

'How Denis Thatcher Went to War with the BBC over "Foul Libel" of His Wife' by Ben Farmer, *Daily Telegraph*, 21 July 2016

'The Political Legacy of Blair Peach' by Jenny Bourne, *Institute of Race Relations*, https://irr.org.uk/article/the-political-legacy-of-blair-peach/

'Benjamin Zephaniah on How Colin Roach's Death Inside Stoke Newington Police Station Sparked a Movement 35 Years Ago' by Emma Bartholomew, *Hackney Gazette*, 23 January 2018

'Britannia Rules the Waves' by Emma Bartholomew, *Hackney Gazette*, 18 January 2017

'I was Engaged to an Undercover Police Officer' by Donna McLean, *Guardian*, 29 January 2021

Fiction

Arnott, Jake, *He Kills Coppers* (Sceptre, 2002)

King, John, *Human Punk* (Jonathan Cape, 2001)

Mantel, Hilary, *The Assassination of Margaret Thatcher* (Fourth Estate, 2014)

Mantel, Hilary, *A Place of Greater Safety* (Fourth Estate, 2010)

Nath, Michael, *The Treatment* (Riverrun, 2020)

Peace, David, *Nineteen Eighty-Three* (Serpent's Tail, 2002)

Peace, David, *GB84* (Faber & Faber, 2004)

Unsworth, Cathi, *The Singer* (Serpent's Tail, 2007)

Film/Television

Babylon by Franco Rossi (1980)

Long Hot Summers: The Story of The Style Council by Lee Cogswell (2020)

Pop into Politics, TV Eye, ITV 30 January 1986

Rude Boy by Jack Hazan and David Mingay (1980)

Small Axe (5-part BBC series) by Steve McQueen (2020)

Speak Like a Child by The Style Council, promotional music video by Tim Pope, Polydor Ltd, 1983

The Filth and the Fury by Julien Temple (2000)

Uprising (3-part BBC series) by Steve McQueen (2021)

White Riot by Rubika Shah (2020)

Who Killed Colin Roach? by Isaac Julien (1983)

World in Action, BBC 1, 27 January 1978

Yardie by Idris Elba (2019)

Notes

40–1 Noble's interview with the suspect is fictional, though based on, and including quotes from, an account by Nye and Bright, BBC News: If we saw a Paki we'd have a go at them. We would ask for money and then beat them up. I've beaten up Pakis on at least five occasions.

42 Noble's interview with Shams Uddin is fictional, though quotes from the same BBC source, as follows: I was feeling excited, I was a big boy, casting my vote for the first time. Nye and Bright, BBC News

42 He told me he needed to go home because he had some cooking to do and after that he was going to go out and vote too. Nye and Bright, BBC News

42 We [knew] there [would be] no place for us unless we [fought] back. So everyone joined together – Bangladeshi people, Caribbean people, Indian people, Pakistani people. Everyone [was] involved. Nye and Bright, BBC News

42–3 It [was] difficult for Bengalis to go out on their own because you'[d] often [be] abused. If you live[d] on a council estate your neighbours [would] be very hostile towards you. They [would] break your windows, they [would] push rubbish through your letterbox – basically make your life miserable. Nye and Bright, BBC News

43 One of our community leaders told us that if we kill racism from the political ground, it will automatically die on the streets. Nye and Bright, BBC News

45–6 There was a marked increase in racist graffiti, particularly NF symbols, all over Tower Hamlets and in the presence both of NF 'heavies' and clusters of alienated young people at key fascist locations, especially in Bethnal Green. Ken Leech, Anglican priest for Brick Lane

… the Bengali youth, who have joined enthusiastically with their white friends in combating a menace which in its ultimate form will spell the death knell of a democratic Britain. Tassaduq Ahmed, educational worker in the East End

How many more racial attacks? Why are the police covering

up? Placard, protest march carrying Altab Ali's coffin to Downing Street. Renton, *Never Again*, pp. 123–5

53–4 Matlock Street, Varden Street, Walden Street and Old Montague Street, in Jubilee Street, Adelina Grove, Lindley Street, Redmans Road, White Horse Road, Aston Street, Flamborough, Westport and for a time Arbour Square. Renton, *Never Again*, p. 124

55 If we saw a Paki we'd have a go at them. We would ask for money and then beat them up. I've beaten up Pakis on at least five occasions. Nye and Bright, BBC News

62 Worse since [the] National Front [came] on the scene. Worse [still] since [Mrs] Thatcher['s]. Renton, *Never Again*, p. 123

63 Single-handedly [she has] recuperated overt racism into the parliamentary tradition. Widgery, *Beating Time*, p. 14

63 An elderly Asian hospital porter sacked for looking ill. A Bangladeshi woman sectioned in the seventh month of pregnancy. A white trade unionist driven to insomnia by window bashing after he's defended his Asian neighbour. Widgery, 'Who Killed Altab Ali?', p. 8

64 It's a coincidence. Extracted from 'Back to Front' by Mike Goulden, Charles Ashleigh and Doris Archer, *Marxism Today*, March 1980

64–5 Stuart Weir quote from *Red Pepper*, redpepper.org.uk via the Radical History of Hackney

65 Quote from Anti-Nazi League pamphlet 'Heroes or Villains' by Anti-Fascist Action, 1992, via the Radical History of Hackney

65–6 Derrick Day rant from *The Filth and the Fury* by Julien Temple

75–6 References to newspaper coverage of the Altab Ali march to Downing Street statistics from Renton, *Never Again*, p. 123

78 Nesta Wyn Ellis tract from Turner, *Crisis? What Crisis!*, p. 272

78 *World in Action*, BBC 1, 27 January 1978, Margaret Thatcher Foundation, www.margaretthatcher.org

78 I think we are trying to get rid of discrimination wherever it occurs. Turner, *Crisis? What Crisis!*, p. 269

82 The most heavily policed area in Britain. Renton, *Never Again*, p. 124

83 I'm forever blowing bubbles, West Ham United club song

84 Based on certain lyrics from 'White Noise' by Stiff Little Fingers

86–7 Contrary to the council's policy of encouraging employment
      opportunities [...] The presence of the front leads to political
      unrest, likely physical clashes, and this will act as a considerable
      disincentive to companies who might otherwise have set up shop
      in Hackney. Added to this, that the racist nature of the National
      Front will discourage black workers from seeking jobs in the area.
      People are frightened, in Hackney south. 'Simon Says' by Ian
      Walker, *New Society*, January 1980

89 Edward Shaw's interaction with Jon Davies is fictional, but quotes
    from 'Simon Says' by Ian Walker, *New Society*, January 1980: We
    work here three weeks. Every morning we clear out the rubbish
    and shit that's filled the hole during the night. It's nasty, wet. It
    stinks of piss. Every night, men leave and call us dirty nigger
    bastards. Some nights, they throw stones.

89 There is no difference, in my mind, between the relatively light
    sooty, or satchy, and their heavier counterparts, coon or wog
    or the n-word, you understand. Adapted from Morton, *Bent
    Coppers*, p. 293

90 Cultivated rhetoric of abuse. Morton, *Bent Coppers*, p. 293

90 Fair deal to all. Morton, *Bent Coppers*, p. 293

92 Parker's reference to Abdul Monan and his account of the abuse
    that Monan suffered is based on Renton, *Never Again*, p. 124,
    specifically the horrific nature of the attack and the injuries that
    Monan sustained; the situation and context of this account in the
    novel – Parker to Noble – is fictional

94–5 Suzi's interview with Jake Burns is fictional but based on and
      quotes from Jake Burns in Rachel, *Walls*, pp. 158–60

104 You ask the housewife ... Perhaps it takes a housewife to see that
     Britain's national housekeeping is appalling. Sandbrook, *Seasons
     in the Sun*, p. 761

104 Dennis Potter quote from Sandbrook, *Seasons in the Sun*,
   p. 760

105 Imagined conversations between Mrs Thatcher and Saatchi &
   Saatchi refer to and quote from Sandbrook, *Seasons in the Sun*,
   pp. 756–8

105 We'd have been drummed out of office if we'd had this level of
   unemployment. Sandbrook, *Seasons in the Sun*, p. 759

120 Whatever you're doing, make sure it's favourably reported. I don't
   want you stitched up by bloody BBC poofs and Trots. From *Daily
   Telegraph*, 'How Denis Thatcher Went to War with the BBC over
   "Foul Libel" of His Wife', 21 July 2016

128 Although the scene and interactions with Suzi are fictional,
   details from conversation regarding booking for RAR 2,
   Brockwell Park, from Rachel, *Walls*, pp. 172–3. The reference to
   Jimmy Pursey receiving death threats is based on Kate Gregory in
   Rachel, p. 174, though the situation is fictional.

132–3 Abdul Noor's interaction with Jon Davies is fictional, but quotes,
   and is based in part on, 'Simon Says' by Ian Walker, *New Society*,
   January 1980, specifically the horrific nature of the attack, and key
   factual details of this, i.e., that Noor was attacked by 'four white
   skinheads who came out of Excalibur House one night while he
   was walking home from work. He lost consciousness, and was
   picked up by an Asian minicab driver.'

133–4 Edward Shaw's interaction with Jon Davies is fictional, but
   quotes, and is based in part on, 'Simon Says' by Ian Walker, *New
   Society*, January 1980, specifically, and as referenced in an earlier
   note above: 'Shaw recounts the harassment he suffered digging up
   the road at Great Eastern Street, where he was working for two
   and a half weeks: spat at, called a "nigger bastard," stones thrown.
   Every morning he had to clear out the rubbish which had been
   tipped overnight into the hole he was digging.'

135 I'm afraid I do, yes. From 'Simon Says' by Ian Walker, *New
   Society*, January 1980

135 Iris Walkinshaw was headmistress at Rushmore School when I attended in the early eighties.

139 Callaghan's television speech quotes from Sandbrook, *Seasons in the Sun*, p. 805

140 He should now properly seek the verdict of the people. This country belongs to the courageous and not to the timid. Sandbrook, *Seasons in the Sun*, p. 806

140 'Jim unfixes it', *Daily Mirror*, from Sandbrook, *Seasons in the Sun*, p. 806

140 She is so beautiful. Quite bewitching, as Eva Perón must have been. Alan Clark, from Turner, *Rejoice! Rejoice!*, loc. 409–10

141 There is no ambiguity at all and no qualification. The TGWU does not support pay restraint … back off and let the unions get on with the job of securing the best settlements they could … [the unions will] behave responsibly. Sandbrook, *Seasons in the Sun*, p. 811

145 Certain details of Excalibur House from 'Simon Says' by Ian Walker, *New Society*, January 1980

147 Instances of Special Patrol Group violence from *The Political Legacy of Blair Peach* by Jenny Bourne, https://irr.org.uk/article/the-political-legacy-of-blair-peach/

147–8 Certain details of Special Patrol Group weaponry, Pallister and Davies, *Guardian*, 7 May 1980

151–2 An edited version of the Soho/Challenor story first appeared in *The Social Gathering* as 'Soho Mornings', 28 May 2020

154–5 Quotes Rachel, *Walls*, pp. 171 and 175

155 No leadership qualities and little loyalty to the Labour Party. Sandbrook, *Seasons in the Sun*, p. 811

155 Courage, mind and energy to work even for mitigation of the mood. Sandbrook, *Seasons in the Sun*, p. 811

156 The only way of avoiding high inflation – and avoiding the monetary squeeze and high unemployment which would inevitably follow such inflation. Sandbrook, *Seasons in the Sun*, p. 815

156 Are you saying, Tom, that 5 per cent would not be best for the country? Sandbrook, *Seasons in the Sun*, p. 815

160 We give them a chance to buy their council house, they'll vote for us, in their thousands. They want that chance to buy their own home. Adapted from Thatcher quote in Sandbrook, *Who Dares Wins*, p. 319

160 The buggers have obviously got jam on it. If you seriously think a few quid on the rent is going to hurt these spongeing sods, you must all be mad. Sandbrook, *Who Dares Wins*, p. 319

161 A few of us will stay at the SWP print shop, just in case. There've been threats by the Front to burn it down, as you know. We've got binoculars and baseball bats; we'll sit on the roof. It's a bit bloody toy town, but better safe than sorry. Roger Huddle quoted from Rachel, *Walls*, p. 176

162 Paul Holborow speech quotes and adapts Renton, *Never Again*, p. 127: the Anti-Nazi League has sent supporters to Brick Lane to make sure it's safe, and it is safe! There is no Front presence now, and if there was, it's been smashed!

164 Misty [were] joyous, lilting and weaving into the rhythms so evocatively [...] Brockwell Park [was] transferred to the Jamaican mountains by their open, rural, spiritual magic. Rachel, *Walls*, p. 177

164 All week you've probably read a lot of things about me and Sham 69. We've been dictated to. Last night I wasn't going to come. But this morning I met this kid who said, 'You ain't doing it 'cos all your fans are National Front.' They said I ain't got no bottle. But I'm here. Nobody's going to tell me what I should or should not do. I'm here because I support Rock Against Racism. Renton, *Never Again*, p. 126

165 Ernie Roberts' speech quotes from and adapts Renton, *Never Again*, p. 127: The Front was at Brick Lane but so were anti-fascists, in their thousands. The NF's feeble attempt to disrupt the carnival and invade Brick Lane [is] completely defeated.

175 Quote from Harrison, *Inside the Inner City*, section: Prologue

186–7 Tracey Thorn quoted from Rachel, *Walls*, pp. 349–350

187 Paul Weller quote from Style Council *Internationalists* tour programme

188 Details/quotes from the Excalibur House planning dispute public inquiry, quotes from 'Simon Says' by Ian Walker, *New Society*, January 1980 and 'Back to Front' by Mike Goulden, Charles Ashleigh and Doris Archer, *Marxism Today*, March 1980

189 The community hated us and we hated them. It wasn't a black thing. It wasn't as complex as that. If you went out in uniform or plain clothes you could feel the hatred [...]

The officers involved in these atrocities can do this because they are not accountable to anybody. They cover up their crimes by picking on the weak – unemployed and uneducated people who do not have any knowledge of the law. There are no rights for black people, and if you are poor it's worse; as far as the law is concerned you have no place in society. You are a dog; when they kick you, you move.

"'They Hate Us, We Hate Them" – Resisting Police Corruption and Violence in Hackney in the 1980s and 1990s' by John Eden, *Datacide* magazine

205 Goodnight moon, goodnight cow jumping over the moon, from *Goodnight Moon* by Margaret Wise Brown (Harper and Brothers, 1947)

213 Monday Club minutes and Thatcher's spy details quote from McSmith, *No Such Thing*, p. 87

215 Willie Whitelaw quotes excerpts from the Police Bill, 1983, and his own *The Whitelaw Memoirs*, pp. 246–7

216 Paul Weller quotes from *Suburban 100*, p. 67, and 'Pop into Politics', *TV Eye*, ITV 30 January 1986

195 We didn't stop racial attacks, far less racism. Widgery, *Beating Time*, p. 1

220–6 Lloyd Manley is a fictional character; details in Noble's interview, however, are based on media reports of the inquest – and build-up to it – into Colin Roach's death.

230   Prince Philip and Grace Ellis quotes from *Hackney Gazette*, 'Britannia Rules the Waves', Bartholomew, 18 January 2017, pp. 209–10

232–4   Noble's interactions with James Roach are fictional, though the account and details regarding the chronology of the night Colin Roach died are based, in part, on 'Bulletin of the Roach Family Support Committee, no. 3' (My son did not commit suicide. He had too much to live for) and on '"They Hate Us, We Hate Them" – Resisting Police Corruption and Violence in Hackney in the 1980s and 1990s' by John Eden, *Datacide* magazine

234–6   Noble's interactions with Keith Scully are fictional; the account is based, in part, on a newspaper article by Nicholas Timmins, from a still image, *Who Killed Colin Roach?* by Isaac Julien, www.isaacjulien.com

237–8   Thatcher/Livingstone quotes from Turner, *Rejoice! Rejoice!*, loc. 1994–5 and Sandbrook, *Who Dares Wins*, pp. 762–3 and 768–70

244   Steve Strange and Chris Sullivan quotes from 'Spandau Ballet, The Blitz Kids and the New Romantics' by David Johnson, *Guardian*, 4 October 2009

245   The phrase, 'the sound of Thatcherism on vinyl', from *Spandau Ballet: The Sound of Thatcherism* by Michael Hann, *Guardian*, 25 March 2002

245   Gary Kemp quotes from 'Spandau Ballet, The Blitz Kids and the New Romantics' by David Johnson, *Guardian*, 4 October 2009

246   The phrase 'White European Dance Music' from 'Spandau Ballet, The Blitz Kids and the New Romantics' by David Johnson, *Guardian*, 4 October 2009

255   Roy Cornwall reference based on still from *Who Killed Colin Roach?* by Isaac Julien, www.isaacjulien.com

255   Delroy Thompson quoted from 'Bulletin of the Roach Family Support Committee, no. 3'

256-7 Details, including quotes, of the background to the motion to defund the police, from 'When Hackney (Almost) Defunded the Police', The Radical History of Hackney

265 Quote from Harrison, *Inside the Inner City*, section: Prologue

266-7 Details in Parker's legal analysis as well as questions fed by Noble quotes and adapted from 'Bulletin of the Roach Family Support Committee, no. 3'

268 'Thatcher' here, in fact, quotes Whitelaw as documented in the 'Bulletin of the Roach Family Support Committee, no. 3'

269-70 Details from *Speak Like a Child* by The Style Council, promotional music video by Tim Pope, and from Munn, *Mr Cool's Dream*, section: February 1983

270 Paul Weller quotes from the Timmy Mallet Show, Piccadilly Radio, 7 March 1983, from Munn, *Mr Cool's Dream*, section: March 1983

271 Details on 'Speak Like a Child' record sleeve from sleeve itself and Munn, *Mr Cool's Dream*, section: March 1983

271 All that scratching is making me itch. Sample included in 'Buffalo Gals' [song] by Malcolm McLaren

272 And throughout the rest of the text, 'Godfrey Heaven' quotes Brynley Heaven, interview with the author, January 2020

275-6 Quotes and details from 'When Hackney (Almost) Defunded the Police', The Radical History of Hackney

278-80 Details of and quotes from John Fernandes' study, and other quotes, including Les Curtis, from Morton, *Bent Coppers*, pp. 293-4

282 Clinton Davies quote from 'When Hackney (Almost) Defunded the Police', The Radical History of Hackney

285 Gardiner singing a West Ham terrace chant

291 Ronald Bell and the Monday Club, details from McSmith, *No Such Thing*, p. 87

291 IRA-loving, poof-loving, Marxist. *Sunday Express*, from Turner, *Rejoice! Rejoice!*, loc. 1994

292 All those who wrote letters ... should be invited to accept (a refugee) in their homes. McSmith, *No Such Thing*, p. 88

292 It's quite wrong that immigrants should be given council housing whereas white citizens were not. McSmith, *No Such Thing*, p. 88

292–3 Suzi quotes extracts from letters to the RFSC in 'Bulletin of the Roach Family Support Committee, no. 3'

297 It is but one painful and monotonous round of vice, filth and poverty. *The Illustrated London News*, October 1863, lookup.london

303 March details based on *Who killed Colin Roach?* by Isaac Julien

305–6 Statistics details and quotes from 'Bulletin of the Roach Family Support Committee, no. 2' and 'Bulletin of the Roach Family Support Committee, no. 3'

320 Here Godfrey Heaven quotes Brynley Heaven, interview with the author, January 2020. The interaction with Suzi, as other instances, is fictional.

325 Details from inquest proceedings from 'Bulletin of the Roach Family Support Committee, no. 3'

328 Ronald Brown quote from 'When Hackney (Almost) Defunded the Police', The Radical History of Hackney

330 Quote Aziziye Mosque, wikipedia.org

337 Put your savings in your socks and they'd nationalise socks. Margaret Thatcher, Speech in Cardiff, 23 May 1983, Margaret Thatcher Foundation, margaretthatcher.org

337 Bernard Levin quote from Stewart, *Bang!*, loc. 3788–90

337 Clive James quote from Turner, *Rejoice! Rejoice!*, loc. 2646–8

337 Quote from *The Sun* from Stewart, *Bang!*, loc. 3791–2

337 Quote from *The Sunday Telegraph* from Turner, *Rejoice! Rejoice!*, loc. 2646–8

338 Quotes from GLC-sponsored pamphlet 'Policing London – by Coercion / Black people and the Police Bill', via movinghere.org.uk, catalogue reference LMA/GLC/DG/PUB/01/164/UO331

339 The Conservative Party has definitively *not* been infiltrated by the National Front or the League of St George, nor by any of the

far-right, rogue members of these political groups. Adapted from Peace, *Nineteen Eighty-Three*, p. 161

340   Alan Clark quote from Turner, *Rejoice! Rejoice!*, loc. 3114

340   Cecil Parkinson rumours from Sandbrook, *Who Dares Wins*, p. 93, McSmith, *No Such Thing*, p. 24, and Turner, *Rejoice! Rejoice!*, loc. 3082

351   Talk show quote based on Stewart, *Bang!*, loc. 3908

360   Details from the procedure relating to Dawn Driscoll's arrest from Morton, *Bent Coppers*, p. 203

361   Professor Stuart Hall quote from the Foreword to the Independent Committee of Inquiry, *Policing in Hackney 1945–1984*

362   Neil Kinnock quote from Turner, *Rejoice! Rejoice!*, loc. 2667–8

363   It is a particular personal triumph for the Iron Lady as she becomes the first twentieth-century Conservative Prime Minister to win successive working majorities. Adapted from Stewart, *Bang!*, loc. 3870–1

364   Quotes from the poem *Who Killed Colin Roach?* by Benjamin Zephaniah

364–5   Professor Stuart Hall quote from Foreword to the Independent Committee of Inquiry, *Policing in Hackney 1945–1984*

With thanks to

Will Francis, Ren Balcombe, and all at Janklow and Nesbit; Paul Engles, Katharina Bielenberg, Corinna Zifko and all at Arcadia and Quercus; Piers Russell-Cobb; Angeline Rothermundt; Rita Winter; David Peace, for his support and friendship; Lucy Caldwell, for her reading – once again! – and her thoughts; Martha Lecauchois and Lucian Thomas-Lecauchois for their love.